BETWEEN PRINCESSES

AND OTHER JOBS

A Tale of Indrajit & Fix

D.J. BUTLER

A Baen Books Original

Baen Publishing Enterprises
P.O. Box 1403
Riverdale, NY 10471
www.baen.com

ISBN: 978-1-9821-9357-7

Cover art by Kieran Yanner

First printing, July 2023
First mass market printing, August 2024

Distributed by Simon & Schuster
1230 Avenue of the Americas
New York, NY 10020

Library of Congress Control Number: 2023005376

Printed in the United States of America

10 9 8 7 6 5 4 3 2 1

Huge thanks to the many editors
who have contributed to the stories in this volume:
Kacey Ezell, Marisa Wolf, Larry Correia,
Christopher Ruocchio, Rob Howell, Chris Kennedy,
Joe Monson, Toni Weisskopf, and
Isabelle "Hell's Belle's" Butler.

Contents

A Short Note of Explanation
ix

Sacrifices
1

No Trade for Nice Guys
31

Backup
55

The Path of the Hunter
85

Power and Prestige
115

The Lady in the Pit
139

Welcome to Kish Part One: The Name of the Monster
167

Welcome to Kish Part Two: The Caveats of Salish-Bozar
197

Welcome to Kish Part Three: The End of the Story
227

Good Boy
259

The Politics of Wizards
287

A Short Note of Explanation

〜⚬〜

This book started as short stories. The heroes of the following tales, the Blaatshi Recital Thane Indrajit Twang and Fix, former Trivial of Salish-Bozar the White, first appeared in the Baen Books novel *In the Palace of Shadow and Joy*. In *Palace*, Indrajit and Fix met, had a joint adventure, endured sundry joint perils, and emerged as partners in a new, small, jobber firm, the Protagonists. (I won't tell you more about the events recounted in *Palace*, because, although the Protagonists' adventures happen in sequence, they're not part of an overarching plot. That means that you can go right ahead and read this book first, and then go back and enjoy *Palace* afterward. Do it, I dare you.)

This volume contains ten short stories, previously published by Baen Books, Chris Kennedy/New Mythology Press, and Hemelein Publications. They're included herein in the order in which they were written, which is also the order in which Indrajit and Fix experienced them. The Protagonists and Kish change over time and the changes persist—once the Kyone Munahim shows up in "Power and Prestige," for instance, he sticks around (indeed, in "Good Boy," he's the point-of-view character). Seven of the stories were written as standalones, but three were written as a tightly linked sequence, comprising, in effect, a novella in three parts. "The Name of the Monster," "The Caveats of Salish-Bozar," and "The End of the Story" are collected here under the title "Welcome to Kish."

I have made some subtle tweaks to the texts of the previously published stories, for consistency.

The novella that closes this volume, "The Politics of Wizards," was written new, for the purpose of inclusion herein.

BETWEEN
PRINCESSES
AND OTHER JOBS
A Tale of Indrajit & Fix

Sacrifices
❦

"That's the shipwreck." Fix pointed at a mass of timbers lying around a cluster of gray, kelp-veiled rocks. The tide was out, and a gull watched the two men from the highest of the timbers.

"It's *a* shipwreck," Indrajit conceded. "How do you know it's the wreck of the ship bearing the Pelthite ambassador?"

The two men stood on the track running along the headland above the sandy, rock-spiked beach. No highways ran straight south from Kish to the Free Cities; most of that traffic went by sea. The land-routes out of Kish ran south and east, toward Ildarion and the King of Thunder Steppes. Toward the bit of coastland where Indrajit's own people lived.

If they still lived.

The late afternoon sky was overcast, the clouds sinking in iron bands to encircle the headland, the rocks, and the waves themselves, so that the breaking surf was only barely visible. In this weather, there could certainly be more than one recent shipwreck.

"Look at the curve of that prow," Fix said. "Pelthite. Aren't your people seafaring?"

"We're fishermen," Indrajit said. "In the first place, that means that we make our own boats for fishing. In the second, we make small boats. We don't need to sail to Pelth or anywhere else, we just get out far enough in the water to catch food. So I wouldn't know a Pelthite prow from a Maliki mainmast."

"You'd better be able to tell a prow from a mast. Don't you have a kenning that would help?"

"I know the parts of a ship." Indrajit sniffed. "I see you missed the alliteration entirely."

"Ah," Fix said. "Pelthite prow, now I hear it. I see alliteration better when it's written down."

"Poetry that has been written down isn't poetry," Indrajit said. "It's just the dead remains of poetry. An Ylakka skeleton is not the same thing as an Ylakka."

"But a century after its death, I can still examine an Ylakka skeleton and learn from it. An hour after a living Ylakka walks across this headland, no one will have any idea that it has been here."

"You belong in the Hall of Guesses," Indrajit said, "with the other scholars."

"If I wanted mere knowledge, I'd have stayed in the ashrama."

"I'm glad you didn't." Indrajit clapped his shorter friend across the shoulders. "Shall we get down in there with the prow and the mainmast and see if the ambassador went down with the ship?"

"If the ambassador died, there's time to find that out." Fix scanned the headland and Indrajit looked with him, spying a cluster of huts at the base of a cliff ten minutes' walk away. "Besides, if he died, he's probably under thirty fathoms of seawater. But if Wopal is right and someone else is interested in the ambassador, and the ambassador is alive, then we need to get to him first."

Grit Wopal was the spymaster of Orem Thrush, the Lord Chamberlain. Indrajit and Fix worked for him, not as spies, exactly, but as men of all competence—investigators, observers, enforcers, messengers, bodyguards, and more. Usually, they worked in the Paper Sook, which was the financial market of the city of Kish, but on this day, Wopal had sent them on an urgent errand to find a shipwrecked ambassador.

"If I wrecked on this shore," Indrajit said, "the first place I'd go would be those houses. For food and shelter, to get wounds tended, to get a message sent off to Kish."

"Unless you just walked straight to Kish," Fix suggested.

"We'd have passed the ambassador on the road," Indrajit said. "With your keen wit and my broad vision, we'd have seen him. What about the necropolis?"

The necropolis stretched to their left. It was larger than the city itself, having once been a city in its own right before being converted into a massive burial complex. From where they stood, it was invisible, shrouded in fog.

"If I knew the lay of the land," Fix said, "and I thought I was being pursued . . . maybe. Or if I was a stranger, and mistook the necropolis for Kish itself."

"So first we try the huts."

They walked to the cluster of hovels. They were on foot because Indrajit didn't know how to ride. But Fix didn't complain, and, in any case, they were close enough to the city that it probably didn't really matter.

But not knowing how to ride limited Indrajit's ability to be effective. He should probably learn how. He had resisted it, partly out of pride and partly because, on the few occasions he had ridden, the placement of his eyes, far apart on the sides of his head, when he was perched atop a big, fast-moving animal, had quickly made him queasy with vertigo.

"I should learn to ride," he said, as they approached the village.

"Fine," Fix said.

There were more huts, visible once they drew close, than Indrajit had realized; half a dozen, all told, none more than twenty cubits to a side and most closer to ten. They huddled around a linear depression in the beach, a slash that created an inlet of water running right up to their doors, fed from a spring in the rocks of the headland. Skin coracles lay upside down beside the huts, which were made of a gray plaster and roofed with bundles of grass.

Indrajit and Fix rattled down a natural staircase made by a tumble of boulders spilling down the headland, hallooing and waving, hands nowhere near their weapons, to catch the attention of a single visible person who huddled in the lee of a cottage beside a tiny fire, smearing pitch from a pot over the fire along a coracle's seams.

"Hello!" Indrajit called. "We're friendly!"

"We're men of peace!" Fix added. His high-pitched, almost feminine voice made him sound very earnest.

The coracle-mender looked up from the work. Indrajit had seen this race of man before in Kish, among the fishermen of the East and West Flats. They had grayish skin, not pale so much as leached of color, with very wide foreheads and very narrow chins, giving their faces a triangular appearance. Along their chins and jawlines, where other men might sometimes have beards, these fishers instead had fringes of noodle-thin tentacles that bounced when they spoke.

"What do you want?" The coracle-mender stood. "We owe no one!"

"We're not collecting taxes," Fix said. "And we're not buying fish."

"Then we have no business!" The coracle-mender cracked his knuckles, but made no motion to return to the work.

"We work for the Lord Chamberlain," Indrajit said. "And we're investigating a shipwreck."

"We're fishermen." Triangle Head sniffed. "Not wreckers."

Indrajit looked at the village, with its rickety boats and its worn nets and its thatch roofs. He noticed that the sand, much disturbed by many footprints, bore the distinct marks of the passage of men with tails. "We believe you. Is it just you and your family here?"

Triangle Head nodded warily. "We're all kin."

Fix was watching the fisherman intently. He must also have realized that Triangle Head was lying, concealing the presence here of other men. Were they wreckers, after all?

"There's a shipwreck just up the coast," Indrajit said. "Recent. I gather you didn't see any survivors."

Triangle Head snorted.

"Can you ask your family?" Indrajit asked. "Maybe they saw someone. Maybe ask them to come out and talk?"

"There's a reward," Fix said, smiling.

Triangle Head grunted and set down the stick he had been using to smear pitch. He shuffled into the nearest and largest of the huts.

"There's no reward," Indrajit said.

"He's lying," Fix answered, "and we're about to fight whoever is hiding in that house."

"Zalaptings," Indrajit guessed, "maybe others."

He shrugged out of his tunic, wrapped his hand in it, and picked up the pot of melted pitch.

"Good idea." Fix drew his falchion in one hand and his fighting ax in the other.

Indrajit thrust the smearing stick into the fire; it ignited instantly. "Why will no one ever cooperate with us? We are so obviously men of peace."

Fix positioned himself in front of the cottage door, a thick slab of knotted wood hanging on leather hinges. He scanned the village with his eyes, making certain no one could shoot him out of any windows. "They think they can get a better outcome by lying to us or killing us."

"I suppose that must be it."

Indrajit touched fire to the pot of pitch, which burst into flame. Then he threw the pitch onto the thatched roof.

"Come on out," Fix called. "We'd rather not hurt anyone. We're just here for the ambassador. But we *have* set fire to the building."

Indrajit heard a whirring sound behind him and dove to the side, trying to avoid the sling bolt that he knew was coming. The projectile struck him in the upper left arm, hard enough to make him drop the pot.

"Get the door!" Fix yelled. The shorter man was already bounding toward the boulders above the spring, where two Zalaptings, short, lavender-skinned men with long snouts and tails, crouched and spun their slings again to fire a second time.

"Come out and die like men!" Indrajit bellowed, in his loudest, angriest voice.

Then he gripped the plaster wall, wrapping his fingers around the faintest of protrusions and sinking his toes into the shallowest of cracks. Indrajit, like all his people, was a good climber, and he quickly vaulted up onto the burning rooftop.

Indrajit drew his leaf-bladed sword, Vacho, the Voice of Lightning. Eyes watering from the smoke, he peeked over the front of the building, but saw no one. Under his feet, the thatch was ablaze. Timbers were exposed, and through the smoke, Indrajit could see an upper loft over half the building's footprint, and a single large room below, with sleeping platforms and pens for geese and pigs.

Stepping as lightly as he could manage, Indrajit dropped onto the loft. It was an untidy nest of sleeping furs, clothing, and personal oddments, and a ladder led down into the main room.

"What was that?" he heard.

"The cottage is burning, you moron," a second voice snarled, deeper than the first. "Soon it will fall down on top of us. Now get out there and kill those two."

"We don't know that there are only two."

"So send the fisherman first. Use him as a shield."

Indrajit crouched and waddled to the edge of the loft, which had no rail. He saw Triangle Head and a group of other people who looked like him; Triangle Head stood with slumped shoulders and bowed head, and the others, seven or eight of them, were tied hand and foot in the corner. He saw six Zalaptings, and a man four times Indrajit's size, with mottled red skin, a carapace, and lobster-like claws where Indrajit had hands. At the red giant's feet lay one more person, a young man with a yellowish Pelthite complexion. The Pelthite wore loose silk purple pants and a bright red sash for a belt.

He seemed a bit young to be an ambassador. Maybe he was politically connected.

"If we wait," one of the Zalaptings was whining to Lobster Hands, "Payot will come down from Kish with more men."

"If we wait, Payot will find us roasted. Go!" Lobster Hands snapped his claws.

Two of the Zalaptings grabbed Triangle Head and pushed him out the door.

Indrajit had to act now or lose the initiative. He jumped.

He crashed down feetfirst, his sandals striking the back of Lobster Hands's neck and driving the man to the ground. Geese honked and pigs oinked furiously, but Indrajit had no time for the livestock.

"The Protagonists!" he yelled, staggering to his feet and sweeping his sword. The name of their jobber company might not yet strike fear into enemies' hearts, but if Indrajit kept bellowing it as he ran into combat, eventually it would. He struck down one Zalapting and the other three scattered, bouncing into the smoky corners of the cottage.

Lobster Hands groaned and rolled over onto his back.

Vacho's blade was sharp, so Indrajit cut through the ropes tying the feet of the triangle heads quickly, and then stood, just in time to meet the two Zalaptings returning through the front door. The first ran at him with a short stabbing sword extended, and Indrajit swung with all his strength. Indrajit was tall, with longer reach than the Zalapting, and had a longer blade—the Zalapting's point was nearly a cubit short of Indrajit's breast when Vacho bit into the side of the Zalapting's head, sending the little lavender man into a silent pile in the corner.

The blow left Indrajit off-balance and exposed to the attack of the second Zalapting, but Triangle Head jumped the little man from behind, dragging him to the ground and headbutting him.

Indrajit turned to menace the other three Zalaptings. They huddled in the back of the cottage, among squealing pigs.

"You burned my house!" Triangle Head yelled.

Indrajit scooped up the Pelthite and slung him over his shoulder. "But I saved your family!"

"You burned my house!"

Indrajit had no time to argue. He stooped to move through the small front door. As he drew breaths of fresh air on the outside, stumbling toward where Fix stood pulling his ax from the body of a Zalapting, a flash of green caught his eye. A lizard, the size of a smallish dog, burst from the flaming cottage behind him and raced ahead, toward the headland.

Lobster Hands would be standing soon. Indrajit wanted to get out of sight before the larger, scary-looking man came looking for him.

Fix gave Indrajit a hand up the boulders, and they scrambled to higher ground.

"Is this the ambassador?" Fix asked.

"We'll ask him when he wakes up," Indrajit said. "Right now, there's a big ugly fellow about to come swarming out of that cottage with blood in his eye, and also someone named Payot coming down from Kish with more fighters."

"We need to hide," Fix said quickly.

"I bet you read that in a book somewhere." Indrajit nodded toward the necropolis, just visible as a wall of gray in the gray mist. "The necropolis it is."

The lizard bounded on ahead. It had a long, muscular tail, a wide ruff around its neck, and a snout like a needle. Its scales were a shimmering green, dimmed by the fog.

When he reached the wall, Indrajit cast his eyes about, looking for pursuit. The sea was invisible behind them, the land simply disappearing where the headland dropped to the beach, and there was no one following. He saw no one on the road, either.

But the damp ground held his and Fix's footprints, glaringly visible even to the eye of someone who had never been a tracker.

"Frozen hells," he muttered.

The wall was low and crumbled at this point. Once it had defended living inhabitants within, in this remote neighborhood of Imperial Kish, or perhaps in this far-flung suburb, or satellite fortress. Now Indrajit climbed up onto the wall without setting down the Pelthite, and the wall defended nothing, but only marked the line between the land of the living and the land of the dead.

Within the wall, crumbling brick houses. Tall, spiny yellow grass thrust its way up into the fog, knocking aside cobblestones and asphalt, and grim, tenacious black lichen sank invisibly tiny fingers into the cracks between bricks, gnawing at the mortar and striving with centuries-slow growth to tear down the remaining monuments.

"We have to get out of sight." Fix jogged deeper into the necropolis, turning twice to get buildings between him and the sea. The lizard scampered at his feet, gazing up at him and Indrajit both with a thoughtful expression.

Indrajit followed, slightly more slowly. His burden was beginning to tire him, but the knowledge that they could be easily tracked spurred him on. "Get onto a highway," he panted. "Let's get a mile between us and the lobster. Or, better still, a league."

"Lobster?"

"That's what he looked like." Indrajit coughed up and spat bitter phlegm. "Really big, reddish, a shell, claws."

"I've seen those before," Fix said. "They come from down south somewhere. Easha or Hith, maybe."

Indrajit grunted. "Makes sense they're from far away." They reached a stretch of tarred road that wouldn't hold tracks—or at least, not any ordinary kind of tracks—and jogged northward along it. This was good, this might let them get on the other side of Payot and his men, and get back into Kish, where the Lord Chamberlain's power would protect them. "I don't know any kennings about such men."

"We need to wake this guy up and confirm he's the

ambassador," Fix said. "Because if he isn't, we have to go back."

Indrajit grunted his reluctant agreement. They took a right turn, heading east, away from the city, to cross a stone-paved plaza whose flagstones were mostly intact. The buildings surrounding the plaza were whole, and had had their windows and doors bricked shut.

Once shops and offices and dwellings of the living, they were now mausolea.

Beneath ancient Kish ran a maze of tunnels and caverns in multiple levels. Stories suggested that was true of the necropolis as well. Did that mean that strange creatures fed on the dead interred here?

Or that if someone was buried who was ... not *quite* dead, he could escape and walk around?

They walked beneath the gaze of a statue. It was carved of marble but thoroughly weathered, and new features had been painted on the statue, and new words painted over the words that had been chiseled into the pedestal. Indrajit couldn't read, but he could see that the statue had been carved as a bearded man, and had been painted to resemble a woman with green skin and long hair.

Fix saw him looking. "Old Imperial sculpture. I don't recognize the name, might be a god or a hero or some long-forgotten banker who was once important. He's been converted into a burial image for a priestess named Artazia."

Indrajit wasn't quite sure where the sun was, given the fog, but he thought it might be getting low in the west by now. He took a deep breath.

"Okay, this is the moment of truth." He knelt and

stretched the unconscious young man out on the stones, as gently as he could. The green lizard rushed up and perched on the crumbled, two-cubit tall remains of a stone column. Its bright pink tongue flicked in and out, and it seemed to watch Indrajit closely. "Wake up . . . How do you address an ambassador?"

Fix grunted. "Your Excellency?"

"I'm going to stick to *sir*," Indrajit said. "If it's wrong, it's at least respectful, and doesn't sound like a comic exaggeration. Wake up, sir."

He cut the ropes binding the young man, listening for indications of pursuit as he did so. Nothing.

He patted the unconscious man's cheeks. He was still breathing, but his breath was a little erratic, and he groaned. The Pelthite had long, dark eyelashes, and curly dark hair that fell around his ears and covered what would have been a very high forehead.

Fix handed Indrajit a waterskin. "Try this."

"It feels impolite," Indrajit said, but he took the water.

"We need to know, and we need to know *now*."

Indrajit nodded, and splashed water in the young man's face. The Pelthite gasped, opened his eyes, and sat up.

"Banus!" he cried.

"No, sir," Indrajit said. "My name is Indrajit, this is Fix. You are not our prisoner. In fact, we rescued you. If you are the Pelthite ambassador whose ship wrecked yesterday, we are here to bring you to the Lord Chamberlain of Kish."

The lizard scampered between Indrajit and the Pelthite, climbing onto the young man's chest and laying its head alongside his. The young man grew noticeably calmer, his breathing slowing and his posture relaxing.

"Are you the ambassador . . . sir?" Indrajit asked.

Then young man hesitated, then nodded.

"You seem quite young." Fix's statement wasn't exactly an expression of doubt, but it wasn't exactly a request for an explanation.

"I am a prince of the blood," the Pelthite said, "born on the rabbit fur. Banus is *my* name."

Indrajit looked at Fix and both men shrugged slightly.

"The Lord Chamberlain is to be my host," Banus said. "How do I know you serve him?"

"We don't carry badges," Indrajit said, "and if there's a password, he didn't tell it to us. So I guess your choices are to go back to those guys who had you tied up, or try to get to Kish on your own, or come with us."

Banus hesitated, doubt in his face. "May I have some water?"

Indrajit handed him the waterskin and Banus drank.

"If you want to strike out on your own," Indrajit told him, "you can take the water. I should warn you, we'll follow you and try to protect you, so you'll still see us. And, if you weren't sure, Kish is that way." He pointed. He didn't like losing the waterskin, but if that was what it took to keep the ambassador alive, so be it.

Fix handed the young man his fighting ax. "Whatever your decision is, you should go armed."

"You should definitely go armed." Indrajit laughed. "Welcome to Kish."

Banus stroked the lizard, pressed his cheek to the creature's cheek, and struggled to his feet. The lizard stayed perched upon his shoulder. "I will come with you."

"That leaves *us* a choice," Fix said. "Walk back in the dark, or hide here for the night?"

"I don't like either of those. If we hide here, they might catch us, or we might encounter worse threats, living among these stones." He peered into the deepening shadows, imagining cannibal cults, walking dead, and evil things too old to have names.

"I'd be tempted to dismiss your fears as ridiculous fantasy," Fix said. "But outlaws and smugglers use the necropolis. We don't have to encounter any eldritch unnamed thing to meet our end out here tonight."

"But between the necropolis and the Caravanserai, on the south side of the city, is open ground. Flat as a frying pan."

"Is that an actual kenning from the Blaatshi Epic?" Fix kept a straight face, and Indrajit couldn't tell whether he was being teased.

"No, it's a cliché. There is an actual kenning for broad, flat meadows, and it's *Earth asleep, still as breathing, wide face of earth unending.*"

"You're a poet," Banus said.

"Sort of," Fix answered.

"I am *the* poet," Indrajit said. "I am the four hundred twenty-seventh Recital Thane of the great epic poem of my people."

"You wouldn't believe how impressive people find that," Fix said.

Banus nodded solemnly.

"If we try to cross the open ground, we're easy targets," Fix said, finishing Indrajit's thought. "Of course, with the fog, it might be hard to see us."

"And it might be hard for us to see Payot, or Lobster Hands, sneaking up on us. And it might be hard to find our way to the city. We might walk all night toward Ildarion."

"Which one of you is the boss?" Banus asked.

"You have divined the weakness in our management structure," Fix said.

"It's not a weakness." Indrajit snorted. "It's a strength. We decide unanimously. But I think there's a third possibility."

"We go south," Fix suggested. "Walk a week to the Free Cities, book passage on a ship, and sail back."

"Close, actually. We sneak back to the fishing village under cover of darkness. We borrow a coracle and paddle it up the coast to Kish."

Fix was quiet for a moment. "Yes. I think that's a good idea."

"Unless they expect it," Indrajit said. "In which case, they might be waiting in ambush for us. Again."

"That's true of any choice we make," Fix pointed out. "And I think this seems like a pretty unexpected maneuver."

"I don't really want to find out what this place is like after dark. And, even if it's just smugglers, I don't want to meet anyone else out here."

Fix pointed. "Back that way is west. If we can get to the wall and take shelter near it, we can easily walk straight out to the coast once it's dark."

"Or a few hours later." Indrajit started walking.

The journey back westward was easier in that he was no longer carrying Banus. The Pelthite prince kept pace with Indrajit and Fix easily, even though the lizard rode on his shoulders. He spoke a lot, but kept his voice down, and most of what he said was innocuous to the point of being vapid. "That's a big building . . . I wonder what kind of people used to live here . . . Ooh, this must have cost someone a pretty penny, once upon a time . . . I can imagine that this would have been a lovely street, with a cooling breeze from the sea."

Perhaps ambassadors specialized in small talk, with no content. Indrajit didn't object, and he and Fix took turns grunting laconic agreement with whatever the ambassador said.

The journey wore on Indrajit's nerves, though, because the shadows grew deeper and darker. Rattling and slithering noises that he had ignored in the afternoon, assigning them in his imagination to birds and snakes and marmochucks and thylacodons, he now imagined to emanate from the footfalls of assassins and cannibals and masked hierophants with stone daggers in their hands.

They reached the wall. Here, it rose to its former height, with a parapet and a walkway. A stone's throw away, a tower stood athwart the wall, its peak staring out over the battlements, a yawning entrance and the bottom of a flight of steps at its base. The sun was down and the entire tower lay in shadow, only the toes of the lowest two steps visible in the gloom.

"Who wouldn't feel safe, surrounded by such walls?" the Pelthite prince asked.

"A prisoner." Indrajit smiled, the expression lost in the darkness that had fallen. The lizard on the prince's shoulder made a rasping sound that sounded like laughter.

"I'll go first." Fix started up the stairs, falchion probing ahead of him in the shadow.

The prince with his lizard followed close behind.

Indrajit turned, leaf-bladed sword in hand, and stood at the base of the stairs. He heard his friend and the ambassador climb, steps fading to hushed whispers the higher they went. He took a single step back into the shadows and scanned the mirk of the necropolis.

He heard Lobster Hands coming before he saw the man. At first, he heard footfalls, and though his imagination conjured up slithering eyeless crypt denizens, toothless eaters of the flesh of the dead, and asymmetrical, lurching monsters with three wings and a single fang, he held still, breathed deeply, and tightened his grip on Vacho. But then he heard the sound again, and knew it for the heavy tread of a foot. And then he saw Lobster Hands, walking directly toward him.

The man came from the north. With him came two Zalaptings—Kish had absolutely too many of the lavender-faced little men, and they seemed to fill out the cheap sacrificial ranks of every jobber company in the city. Should the Protagonists get a few Zalaptings? If they died, you didn't have to pay them, and in Indrajit's short experience working as a jobber, the Zalaptings always seemed to die first, and in greater numbers.

But until they died, they'd want to get paid. And if he asked Fix, Indrajit expected to hear that, with employees, the Protagonists would have to enter into more risk-merchantry contracts, to be able to pay out death benefits to the families of jobbers who were killed while working. Which might make Zalaptings a spectacularly *bad* choice for employees, since if they all died, you'd have to pay benefits to all their families.

But maybe less, since their deaths were so likely? Indrajit shook his head, trying to shake thoughts of risk-merchantry from his head. A few short weeks in the Paper Sook had already left their mark on him. Like a man immersed in a latrine, he now carried the stink of joint-stock companies and risk-merchantry contracts and future currency purchases with him everywhere he went.

In addition to the two Zalaptings, Lobster Hands walked with three Kishi, the dark-haired, brown-skinned, common man of the city of Kish. Lobster Hands appeared unarmed—other than his giant claws—but the other five carried spears. They walked scanning the shadows, swinging their spear blades back and forth at the darkness, prepared for a fight. They had numbers, and they had reach.

Indrajit had the advantage of surprise. Jump out and attack them from behind? Or try to quickly kill one or two, and then lure the others into a narrow fight up the stairwell?

But they were too many. He faded back up the stairs, intending to let them pass unmolested.

Only the step behind him crumbled as he put his weight on it, dropping a tiny avalanche of rubble onto the step below it. Lobster Hands heard the falling stone and looked into the opening at the tower base—

Locking eyes with Indrajit.

"Frozen hells," Indrajit murmured.

The six men charged. In a desperate bid both to warn Fix and to misdirect his attackers, Indrajit stepped out of the doorway and waved his arm as if signaling to someone deeper inside the necropolis. "I'll meet you at Kish!" he hollered. "Run!" If Indrajit was to be sacrificed, at least his sacrifice would accomplish something.

Then he scooted back up the stairs.

He held his ground first just a few steps up, at a point from which he could see an irregular rectangle of light, or, if not light, then lesser gloom, around the entrance to the bottom of the staircase. From the outside, he knew, his own position would be concealed in complete darkness. Kishi had very ordinary powers of vision, and as far as he knew, so did Zalaptings.

There was the possibility that Lobster Hands had special sight and would be able to attack Indrajit in the darkness. There was also the possibility that any of the five attackers had some magical ability to detect him in ambush, but he was willing to take those risks.

He raised Vacho, ready to chop downward with the blade, and tried to control his breath.

The scuffle of feet raced to the opening—and then halted.

"Get in there," a deep voice growled. Lobster Hands.

"But shouldn't we . . . ?"

Lobster Hands bellowed, and a Zalapting flew in through the opening. He wasn't running, he was being thrown, and he slammed against the wall and crumpled onto the bottom steps.

Indrajit had planned to attack the first man onto the stairs, but this was no attacker—this was bait. And because the Zalapting was lying on the steps rather than standing, attacking him would require Indrajit to expose himself more fully than he liked.

Grinding his teeth silently, Indrajit eased back up the stairs, away from his attackers.

The Zalapting looked up at him. "Fish Head!"

Indrajit wanted to hit the Zalapting, but instead he ran. Taking advantage of his long legs and risking the unseen hazards of the steps in the darkness, he pressed his left hand against the central column around which the stairs spiraled and raced upward.

Below, he heard his attackers fumbling on the first steps, and the squeal of at least one Zalapting getting trodden upon. Good; that meant his enemies couldn't see in the dark, any more than he could.

Awkwardly, he made it up the stairs and emerged onto a narrow stone walkway with crenellations to one side and empty space to the other. He forced himself to reason; the wall must run north and south, with the crenellations outside, hence on the west. Fix and the ambassador should be moving south, to meet at the fishing village, so Indrajit should lead Lobster Hands and his crew north. Which meant crenellations to his left.

He turned, touched the stone defenses to be sure they were there, and jogged. "I do not have a fish's head!" he yelled. "My eyes are just set farther apart than yours, you pink rat!"

The stars were still obscured by the fog, and Indrajit could barely see the walkway before his feet. If he ran too fast, he risked falling off the side, or running off the end of the walkway if the wall failed.

Had he given his pursuers enough indication that he was running northward?

He'd risk it.

Indrajit sheathed Vacho and levered himself up into the crenellation. The wall wasn't higher than twenty cubits, he was sure. He was a tall man, and he lowered himself over the other side, letting his legs dangle to their full extent. Subtract another five cubits from the drop for his height, it shouldn't be more than a fifteen-cubit fall.

Unless there was a ditch.

He heard feet running toward him along the top of the wall.

There could also be rocks.

Help me now, Sea Mother. Indrajit let go of the wall.

He hit water. It wasn't the sea, but he splashed down into marshy earth. Stagnation filled his nostrils, and something slithered away across the mud. He stood and his feet sank. Indrajit trembled with the excitement of the chase and with fatigue, but he wasn't injured.

Thank you.

"Something jumped off the wall!" Lobster Hands bellowed.

Frozen hells. Indrajit yanked one leg up, trying to move out of the bog—

And left a sandal behind.

"No way of knowing how far the drop is!" a Zalapting whimpered.

"There's one way," Lobster Hands rumbled.

Indrajit scrambled and got out of the marsh, onto dry land. He kept his second sandal on his foot, but there was no going back for the first one. He ran, southward, back along the wall.

Splash!

"You aren't dead, are you?" Lobster Hands called.

"I don't think so!" The Zalapting's voice wavered.

Behind him, Indrajit could hear his pursuers continue to come down the wall. He turned right, crossed the road he'd ridden south with Fix, and then nearly ran over the top of the headland in the darkness. The sounds of pursuit behind him were indistinct, and as the waves grew closer, they faded further. Dropping to his backside and then flipping over onto his belly, Indrajit kicked off the second sandal and probed with his toes, lowering himself down the steep pile of clammy boulders.

The tide had come in. Come in and probably was now going back out, because when Indrajit reached the bottom, he was standing on wet sand. Turning southward again, keeping the mass of boulders on his left, he was able to see a narrow, winding strip of sea-licked beach before him.

The gray strip led him around a small bay and then a promontory, and Indrajit could see that the waters were receding quickly now, so that the sand on which he ran felt cool and firm, but not wet. He didn't hear voices behind him, but the fog got thicker as the night went on, and he didn't dare slow his pace to see whether he was being followed. The beach got noticeably rockier as he traced the edge of a second promontory, and then he ran into the fishing village.

He knew it was the same village that he'd been in earlier, because one of the buildings had burned, its thatch and timbers entirely gone and its plastered rocks scorched black. There were no lights, and there was no sign of any of the triangle-faced people who lived here.

Indrajit stepped on a stick.

Looking down, he saw an arrow, made by laying out sticks, that pointed down the narrow channel of water toward the sea. He could barely make it out, but scratched into the sand beside the arrow was the heraldic image of Orem Thrush, the Lord Chamberlain: a horned skull.

Indrajit looked down the stream and saw a dim flicker of movement, halfway down the lengthening beach to the rolling waves. That had to be Fix.

His legs ached, but he forced them to run. At least here, the sand was smooth and pure and his bare feet were not a disadvantage. He was just leaving the huddle of cottages when he saw a smudge of movement in his peripheral vision. Turning his head, he saw a creature like a centipede—long, segmented, chitinous body, many legs—emerge from the burned hovel, climbing right out of the top of the building.

It was like a centipede, only it was the length of a horse and the height of a dog, and it had a man's face on the front end. A man's face with two long mandibles.

Indrajit stopped and pointed at the thing. "Payot!" he shouted. "They need you up at the necropolis!"

It was a guess, and a bluff, and it almost worked. The thing—or rather, Payot—stopped and stared at Indrajit. There was enough dim light on its face that Indrajit thought he could see Payot frown and then blink.

"The Lobster Hands guy," Indrajit said, pushing his luck. "He sent for you."

Payot laughed and charged.

Indrajit turned and ran. He gripped the sheath with his left hand as he galloped and pulled Vacho out. Payot didn't want him, he reminded himself. Payot was after the ambassador. Indrajit could slow Payot down and then get out of his way, and Indrajit could probably slink off without being pursued.

"Run!" he bellowed.

He could see Fix and the Pelthite prince now. They were carrying a coracle between them and they were lurching down toward the waves, ever slipping away. They raised their heads when Indrajit yelled, and then ran faster.

A chitinous rattle rose in volume behind Indrajit, and he spun about. Payot lunged toward his legs, mandibles clacking together—

Indrajit leaped into the air, vaulting up and over Payot's head. He came down with both bare heels in the center of the centipede's back.

Payot squealed and veered sideways, throwing Indrajit off. Indrajit managed to keep his grip on Vacho and land on a shoulder, then roll to his feet. Payot swerved and spun himself in a continuous circle, hissing angrily.

Shouts from the top of the beach told Indrajit that others were coming. He sped down the beach again.

He nearly stepped on the lizard, which ran just behind Banus, but the creature leaped nimbly aside as Indrajit caught up.

The shouts behind were closer.

He could hear Payot's hissing and the chitinous rattle again.

Their feet splashed into water. Fix and the prince threw the coracle into the waves and the lizard leaped in first.

"This won't hold all of us," Fix grunted.

"I'll swim," Indrajit said.

With a sudden scream, Banus tripped and fell into the surf.

"Frozen hells!" Indrajit sloshed to a stop and turned. Zalaptings rushed down the beach in his direction. Behind them came Lobster Hands and Payot. He grabbed Banus by the elbow and tried to raise the young man, but the Pelthite only thrashed about and whimpered. "Hold the coracle!" Indrajit shouted to Fix. "I'm coming!"

Only he wasn't coming. He was stuck, trying to get Banus to his feet, and exhaustion or panic or some cause Indrajit didn't know was keeping the young man trapped.

Indrajit was going to be overrun and killed. He spread his legs and stood over the prince, swinging Vacho before with a bravado he didn't feel in his heart.

The lizard appeared, thrashing through the waves, and climbed onto Banus's face. Would the comfort of his pet reptile help the prince rise? Indrajit stepped aside as the prince rolled over—

And then the lizard tore open the veins of the young man's throat with its teeth.

The surf was cold and the young man's blood was a hot jet on Indrajit's ankle. "No!" he roared.

The lizard rose onto its hind legs and looked him in the eye. "*I* am the ambassador," it said in a low whisper. Then it raced into the water.

Indrajit stared at the young man in his death throes, but only for a moment. He had no choice but to believe the lizard—it could be telling the truth, and in any case, Banus was dead already. Indrajit sheathed his sword, ran until the water was up to his thighs, and then dove in. The salt water was cold and bracing, the strength of the waves gave Indrajit something to push against, and the swim invigorated him.

A bowshot from the coast, he met up with the coracle. Was he just getting used to the darkness, or was the fog lifting? Overhead, Indrajit saw several of the brighter summer stars.

Fix paddled the coracle and talked with the green lizard. On the beach, Payot and Lobster Hands and a dozen Zalaptings dragged the body of Banus up the sand; none of them followed into the water.

"I would have left a written message," Fix said, amusement in his voice, "only you insist on refusing to learn to read."

Indrajit ignored him. "How do we know you're the ambassador?" he asked the reptile.

The lizard fixed him with a cold eye. The ruff around its neck splayed out and grew stiff, which made the lizard look formal and important. "In fact, it doesn't really matter. The boy is dead and you'll take me to Orem, because I am all that remains of this task of yours. But since I *am* the ambassador, Orem will be pleased at your success. But if it helps you in the meantime, ask yourself this: What is more likely? That the ambassador's pet lizard killed him to escape, when no one was seeking the pet? Or that the ambassador sacrificed his pet man to aid his flight?"

"Banus never claimed he was the ambassador," Indrajit said thoughtfully, "but he did tell us he was a prince."

"Do you know how many princes Pelth has?" the lizard asked. "He was a *disposable* nobleman, with no wealth and no power. He was given to me at my appointment, to be my bearer."

"How does one address a Pelthite ambassador?" Indrajit asked.

"'Sir' will do fine," the lizard said. There might have been a hint of a grin on its needlelike snout.

"That's not the strangest thing I've ever heard," Fix said. "It is . . . a little surprising."

"Why kill your . . . bearer?" Indrajit asked.

The lizard made a rattling sound in its throat that might have been a sigh. "I saw your compassion and self-sacrifice. You gave the prince a weapon. You offered him your water. You split up and tried to divert pursuit. You stayed behind to slow them down. You risked yourself for him, or rather, for the ambassador you thought he *was*, before, and you would have done it again. I admire your impulse to sacrifice yourself, it is noble. But in this case, I could not permit you to indulge it.

"And Banus had to be left behind. They thought he was the ambassador; he was the only sacrifice that would stop pursuit.

"If I had tried to persuade you I was the ambassador, you wouldn't have believed me. Even a delay while I tried to persuade you likely would have proved fatal. You both would have stayed and died on the beach, fighting for that pretty, but useless, young man. Then I would have been left alone, to try to make my way to the city without a guide and without protection. My work and my mission are too important. It was time for a sacrifice, and the sacrifice had to be my poor Banus."

Indrajit had nothing to say. In other circumstances, the sacrifice could just as easily have been him, and then this lizard would have been sitting in the coracle, explaining to Banus and Fix how important it had been to kill Indrajit.

Fix just paddled.

"Let us finish the journey in silence, then," the lizard said. "We will grieve Banus together, and drink a cup with the Lord Chamberlain. For Banus, and for sacrifices."

Indrajit shook his head. He held the back of the coracle and swam.

No Trade for Nice Guys

〜◦〜

"Look," Indrajit Twang said, "this isn't hard. You can tell us where you got the necklace. We know it was a black-market dealer of some kind, someone willing to sell stolen goods, and that's who *we're* looking for. We don't care about you. Our *patron* doesn't care about you."

"Patron?" Fibulous Mosk, the pottery merchant, was pale green, nearly spherical, and sweating. The fingers of all four of his hands, sixteen digits in total, drummed on his countertop.

"Yes, our patron." Indrajit took a large red vase from the shelves and hefted it. Imitation astrological Bonean glyphs were painted around the vase's mouth in gold to add class, but the color of the glazing clearly said that the work was local. He swung the vase experimentally, as if considering how he might smash it on the floor. Indrajit's partner, Fix, joined in the implied threat, hoisting a pair of red clay jugs by their handles. "Did you think we were here on our own? What, just looking for a little stolen jewelry?"

Mosk shrugged. "I don't know you guys."

"You haven't heard of us? The Protagonists? We're a famous jobber company. We're the terror of risk-merchants and joint-stock promoters throughout the Paper Sook."

The merchant shrugged again, helpless.

"Anyway," Indrajit continued, "we *are*, and our patron is looking for the thief who stole this necklace. Our patron spotted the jewelry at a ball of some kind, around your wife's lovely green neck." In actuality, the necklace had been spotted by Grit Wopal, the Yifft who was the head of the Lord Chamberlain's Ears, and to whom Indrajit and Fix reported. And also, in actuality, Mosk's wife didn't have a neck. Indrajit had no idea how she wore the necklace, which he and Fix had retrieved from her wardrobe. "To track our way back to the thief, we need to find the vendor. So just tell us where you bought it, and we'll have no more trouble."

Fix flashed the jewelry to remind the merchant and sharpen his wits.

Mosk hissed, the upturned cups that sprouted on his head like grass on a picnic field trembling. "What did you do with my wife?"

"Nothing," Indrajit said.

"But you're going to hurt her, if I don't turn over my... jeweler? You stole her necklace to show me you could hurt my family if you want to?"

Fix met Indrajit's gaze and squinted. He could do that, even standing to Indrajit's side, because Indrajit's eyes were set so far back on the sides of his skull, Fix sometimes teased him that he was descended from a fish.

Fix shook his head, a subtle warning to his friend.

"We're not going to hurt your wife," Indrajit said.

The green shopkeeper's eyes narrowed. "Nice guys, is it? Yours is no trade for nice guys."

Fix smashed a jug against the countertop, sending baked clay shards flying in all directions.

"Okay, okay!" The merchant waved his hands in surrender, to avert any more destruction. "I'll tell you!"

Fix raised the second jug over his head, and Indrajit set the necklace on the countertop. "We're listening," Indrajit said.

Mosk cocked his head at Fix. "Does he *ever* talk, then?"

"He talks more when you get to know him," Indrajit said. "It isn't an improvement."

"Do I get the necklace back?" Mosk licked his lips. In contrast to the pale green of his skin, his tongue was a bright crimson.

"If the information pans out—" Indrajit started to say.

"No," Fix said. Indrajit's partner was shorter than he was, but broad-shouldered and stocky. The high-pitched, soft voice that came out of him still surprised Indrajit, though they'd been partners now for weeks. Feminine though the voice could sound, it was still forceful. "We keep the necklace."

"No?" Mosk was disappointed, and the thin blue ridges over his eyes rose up and wrinkled together. Then they coalesced into a stony glare of resolve. "In that case, I can't see that I have any reason to help you."

"Sure you do," Indrajit said, thinking fast. He had planned to give the man back the necklace, provided that his information proved to be accurate. "You'll help us *because* we're the good guys."

Mosk shook his head. "If I help you, then my source gets angry with me."

"Maybe." Indrajit shrugged. "But you know that we'll play nice with your jeweler, just like we're being nice with you."

"That doesn't guarantee my source will forgive me."

"True," Indrajit agreed. "But if we have to go back to our patron and report failure, he'll be angry."

"Our patron is Orem Thrush," Fix said. "The Lord Chamberlain."

"Thrush?" Fibulous Mosk grew visibly paler.

"Orem Thrush," Fix said again. "The beast with a hundred faces, who walks unseen among the people of Kish because he can take any face he wants."

That wasn't completely accurate, but there was truth in it; Thrush's face could metamorphose into masks resembling the faces of those around him. Indrajit wasn't really sure whether Thrush consciously controlled the phenomenon, but it allowed the Lord Chamberlain to move about Kish anonymously. It also gave rise to extravagant rumors.

"He'll probably kill us," Indrajit said. "And then he'll send some other jobbers to catch the thief. And those guys will be better armed, more numerous, and probably really mean. You know, typical short-tunic bruisers. And just like *we* found you and your wife, *they'll* find you and your wife."

"They'll beat the information out of you," Fix said. "Or out of her."

"And your jeweler will meet them, and be really unhappy."

Fix nodded solemnly. "We're gentle. We're your best option."

"We really are." Indrajit recovered the necklace and slid it into the pocket of his kilt. "So save everyone the trouble, won't you? Just tell us who sold you the necklace."

"Was it in the Spill?" Fix suggested. "In the Alley of Ten Thousand Eyes?" The street he named was a narrow avenue that was home to a dozen jewelers. It was located near the Paper Sook, where Indrajit and Fix spent much of their time, because the presence of so much money meant the area crawled with armed guards, and crime was rare.

Or anyway, some crimes, like robbery and burglary, were rare.

Fibulous Mosk shuddered. "It's in the Dregs."

Indrajit frowned. "I don't know a jeweler in the Dregs. Do you?"

"There are no jewelers in the Dregs," Fix said. "Pickpockets, lepers, burglars, madmen, whores, beggars, cutthroats, sell-swords—"

"Cheap sell-swords," Indrajit said.

Fix nodded. "—smugglers, kidnappers, arsonists, poisoners, rabble-rousers, madmen, and drug addicts, yes. Also the Vin Dalu. But no jewelers."

"My source isn't a jeweler," Mosk said. "He's a fence. I...needed to impress my wife. Buying goods that were... previously owned..."

"*Stolen*," Fix said.

"...was the only way I could afford what she wanted."

"That makes more sense," Indrajit said. "A fence would be right at home in the Dregs."

"What fence?" Fix asked.

"His name is Jaxter Boom."

"Jaxter Boom," Fix said. "The Puppeteer."

"Whoa." Indrajit shook his head. "A jeweler, I believe. A fence, that makes sense. But puppets?"

"They call Boom the Puppeteer because he controls so many other fences," Mosk said. "As well as smugglers and thieves. The Puppeteer is a gangster, a crime lord, one of the Gray Lords of Kish."

"My kind of people," Indrajit lied.

"I don't think Boom is one of the Gray Lords," Fix said. "Not that I have thorough knowledge of the city's thieves' guilds. But I don't think he's that important."

"Well, then," Indrajit said, "tell us how to find this Puppeteer, and we're on our way."

The green drained right out of Mosk, leaving him looking nearly white.

"Come on." Indrajit tapped his thumb against the pommel of his leaf-bladed broadsword, Vacho. "Give us the streets, and our business here is done. You never have to see us again—or at least, not until you commit risk-merchantry fraud, or swindle your investors."

Fix was looking intently at the pottery merchant.

Fibulous Mosk trembled.

"One last time," Indrajit began, swelling his voice up to trumpet level.

"No need," Fix said. "I know where Boom lives."

"Really?" Indrajit felt caught off-balance. "They can't have taught you that at the ashrama, as one of your ten thousand useless pieces of lore." Fix had been plucked from the street as a child and raised to become a priest of Salish-Bozar the White, god of useless knowledge. He'd walked away from the priesthood for a woman, who had then married someone else.

Mosk shook so violently, he knocked his ledger from his countertop.

"You forget that I'm *from* here," Fix said. "I was a street urchin for years before I was ever a devotee of Salish-Bozar. Everyone knows the lair of the Puppeteer. That was a useful piece of information, especially for any kid who ever aspired to be a thief."

"Lair, that's good. We should call our offices a 'lair.'" Indrajit looked back at the shopkeeper, who was melting into the corner, the gnarled ridges on his face softened and gone flat. "We're done here, then?"

Fix nodded. "We're done. And you, Mosk," he added, his voice tightening into a high-pitched snarl, "don't you dare warn the Puppeteer that we're coming."

Indrajit and Fix exited onto the street. Outside, the summer sun baked the cobblestones of the Lee even through the thick, wet swaddling of summer haze. Indrajit followed Fix as the shorter man turned right, downhill, and then ducked into a large cloth merchant's tent just down the street and across from the potter's shop.

"I'm glad you caught on," Fix whispered, as the two men turned to look back at Mosk's shop. "I was worried you were going to push him too far and make him snap."

"*I'm* worried you played that last line a little too hard." Indrajit sniffed. "You can tell a *child* not to do exactly the thing that you want it to do, but a grown man?"

"I had to plant the thought in his head," Fix said. "It will work, and it will work quickly. He'll send his shop boy, any minute."

A third person intruded into their conversation; the shop's clerk was tall and thin, with luminous circles under her eyes and dry, scaly skin. An orange tail whisked the cobblestones behind her. She smiled. "Can I show you gentlemen any fabric?"

Fix grunted.

"Yes." Indrajit sighed. "Bring me a bolt of your cheapest, coarsest cloth. Burlap, if you have it. I mean really, the worst you have."

The clerk sniffed. "We don't carry cheap cloth here. Perhaps you'd prefer to shop in the Caravanserai."

"Your least elegant, then," Indrajit said. "Whatever no one else is buying." He pressed two asimi into the clerk's hand; she sniffed, but didn't return the money, and disappeared into the deeper chambers of the tent.

"You're a prodigal," Fix said, "a spendthrift."

"I know what a prodigal is."

"You didn't have to give her money."

"I'm pretty sure it wasn't very much." Indrajit kept his eyes pinned on the door. "Besides, we might be gone before she gets back, and I don't want to ruin her day."

"You didn't want to ruin Mosk's day, either, so you were going to let him keep the Lord Chamberlain's stolen necklace."

"Which the Lord Chamberlain doesn't care that much about, because *he's* willing to let *us* keep it."

"Let me rephrase myself. You were willing to give away the biggest part of the payment that Orem Thrush promised us, three-quarters of our reward, if I'm any judge of jewelry at all, for finding this thief."

"Which we're only entitled to if we actually bring back

the thief. Alive. Thrush really emphasized the *alive* part."
Indrajit shuddered, thinking of the beating he'd received
the first time he'd entered the presence of Orem Thrush.
"To be tortured, presumably."

"Think about what you're saying. You were willing to
spend money we haven't actually earned yet, and might
not earn at all."

Indrajit sighed. "Now you're going to tell me we have
a business to run and expenses to cover."

"I'm glad to see that I don't have to." Fix snorted.
"Mosk isn't entirely wrong when he says this is no trade
for nice guys."

"He's right about that," Indrajit said. "This is a trade
for *heroes.*"

The clerk returned with a bolt of cloth. It was undyed
linen, and Indrajit wasted only moments fingering it.
"Fifteen cubits," he said to the clerk. "One ten-cubit
length, and one five-cubit."

The clerk cut the lengths of fabric, named a price, and
Indrajit handed over the coins.

"You could have bargained," Fix said. "Now you've got
two lengths of cheap fabric that was surprisingly costly."

"False." Indrajit tossed the ten-cubit length to his
partner. "Now *you* have a toga, and *I* have a cloak.
Assuming they taught you to tie a toga at the ashrama."

At that moment, Fibulous Mosk himself scurried out
of the front door of his shop, and turned uphill, toward
the Crown, the finest quarter of Kish and the one that lay
within its walls at the top of the hill upon which Kish
sprawled. Through the Crown was the shortest, and the
safest, route to the Dregs. The potter had a broad hat on

his head, with a scarf swathed around his neck and chin to screen him from the sun, and also to hide his face. Indrajit recognized the merchant from his green forehead and the pale green skin of his four forearms.

Fix quickly folded himself into a toga; he was Kishi, the most common race of man in Kish, so the toga ought to make him essentially invisible, especially in the wealthier quarters of the city. It also nicely hid his hatchet, falchion, and long knives, and his spear might be mistaken for a walking staff, especially at a distance. Indrajit, on the other hand, was tall, with wide-set eyes, a bony ridge for a nose, and a faint greenish tint to his mahogany skin, so he had a hard time disappearing into a crowd, even in Kish, where half the thousand races of man passed through the streets every day; instead, he wrapped the linen about his head and shoulders as a cloak and hood.

Then they slipped into the street and followed the potter.

The Lee, lying on the landward side of Kish, was sheltered from the brunt of the weather that came in from the sea. On the south-facing slopes of Kish's mound, it got the largest share of heat and light in all seasons. The summer sun hammered on Indrajit and Fix both, but Fix was a native, and underneath his toga he wore only his kilt, and the hike up into the Crown brought only the faintest trace of a crown of sweat to his brow. Indrajit, who was from cooler and wetter climes, and who now isolated his face from what breeze there was behind a linen hood, was soon panting.

They passed through the usual commercial traffic of the Lee: Droggers carrying burdens to or from warehouses, tradesmen shouting the virtues of their wares, shoppers in togas followed by their servants. Indrajit accidentally stumbled into a scab-eyed Gund, provoking a bellow and a hiss from the pale giant, but Mosk didn't turn around.

Jobbers in green and gold, wearing the hammer and sword device of the Lord Farrier, watched the gates. Indrajit ignored them and was ignored in turn, shuffling through the gates a stone's throw behind the four-armed potter.

Chanting came from Indrajit's right as they passed within a few streets of the Sun Seat. Celebrants there would be preparing to receive the procession that marked the longest day of the year and one of the two turning points of the city's calendar. The summer procession, like its winter counterpart, was a holdover from the old Imperial days, when Kish had indulged in much more ceremony.

Turning right shortly beyond the Sun Seat, Indrajit and Fix followed the pottery merchant through another gate and into the Dregs.

Several quarters could reasonably vie for the title of "worst quarter of Kish." The Dregs did not *smell* the worst—that distinction belonged to either the East or West Flats, where the city's fishers lived and hauled in their catches. The city's worst abuses of power were likely planned in the Crown, and its financial crimes were committed in the Spill. But the Dregs was home to the contagious, the footpads, the poxy, and the murderous. It was the weeping sore of Kish.

"You didn't really live in here as a street urchin," Indrajit murmured to his partner.

"I was a homeless beggar child," Fix said. "I slept wherever people wouldn't kick me out. Believe it or not, yes, some of the more welcoming corners I slept in were here."

"Ugh." Indrajit raised his knee to step carefully over a pile of droppings whose species of origin he couldn't even guess at.

Mosk turned and turned again. At each change of direction, Indrajit and Fix rushed to catch up and then carefully watched at the merchant turned down a narrow alley, and then into a tiny plaza, choked by buildings that rose around it and leaned inward as they climbed, leaving a patch of bright sky at the top only a quarter the size of the stained cobblestones below.

Within the plaza, Mosk stood at a broad, unmarked door, talking to a tall figure wearing a black cloak. A drooping mass of flesh like an elephant's trunk descended from the open hood and twitched as Mosk whispered urgently.

Indrajit's long legs took him across the plaza in three quick steps. "Friend Mosk!" he called, letting his hood fall back to reveal his face. Just in case, he kept his hand on Vacho's hilt, concealed under his cloak. "Friend Mosk, thank you!"

Fibulous Mosk wheeled. His scarf fell away from his face, and terror twisted his green features. "But! But!"

Indrajit addressed the cloaked guard. "Our friend Fibulous has such a quick pace, he nearly left us behind. But you'd have looked a little silly, coming into Jaxter Boom's … office … to introduce us to Boom … without us!"

Fix caught up, throwing an arm around the pottery merchant. Indrajit heard the man's knees knock.

The doorman shook with slow laughter. Long, shaggy hair hung down around the proboscis, trembling like leaves in the wind. "The Protagonists. You would be Indrajit Twang, and the shorter one is Fiximon Nasoprominentus Fascicular. The scholar."

"Dammit, Twang," Fix snarled. "Stop telling people that's my name."

"It's not my fault your name is so short," Indrajit protested. "It's an undignified name for a literary man."

The guard laughed again. "You've arrived earlier than we expected. My master will be pleased. But you don't need an introduction."

Indrajit felt uneasy. "In that case," he said slowly, "we should probably let our mutual friend go. He has pots to sell."

Fibulous Mosk made a squeaking noise as he escaped, that might have been intended to communicate relief or gratitude.

The doorman opened the door. Within the hood, two twinkles briefly flashed in Indrajit's direction, hinting at unseen eyes. Indrajit discreetly checked that the necklace was safely stowed in his kilt pocket, smiled at the guard, and stepped through the door. Fix followed.

The steps immediately behind the door descended steeply, each step so narrow it could barely accommodate one of Indrajit's sandaled heels. The ceiling overhead was low, forcing him to stoop.

"Be glad you're not a Grokonk," Fix said.

"The existence of low ceilings is the least of *many*

reasons why I am relieved not to be a Grokonk. The choice between being voiceless and sexless is a much more serious drawback."

"I don't know," Fix said. "I think you would do fine as a voiceless man."

The stairs ended in a high-ceilinged, long chamber, with arches opening onto dark passages along both sides. At the far end of the room, two coal-filled braziers gave light, illuminating a glass wall, behind which sloshed dark water. The glass didn't rise all the way to the ceiling, and its depths were dark, suggesting that Indrajit was only seeing the very end of a large tank. Left and right, two low pedestals stood pressed against the glass. Two young Kishi, a woman and a man, stood on the pedestals. They wore tattered shifts and leaned back against the glass as if they needed the support; their bodies were emaciated, their eyes vacant.

Indrajit and Fix strode forward. Behind him and to his right, Indrajit heard the steps of the guard with the long nose.

"Surely, neither of these wretches can be the famed Jaxter Boom," Indrajit said.

"Boom is coming," Proboscis told them.

Indrajit heard many footfalls. Keeping his facial expression light and cheerful, he turned his head slightly. In his excellent peripheral vision, he saw all the arches exiting the room, as well as the exit to the staircase, filling with armed men. They wore no uniform and their weapons were irregular, suggesting they weren't a jobber company or any other kind of irregular force—just thugs hired by Jaxter Boom, armed with long knives, short spears, clubs, and axes.

"Good," he said.

With a muted *whoosh* sound, something pressed itself against the glass. For a moment, Indrajit saw only indistinguishable flesh, pink and so pale it was almost white, but then a lashless blue eye opened, pressing itself against the glass. With a soft *splash*, two masses of pink flesh rose above the glass wall, unfurling themselves until Indrajit could see they were tentacles. The tentacles reached forward, each touching the back of the skull of one of the Kishi standing on the pedestals—

And then pushing forward, entering the heads of the Kishi.

The two Kishi straightened their backs, standing up. Energy seemed to fill their frames; their backs straightened and their vacant eyes lit up, but the light was unnatural and sickly.

"I am Jaxter Boom," the Kishi said. Their voices spoke at the same pitch and in perfect unison, but somehow managed to clash with each other.

Indrajit took a deep breath.

"I assume you are the . . . person in the tank, and not the people standing on pedestals in front of us," he said.

"Correct," the Kishi answered in unison.

"That must be uncomfortable for *them*," Indrajit said.

"They have neither comfort nor discomfort," the Kishi said together. "They have ceased to be men, and are now simply the Voices of Jaxter Boom."

"You have two for the symmetry?" Indrajit asked. "Or because it lets you shout louder?"

"You have two because they wear out quickly," Fix said softly. "Look at them, they're wasting away. And with two at all times, you won't be left without a Voice. You must keep . . . spares."

"Correct, Fix of the Protagonists," the Voices said.

Indrajit wanted to know more, out of natural curiosity and because, as Recital Thane, he had yet to compose his additions to the Blaatshi Epic, and this strange race of men was not one that yet appeared in the Epic. Indrajit wanted to know more so that he could construct pointed kennings and compose stock epithets.

In addition, Indrajit was curious how Boom knew their names and expected their arrival.

But he also didn't want to aggravate this crime lord in his own lair.

"A thief sold you this." He held up the necklace so that the lashless eye could gaze directly at it. "We're hunting the thief."

"I have the thief," the Voices said. "She tried to cheat me. If you're seeking justice, be assured that the thief shall receive it."

The thief was a woman. "We've been tasked with bringing the thief back alive," Indrajit said, smiling. "Perhaps you could surrender her to us, and rest easy in the knowledge that the Lord Chamberlain will have her punished thoroughly enough for the wrongs she has committed against both of you."

There followed a long moment of silence.

"No," the Voices said. "I do not think I shall surrender my prerogative of justice so easily."

What could the thief have done to so irritate this crime lord, that it wanted her punished, and hadn't killed her already?

"We're prepared to pay," Indrajit said.

Fix groaned in disgust.

"How much?" the Voices asked.

"Nothing," Indrajit said, "until we see the thief and can ascertain that she's really the one who robbed the Lord Chamberlain. And then, we're willing to negotiate. Where is she? In some cell? Stretched on the rack? You're not planning on using her as one of your Voices, are you?"

"I'll permit you to see her," the Voices said, "for the price of the necklace."

"We may be willing to pay for the necklace," Indrajit said, "if you give her to us first."

"The necklace for a look." The Voices made a horrible rasping noise that might have been laughter.

"What kind of spendthrifts do you take us for?" Indrajit scowled.

"Agreed," Fix said. "The necklace for a look."

Indrajit stared at his partner.

Fix whispered, "I think more is going on here than appears."

"So it's bad if I spend money, but prudent if you do it?" Indrajit asked.

"In this case, yes."

"Throw the necklace into the tank," the Voices commanded.

"If I'm wrong," Fix continued, "I'll take responsibility for the necklace."

"Don't be an idiot," Indrajit told his partner. "If you're wrong, we tell Grit Wopal we never found the necklace."

He threw the jewelry into the tank. It sank past the

staring eye, settling on the bottom, still visible as a dull, brassy glow.

"Bring in the thief," the Voices commanded.

A rustle of grumbled complaints and padding feet to Indrajit's left ended as a young woman stumbled out into the room. Her hands were tied with a thong, and she wore a simple tunic and skirt, both of silk, that had once been elegant but were now ragged and filthy. She had an ordinary Kishi complexion and an unremarkable, rather blocky face beneath long black hair. As she glared at Indrajit, something flashed through her eyes.

Hope? Recognition?

Then the woman straightened her back and snarled. There was something familiar about her.

"How about it, then?" Indrajit asked. "Did you steal from the Lord Chamberlain?"

"The hells with you!" the girl snapped.

"Well, *that* was certainly worth three-quarters of our pay," he murmured to Fix.

"Look again," Fix murmured back.

The young woman's face was subtly shifting. Her skin grew darker, and her nose began to bulge up in a bony ridge as her eyes seemed to swim toward her ears.

"Frozen hells," Indrajit said.

"Do you understand what you are seeing here?" the Voices asked.

Indrajit thought furiously. They were vastly outnumbered. Jaxter Boom was not going to surrender his prisoner; he was going to use her to get leverage against the Lord Chamberlain, and possibly for nefarious purposes.

Certainly for nefarious purposes—what other kind of purpose could such a creature have?

"You'll recall that you once had questions about my people's ancestry," Indrajit said softly.

"I still maintain that you are descended from your goddess," Fix answered.

"Good. I see only one way out by which we are not outnumbered, oh, about twenty to one."

"I'm ready," Fix said.

"Do you *understand*?" the Voices demanded.

Indrajit played dumb, just a little longer. He stepped closer to the young woman who had to be kin to Orem Thrush—a daughter? A niece?—and pretended to examine her as he would a Ylakka he was considering purchasing.

He needed to get into position.

And besides, maybe they could still get out without violence.

"She looks poor, more than anything else," Indrajit said. "She's wearing someone else's stolen clothing, obviously, but she can't be a very good thief, because she's worn that to rags and hasn't been able to buy or steal a replacement."

"I'll wear your head for a helmet," the girl said to him, "and make a kilt of your hide."

She certainly sounded like Orem Thrush.

While all eyes were on Indrajit, Fix drifted back, positioning himself close to one of the Voices.

"You have the necklace," Indrajit said to Jaxter Boom. "On top of that, I'll give you ten Imperials to let us take her back to the Lord Chamberlain for *punishment*." He met the girl's gaze as he spoke, and saw again the flicker of emotion.

"You idiot," the Voices boomed. "How well do you know your master?"

Indrajit shrugged, took a deep breath, and sighed. "I know him well enough to *go*!"

He shouted this last word, and as he did so, he grabbed the young woman, wrapped his hands around her hips, and hurled her up and over the glass.

At the same moment, Fix leaped onto the pedestal and stabbed a long knife into one of the tentacles, just beside the Voice's skull.

Men roared and drew weapons. Indrajit kicked over the nearest brazier, sending glowing coals in an arc toward the center of the room, and then grabbed for the second tentacle.

Jaxter Boom yanked both his tentacles back. This had the effect of pulling Fix into the tank, and as the short man hit the water, he was raising his spear over his head with his right hand, preparing to stab. The disappearance of the tentacles also meant that Indrajit missed his grab, seizing instead the top of the glass and scrabbling to drag himself up and over—

But hands seized his ankles.

Indrajit dragged his upper body closer to the tank, touching the glass with his chin. Dark ichor clouded the water of the tank as Fix stabbed into Jaxter Boom's eye. The two Voices staggered forward into the crowd of criminals, knocking some men down and tripping others. Blows landed on Indrajit's back and legs. He bellowed and shook himself, trying to writhe free. Looking back, he saw the doorman with the long nose, holding tightly to Indrajit's right leg. Indrajit lost both sandals, but was also losing his grip on the glass—

The thief grabbed Indrajit by the head. Placing her feet against the glass, she kicked herself back and down, and with the weight of her body, she hauled Indrajit away from the men grabbing him.

Indrajit kicked, landing a blow on Long Nose's face.

Then he splashed into the water just ahead of two sword points. Through the glass, he saw men with spears plowing through the crowd.

"Are we sure there's a way out?" the young woman asked.

"No," Indrajit said. "Take a deep breath!"

She did, and he grabbed the cord that tied her hands together. It made a convenient handle by which to pull her, and Indrajit dove.

Fix's kicking feet ahead of him indicated the path, and Indrajit followed. Thin, wispy clouds of black ichor dissipated as Indrajit swam directly into them, shattering them with his one-armed stroke. He fought his way out of his own burlap cloak, and then through the clinging film of Fix's burlap toga.

Fix plunged into darkness and disappeared.

Were they going to die? Had Indrajit made a terrible, final mistake?

For long moments, he struggled against black despair as he stroked. The rescued prisoner had taken a breath as directed, and she was cooperating, kicking her feet behind her, but she was doing so awkwardly. She wasn't a great swimmer, and if she started to run out of air she might panic.

Behind him, Indrajit heard faint splashes. Looking over

his shoulder, he saw the heads and shafts of long spears being stabbed into the water. Then he heard a larger splash and saw the first of Jaxter Boom's men plunge into the water.

He focused on the path ahead, and saw a glimmer of light. Fix wiggled, a dark silhouette on the right side of Indrajit's frame of vision. Then the light shone down directly on Fix's body, and Indrajit saw his partner stop, look upward, and then swim up toward the light.

Toward air, hopefully. Indrajit's lungs ached.

Four long tentacles reached out from the darkness and grabbed Fix.

Indrajit yelled out of pure instinct, and shouted the last air from his lungs out into the water. Instantly, he felt dizzy, and sank. He was going to die, suffocated, or crushed by the same arms that were now drawing Fix out of the light and back into darkness.

His foot touched rock and he felt the young woman thrashing. Bracing himself, he pushed her forward, toward the light, and then with his right hand he drew Vacho from its sheath.

Inanely, some part of him wanted to shout a battle cry, like the heroes of the Epic. Vacho was, after all, named after the lightning-sword of Inder, an ancient name of the city's great storm god, Hort. Fortunately, Indrajit had mastered his instinct to yell again, and instead lunged upward through the shaft of light into the darkness, left hand extended and groping, right hand tucked under his shoulder, ready to stab.

To his left, the young woman's feet kicked as she swam up to the light.

Indrajit's fingers found something elastic and smooth, something that tensed as he touched it. His head swam; much more time without air and he would pass out. He closed his hand, found his fingers wrapped around something ropelike, and then pulled himself toward it. In the gloom, he saw Fix, shuddering, a tentacle wrapped around his neck. He saw pale skin, and then an eye.

Indrajit stabbed.

Black ichor jetted from the eye and struck Indrajit in the face.

Darkness. Lights flashed in his vision.

Something hit Indrajit, but he wasn't sure.

What it was.

Warm. He felt.

Warm.

Air forced its way into Indrajit's lungs and he coughed.

Hands gripped his face. Indrajit spat out water and the hands shifted, turning him over onto his side. He gagged, coughed again, and then suddenly he was sucking in warm air. His limbs felt numb and leaden.

"See?" he heard Fix's voice say. "He's at least half fish."

His vision returned, and Indrajit struggled through more coughing to sit up. He was sprawled on a stretch of rocks, and the air reeked of salt and decay.

Fix and the young woman they had rescued stood over him.

"I guess Boom must live in the sea," Fix said, looking out at the water.

Indrajit decided he didn't want to know which of the two had breathed air into him. He wobbled, but with Fix's help he was able to stand up, and then Fix handed him Vacho, hilt first.

"Thanks." Indrajit sheathed his weapon. Sensation was gradually returning to his arms and legs.

"I only ever saw it in the water," the woman said.

"Ouch." Indrajit shook a sharp, stabbing rock out of his foot.

"You guys work for my father," the young woman said.

"You're not a thief." Indrajit took deep breaths, trying to shake a lingering feeling of dizziness.

She shook her head. "My name is Yasta, and that was my necklace. I was kidnapped."

"Boom sold the necklace as a signal," Fix said. "He wanted us to find him, and learn he held Yasta, so that he could have leverage over Yasta's father."

"I guess your father didn't want to tell anyone his daughter had disappeared," Indrajit said to the girl. "And he sent us because he knew we wouldn't want to kill anyone, even someone we thought was a thief."

Fix shook his head. "He sent us because we're the best." He raised a hand, and in it he held Yasta Thrush's necklace. He held it out toward the girl.

"We'd better get moving," Indrajit said. "By the smells, we're near the East Flats, which means we have a bit of a run to get you home. And some of those fellows might be able to swim."

"Keep the necklace," Yasta Thrush said. "It's a fair trade."

Backup

~oo~

"You really shouldn't rely on me to say anything that sounds remotely intelligent in this meeting," Indrajit warned his partner.

"Believe me," Fix said in his high-pitched voice, "I know. You're just the backup."

Both men wore togas. Indrajit's was a dark orange and Fix's was a rich purple, with strong notes of blue. They weren't the false togas that were really just robes, easier to move in and adopted by the merchant class when they wanted to appear wealthy, but wrap-around-the-body-and-pin-over-the-shoulder togas. They weren't uncomfortable; if he were compelled to pronounce on the comfort of the garment, Indrajit would even have said that it felt good. Air flowed around his thighs as it did when he wore his customary and preferred kilt, and under his arms as it did when he wore the loose tunic he liked, and he felt at ease.

But if he ran, he worried that the toga would slip and trip him. And there was no room in the toga to hide his legendary sword, Vacho, so Indrajit was reduced to wearing a stiletto on a belt wrapped around his thigh.

The thought that he would be unable to either fight or run made the Recital Thane nervous.

Also, he was wearing perfume. It was a floral scent, though he didn't know the name of the flower.

A bright-blue-skinned wine peddler on the other side of the street caught Indrajit's eye and started across, the tray hanging at the level of his sternum from a strap around his neck jostling only slightly, the cups not even rattling. He raised a jug in one hand, and his face fell when Indrajit waved him off.

"I'm probably being too harsh on myself," Indrajit continued. "I mean, when we were investigating those indoors traders last month—"

"In*side* trading," Fix corrected him. "Not in*doors*."

"Yes, and I was the one who realized what they were up to."

"To be fair," Fix said, "I knew that something was off, since the inside traders in question had already tied me hand and foot and dropped me into a hole underneath their offices."

Indrajit nodded. "Fortunately, I was able to put two and two together, realize exactly what they had been up to, and come to your rescue."

"Yes. If by 'put two and two together' you mean that you overheard Samwit Conker say, 'I am very excited to get rich by this inside trading scheme, just as soon as we kill that fellow Fix, whom we have stashed in the basement.'"

"Not in so many words."

"But almost."

"I was very pleased to be able to rescue you."

"I was pleased, too," Fix said. "I remain pleased. I hope that in the future, every criminal we come up against will have the decency to confess in your presence. It really simplifies the investigative process."

"Also, when a high level of general culture is required, I'll contribute." Indrajit cleared his throat. "But if we need to say something about the horoscopes that were provided to us, I'm right out."

"Projections," Fix said.

"Right." Indrajit nodded. "Papers telling the future."

"Yes, but not by stars or entrails." Fix, too, had to forego his usual falchion and hatchet, and wouldn't be carrying a spear, either. Indrajit didn't think he had so much as a knife on his person. Still, arms folded over his chest, he seemed at ease. "But the real question is whether what we got is a bottom-up or a top-down projection."

"I assume we prefer top-down." Indrajit put on his thinking face, the one he wore to communicate that he understood, that he was taking the conversation very seriously, and he knew the answer to the posed question was likely something sophisticated and nonobvious. "But I am anxious to hear your view."

"The real point is, did someone just bump the revenue number up five percent each year, or did they actually analyze the underlying business on a contract-by-contract basis, in the light of recent Auction House trends, to determine what they thought would happen, and by chance arrive at a round five percent figure?"

"Correct." Indrajit touched a finger to his pursed lips.

Fix snorted. "Don't worry, I'll do the talking."

"I'm just showing you that I can fake it," Indrajit said. "For a little while, at least."

The two men waited for their palanquin to arrive. The sedan chair was being sent by their master, Orem Thrush, the Lord Chamberlain of Kish, but it wouldn't bear his horned skull emblem. It would look luxurious and anonymous, as Fix had specified.

To be precise, the palanquin was being arranged not by Orem Thrush himself, but by Grit Wopal, the Lord Chamberlain's Yifft spymaster. Indrajit and Fix reported to Wopal, not as members of the Lord Chamberlain's espionage organization, the Ears, but as their own separate unit. They formed a two-man jobber crew, nearly anonymous, with the flexibility to undertake a wide range of missions in and around the Paper Sook.

Of all the places and institutions of Kish, the Paper Sook might be the one Indrajit hated the most.

"You must realize that I value you for qualities other than your understanding of how the Paper Sook works." Fix raised a hand as the palanquin hove into view around a corner. It was picking them up at a swanky tavern in the Lee, as arranged, rather than at their quarters at an inn in the Spill.

"But I *do* know how the Paper Sook works."

"Yes," Fix said mildly.

The palanquin stopped. Its six bearers were all thickly muscled men with scaly shoulders and four arms. They ran on their legs and on their middle set of arms, which had horny, callused knuckles. A short, thick tail swished back and forth behind each bearer.

Fix crossed to the far side of the palanquin to enter and Indrajit climbed in where he stood, settling himself with a bolster behind his back and a cushion under his raised knees. With his widely spaced eyes, Indrajit could face forward and still see out the door of the palanquin with his left eye, while his right rested its gaze on Fix. Fix, who had a very ordinary Kishi arrangement of his facial features, looked out his door as the six-limbed palanquin bearers picked them up and began to jog toward the Crown.

"What qualities?" Indrajit asked.

"Hmm?" Fix seemed distracted. Outside the palanquin, the Kish evening was lit with torches, oil lamps, and fires. A three-armed juggler tried to rush the sedan chair, perhaps hoping for a gratuity, but the bearers hurled him back into shadow. A scaled Shamb leaped aside to avoid being struck, and hissed an objection.

"What qualities do you value me for?" Indrajit pressed.

Fix cleared his throat. "Well, for one, you're not needy. You feel very confident in your contributions to our joint enterprise, which makes it always easy to deal with you. I don't have to be gentle to your wounded vanity, or overstate your excellence. I think it's easy to underestimate how attractive that quality is in a partner."

"Yes." Indrajit nodded. "What else?"

"Well, you're tall. And you have good peripheral vision."

"Those traits could prove extraordinarily useful. There is also my knowledge of poetics."

"Though I understand your poetry sounds better in the original Blaatshi."

"Everything sounds better in Blaatshi."

"You're good in a fight," Fix pointed out.

"We're not going to get into a fight tonight," Indrajit said. "We're going to pretend to be investors considering funding the joint-stock company of a new jobber band, while actually investigating the promoters."

"Listen to you," Fix said. "Talking the language of joint-stock companies so well."

"You're trying to distract me."

"We might get into a fight. This is supposed to be a private pitch session, part of what is sometimes called a *road show*, so it should just be us and the promoters."

"And we think they're from out of town."

"Wopal thinks they're foreigners, gathering up local money to pay for an assassination attempt on Orem Thrush."

"Why not just outlaw joint-stock companies?" Indrajit suggested. "Nip this whole thing in the bud?"

"That would have other consequences." They passed the Spike, with its cluster of five temples. They were nearly at their destination now. "Legitimate businesses would be hurt. The assassination organizers would just raise money some other way. And besides, the Lord Chamberlain can't just make things illegal by decree, he's not a king. He'd have to get the heads of the other Houses to agree, or at least four of them, and that never happens. And if it did happen, then they'd have to pay the Auction House to inscribe the new law into the legal code."

"We might get into a fight tonight if the promoters really are crooked, and they conclude that we work for Thrush."

"Correct. And one way they might be led to conclude that is if there are real investors there, and they recognize us. We're anonymous in many places in this town . . ."

"But not in the Paper Sook. Frozen hells." Indrajit sighed. "If I could pick one place in Kish to be well-known, it wouldn't be that one."

"Because all they do in the Sook is yell and trade chits, and that gives you a headache."

"I know what they do in the Paper Sook. They trade shares in companies and they make bets on the future prices of company shares, and they trade currencies, and . . . Hey."

"See?" Fix elbowed his partner. "You *do* understand the Paper Sook."

"Like I said. It still gives me a headache."

The palanquin stopped; they had arrived. The two men climbed out.

"But this road-show meeting," Indrajit said, straightening his toga and looking up at the rectangular palace above them. "It's not being held anywhere near the Sook."

"That would be entirely too unimaginative," Fix said. "The promoters are trying to convince rich men to invest some of their wealth, so they want to radiate wealth and success themselves." From within his toga, he drew the letter of invitation Grit Wopal had given them. "Ergo, we meet in an elegant building, in a fine old neighborhood."

The palace porter looked at the seal on the letter and waved the two men toward a staircase at the back left of the building's inner courtyard. There stood two tall men, bright yellow in color, with narrow eyes, blue on blue, tall feather headdresses, and long spears. The smaller of the two, who had a bent nose and one eyebrow permanently arched high on his forehead, took the letter.

"The Bilzarian Partners?" Bent Nose asked.

"Obviously," Fix said.

Indrajit snorted his contempt for the process.

The palace was four stories tall and six at the corners, so Indrajit was dreading a long and breathless climb. In the event, they shuffled up two flights of stairs to a landing where two more of the tall, blue-eyed yellow men with spears stood. They patted down Indrajit and Fix both, but the search was perfunctory; another beauty of the toga was that it tended to communicate *harmless noncombatant* and therefore discouraged the searchers from carrying out their task with too much zeal.

Indrajit followed Fix under an arch, passing from the landing into an airy, high-ceilinged chamber. A low table in the center of the room was laden with food: roasted tamarind, coconut, mango, rose-apples, apricots, cubes of lamb and goat meat on skewers, a soft white cheese, flatbreads. A pitcher of chilled tea sat surrounded by huddled stone cups. Surrounding the low table were reclining couches and divans piled high with cushions. To Indrajit's left was a taller table, on which rested an open ledger beside an inkpot and a quill.

Two yellow spearmen stood in each of two arches exiting the room.

Beside the low table stood two Xiba'albi men, one wearing a gold collar and the other wearing multiple gold rings. Both had gold hoops in their ears.

Beside the ledger stood a lavender-skinned Zalapting

with a small hump on his back and a gray beard. He wore a simple tunic and kilt, gray in color, and the gray of his tunic and beard and the fading lavender of his skin blurred into a nondescript bland smudge. Beyond him and the table bearing the ledger was an open doorway leading to a balcony. Potted palmetto plants on the balcony muffled the street sounds rising from below.

"Mr. Bilzarian?" one of the Xiba'albi asked.

"Yes," Indrajit and Fix both said.

Oops.

"We're brothers." Indrajit smiled.

"Different mothers," Fix said to the immediately raised eyebrows.

"And we're an exotic race of man," Indrajit continued. "Our appearance varies widely."

The Xiba'albi both bowed deeply. "We are but the subscription agents," one of them said. "Give us a few minutes, and we will bring the issuer out to meet with you. In the meantime, please refresh yourselves. The tea is delicious."

The Xiba'albi swept from the room in a tinkle of gold.

The Zalapting cleared his throat.

"Do we know each other?" Indrajit asked.

The Zalapting inclined his head, a stiff gesture. "I have some familiarity with many of the professionals of the Paper Sook."

Indrajit smiled, but he wasn't sure whether the Zalapting was intimating that he might be a threat. Was he saying he knew that Indrajit and Fix were not who they said they were? Or was the Zalapting bluffing? Or just being polite?

"Perhaps the Bilzarian Partners would care to examine the company's registry while they wait?" the Zalapting suggested, tilting up the book beside him to show the present page.

Indrajit waved fingers, feigning indifference to cover the fact that he couldn't read. This was a good sign, though—it might mean that the Zalapting didn't really know who he was.

Fix peered at the page. "I see."

The Zalapting replaced the book on the table and shifted from foot to foot.

"So . . . you don't work for the issuer, then?" Fix asked.

"I'm a notary's clerk," the Zalapting said. "I'm just here to witness in case any shares are transferred tonight."

Indrajit stretched himself out on a divan and took a handful of apricots. Fix glared at him.

"What?" Indrajit asked.

"We just ate . . . and drank," Fix growled. "How can you still be *thirsty*?"

"Just having a few pieces of fruit," Indrajit said. "To be polite. Welcome to Kish: eat when you can."

His words seemed to irritate rather than calm Fix, and then the shorter man was stalking across the room. "Perhaps you would like to read the register yourself," Fix grunted.

Fix knew very well that Indrajit couldn't read. Indrajit was an oral poet, who could spin out thirty thousand lines of his people's Blaatshi Epic on the toss of a coin, but couldn't read a word of any language. Fix knew this, and had mocked Indrajit repeatedly for all of it.

What was Fix getting at, suggesting Indrajit might like to read?

"Fine," he said, and as he stood, he reached for the tea.

"I'll get that." Fix knocked the pitcher over, spilling tea across the table.

"How clumsy," Indrajit said, waving fingers again to feign . . . being rich, basically. "We shall have to subscribe to more shares, to make up for the tea we have spilled."

The large yellow men looked impassively at him.

"Yes," Fix said, "that's no problem. But first, come take a look at this."

The Zalapting stepped aside and Fix drew Indrajit close to the registry volume.

"What are you trying to say, Fix?" Indrajit murmured under his breath.

"That it's past time you learned to read, for one thing!" Fix snapped.

"This is an awkward time and place to have this argument." Indrajit looked over his shoulder at the nearest yellow spearman and smiled.

Fix jabbed his index finger into the blue ink swirls written on the page to which the registry was opened and lowered his voice. "What our new Zalapting acquaintance here has written is, 'The tea is drugged.'"

"Frozen hells."

"The Bilzarians." These words came from behind them, but they were spoken by a familiar voice.

"Samwit Conker." Indrajit turned around.

Conker was a Wixit, one of the most common races of man in Kish. If Wixits walked on all fours and kept their mouths shut, they might easily be mistaken for some forest-dwelling species of beast, or pets of Kish's wealthy.

Wixits were furred, and looked rather like ferrets. Some might even find them cute.

But Conker stood upright, on his hind legs, on the back of a divan. His hands were on his hips, and he appeared to be in no mood to keep his mouth shut.

"Fix *Bilzarian*," the Wixit said. "The last time I saw you, I was locking you in my basement while I decided what to do with you."

"Apparently, you decided to sell me shares," Fix said.

"Wrong." The Wixit shifted his gaze to Indrajit. "And Twang *Bilzarian*."

"Indrajit is my first name," Indrajit said, "if you care." He longed for his sword.

"I don't. I do care that my rather elaborate plan to drug you and feed you to my lizards has been thwarted."

"You were exiled from Kish," Fix said. "Kish can stand its share of murder and robbery, but your insider trading scheme made the Lord Stargazer lose a lot of money."

"I was too enthusiastic." Conker curled his lips back to show his teeth. "I got greedy."

"I bet he just put a leash on his own neck," Fix continued, "and had one of those Xiba'albi walk him through the gate like a cat."

Samwit Conker arched his back and hissed. "I am no one's pet."

"Or just curled up on some prostitute's lap, pretending to be a handbag," Indrajit continued. "You'd be a good handbag."

"Kish is as porous as a sponge," Conker said. "Nothing easier than to move in and out."

"Welcome to Kish," Indrajit said, quoting one of the

dozens of epigrams featuring the ancient city's name. Some bore wisdom, others humor, but most of all, they told hard truths about the hard city. "Or not, as you please."

"Today the answer will be not." Conker raised an arm and spun one finger in a quick circle. This gesture summoned the yellow spearmen to surround Indrajit and Fix. More of the men slipped from the arched doorways in the process, and Indrajit and his partner found themselves detained by eight warriors.

"You came in through Underkish, didn't you?" Fix asked. "Through the tunnels?"

The Wixit squinted at him. "Why do you say that?"

Fix shrugged. "You stink."

Samwit Conker laughed.

"Welcome to Kish," Indrajit said. "Hold your nose."

"Kill the Zalapting," Conker ordered.

One of the spearmen turned and took a step in the clerk's direction, but Indrajit reached out and touched the man on the chest to restrain him.

"Hey," Indrajit said.

Three spearpoints pressed into the flesh of his chest and arm.

Indrajit swallowed, his throat dry. "You don't need to kill that guy. He's not going to tell anyone anything and he can't stop you. No point in making more enemies than you have to."

Conker stared at Indrajit. "So the clerk is one of Wopal's Ears, too?"

Indrajit shook his head. "None of us are the Lord Chamberlain's Ears. Fix and I are jobbers, you know that. The *Protagonists*."

"Ah, yes." Conker's smile was cold. "The heroes. And you don't want me to kill this innocent registry clerk."

"Just let him go. Or tie him up if you need to."

"He's only a Zalapting. In the time it takes me to kill him, they'll have bred a thousand more."

Indrajit grinned. "Just because he's short, it doesn't mean his life is worthless."

Samwit Conker snarled, but then his snarl broke down into a tittering laugh. "You've got wit, Twang. Perhaps when we are done, I'll keep you. Blinded and gelded, chained to a pit in my throne room, forced to entertain me until you die."

"When you say 'throne room,' I imagine you squatting on a hat box."

"Tie them all up," Conker said to one of the yellow men, a fellow with a taller headdress than the others wore, full of white and purple feathers. "Leave them conscious, if possible."

Indrajit ground his teeth as the yellow men bound his hands behind his back. The fabric of the toga at his shoulder tore around the pin of the brooch as they handled him, but it didn't rip all the way through. "Good move," he told the Wixit. "Hold us for ransom. And you can use the registry clerk as a little kicker during negotiation, if the Lord Chamberlain doesn't want to meet your demands."

"Yes," Samwit Conker said. "Something like that."

Then spears in Indrajit's back prodded him forward.

The captain of the yellow men went first, followed by Fix. Two yellow men held Fix, one gripping each arm, while a third walked behind him, holding a knife to his kidneys. Then a single yellow warrior dragged the Zalapting, and finally three brought Indrajit along.

"Where are you brightly colored fellows from, anyway?" Indrajit asked.

"Why do you care?" Samwit Conker snapped. He must be bringing up the rear.

"Indrajit is probably trying to compose an epithet," Fix said.

"I'm wondering whether I already know one," Indrajit countered. "I don't recall anything about men with yellow skin, but there is an epithet that goes, *Tall men and feathered, who sail the Sea of Rains*. So I would be interested to know if you guys are from Thûl or Xiba'alb or somewhere near the Sea of Rains."

"On second thought," Conker said, "I'm going to have to kill you. Nothing else will shut you up. Do you never tire of this, Fix?"

"When it seems tedious," Fix called over his shoulder, "I just try to imagine how Indrajit feels when I explain option contracts to him."

"I understand option contracts," Indrajit protested. "That's the one where you sell something you don't actually own, right?"

The Wixit cackled.

"Close," Fix said.

They passed through several rooms with weighted silk curtains. Indrajit could smell the sea. At the back of the apartment, a blank door of solid *yetz*-wood was shut by a thick iron bar. The captain heaved the bar up with visible effort and set it aside. When the door opened, it revealed a narrow chute lined with orange bricks, leading down.

Faint yellow light rose up the shaft. Iron ladder rungs bolted into the bricks provided a means of descent—

For a person with free hands.

"Do our ways part here, then?" Indrajit asked.

For answer, the yellow captain pushed Fix into the chute.

Indrajit's short, muscled partner fell, but landed on his buttocks on the floor, legs jammed down the chimney and hands behind him.

"Get a move on," the Wixit growled.

"His hands are tied," Indrajit protested.

"He has shoulders and feet," Samwit Conker said. "And I only need one of you to survive, anyway, so if he falls and dies . . . it's your lucky day."

Fix scraped his way down the chute, grunting with effort and pain. After a minute of listening to his partner's efforts and imagining flesh being scraped off by old brick, Indrajit heard the dull thud of Fix falling to the floor at the bottom of the shaft.

The yellow captain went next, much easier.

"It isn't far!" Fix called up from the pit. "When the wall starts moving away behind you, just drop!"

Indrajit seated himself at the chute before he could be forced to sit. There was only one yellow warrior in the chamber below—if Indrajit could get his stiletto into his hand and surprise the man, this might be his and Fix's best chance to make their escape. He felt the cold weight of the weapon, and the pinch of the belt around his thigh as he scooted forward.

"At least untie the Zalapting," he said as he probed with one sandaled foot for his first hold. "What's he going to do, attack your eight huge mercenaries with his bare hands?"

"We are a ferocious people," the registry clerk said, "driven by our inborn wildness to war. War proves which Zalapting men are fit mates, and war also keeps the population down. All our poetry exalts war, all our childhood play trains for it. We are driven by our mad bloodlust until the Turning."

"Then what happens?" Samwit Conker asked.

"We become even more ferocious."

The Wixit laughed. "Twang is right. Untie the Zalapting, or he'll break his neck."

Indrajit heard the cords around the clerk's wrists being snipped as he lowered his weight onto the iron-rung footholds and sank into the chute. He felt the skin of his shoulders being scraped raw as he used them like feet, inching downward with his weight first on one shoulder and then on the other.

He tried to keep his legs together, without appearing that he was trying to keep his legs together. He didn't feel especially self-conscious about another man seeing up his toga, except that today he wore a secret knife wrapped around one thigh.

He almost lost his foothold twice.

Then, when his head was maybe three cubits below the surface of the floor above him, he felt the wall behind him begin to bow out and away from him. Smooth, time-gnawed brick gave way to a rougher surface that cut into his flesh. The chute was opening into a room.

"Drop!" Fix called.

Indrajit let himself fall. He landed on his feet, feeling

the hard impact through his soles and his legs and crashing into his pelvis, knocking him to one knee. But the knife stayed in place and his toga stayed on.

He stood.

"Get up," the yellow captain said, prodding Indrajit in the shoulder.

Indrajit stood. He and Fix and the yellow man were in a brick chamber that seemed to suffer from centuries of neglect; bricks lay heaped in the corner, and gaps in all the walls showed where the bricks might have fallen from. Light came from an oil lamp that burned in the corner; the slight flicker of its flame testified to the presence of an air current, but there were no windows, and the only other opening was the mouth of a second chute in the floor.

"We are from Boné," the yellow captain said in a low voice. "We are Udayans. We come from the hill country, and we serve only the greatest noblemen."

"Why are you satisfying my curiosity," Indrajit asked, "if you only plan to kill us?"

"They don't plan to kill us," Fix said.

Indrajit snorted. "We aren't worth much ransom."

"They want us to do something," Fix continued. "My guess is an assassination."

The captain of the yellow warriors gave no hint that the guesses were at all correct. He stepped to the other side of the steel rungs bolted into the bricks, keeping his spear pointed at the Zalapting clerk for the last few cubits of his descent.

"That's sort of a funny joke, on Conker's part," Indrajit said. "Luring us to this meeting, thinking we were going to prevent an assassination, and then trying to make us carry one out. Do you think the Lord Chamberlain is the target?"

"It's a good guess," Fix said. "Maybe they hold one of us prisoner to force the other to kill Thrush."

"Or maybe they send the Udayans with us, we commit the murder together, and then the Udayans leave, and we're left behind to take the punishment."

Fix watched the yellow man closely. "Or they murder us on the scene, so it looks like the Lord Chamberlain killed us in self-defense."

"These scenarios all sound bad for us." Indrajit sighed. The Zalapting clerk reached the floor and padded over to join Indrajit and Fix. The captain didn't retie the clerk's hands. The yellow warrior stayed beneath the chute, looking upward and calling instructions to someone who was now beginning to climb down. "I apologize for not asking earlier, but what's your name?"

"Tufo," the clerk said.

"What was that you were talking about, the Turning?" Indrajit asked. He kept a close eye on the yellow captain, who, for his part, was looking intently up the chute, engaged in a conversation in a language Indrajit didn't understand. Indrajit's hands were tied behind him, but he was able to gather up a large handful of toga material, which was in any case coming loose from movement, and from the brooch pin tearing through the toga fabric. Leaning forward slightly and yanking, he managed to ruck the cloth up around his hips, exposing his thighs and, he hoped, the dagger strapped to one of them.

Which he couldn't mention verbally.

Fix helped, though, raising one foot off the ground to point at Indrajit's weapon.

"You smell nice," Tufo said.

"It's a flower," Indrajit said. "I forget the name."

"It means," Tufo said, "that when we become too numerous, so that war does not prune our numbers and our warrens can no longer hold us, something happens to our births. Our males are then born overwhelmingly homosexual."

Tufo missed the stiletto in the dark and started patting around on Indrajit's thigh.

Indrajit felt exposed. "I . . . ah . . ."

"What an interesting way to keep your numbers in check," Fix said. "'Homosexual' means that the men are attracted to other men, Indrajit."

"I know what homosexual means." Indrajit cleared his throat. "Can't you see it?" he hissed. "A little higher. Not there. Are you saying—is that happening now, the Turning?"

"No. The warrens of Kish are large, and there is much violent work among the jobber companies to keep the numbers of our males pruned. We have relatively few homosexuals in these times." Tufo finally found the stiletto and drew it. "I am one, of course."

Indrajit let his toga drop around his legs.

"You said you become more ferocious in the Turning," Fix said.

"We homosexuals are noted for our savage prowess in combat." Tufo cut through the rope around Indrajit's hands with a single firm motion, then moved to stand behind Fix. Indrajit held the sliced bits of cord around his wrists, trying to maintain the appearance that he was tied.

The person coming down the chute was Samwit Conker himself. He was nimble, as Wixits generally were, but the iron bars were large for his small hands, so the yellow captain took care to stand beneath him, prepared to break his fall. Conker himself focused on his hand- and footholds.

Tufo walked around to stand beside Indrajit, hands behind his back. Presumably holding the stiletto there. Indrajit couldn't ask for his knife back, but he was about to reach over and take it when Conker dropped to the floor, and the Wixit and the yellow Bonean both turned to face Indrajit and his companions.

"They almost figured it out," the yellow captain said to the Wixit. "But then they got distracted talking to the Zalapting about how ferocious Zalaptings are."

Samwit Conker laughed. "Oh? How ferocious *are* Zalaptings, then?"

Tufo attacked without warning, leaping at the yellow warrior. As the larger man tried to step aside, Tufo reversed the stiletto and slashed it through his right hamstring. Shrieking a string of syllables in his foreign tongue, the warrior sank to his knees. He tried to bring his spear into play, but it was too big to get between him and the Zalapting.

Conker leaped forward, and Indrajit kicked him against the wall.

The Wixit bounced, snarling and yapping. Indrajit's brooch pin chose that moment to finally eat its way through the cloth of the toga and the garment collapsed around Indrajit's body, tangling his legs and tripping him.

Indrajit stumbled. He stood at the edge of the shaft in the floor, arms flapping as if he might take flight.

Tufo wrapped his left hand in the yellow warrior's hair, stepped onto the man's thigh to raise himself, and plunged the stiletto up to the hilt into the man's throat. Blood spattered across the brick floor, the Zalapting, and Indrajit.

Fix grabbed Indrajit's toga and yanked. He pulled the poet back from the edge and Indrajit reeled across the room into the far corner. The toga pulled away from Indrajit's body into Fix's hands, and Fix turned, holding the cloth up.

Tufo grabbed the dead man's spear and looked up the chute. A second warrior was descending, yellow legs vivid in the flickering lamplight. Above them, shadowed movements suggested the presence of a third, coming down the shaft. Tufo braced himself.

Samwit Conker leaped at Fix, fangs bared and limbs splayed, a raucous war-shriek unrolling from his lungs.

The second yellow warrior dropped, and fell impaled through the chest on Tufo's spear. He died with no sound other than a heavy thud as he and the Zalapting fell over sideways.

Fix swung the toga like a net. He wrapped it around Conker, snatching the little furry man from the air and wrapping him entirely into a squirming bundle.

Indrajit found himself wearing only a loincloth and sandals, with an empty knife sheath strapped to his thigh. Tufo climbed out from under the dead Udayans' bodies, straightening his disheveled clothing, and Indrajit started to laugh.

A voice called down from above in an unknown language.

"Your two friends are dead!" Indrajit yelled back up. "And we have your employer tied up in a sack. Time for you to go home!"

He eyed the descending shaft. Presumably, it must drop below the level of the street, into the Underkish— the sewers and other passages that honeycombed the enormous hill, part natural and part man-made, built of the accumulated detritus of millennia—beneath the city. Presumably, the yellow men or the Wixit knew a route through that maze that would have let them attack Orem Thrush, which meant that they probably also knew a way out, but Indrajit didn't want to put a single foot down there, if he could help it.

At least, if he had to, he'd go armed. He unbuckled the sword belt of the yellow captain and then rebuckled it around his own waist. He took a spear in hand, too, though in his life, he had mostly used spears for fishing.

Tufo kept the stiletto, saluting Indrajit with it by touching it to his eyebrow.

Fix handed Indrajit the bundle of toga cloth. Indrajit gripped the balled cloth firmly, letting the excess material fall over his elbow; the Wixit squirmed inside, and Indrajit buffeted him gently with the knuckles of his other hand. "I've got a blade now, Conker," he whispered. "Hold still, or I will cut you."

Fix armed himself, pulling the bloody spear from the yellow corpse and belting a sword around his shoulder.

"Let the Wixit go," a voice from above called, "or we'll come down and make you regret it."

"Oh, yeah?" Indrajit laughed. "We killed two of you unarmed! How much damage do you think we'll do to you now that we have your friends' weapons?"

"Counteroffer!" Fix shouted. "Get out of here, and we'll leave you alone!"

"No!" Conker shrieked, the sound muffled by the toga. Indrajit boxed the bundle lightly and was rewarded with an angry hiss.

The murmur of discussion drifted down from above.

"What do you think came of those Xiba'albi?" Fix whispered.

Indrajit frowned. "I assumed they were just hired to lure us in, and then left. You don't think maybe they're down there, do you?" He pointed at the shaft leading down.

"We have no idea what's down there," Fix said.

"Right." Indrajit nodded. "And we don't know the way. Underkish is an impossibly complicated maze in three dimensions."

"But Conker probably knows the way," Tufo said.

Indrajit stared at the Zalapting. "What kind of notary's clerk *are* you?"

"I work for Wopal," the clerk said. "I was here as your backup."

"Backup?" Indrajit harrumphed. "Do we *always* have backup?" He looked at Fix for an answer. "When did we ever have backup before?"

Fix shrugged.

"All those things you told us about Zalaptings," Indrajit

said to Tufo. "You know, warrior poems, and the Turning, and you being . . . an especially ferocious sort of Zalapting."

"All true," Tufo said.

"We'd better be more careful around Zalaptings," Fix suggested.

"You two are also quite ferocious," Tufo said. "I wouldn't worry too much."

"We're not ferocious," Indrajit objected. "We're the good guys."

Conker snarled and thrashed about in his cloth cage.

"We haven't been paid," a voice called down. Indrajit peered up the chute and saw light from the floor above, unobstructed by any bodies, so whoever had been in the process of climbing down the shaft had thought better of the idea.

"Not our problem!" Indrajit called back.

"It *is* your problem, because you're holding the man who owes us!"

Indrajit rapped a loving knuckle where he thought Samwit Conker's head was. "Don't think that we're going to just let him come on up to you. We like having him as a hostage!"

More murmuring. "We could allow you to ascend. We would promise not to hurt you."

Indrajit met Fix's gaze and frowned. "The more you talk, the less I trust you!" he yelled. "You could just stab us as we climb up!"

"I'll pay you myself!" Conker shrieked. "Ten Imperials, I'll lead you out through the tunnels, and then you let me go!"

"Well, that's odd," Indrajit said softly. "Why would you pay us? I'm pretty sure you planned to kill us."

"Because if we give him to his yellow boys," Fix said thoughtfully, "he knows they'll shake him down for more. Since he hasn't got the assassination he wanted in any case, he's just trying to get out alive at the cheapest price."

"But he might have more fighters in the tunnels," Indrajit said. "The Xiba'albi, or someone else."

"I have no fighters in the tunnels," the Wixit said.

"Maybe a trap," Fix suggested.

"I have no traps, either."

"It would be nice to get paid," Indrajit said.

"Twelve Imperials!" Conker cried.

"We could climb down in there with you!" an upstairs voice called. "You could leave the Wixit with us and climb out!"

"I don't trust you not to attack us as soon as you have Conker!" Indrajit shouted. "I'm pretty sure that's what he'd want!"

"The hole in the floor is looking better all the time," Fix said.

"What if you all climbed down unarmed?" Indrajit yelled.

"That's not going to happen!" the unseen Udayan called back.

Indrajit lowered his voice and stepped in close to Fix and Tufo. "We seem to be at an impasse."

"We can take our chances with the hole in the floor," Fix murmured.

"I'll still pay you ten Imperials!" the Wixit squeaked.

"I have a plan," the Zalapting said. "Perhaps we should be careful to bind the Wixit's mouth shut before I say any more."

Cho'ag Yoom was the youngest of the eight Udayan warriors who remained in this ancient, rotting city. They had been the bodyguard of a pasha, once, but he was dead and their numbers had dwindled from their former thirty-six (to match the thirty-six houses of the night sky) to eight, as the pasha's enemies had driven him from his lands across the Serpent Sea, and then to this city, and then had made repeated assaults on the pasha before he finally took his own life, leaving his prized Udayan warriors to become mercenaries.

And perhaps only six remained, if the fish-headed man and his companions were to be believed. The gods had hated the Bonean pasha so much, they had not been content to kill him alone, but were now sating their last appetite for vengeance upon his bodyguard.

Leaning on his spear and waiting, with his five companions, for the fish-head's answer, Cho'ag shook his head.

Cho'ag was a member of the band only because his uncle Zhan had chosen him and sworn him in. Zhan was the headman of the band. Cho'ag had survived under Zhan's protection, only gaining tentative acceptance, if that, from the other warriors, and now Zhan was likely dead.

A scream sounded from the chamber below. "No!" a voice shouted. "Don't leave me here, they'll kill me!"

"That doesn't sound like the fish-headed man," Hakk

said. Hakk was the senior surviving member of the band, and had been their spokesman in communicating down the shaft. He had a bent nose, and low cunning.

"Please!" the voice called up the shaft. "The two jobbers are running! They're fleeing down into the tunnels with the Wixit, who promised them ten Imperials! Please don't hurt me!"

"This could be a trap," Churt suggested.

"Yes," Hakk said. "That is why we will send Cho'ag."

Five spears dropped to level at him, and there was no arguing. Cho'ag took his spear into his left hand and looked down into the shaft. Seeing the Zalapting looking up at him, covered in blood, he eased himself into the chute and rapidly descended into the chamber below.

A flickering lamp sat on the edge of a second shaft that dropped farther, in one corner of the orange-walled room. In the center of the room stood the Zalapting clerk, flailing his arms. Near the foot of the ladder, obscured by shadow and blood, lay two bodies. Cho'ag couldn't see their faces, but he saw their Udayan headdresses; one bore the purple and white headman's feathers.

"Uncle Zhan," he murmured, and sighed.

The Zalapting pointed down the hole. "They left me!"

"Do you live, mighty Cho'ag?" Hakk called down from above.

Cho'ag did not appreciate the sarcasm. "So far!"

He knelt to examine the corpses. These were the bodies of his uncle Zhan, and of his former fellow guard, Ferut. Strangely, Ferut's loincloth was missing. Barbarians. "Safe sailing, Uncle," he murmured. "I will sing for you when next I see the Celestial River."

Hakk now climbed down the ladder. "Why are you not pursuing the fish-head down the hole?" he demanded.

Cho'ag stood. "I was saying farewell to my uncle." He crossed to the opening of the second shaft and began to climb down it. His feet descended below him into darkness, and he imagined the feeling of spears stabbing into his flesh with each step.

"Shall I kill the Zalapting?" Hakk sneered.

"As you wish," Cho'ag said. "But if you want to be useful, hold the lamp so I can see where I climb."

He didn't wait for Hakk, continuing his descent into darkness.

"They are gone," Tufo whispered.

Indrajit and Fix dropped the toga. They'd been holding it up to screen themselves from view, standing in the darkest corner of the chamber and counting on the orange dye in the toga and the orange brick of the wall to blend enough, in the shadow, to escape notice.

It had worked.

Samwit Conker's muzzle was bound shut with the loincloth of one of the dead yellow men. Indrajit had held the Wixit close to his chest with one hand while all six warriors had passed through the chamber on their way down, making certain the Conker was still, and was still breathing.

Only a trickle of light came up from the shaft in the floor; the Udayans had taken the light with them.

"Up the ladder quickly now," Fix said. He led the way.

"We bar the door once we're through," Tufo added, following.

"I have thought of an epithet," Indrajit announced.

"This," Fix said, "this is why I like being your partner. Tell us the epithet."

Indrajit cleared his throat, climbing the iron rungs out of total darkness toward the square of light where Fix and Tufo now waited, the squirming Samwit Conker clutched under one arm. *"Yellow-skinned Udayans,"* he chanted, *"blue-eyed and deadly."*

There was a brief pause.

"It probably sounds better in Blaatshi," Fix said.

"Everything does," Indrajit said. "This epithet, in particular, is highly alliterative."

"Perfect," Fix said.

Indrajit handed the Wixit to his partner. Once they had climbed out of the chute, they barred the door.

The Path of the Hunter

⁓

"Fifty Imperials if you bring my partner's killer to justice," the caravan merchant Ripto Shabam said. "I trust you know the path of the hunter."

The trader was a Thorg, squat, thick-skinned, and a dull orange color. His eyes were narrow slits that occasionally leaped open wide to emphasize a point, and he had no visible ears. The top of Shabam's head was a thicket of tiny stalks that ignored the gusts bringing seaport smells in through the merchant's open window, but trembled in response to sound.

Shabam sat at a wide table. On the table beside him rested a bronze cage a cubit in all dimensions, containing a black kitten. The little creature lay coiled up on its side, but it looked at the conversation with wide yellow eyes set in a flat face.

Indrajit Twang and his partner Fix—adventurers, thinking men, and sometimes agents in the employ of Kish's Lord Chamberlain, Orem Thrush—stood in front of the table. Indrajit was taller than his partner; Fix looked Kishi, but for his large nose and his broad Xiba'albi-like shoulders. The shorter man was very muscular. Indrajit and Fix were both dressed in kilts and tunics of undyed gray-brown linen. Indrajit wore his leaf-bladed sword at his belt, and Fix carried two knives and a hatchet; he'd left his spear at the front door.

They didn't have uniforms, despite the fact that they were a bonded jobber company, because they generally undertook tasks that required discretion.

"Justice is tricky." Indrajit was wary of the phrase *the path of the hunter*. "Do you mean you want the killer to be tried before an Auction Court?"

Fix smiled blandly as he and Indrajit sat.

The Thorg snorted, the sound causing his head-stalks to part left and right for a moment. "Who has time for *that* bureaucracy, not to mention coin for the cost? No, I want you to find him and kill him."

Indrajit exhaled thoughtfully. "That course of action brings a different set of complications. I mean, killing someone might get us dragged in front of an Auction Court ourselves." He looked at Fix. "Not to mention the possibility of friends and relatives who might want revenge. Which they would call justice, in turn."

"Bringing a murderer to heel does sound attractive, though." Fix's voice was high-pitched and faintly melodic. "It sounds like the sort of thing heroes would do."

Indrajit nodded. "We do like the idea of being heroes. On the other hand, we definitely don't have the resources to go up against the House of Knives."

"It's not the House of Knives!" Shabam sputtered.

"How do you know?" Fix asked. "The House of Knives employs a lot of assassins."

"They don't have a registry, like the Paper Sook?" Indrajit asked. He had no experience with Kish's assassins' guild.

Fix shrugged.

"Because the killer dogged our trail all the way here along the Endless Road." The Thorg hesitated. "We acquired . . . something exotic . . . in the east, and the killer wants to take it from us."

"Oh, I see. You want justice, and you want to protect yourself." Indrajit scratched the bony ridge of his nose. The role of bodyguard was more familiar. "How much do you know about this assassin?"

Ripto Shabam shook his blocky head. "Nothing. But he must be very good, if he could sneak past my partner's servants and kill him in his own office."

"And what is it you bought in the east that's so valuable an assassin would be dispatched to recover it?" Fix's eyes narrowed. "Or *did* you buy it, in fact? What do you mean by 'acquired'?"

The Thorg chuckled. "Now, now, you're starting to ask questions that get awfully close to what we in merchantry call 'trade secrets.' *What* we brought back is not relevant, nor how we acquired it. Though I am pleased that you are quick enough to guess that it wasn't a simple purchase. No, we acquired something we believe the Lord Marshal or the Lord Stargazer will pay a lot of money for."

"And would the Lord Marshal or the Lord Stargazer be willing to send an assassin after you instead?" Fix asked. "It might be cheaper."

Shabam snorted. "And risk getting that kind of reputation in the Caravanserai? No one would ever do business with such a man again."

Indrajit nodded. "Well, we're going to have to insist on the option not to kill the assassin, but just to bring him to you. And then you can do the killing, if you want, or file for a court."

"Fine," Shabam said.

"But you'll admit there's legal risk to us," Fix added. "So our fee will be one hundred Imperials. Thirty up front."

"And I think you're going to want to give us a key to your house," Indrajit said. "We'll have to be able to come and go, so we can better protect you."

The Thorg shook his head. "I could hire a whole jobber company for a hundred Imperials."

"You *are* hiring a whole jobber company," Indrajit said.

"You are hiring the jobber company that is famous among all the better classes of Kish." Fix smiled. "We're the ones who are so committed to client service that we went into battle on the stage of the Palace of Shadow and Joy, reckless of the danger to ourselves."

"Really livened up the opera season, they say," Indrajit added.

Shabam sucked at his teeth. "Seventy-five."

Indrajit stood. "We do work at discount rates," he said, "for widows and orphans. Damsels in distress, that sort of thing. Call us when you're ready for premium service."

Fix stood, too. "Good luck with whatever cut-rate jobbers you choose to hire."

"We hear Mote Gannon has capacity," Indrajit said. "He recently lost some of his contracts with the Lord Chamberlain."

"His poor Luzzazza lost his lower arms." Fix tsked.

"Why do you say 'lost' when you know I enjoy getting credit for my deeds?" Indrajit said.

"Fine, you took his arms in single combat. I'll make sure your successor Recital Thanes get the details right."

"The details are less important than the spirit. The spirit should be heroic. High risk, last minute, personal danger, swooning maidens. And how do you plan to tell my successors what to recite? Your race is no longer-lived than mine is."

"I plan to *write* the instructions *down*, Little Hort."

Indrajit sucked in air past his teeth.

"Gentlemen, gentlemen." The Thorg spread his arms in a gesture that disavowed his earlier offer. "You must forgive an old camel trader his habits. I meant no offense. Of course, I recognize the best when I see them, and I am willing to pay for quality. Ninety Imperials!"

"Goodbye," Fix said.

"One hundred Imperials it is!" The trader opened a purse at his belt and counted out thirty of the silver coins.

"We'll watch your house tonight," Indrajit said. "In the meantime, give us all the information you have, and we'll see what we can find out."

Ripto Shabam produced two long keys, one to his own house and a second to his partner's. He also summoned a violet-skinned, long-snouted, red-robed Zalapting servant named Shunt, introduced Indrajit and Fix, and told Shunt to take them to "Jak's office."

To Indrajit's surprise, the Zalapting didn't lead them down to the street. Instead, he took them along a short hallway to a small door. On a staircase as they passed, Indrajit saw a gray-skinned servant sweeping the floor with a long-strawed broom. Big as this house was, it was quiet. Unlocking it, he led them out onto a catwalk that crossed over the street two stories below to another building.

The sky overhead was clouded, the scowling dark blue underbellies of the cloud promising rain. From the street below drifted the smell of roasting nuts and the neighing of horses. The two buildings were built of matching yellow bricks, irregularly sized but in a pleasing way that made the houses look bespoke. Their rooftops were made of matching red-clay half-pipe, with lead gutters around the edges.

"These men are close partners," Fix murmured, "if they literally joined their houses."

"These men are rich," Indrajit said, "but we already knew that."

They shut the door behind them and crossed the catwalk. Shunt unlocked the door on the other side.

"You and I live in the same chambers," Indrajit pointed out.

"Because we're poor." Fix grinned. "As soon as we're rich, you'll buy your own palace where you can have a stage to act out your Blaatshi Epic with a dozen apprentices."

"And you'll marry that widow you're crazy about and move to a farm in Ildarion where you can have a dozen children and inflict literacy upon them all."

"She's not a widow yet."

"In due time."

In his excellent peripheral vision—Indrajit's eyes were set far apart in his head, as were the eyes of all Blaatshi—Indrajit noticed a smudge of black in motion above the door from which they'd exited. Turning, he saw two black cats crouched on the rooftop. One was large, and the other small, perhaps a kitten.

Fix followed his gaze. "Don't worry, that's a city cat. It probably eats rats and street-fowl, snakes, maybe even big beetles in lean times, but you're safe."

"I do *not* look like a fish," Indrajit said.

"I know how uncomfortable you must feel, resembling food as you do."

The Zalapting Shunt snickered.

"That's it," Indrajit said. "Take us to the latrines, Shunt. I'm throwing you both down, and the Druvash can eat you."

As they entered the adjoining building, the black cats disappeared. Indrajit had the uncomfortable sensation that the creatures hadn't moved, but had in fact simply ceased to be visible, but as good as his peripheral vision was, the edge of his field of vision was still tricky.

And besides, this was Kish. A cat that could turn invisible would fit right in.

The building that had belonged, apparently, to the dead partner Jak was completely silent. Shunt led them down a short hall to an office, both hallway and office the mirror image of what they had seen in the Thorg's house.

"Did Jak have no servants?" Fix asked.

"On Jak Furbit's death, his belongings all became the property of my master," the Zalapting said. "My master promptly fired all the staff."

"For failure to defend Furbit?" Indrajit asked.

"To control costs," Fix suggested.

The Zalapting nodded.

Like Shabam's study, Furbit's office had a broad table and large windows letting in the sea breeze. On the table stood an open inkpot, a ledger, and a bronze cage just like the one the Thorg had, except that several of the bars had been pried out.

Furbit himself lay dead on the floor. He looked Ildarian, fair-skinned and with light brown hair that was almost blond. His throat was ripped open savagely and he lay centered in a circle of dried brown blood. He clutched a book to his chest, spine cracked open so that the book's plain black cover was visible.

"Oh, look," Indrajit said. "Another victim of reading."

Fix stooped to pick up the book. "I hate to disappoint you, but I'm pretty sure he was *writing*." He pointed at a quill pen lying on the floor halfway across the room. "And look, ink on his fingers."

"Another iniquitous practice." Indrajit waited. "Well, go on, tell me what he was writing. Was it by chance his killer's identity?"

"Don't you want to take this opportunity to admit how important it is to be able to read?"

Indrajit smiled. "No."

"Leave the keys," Fix said to the Zalapting. "And you can go."

Shunt gave both keys to Indrajit and left the way they'd come.

"What is this on the floor?" Indrajit picked his feet up, looking at white dust that now coated the sole of his sandals.

"Powdered sugar, I think," Fix said. "Don't suggest that I taste it."

"I wasn't about to." Indrajit pointed to a crossbow that lay on the floor, and then at the feathers of a crossbow bolt embedded into a wall timber on the other side of the room. "Just like I wasn't about to suggest you taste Furbit's weapon."

Fix pointed to a confectioner's bag sitting on the corner of Furbit's table.

"Touché," Indrajit said.

"Hmm." Fix looked into the book. "This is a narrative."

"You mean a *story*?"

"There's a heading. It says 'dictated' and then has today's date."

"And does the narrative come to a satisfactory conclusion?"

Fix looked. "It ends mid-sentence."

"So he was taking dictation from the killer."

"Or if not, then the person telling the narrative might have been a witness."

Indrajit stepped to the window and peered out, assessing the difficulty of climbing up from the street. The walls were sheer, without handhold. "Clearly, you should read this narrative and see what it says."

Fix's eyes scanned the page.

"Out loud," Indrajit said. "And try performing it. Maybe do a voice or two, make some theatrical gestures, as appropriate."

Fix read. "'Once, there was a dama who gave birth to a litter of six kitas. This birth was exceedingly rare, even miraculous.'"

"What is a 'dama'?" Indrajit asked. "And a 'kita,' what's that?"

"The text doesn't say. Shall I keep reading?"

"Please."

"'Wise men and wealthy men and rulers came from all the . . .' Here now, what's this?"

Indrajit frowned. "Is that what the dictation says? Men came from all the 'here now, what's this'?"

Fix squinted at the page. "No, he originally wrote 'planets of that system and all the nearby systems.'"

"Gibberish. Or some kind of incantation."

"Maybe Shabam should have hired the Collegium Arcanum rather than the Protagonists."

"I think wizards charge a premium. Maybe Jak just made a mistake."

Fix nodded. "I guess that's why he scratched out that phrase and wrote 'lands near and far' instead."

"Translation problems. Go on."

". . . 'came from all the lands near and far to honor her. The gifts rendered to the dama made her and her clan wealthy, and the offers of alliance that she received made her clan powerful, as well. Her many well-wishers feasted her and her litter for seven cycles of the earth around the sun.'"

"Clearly a fairy tale," Indrajit said. "Or another mistake. In what kind of world would the *earth* move around the *sun*? But a seven-day feast sounds delightful."

"One of the Selfless of Salish-Bozar in the temple where I was a foundling had mastered a series of obscure astronomical texts. Apparently, they accounted for nearly half of the useless facts he had to master to become a Selfless."

Indrajit snorted. "Someone made a mistake in signing

off on his ordination. Astronomy is supremely useful. You can navigate with it, and tell the seasons. It also makes an excellent theater of the mind for memorizing large amounts of information."

"If you can't be bothered to write it down."

"Or you don't want to weaken your mental faculties."

"But these astronomical texts," Fix continued, "argued that the earth moves around the sun."

"So your Selfless had memorized not ten thousand useless facts, but ten thousand useless theoretical conjectures?"

"There is nothing so useless as a hypothesis that has been disproved." Fix looked at the page again. "But what I'm saying is, maybe the feast didn't last seven days, but seven years."

"Ah, so we *are* firmly in the realm of fairy tales. Go on."

"'At the end of the seventh cycle, when all the well-wishers departed, the dama discovered that one of her kitas was missing. Had she been of another race, the dama might have sworn grand oaths of vengeance or commitments to recover the kita. Instead, she simply noted the disappearance to one of her clan.'"

"Disappointing," Indrajit said. "Rookie move. Grand oaths have lots of dramatic potential, your characters should always swear them."

"Is this how your recitations go?" Fix asked.

"The audiences are generally larger. When the news gets out that the Recital Thane is going to perform, people assemble in a hall to listen. Everyone brings food and drink, and each family competes with its neighbors to provide the best wine or beef or fish."

"No, I mean, do you get interrupted this much when you perform?"

"No," Indrajit said. "But the Blaatshi Epic is more exciting than this."

Fix arched an eyebrow. "I've heard you recite for an hour straight once, and say nothing but genealogy. I lost count at three hundred instances of begetting."

"Yes, and wasn't it exciting?"

"Stop interrupting."

Indrajit grunted.

"'That very same night,'" Fix continued, "'every hunter of the clan departed. Each left alone in his vessel, and they'—scratched-out words here—'sailed the oceans around, tracking down every single guest at the feast. Those who gave aid were honored, and some even adopted into the dama's clan. Those who refused aid, or lied, were dispatched, as surely and as easily as a corn-mouse.'"

"That *is* dramatic," Indrajit conceded. "But one could hope for a little more detail in the description. Also, the hunters should suffer setbacks, so that we the listening audience are not totally convinced that in the end they will succeed. For instance, maybe have some hunters die, or get lost and wander for forty years. Also—"

"Shut up. 'Finally, a lone hunter, a Depik named Mrowf with over one hundred kills to his credit, found the missing kita. The kita lay imprisoned in the—' Oh, what is it now?"

"What's a Depik?"

"Obviously, I have no idea. 'The kita lay imprisoned in the dungeons of a prince who was also a mighty warrior, and who enjoyed pit-fighting. Every year, the prince held a grand tournament in which fighters from'—scratched out—'many lands battled, always to the death, and the winner faced the prince himself.'"

"Heroism." Indrajit nodded his approval.

"'If the winner of the tournament could survive three minutes in the pit with the prince, then the winner received his freedom. The hunter strode boldly into the prince's hall and demanded the kita's freedom, but the prince rejected his plea. There were too many warriors around the prince to attack him directly, and the dungeons were too well guarded to sneak into, so the Depik made the prince an offer. He proposed that he would enter the arena in place of the kita.'"

"Of course he did." Indrajit rubbed his hands. "See, Fix, this is the sort of thing I want my successor to write about me."

"You'd better take up pit-fighting, then. 'The prince agreed, but it was a trick, and he threw the hunter and the kita into separate cells, and forced them both to fight in the tournament, which began the next day. No one was surprised that the Depik was a skilled warrior, but the crowd cheered with delight when the tiny kita dispatched heavily armored warriors on her own. Both the hunter and the kita advanced, killing foe after foe, until the final round of the tournament, when they were forced to face each other.'"

Indrajit chortled. "Ah, now the story is reaching its climax. The tragic, impossible choice!"

"'But Mrowf would not fight, and neither would the kita. They stood there, enduring the insults of the crowd, until the prince told them that they would starve to death together in the pit. Then Mrowf knelt, and begged the kita to take his life, and then avenge his death on the prince. With tears weighing down her whiskers, the kita bit the hunter's throat, and he fell to the sand.'"

Indrajit unexpectedly felt tears in his own eyes.

"'When Mrowf's body had been carried out, the prince entered the arena. His armor was strong and his weapons devastating and he, too, had killed over a hundred men. Despite her agility and toughness, the kita found herself overmatched and backed into a corner. As the prince was about to deliver the killing blow, Mrowf appeared. His death had been feigned; he had vanished before the very eyes of those who had thought to bury him, and he now leaped down into the pit and...'"

"And what?" Indrajit asked. "And what?"

"And that's the end," Fix said. "It stops in the middle of a sentence."

"Well, clearly the end is that Mrowf kills the prince, takes his wealth, and sails with the kita back to the dama, to be honored for his heroism for the rest of his days." Indrajit frowned. "Hey, wait a minute."

"You're considering an alternate ending?"

Indrajit pointed at the ruined cage on the table. "Who was Jak Furbit taking dictation from?"

Fix scratched his jaw thoughtfully. "You're putting pieces together. Hold on. You think he was taking dictation from someone in the cage..."

"Who was distracting him so that he wouldn't notice the real killer," Indrajit considered. "Or possibly someone was dictating to him to distract him from the fact that whatever he had caged was escaping."

Fix picked up the bag of sugar and crouched to examine the floor. "There are tracks here. Wixit?"

Indrajit shuffled to the spot his partner was looking at. Small tracks crossed the floor, apparently at a run, since they were very far apart, given their tiny size. They didn't look like Wixit tracks, though.

"Those look like handprints," Indrajit said. "Or—what do you call them?—feet with thumbs. Like monkeys have, but Wixit don't have feet like that."

"Opposable thumbs," Fix murmured.

"Lucky for us Furbit spilled sugar all over his floor."

"Not luck," Fix said. "Furbit did it on purpose. So he could see the killer coming."

Now it was Indrajit's turn to guess his partner's mental leaps. "So you're guessing that otherwise, he wouldn't have been able to see the assassin. So the assassin is . . . someone who is on the mystic path of the Luzzazza, but he's so far along it, he can become entirely invisible, rather than just having invisible arms. And Furbit knew it."

"Something like that." Fix pointed. "I think this is the spot where the assassin jumped up on the table and ripped out Furbit's throat."

Indrajit tried to picture a Wixit—short, furry men who seemed generally to be business owners and merchants in Kish—leaping up to the table and biting Furbit's throat. "I think Wixit eat carrion," he said.

"It's not a Wixit," Fix told him. "Stop imagining a Wixit. It's something the size of a Wixit, that can turn invisible, that's a natural-born killer."

"Frozen hells," Indrajit said.

"The cats," Fix answered.

Indrajit broke for the exit first, and he had longer legs, but Fix was muscular and a powerful sprinter. They charged down the hall and threw open the door, revealing the narrow bridge connecting the houses again. Rain had begun to fall.

The felines on the opposite rooftop were gone.

"They captured two," Indrajit said. "They brought home two cats, and each of them kept one. And an adult cat has hunted them down to rescue the kittens."

"Only they're not cats," Fix said, "since they have opposable thumbs."

Indrajit's thoughts spun. "The cat-killer sat there and narrated a story about cat-killers to distract Furbit while another cat-killer crept up to murder him."

"Cold bastards," Fix said.

"Hunters."

They raced across the bridge, nearly slipping because the surface was now slick with rain. Indrajit fumbled the key into the lock and opened the door. "If they're not cats," he asked, "what are they?"

Fix had a knife in one hand. "According to the transcript, they're Depik."

"Welcome to Kish," Indrajit said. "Nothing is what you expect."

"Did these guys plan to sell the kittens to the heads of the families as pets?" Fix asked. "Worth so much because they're rare, and come from the far end of the Endless Road?"

"Or worth so much because they're lethal assassins?"

"This was a terrible miscalculation on their part."

They entered the building at a run. The Zalapting

Shunt lay dead on the hallway floor, his throat torn out, and there was no sign of any other servant. Indrajit and Fix burst into Ripto Shabam's office—

And saw Shabam, staring transfixed at the kitten in the cage on his desk.

Only the kitten was standing, like a man, and gripped the bars of its cage with both hands. Tiny furred fingers were clearly visible, wrapped around the bronze. Shabam leaned over a ledger book and scratched out words as the kitten said them. On Indrajit's entry, the kitten stopped talking and glared at him and Fix.

"Stop!" Fix cried at Indrajit's shoulder.

"Mrowf!" Indrajit called. "Mrowf, come out! You don't need to do this!"

Suddenly, Indrajit's own actions struck him as ridiculous. The kitten had fingers, but did that mean that a tiny cat-man had murdered Jak Furbit and was preparing to murder Jak's partner? A tiny cat-man who could turn invisible?

He felt vaguely embarrassed at the thought.

The pages of the ledger in Shabam's hands ruffled, though there was no breeze.

"Mrowf!" Indrajit shouted.

Fix threw the sugar.

It was good that Fix had picked up the sugar, rather than Indrajit. Indrajit's wide-set eyes gave him excellent vision to his sides and even somewhat behind his own back, but it also meant his aim with missile weapons and thrown objects was poor at best.

But the sugar bag, thrown by Fix, hit something unseen directly in front of the Thorg merchant and exploded. The invisible thing let out a sound that was half yowl and half curse, and then Indrajit heard the soft pattering sound of something landing in a far corner of the room, near the door.

Indrajit and Fix charged the table. Sugar coated Ripto Shabam and his open ledger, the surface of his table, and the floor all around. Fix dragged the merchant by the twitching fronds of his head into the corner of the room. Indrajit grabbed the bronze cage, holding it carefully by a ring at the top, so as not to put any of his fingers within biting range of the kitten.

The kitten glared at him, the white powder on its fur making it look like an aged cat, and uttered one word in perfectly intelligible Kishite: "Peasant."

Then the kitten disappeared.

"I know you're still in there," Indrajit said to the kitten, and hurled himself into the corner of the room. He and Fix stood shoulder to shoulder, the merchant squeezed behind them into the corner of the room. Indrajit held the cage in his left hand and with his right drew his leaf-bladed sword, holding it out in front of him, while Fix held a knife in each hand.

Indrajit kept his eye on the sugarcoated floor.

"They're not like Luzzazza," Fix murmured.

"What?"

"Luzzazza change color," Fix said. "Or their second set of arms do. If you coated a Luzzazza's lower arms with sugar, they would become visible, and appear white. But I hit that thing squarely, and it didn't become visible, even for an instant."

"So it's not a Luzzazza," Indrajit muttered. "The fact

that it isn't seven feet tall and blue might have been a giveaway."

"I'm just saying that its mechanism for disappearing is different."

"Save it for the Hall of Guesses," Indrajit said. "Right now, we have a bigger problem."

"Or a littler one," Fix countered.

"Mrowf," Indrajit said, addressing the apparently empty room. "Can I call you that?"

A soft, disembodied chuckle sounded somewhere in the room. "It's not my name, but I rather like the conceit." The voice was low and throaty, like a purring sound.

"Well, you *are* the hunter who has come all along the Endless Road to rescue two kittens from a litter," Indrajit said. "That's twice as big a rescue as Mrowf carried out, in the story I heard. I can appreciate the heroism."

"Your appreciation might be a little misplaced," Fix muttered.

"Kitas," the voice said.

"Kitas," Indrajit agreed. "Not kittens."

"You are supposed to kill him," the Thorg merchant growled from behind Indrajit and Fix. "Not make friends!"

"Kill him or bring him to you," Indrajit said. "I suppose, technically, we've brought him to you."

"Hmm," Fix said. "Taking my payment now and walking away, contract fulfilled, sounds very attractive at this minute."

Indrajit kept his eyes fixed on the sugar. Something bothered him at the back of his mind, something he'd forgotten, but he couldn't quite figure out what.

"Hey!" Shabam squawked. "You can't do that!"

"We *can*," Fix said slowly.

"But you *won't*!"

"We don't want to," Indrajit acknowledged, "but you're making things a little awkward for us. Maybe you should stop trying to get us to kill the Depik, and focus us more on the saving-your-life part of the contract."

"He knew what he was getting into," the unseen hunter purred.

"I did not!" Shabam shrieked.

"You did," Fix said. "You knew these were assassin cats. Cat . . . people. So did Furbit, judging by how excited he got when that kita started telling him a story. That's why you thought they had value, especially to—who was it, you said? The Lord Marshal or the Lord Stargazer?"

"Did you not realize there were adults who would follow and try to recover the kitas?" Indrajit asked. "Did you . . . You didn't kill the rest of the family, did you?"

"No!"

"That sounds genuine," Indrajit said. "Mrowf, how about it?"

"He and his partner killed none of my people." The hunter's voice was cold.

"If you're going to say something like, 'but in kidnapping one of my people's young, he has committed an unpardonable wrong, and now he must pay for it with his blood,'" Indrajit suggested, "I just can't agree."

"It is not yours to judge," the hunter purred.

Was the voice coming from a new direction? Indrajit deliberately didn't shift his grip on his weapon, so as not to give away that he'd noticed a change.

"Maybe not officially," Indrajit admitted, "but since I'm the guy standing in your way with a naked sword in my hand, maybe we ought to come to a reasonable agreement."

"You find that having weapons drawn increases reasonability?"

"I know my own mind," Indrajit said, "and I feel more comfortable going about learning yours if I'm not defenseless. I saw what you did to Jak Furbit."

"Hmm," the hunter hummed. "And what *is* your mind, fish-man?"

"I'm not a fish," Indrajit said. "Have you ever seen a fish this pleasing shade of mahogany?"

"Yes," the hunter said.

"Well, I don't know what's at the far end of the Endless Road, maybe you have mahogany-colored fish, but around here, the fish are silver and green and blue."

"I come from considerably farther away than the end of your Endless Road." For a moment, the purring voice sounded tired. "In pursuit of these kitas, I have come from places you cannot possibly imagine. They had fallen into the hands of eunuch bureaucrats in one of your world's temple-states, but by the time I caught up, this man and his partner had paid lesser temple servants to steal the kitas and sell them."

"What temple-states are you talking about?" Indrajit asked.

"I think he means whatever is at the end of the Endless Road," Fix said.

That seemed right. "Someday," Indrajit said, "we need to go explore down there."

"I grow weary of this," the voice said.

"That's not very catlike." Fix shifted his stance slightly. Had he seen something? "Cats are patient."

"I am not a cat."

"Ah-ha! See how it feels?" Indrajit cleared his throat. "Okay, here's my thinking: You become visible, and you and I walk down together to the street, and I give you the kita, and you leave. No harm done, no one else needs to die."

"Harm *has* been done," the Depik purred. "I killed the eunuchs because harm had been done. You have seen Jak Furbit's end. Ripto Shabam must also die. We are a small species, and few in number, and it is only the complete and overwhelming obliteration of anyone who harms a Depik kita that keeps future kitas safe."

"I'm sympathetic to your plight," Indrajit said. "I'm one of the last of my people—we're down to three hundred or so, as far as I can tell. So I know how important it is to protect the young, and keep them on the right track. But I just can't let you kill my client. Even if, maybe, he should have seen it coming."

"Even if he might deserve it," Fix added.

"Hey!" Shabam blurted out.

"You would die for pay?" the hunter asked.

"Well, there is that. It's awkward, I don't like it, but that is sort of the deal. I get paid, and I take certain risks. But there's more than that. See, we're not the guys who get paid money to kill people. We're the guys who get paid to save people, and to stop killing."

"We're heroes," Fix said.

"Like you," Indrajit hastened to add. "Maybe with slightly different ethical codes."

"You are right to say that I must show the young the correct path to walk," the hunter purred.

"Yes," Indrajit said. "In my case, I suppose I'm failing, since I haven't convinced any of the young of my people to follow my example and become a Recital Thane."

"I will not fail," the voice said. "I will show the young of my people the path they must walk. That is the path of the hunter."

"Uh . . . this doesn't sound like an offer to compromise."

"The path of the hunter tells me that Ripto Shabam must die."

"Look—" Indrajit said.

A howl of pain, right in his ear, cut him off.

Turning with his shoulders, he saw blood spurting from Ripto Shabam's neck. The merchant slapped at his own clavicle, trying to free himself of an unseen attacker. Fix plunged into the semi-visible fray, grabbing the invisible creature with his hands and yanking it free of its prey as his knives clattered to the floor.

The other kita, Indrajit realized, that's what had escaped his mind. The other kita must have been standing in the corner with them all along.

Thinking of the second kita reminded Indrajit of the adult hunter. Turning back to face the room, he saw prints like tiny handprints appearing in quick succession in the sugar, racing toward him.

If he raised his sword, the Depik would likely scoot under it or leap over. Indrajit needed a bigger weapon.

He stepped forward and swung with the bronze cage.

Indrajit made contact with an unseen mass and knocked it across the room. He heard three voices yowl in complaint—one from Fix's hands, one from the cage, and the third from the far corner, near the window. Indrajit saw an irregular whorl of sugar disturbed as the hunter landed, and he sprinted immediately for the exit.

"After me!" he shouted.

Fix followed, unseen Depik kita in one hand, still yowling and hissing, and his second hand wrapped around Ripto Shabam's belt so he could drag the man.

"Where are we going?" Fix barked as they charged up the hall, toward the catwalk connecting the two houses.

"Away from here!" Indrajit held the door to the narrow bridge open as Fix and the trader stumbled through and into the rain, then stepped in after them and shut it. "If we can escape this hunter, maybe we can release the kittens and they'll all calm down and just leave."

Meaning to sheath his sword, Indrajit fumbled and lost his grip on it.

The weapon fell to the street below, making a clear ringing sound on the cobblestones.

"Frozen hells!" Indrajit locked the door and turned to his partner. "To the other house!"

Indrajit heard the faint *whoosh* of something moving rapidly through the air, and then the soft *plop* of it landing on the catwalk ahead of them. The hunter became abruptly visible, standing on the center of the bridge and blocking their path.

Standing, the hunter came to mid-thigh height. His fur was black and his tail long and curled upward like a jug handle. Hands and feet looked very similar, the same dark fur with opposable thumbs. Now Indrajit could see that the Depik wore a brown leather belt, carrying several pouches.

Fix stepped between the hunter and the merchant, holding the kita in his hands before him. "This might have been a tactical mistake."

"You are brave men," the hunter said. "I am willing to let you two go."

Indrajit's heart sank. "That's not good branding. We can't be the jobbers who let a client die."

"I'm not so sure about that," Fix said. "Every jobber company fails at a contract now and then."

"Hey." Shabam's protest was weak. He was losing blood.

Indrajit shoved the bronze cage against the door and stripped off his tunic, wrapping it around Shabam's neck like a bandage. It didn't seem very effective. The hunter might not have to kill its prey at all, it might merely have to stop Indrajit and Fix from summoning effective aid, and watch as Shabam bled to death.

Indrajit eased forward along the bridge until he stood directly behind Fix. "No one has to get hurt." As he spoke, he despaired of the possibility of persuading the little cat-man assassin. He shouldn't be surprised, he told himself. Cats were homicidal little predators that left trails of corpses in their wakes—why should cat-people be any different? "We let the . . . kitas . . . go, and you let us go. We all just walk away."

The hunter stared past Indrajit at his client. "Your client is not worth your loyalty."

"True." Indrajit shrugged. "But, you know, I'm trying to be a hero."

"Not . . . worth . . . it!" Ripto Shabam bellowed.

"No!" the Depik hunter howled.

Indrajit spun about, just in time to see the Thorg merchant lift the bronze cage and throw it off the bridge. In his weakened state, he couldn't throw it far, but the kita inside yelped piteously and winked in and out of sight as its cage spun sideways and fell toward the hard street, two stories below.

Indrajit knocked the Thorg aside and lunged. He dove toward the glittering cage as it dropped, and as he closed the fingers of his right hand around the ring atop the cage, he realized that he had completely surrendered his balance, and was falling himself.

He threw out his left hand, scrabbling against the side of the building for any purchase. His skin tore and he painted the yellow brick red with his blood. For a moment, his fingers caught at the edge of a large brick that protruded slightly. His heart beat once, twice.

"Drop it!" Shabam yelled. "Drop—!" A loud *crunch* shut him up.

Indrajit lost his grip and fell again.

He toppled slowly, head and cage pulling downward until he was pointed face-first at the cobbles, his toes still maintaining an ephemeral purchase on the catwalk, and then he lost all contact with the building—

But someone grabbed his legs.

Indrajit fell and bounced, supported by a strong grip around his ankles.

"Frozen hells," he heard Fix grunt above him. "You are *big*."

Indrajit looked up. Framed against storm clouds, he saw Fix. His partner lay on his belly across the catwalk, perpendicular to the span so that his legs poked out the other side. The Depik hunter stood at Fix's side, holding a black-furred kita in his arms. The kita had blood on its muzzle. Ripto Shabam lay slumped against the doorway.

Indrajit tried to raise the cage and couldn't. "It's too heavy!" he called. Rain filled his mouth and nostrils. Below him, the rain had emptied the street and polished the cobbles to a gray shine.

"I can climb down!" the hunter yelled.

"No," Fix grunted.

Indrajit looked down into the cage at the second black kita. It was wet and bedraggled, but it stood upright, looking at him with a fierce light in its eyes.

"How about it, little kita?" Indrajit asked. "If I open the cage, can you climb up?"

"Yes," the kita said. "Peasant."

Indrajit laughed.

"Stop shaking!" Fix urged him. "Your legs are slippery!"

Indrajit's head was full of blood, making it tingle. He shifted the bronze ring to his left hand, and with his right he gripped the wire of the cage. He pulled with all the strength he had, and the wire snapped from its anchor, bending open.

"Two more," the kita said.

"You could help," Indrajit suggested, but he knew it wasn't true. If the kita had been able to pry open the bars itself, it would have already escaped.

He ripped a second wire from its place.

"Hurry!" Fix roared.

Would the hunter kill them, once he had his kitas? Would he let Indrajit fall?

It didn't matter. The kita was innocent.

Gritting his teeth with pain and exhaustion, Indrajit ripped out a third bar. He choked on the rain filling his windpipe.

The kita scampered out, quickly ascending Indrajit's arm and back, and Indrajit released the cage. The bronze hit the cobblestones below and shattered into a thousand pieces, and then the weight of the kita was lifted as well, and then Fix heaved a sigh of relief.

Indrajit looked down at the hard street. "I don't suppose you can pull me up?"

Even as he asked, Fix began to hoist him. The smaller man was heavily muscled, and as he worked, Indrajit felt other hands—tiny hands—grab his legs and help.

When he cleared the surface of the bridge, Indrajit managed to drag himself onto it and stretch out flat, heart beating fast and lungs gasping for air. Fix lay next to him, breathing hard, and the Depik stood over them. Indrajit wanted to say something, but he was all out of words. The eyes staring from the hunter's flat, catlike face glittered with hard curiosity, and then with something else.

The hunter turned and knelt beside the fallen merchant. He produced several small objects from one of his belt pouches, all glittering, and applied them to Shabam. He pushed one object several times into the flesh where Shabam had been wounded, each time producing a neat *snick* sound. Then he ran a second thing over the wound, leaving an oily sheen behind, and finally he pressed a third object into Shabam's upper arm. The thing hissed and Shabam groaned.

Indrajit groaned, too. "That doesn't *sound* like you just killed him."

The hunter stood over him again. One kita climbed up onto the hunter's shoulders and the other clung to the side of his leg. "The path of the hunter is to kill his prey," the Depik said. "But the hunter kills to feed his clan, and the hunter must always be able to recognize his friends."

Indrajit found he could only nod.

"Get your client to a physician. The best he can afford. Make him drink lots of liquid."

"Thanks, Mrowf."

The Depik hunter disappeared from Indrajit's field of vision. Had he turned invisible, with his mystical power? Had he simply walked through one of the doors and out of sight?

"I like that you call me that," the hunter said.

Power and Prestige

~∞~

"I feel I should warn you," the man with the doglike face said. "There's a possibility I may eat my feces."

"That's it," Indrajit said to his partner. "We're not hiring this guy."

Fix frowned. "Why do you say there's a 'possibility'? Remind me your name... Munahim?"

The three men sat at a table in the common room of the nameless inn where Indrajit and Fix rented a room to serve as both their sleeping chamber and the headquarters of their two-man jobber company, the Protagonists. The barkeep, a broad-shouldered Kishi with a black topknot and tattoos of snakes across his shoulders, was polishing his counter. A messenger stood in the doorway, shifting from one foot to the other. The sounds of camels and gulls drifted in through the windows.

Given the heat, all five men wore simple kilts.

Munahim nodded, the motion making his long ears bounce and his eyes fill with liquid. "I've done it before. I'm not proud of it, but you know, there it is. If it's going to happen, I want you to know about it in advance."

"You make it sound like an impersonal phenomenon," Indrajit said, "like rain. It might rain, so you should be warned. I might munch on my own waste, so don't be surprised. How about you just choose *not* to eat your feces?"

"I get caught up in the moment." Munahim hung his head.

"Speaking of the moment," Indrajit said to Fix, "we don't have any moments left. We need to get over to the Hall of Guesses and look at that hole in the basement, now. We don't have time for this guy."

"Wrong," Fix said mildly. He was shorter than Indrajit and stocky, with a high-pitched, womanlike voice. "We don't have time for any other jobber. But since we're already interviewing Munahim, and he happens to be a tracker, he's the one person we have time for right now. It's just a bit of good luck that we happened to be talking to Munahim when a job offer came through."

"We really must go." The messenger from the Hall of Guesses nodded anxiously in the doorway.

Indrajit scowled at Munahim, who was nearly as tall as he was, and similarly rangy. "Can you track by smell?"

Munahim nodded.

"But I mean . . . really well? Are you good at it?" Indrajit pressed.

"I'm the best," Munahim said.

Indrajit sighed. "Okay, here's the offer. If we get this lecturer back, you get one share. Fix and I each get two. No promises that we retain you any longer term than that, but consider this a trial period. Does that work for both of you?"

Fix nodded.

Munahim held out a hand to Indrajit. Indrajit hesitated, uncertain exactly how this dog-headed man might eat his own excrement and whether his fingers were really clean, but then clasped his hand around Munahim's forearm.

"If I see you eating your own waste," Indrajit growled, "or anybody else's, you will not get paid, and this will, by every frozen hell, be a onetime engagement."

The messenger from the Hall of Guesses was a very ordinary-looking Kishi, skin coppery-brown and hair cut short like an upside-down bowl. Indrajit might have lost him in the crowd, but for the vermilion color of the messenger's kilt. Indrajit loped ahead of his partner Fix, keeping an eye on both Fix and Munahim with his excellent peripheral vision. All three men were armed: Indrajit had his leaf-bladed sword, Vacho; Fix had an ax and a falchion at his belt; and Munahim had a long, straight sword slung across his back.

"Have you worked in a jobber company before?" Fix asked, continuing the interview.

"I was a mercenary," Munahim said. "We fought in Ildarion for two years."

"And then gave it up?" Indrajit asked over his shoulder. "Didn't like the life of living and dying for contracts, eh?"

"I didn't think I was really fulfilling my potential," Munahim said. His voice had a mournful quality, consonant with the melting look of his face. The fur covering his muzzle and forehead and running in a tapering diamond shape down his shoulders and back was black, as were his nails, and his skin was a grayish-blue.

His eyes were golden brown. "I'm a tracker, really, and an archer. All the Ildarion barons wanted from me was to swing a sword."

"We definitely want to use all the skills of all our team members," Fix said.

Indrajit grumbled without words.

"Did you read that we were looking for men in one of our posted notices?" Fix asked.

"I can't read," Munahim said.

"Ah, excellent," Indrajit said. "Finally, a point in his favor."

"I wouldn't mind learning," Munahim said. "It seems very useful."

"That's interesting," Fix mused. "I suppose I could teach you. I could teach everyone we eventually hire into the Protagonists. You never know when reading might come in handy."

Indrajit grumbled wordlessly again.

They climbed from the alley off the Crooked Mile up through the Spill, through clouds of spice and smoke that smelled of fish. Alleys and side streets shot off in all directions like the strands of a spider's web, but the messenger picked the shortest route upward. The walk was steep and Indrajit worked up a sweat.

They passed through the gate, held by jobbers in yellow tunics, and into the Crown. Here the merchants were fewer, the buildings were larger, and the plazas were pleasant with green amalaki trees, ketakas, and aloes. A troupe of actors on a corner recited famous dramatic speeches; jugglers on another leaped upon each other's shoulders and wrestled flaming torches up and down into the afternoon sky. As they approached the solid block of buildings that comprised the Hall of Guesses—walled off within its own stone curtain, complete with battlements and arrow loops—Indrajit found himself grinding his teeth. He wasn't quite sure why. He didn't object to the scholars of the Hall of Guesses cutting open dead bodies and pressing plants between panes of glass and whatever else they did.

He did find it somewhat silly and effeminate that they felt the need to write it all down, and to take it all so seriously.

The messenger took them through the front gate of the Hall of Guesses. The men on guard here weren't jobbers, but warriors on the payroll of the Hall itself. They wore vermilion kilts and tunics and leaned on long spears. Most were Kishi, but one of their number was a pale, hulking Gund with its extra eyes scratched out. They all glared at Indrajit and his colleagues, but when the messenger shouted a few words of authorization at them, they stepped aside.

Indrajit had imagined that the interior of the Hall of Guesses would be a single large courtyard, with tall buildings standing around the outside, against the wall. Instead, the center of the fenced-in area was filled with numerous buildings, the height of the outer wall or shorter, and a maze of lanes and alleys winding among them. Women and men paced deep in thought, conversed with one another beneath arched porticos, yelled over coffee mugs, or lay sleeping on the ground.

"One thing that is immediately apparent," he said to Fix, "is that these reading-scholars have no dignity. Look at that fellow over there, he's lying beneath a bench like any public drunk! All of them together don't have the respectability of a single Recital Thane."

"So you have doubled their respectability by merely entering," Fix said.

"What's a Recital Thane?" Munahim asked.

"Indrajit is the epic poet of his people," Fix explained. "He can recite their epic from memory. A hundred thousand lines about fish-headed warriors."

"Thirty thousand," Indrajit said, "give or take." He let the jibe about his resembling a fish pass.

"Perhaps some of these people might be interested in studying at your feet," Fix suggested. His expression looked serious. "You're looking for apprentices."

Indrajit scanned the area. "I would prefer people of my own kind, if possible. And in any case, committing the art of the Blaatshi Epic to memory is a serious undertaking that requires real discipline, hard work, and self-sacrifice. No one I see here seems capable of any of that."

"A few times a year, the Hall of Guesses puts on its formal robes," Fix said. "When they award each other degrees, and for major cult processions. Then they look impressive. The rest of the time, they mostly care about what's inside. Thoughts and ideas. That should appeal to you, no?"

"No thought is so noble that it matters a whit," Indrajit said, "unless it is matched to noble deeds."

The messenger stopped. They were somewhere in the center of the maze—within the larger warren of the Crown, and again within the still-larger labyrinth of Kish—beside a small brick building. Next to the building's open door hung a bronze sign stamped with letters, and in front of the sign stood a man.

He was shaped like a cone, with the narrow tip pointing up. The wide base of the cone sagged on all sides, and the gray toga hanging over everything nearly obscured tree-trunk-like legs that terminated with nails but no apparent feet, like elephant's legs. A whiskered tail swished quickly back and forth, agitating the lower folds of the toga. Long, muscular arms hung at his side, and his head was thick and boxy, with a prominent, bulging forehead and four yellowing tusks. His skin was pale white, callused, and speckled here and there with thick stands of black bristles.

Indrajit cocked his head to one side. "What race of man are you?"

It was not entirely a polite question.

"I'm an Olifar." The man's voice sounded like an iron sheet dragged over gravel. "Jat Bighra is my name. First Lecturer in Druvash Technologies. And you are Blaatshi. We see few of you in Kish."

"Few, or none?"

"You're the first I've seen, I admit."

"And you are my first Olifar."

The messenger bowed and retreated.

"Why did you send for us?" Fix asked.

"I wouldn't have sent for anyone." Bighra shrugged. "We have our own men. But the Lord Chamberlain was here, meeting with the Prime Magister, and apparently he felt strongly that you might be able to help. He insisted. We are grateful for the help, of course."

"And what are you paying?" Fix asked.

"The Prime Magister has authorized ten Imperials for

the investigation, and fifty Imperials if you bring her back."

"Show us the hole," Indrajit said. "And tell us who the 'she' in question is. The messenger said a group of your scholars that went down a hole in the basement never came back up."

Munahim sniffed.

Bighra led them into the building. Through open doorways, Indrajit saw large rooms, each with a low stage at one end. The narrow halls connecting the rooms were decorated with drawings on the walls, but Indrajit couldn't figure out any of the images. They seemed to be of objects, but the illustrations were cunningly conceived to reveal both the insides and the outsides of the objects at the same time. Universally, the insides were much more complicated, consisting of wires and tubes and nodes that resembled gemstones and plates. The outsides mostly looked like rounded stones or boxes.

"What is this place?" Indrajit asked. "What are these drawings?"

Jat Bighra led them down stairs. "Ironically, one of the subjects studied in this building is Druvash Technologies."

"Of which you are First Lecturer," Fix said.

Bighra nodded. "And Sari was Second Lecturer. Her work was promising, if a little radical."

"I don't care about her work in Druvash sorceries," Indrajit said. "Tell me about how she disappeared."

Bighra nodded, leading them down a second flight of stairs. The light down here came from oil lamps, set into niches in the walls. Kish was an ancient city, with multiple levels of previous occupation hidden beneath its streets in the form of mazelike underground ruins collectively referred to as Underkish. The Hall of Guesses, or at least this building, seemed to have been constructed by sinking several levels of basement down into those ruins. That meant that beyond the walls surrounding Indrajit now, there might be flowing sewers, rapeworm nests, and worse.

It also meant that the Hall of Guesses was bigger than it appeared, and potentially *much* bigger.

"I care," Fix said. "What was the Second Lecturer studying?"

"Power," Bighra said. "Power generation. She had a theory about what powers Druvash artifacts that had managed to garner a few influential adherents."

"You don't agree with her theory?" Fix suggested.

Munahim sniffed.

Bighra shrugged. "From my work in Druvash weaponry, I can't see how her theory explains half of what it would need to explain, even to be taken seriously as a hypothesis. I encouraged her to continue to think boldly, but . . . no, I don't think she was ever going to prove anything."

"Druvash weaponry?" Indrajit asked. "I don't suppose that's available for purchase, say, to employees of the Lord Chamberlain?"

Bighra laughed. "Oh, heavens, no, it's far too destructive. Also, we have precious few pieces, so they have to stay available to us for study."

"Did Sari have an office in this building?" Munahim asked. "Or can you show me where her personal effects are?"

"Er . . . yes, hold on, we have to go back up one flight." Jat Bighra turned and led them up stairs and down a hallway to a narrow rectangular room with a desk at one end.

"May I have a moment alone in here?" Munahim asked.

Bighra shrugged and Munahim shut the door.

"Frozen hells," Indrajit said. "He's defecating."

"What?" Bighra blinked. "Why would he do that in Sari's office?"

"So we can't see him eat it," Indrajit grumbled.

"First of all," Fix said, "you don't know that's what he's doing. This is just your grumpy side coming out. And second, if that is what he's up to, then he's having the decency not to do it in front of you."

"Ah," Jat Bighra said. "He's a Kyone. I've read about their coprophagy."

"I don't know what the word means," Indrajit said, "and I think I'd rather not find out."

"Eating excrement is far from the most bizarre or repellent eating habit of the thousand races of man," Jat Bighra said. "Anthropophagy and cannibalism, surely, must rate at the top. I've read of a race of man whose members eat their own flesh as a means of suicide, when they become too old, and a burden on their communities."

"It isn't a competition," Indrajit said. "That's all disgusting."

"There are different hypotheses about why the Kyones do it." Bighra scrabbed the thick, scabby skin of his jaw reflectively. "Some say it aids in digestion. Others think they do it when their diet is lacking some important nutrient."

"This is what's wrong with the Hall of Guesses," Indrajit said. "You sit around thinking about things like this."

"He said he gets caught up in the moment," Fix said.

"Which sounds like compulsion or madness." Bighra nodded. "But you see, that only raises more questions. Why would a race of man be constituted so as to feel compelled to eat feces? And why do some of them prefer their own, and some prefer the excrement of others?"

"Shut up right now," Indrajit said, "or I'll draw my sword and attack you both."

The door opened and Munahim emerged, his face mournful.

"I'm not going to ask what you were doing in there," Indrajit said, "and I'd prefer you not tell me."

Munahim's shoulders slumped, and he nodded.

"Right." Jat Bighra cleared his throat. "Just back down one level, and we're there." He turned and walked, and they followed him. "It was renovations, you see. The Hall had a jobber crew in here, fixing some corroded heat ducts behind the walls, and they accidentally broke through the floor."

He stopped in front of a door with a lock, and took a ring of keys from inside his toga. Indrajit guessed they must be in the corner of the floor, several levels down from the street . . . maybe five levels? If he exited the building horizontally, and could keep moving until he saw daylight, he'd come out in the Spill or the Lee or the Dregs.

Welcome to Kish. It's as hollow as its people's hearts.

"Beyond that door," Indrajit said, "are we still in the building?"

Bighra shrugged. "I think you would say no, we will have left the building, and be underneath the city. But the pipes and ducts and crawlspaces that serve the building pass through that space, so I'm not so sure. Where does the building really end?"

Indrajit took the oil lamp from the nearest niche. He held it in his left hand and drew his sword. "I really meant, will I need a light?"

Jat Bighra opened the door. Beyond lay a packed-dirt floor, crumbling brick columns and arches, and bronze ducts. Indrajit's light proved to be unnecessary, because the space was lit. A few paces from the door, two brick arches came together, and where a column should have stood, there was only a crumbling orange stalactite, and beneath it, a hole in the floor. A splinter of green light came up through the hole; it wasn't much, but it was enough to see by.

"You might get along fine without a light," the First Lecturer said. "The workmen accidentally broke through the floor, with the result that you see."

Indrajit held on to his lamp anyway.

"And Sari went down there?" Fix said.

"Yes," Bighra said.

Munahim sniffed.

"Something to do with her research?" Fix suggested.

Bighra shrugged. "I suppose. She got excited, and she took two of the most experienced students who were reading with her and went right in."

"Not you?" Indrajit asked.

"I stayed up here," Bighra said. "I had work to do."

"What, this morning?" Fix asked.

"Yesterday," Jat Bighra said. "We shut the door to keep anyone else from getting hurt, or wandering off into the maze, of course. But she never came back."

"You didn't post a guard or anything?" Indrajit asked.

Bighra shook his head. "This door is always here. It's locked, and nothing has ever come through, other than our own people."

Fix rubbed his chin. "So Sari hoped to find a Druvash power source."

"Or perhaps she was finally ready to give up on that idea," Bighra suggested, "and hoped to find something new to study. Or perhaps she was just curious. It takes a lot of natural curiosity to make someone a good lecturer at the Hall of Guesses. Just because something is glowing green down there, that doesn't mean it's Druvash."

"It might not even be sorcery," Indrajit said. "It could be some creature that glows in the dark."

Bighra nodded.

"Why don't you give us the key?" Fix suggested. "You can stay here. We'll come back and report what we find."

"I'll come." Bighra smiled nervously. "She was my colleague, and I'd like to know what happened. And I'll have to make my report to the Prime Magister, so it's best if I'm actually a witness."

They all stepped into the crumbling brick maze and Jat Bighra locked the door behind them. Indrajit kept his sword in his hand. The air smelled sour, with a hint of charnel and ash, and it wasn't moving at all.

Fix and Munahim went first. Bighra gestured politely to Indrajit to go next, and Indrajit shook his head. "You're the client," Indrajit said. "You go in the middle, and I'll bring up the rear. In case anything tries to ambush us, you get the maximum protection."

"I'm quite capable," the Olifar grunted.

"Yes, you're a Druvash sorcerer." Indrajit pointed with the tip of Vacho. "You really look the part, in that toga. Now get moving, or else give me the keys and go back."

The hole in the floor opened at the top of a scree-cluttered slope. The source of the light was not visible as Indrajit stooped to avoid banging his forehead, and entered. Ahead, along the slope below him, he saw Munahim close behind Fix. The Kyone walked bent over, as if bringing his nose close to the ground. Was he really able to track by scent? And, if so, was he following Sari and her two readers now?

Readers. Indrajit harrumphed.

A hundred cubits or more separated the two in the lead from Indrajit and the scholar. With his peripheral vision, Indrajit watched for exits on the left and right sides of the slope of rubble, and saw none. About halfway down the slope, a long black scorch mark blighted one wall. Because he saw better to the sides than immediately in front of him, when he needed to be extra careful about his footing, he turned his head slightly to one side.

"What do your Druvash weapons do, then?" he asked.

"Some of them, we don't yet know." Bighra stumbled, but caught himself. "Indeed, some of my papers have presented arguments that unidentified objects may, in fact, be weapons that we do not yet understand."

Papers. Indrajit snorted.

"But surely you must know how some of them work," Indrajit said, "or you couldn't be certain there were any

Druvash weapons at all. Maybe someone would present the theory that the Druvash were entirely peaceful."

"That theory *has* been argued," Bighra said. "It was vigorously maintained by a Pelthite scholar named Umaltes Sog, about a century ago. But the blasted quality of Druvash ruins told against him; there's simply no way that the Druvash succumbed to a disease, or economic depression, or existential malaise."

"I don't know," Indrajit said. "Never underestimate the deadliness of existential malaise."

"And once we finally started to be able to use some of the Druvash artifacts and learned that they were efficient killing machines, his theory imploded."

"So you know how they work."

"That's not quite right. We can *operate* some of them. We're a long way from knowing how they *work*."

Indrajit nodded. Fix and Munahim had reached a flat space below the stones. Ahead of them stretched a featureless stone wall, through which were bored perfectly circular holes. The green light shone from the hole on the left-hand side.

Indrajit and Jat Bighra were nearing the bottom of the slope, too. The air here still felt stale and motionless, but the smell of ash was gone.

"And you say they don't kill by inflicting existential malaise."

"Some throw projectiles. Like Thûlian black powder weapons, only the projectile is packed in metal."

Indrajit grunted. "No pouring in the fabled powder, eh?"

"No. Other weapons fire heat rays."

"Heat rays?"

"Imagine a ray of the sun, but greatly intensified, so that it burns flesh to ash upon contact."

Something tickled at the back of Indrajit's consciousness.

"Have you ever seen the body of a Druvash?" he asked. "Or the skeleton, or the mummy, or whatever? Even an image, say a sculpture or an old mosaic?"

"No one has," Bighra said. "The discovery of an intact Druvash body would be a world-shaking step forward in learning about them. Scattered bones have been recovered to date, but not enough even to be certain how big they were."

"Is that because of the nature of their weapons?" Indrajit asked. "A ray of heat, if it was hot enough, might incinerate bone as well as flesh."

"*I* think some of the artifacts we haven't yet figured out are explosives," Jat Bighra said. "Others seem to be airborne poisons. One is said by a very old source to cause transformation of its targets, whatever that might mean. I've read an account of a mobile, controllable cloud of acid. Other weapons attack by *sound*."

"Fearsome, indeed," Indrajit said. "Do the lords of the great families know about all this? I would think they would be interested in controlling these weapons. Especially if it came to a war. If Ukeling pirates sailed up to the West Flats, I bet Orem Thrush would love to be able to sink their ships by hitting them with Druvash sunbeams."

"The Lords of Kish are aware of my work." There was pride in Bighra's voice. "It may be that Orem Thrush was meeting with the Prime Magister this morning to be updated on my research."

"And this is how he heard about a missing second lecturer," Indrajit said. "And this is why he cares."

"I suppose." Bighra sniffed. "It's not every lecturer whose work is noticed by the powerful."

"What's the difference between being first lecturer and being second?" Indrajit asked. "Better pay?"

"People in my position can hardly be bothered about such things as pay," Jat Bighra said. "We get paid enough, and there is a pension, and living quarters within the walls of the Hall. All the food I want, of the best kind. Girls, if we want them. I suppose the first lecturer in any department has more honor."

Fix and Munahim were well along the length of the left-hand passage, appearing now as mere shadows. Indrajit and Bighra approached the tunnel mouth. Not only was the opening of the tunnel perfectly circular, but the passage beyond maintained the same shape all along its length, its walls completely smooth.

"Better job security?" Indrajit suggested.

"We're all pretty secure, as long as the wealthy of Kish are willing to pay to send their useless children here to be educated." Bighra laughed, a short, sharp bark. "And as long as we are patronized by the Lords of Kish."

"But you get to go first in the parades, as First Lecturer," Indrajit said. "Your name is read from the roll before anyone else's. You stand foremost in the . . . I don't know, the ceremonies. You get the better seating at the opera. You get prestige."

"All of that, yes," the First Lecturer said. "Prestige, yes."

"Prestige is worth a lot to some people," Indrajit suggested. "Many would envy you."

"Well, hum, ho," Bighra said.

"When would Sari have become first lecturer?" Indrajit asked. "Only if you died or retired, I guess?"

"Based on how her research was going, yes," Bighra said. "She was chasing a dead end, though I don't think she would ever admit it. I suppose if I had moved into administration, somehow, she might have become first. But I'm not the type."

The First Lecturer was nearing the end of the tunnel. His step was becoming slower, more hesitant. The silhouettes of Munahim and Fix had disappeared from view. A bass hum rolled into Indrajit's hearing and made his bones tremble.

"Did you go down this far?" Indrajit asked.

Bighra shook his head. "I stayed above, as I said."

"Should we be calling for them?" Indrajit said. "I mean, we don't want to attract the attention of anything nasty that lives down here, but, on the other hand, that's why we're armed. And Sari and her readers might be lying injured somewhere."

He adjusted his grip on his sword and raised it, resting the blade on his shoulder.

"Sari!" Jat Bighra called. "Chumble! Tom Tom!"

The names echoed up and down the circular stone tunnel, but there was no response.

Bighra exited the tunnel at the far end and his body seemed to acquire a green halo, surrounding the scholar entirely, for just a moment. Indrajit moved slowly into the next chamber, casting his eyes around while still keeping his attention fixed on Bighra.

To the right, a stone wall was incised with deep grooves

in complex patterns. Was that some kind of writing? Bronze spheres sat poised atop those grooves, which might be the handles on levers, which might then . . . ride within the grooves? Indrajit shook his head. At a quick glance, there were maybe a hundred of the balls, and enough groove-cut wall to make a decent Rûphat court, if it were laid horizontal.

To the left, a handrail marked the edge of the flat shelf on which they all stood. Behind the rail, the floor dropped away and the ceiling rose, and the walls on the far side were smooth, without railing, walkway, or grooves. In the center of the resulting space, a green fire burned. It was the size of a large bonfire, or a small one-room hut. Indrajit blinked and his eyes watered, but he couldn't tell whether the fire was contained within some kind of glass, or whether instead the fire was simply so glossy and iridescent that it gave the impression of being bottled. Indrajit could see no bottom of the fire, and no fuel. The green flame seemed simply to exist, floating in the air.

It gave off no heat.

Fix turned to face Indrajit and Bighra. "Sari came down here with her readers because she thought the green light might teach her something about Druvash power. It looks like she was probably right."

"I suppose so," Bighra said slowly. "Have you seen any sign of her?"

"One thing did strike me as strange," Fix said. "Why would she come down here with just a couple of students? Why not some of your Hall of Guesses guardsmen, or a jobber company? I saw a Gund up there, so I know the Hall has muscle to spare. Indrajit and I are tough, armed men, and we avoid coming down into Underkish whenever we can, because there are dangerous things down here. Why would a second lecturer rush down here with so little protection?"

"Oh, that's obvious," Indrajit said. "You just have to stop imagining that the scholars in the Hall of Guesses have some kind of magical selflessness. These aren't the adepts of Salish-Bozar the White, Fix, these are ordinary, petty, ambitious men."

"Hey," Bighra objected.

"And how do men get power in this world?" Indrajit asked. "By controlling access to a resource. By controlling the contracts, in the case of the Lords of Kish. By controlling access to—what do you call it, in the case of the Paper Sook?"

"Capital," Fix said.

"Capital. And by controlling access to knowledge, if you're a lecturer in the Hall of Guesses. Sari wanted the information for herself and her best students, and no one else. She wanted to prove she was right, after all, or get new information for her theory, whatever it was. She wanted work for her students to control and carry out, and this was a golden opportunity to have that. Bringing along anyone who might steal the information, or accidentally pass it on to someone on the outside, jeopardized that opportunity. And look, it was so close. What did it take us to climb down here, a mere twenty minutes?"

"Too bad she got lost," Jat Bighra said. "Wandered off and got eaten by some unknown beast."

Indrajit nodded. "She made one mistake."

"What do we do now?" Bighra said.

"Now," Fix said, "we have to go tell the Prime Magister that his First Lecturer of Druvash Technologies committed three murders."

Jat Bighra pulled something from inside his toga. It looked like a flat white disk, smooth and small enough to fit in the palm of his hand. One end was truncated and flat, and rimmed with black. He pointed it at Fix.

Munahim leaped, dragging Fix to the floor.

A white sheet of flame burst from the disk for a split second, melting a section of the railing ten cubits wide, and then Indrajit brought his sword Vacho down in an overhand motion. He meant to strike with the flat of his blade, knocking the strange weapon from the scholar's hand, but in the excitement of the moment, he struck with the blade instead. Vacho sliced through skin and bone and bit deep into the disk.

A blinding flash of light and a wall of force hurled Indrajit backward. He struck the stone wall headfirst, and for a time he lost track of his surroundings.

"Indrajit. Can you hear me?"

"I can hear you," Indrajit said, his voice slurring. Blinking, he climbed to his feet with the help of the wall. Fix and Munahim helped him up; Fix's eyebrows and the hair on the Kyone's muzzle were singed nearly bare, but otherwise they seemed unharmed.

Jat Bighra, on the other hand, was dead. His nose was smashed flat and his eyes jellied, probably by the same blast that had hurled Indrajit off his feet. His windpipe was also crushed, which was likely the wound that had killed him.

"You could have just knocked him down," Fix said.

"I got caught up in the moment." Indrajit shrugged. "Be grateful that you're alive, after you called him out like that."

Indrajit found Vacho lying on the floor and picked the sword up, returning it to his belt. The oil lamp lay shattered and he left it in its puddle of fuel.

"How did you figure it out?" Fix asked Indrajit.

"It seemed pretty clear that he wanted Sari to fail," Indrajit said. "And there are flame marks on the wall back up there. And I couldn't figure out why he was accompanying us down here, unless it was to make certain we failed, too. I think he followed Sari and her readers down here and burned them to ash with that flame weapon before she even saw this thing. Frozen hells, maybe she was on the path to overtaking him as first lecturer, and he had no other way to stop her. How about you?"

Munahim shrugged. "I could smell from the trail that Bighra had been down here before. He was lying to us."

Indrajit almost shot back that the Kyone's sense of smell had been redundant; that he, Indrajit, had divined Bighra's guilt with no help. But he decided not to, and instead clapped the Kyone on the shoulder.

Munahim grinned, tongue lolling from his mouth.

"Do we tell the Prime Magister about this?" Fix pointed at the green flame.

"If we tell him," Indrajit said, "he can block off the passages around it, and stop anyone else from getting to the flame and . . . I don't know, causing an explosion. Lighting Kish on fire."

"But if we tell him," Fix said, "then his scholars will

have access to this energy, which looks like it could be really dangerous."

"Hard choices." Munahim shook his head.

"On the plus side," Indrajit said, "the two leading scholars studying Druvash sorcery are now both dead. That probably sets the field back twenty years."

"Maybe more," Fix said, "depending on how jealously they guarded their knowledge from each other. So maybe the Hall of Guesses will come down here and fence in this green flame, but there will be no one who can do anything with it. Not for years. Maybe decades."

Indrajit sighed. "I guess that's the solution, then. Why does it feel like, no matter how hard we try to do the right thing, the powers that be always remain the powers that be?"

"The powers that be are not necessarily evil," Fix said.

"And the powers that be have cash to pay," Munahim said.

"That," Indrajit said, "is a really good point. And today, the powers that be owe us ten Imperials. I assume your math is good enough to know how many Imperials you get, Munahim?"

"One of five shares means that I get two," the Kyone said.

"Yes," Indrajit agreed. "As long as you don't slip up and eat feces between here and the Prime Magister's office."

Munahim grinned, somehow still managing to look mournful in his eyes. "I'll try."

The Lady in the Pit

"I need your help."

The woman sitting across the round wooden table wore a black cloak. The hood was up, entirely obscuring her face, other than her slightly pointed, pale slip of a chin. Her voice was soft, but firm, with a whisper of silk in its tones.

Indrajit turned to look at his partner. Fix nodded. "Tell us more." Fix was Kishi, or something closely related to Kishi; he was short, with brown skin and straight black hair cut in a simple bowl shape. His voice was soft, almost girlish, belying his broad frame and the array of weapons hanging at his belt.

Their sole employee, the only member of the jobber company called the Protagonists who was not a partner, stood across the street. Munahim was tall and had a doglike head covered in black fur, so he was hardly conspicuous, but from behind the flap of a tack shop's tent, he watched, ready to intervene if the client pulled any untoward tricks. He'd secreted himself in that station well before the client had arrived for her appointment.

"We don't specialize in damsels in distress," Indrajit added, "but it's definitely in our portfolio."

"My name is Oleandra Holt."

"Your message said that you're a priestess of the Unnamed," Fix suggested.

She purred. "An acolyte. It's unlikely I'll ever make priestess proper."

Indrajit rubbed a finger along the bony nose ridge that rose into a crest along the top of his hairless skull. It pushed Indrajit's eyes out to the side of his skull, but definitely did not make him look like a fish. Also, no fish had Indrajit's pleasing complexion, mahogany with nuanced hints of green. He was the tallest of the three Protagonists, though maybe the least muscle-bound.

"Is that because you're not an assassin?" Indrajit had no idea whether the rumors about the worshippers of the Unnamed were true, but sitting in the common room of the tavern below his own lodgings, with broad beams of afternoon sunlight and the smell of camels wafting in through the windows, he felt brave enough to ask.

Oleandra laughed. "If I deny the substance of the rumors you're alluding to, you won't believe me. An assassin-thief sworn to lie, steal, and kill in the service of the New Moon would lie in any case, wouldn't she? That's what you would tell yourself, if I offered a denial."

"And yet you deny nothing," Indrajit said.

She purred again.

"In any case, the message was eye-catching." Fix cleared his throat and shot Indrajit a withering look, probably reminding his partner that Fix was literate, and Indrajit was not. "The devotees of the Unnamed, the

Unseen, the goddess of the New Moon, rarely disclose their affiliation in public."

"Rarely," Oleandra Holt agreed. "Not never."

"May we see *your* face?" Fix asked. "I find it disconcerting to speak to someone whose eyes I can't see."

Oleandra didn't touch her veil. "You were recommended to me by a certain . . . woman. A rich woman."

"Connected with the Lord Chamberlain?" Indrajit asked.

Fix said nothing, but his eyes narrowed and his nostrils flared.

"One of the scholars of the Hall of Guesses?" Indrajit tried again.

"No," Oleandra said. "But a wealthy woman, and a friend."

"Will you name her?" Fix's muscles were visibly taut, as if he were prepared to leap into hand-to-hand combat at any moment. "Are she and her husband connected with the Paper Sook?"

"You ask too many questions." Oleandra stood as if to leave, her black cloak falling over her shoulders and framing a body clad in white linen. Her limbs were well muscled, but she hunched forward slightly as she stood. Was that why she covered herself with a cloak? She had a tail, too, barely visible as a bulge in the fabric around her ankles.

"Please," Indrajit said, "we're investigators by nature. I apologize if our questions are intrusive."

Fix's eyes burned.

Oleandra Holt seated herself again, slowly.

With exaggerated slowness. And she'd never really

moved toward the door, and she hadn't picked up the canvas sack sitting on the floor beside her.

A bluff.

"My friend said that you were bold men," she said. "The Protagonists, you call yourselves. I have heard that you are valiant fighters in the causes of other people. That you risk life and limb to rescue kidnapped and threatened people, for instance. That you uncover mysteries and bring justice to wrongdoers. That you are dogged, reliable, honest, and highly skilled."

"Ah, good," Indrajit said. "Those rumors I spread are working. Only you forgot the part about how handsome we are."

Oleandra purred again.

"Does your friend need help for herself?" Fix asked. "Rescuing from her . . . husband, for instance?"

The acolyte of the Unnamed shook her head. "I come on my own behalf."

Fix slumped the tiniest bit. "Go on."

Despite their many weeks of working together, Indrajit didn't know the entire story of Fix's unrequited love. He knew the woman had married. He knew Fix still pined for her, and that one reason Fix wanted to become wealthy and successful was to be in a position to woo her back.

"Like all the women of my family," Oleandra said, "I have served the Unnamed since the moon first turned for me."

"What?" Fix asked.

"You need more poetry in your soul," Indrajit said. "She means since she reached womanhood. Only she said it in a very moon-mystical kind of way."

Fix frowned, then nodded.

"Like all the women of my family, my first encounter with the goddess was on my entry into her temple at that time. As is the custom, I took with me a votive, and deposited it there. There is a niche that my mothers before me have all used, in the temple. They passed down knowledge of it to me, and when I knelt and consecrated my votive to the New Moon, I laid it among many other objects placed by my forebears."

"This was what?" Indrajit asked. "A statue? An offering of money? A stolen item?" He didn't know what votive offerings the worshippers of the Unnamed would make. "An assassination victim?"

Oleandra hesitated.

"You don't have to tell us," Indrajit said. "Unless, of course, it's relevant to what you're going to ask us to do."

"It was a statue of the Unnamed," Oleandra said. "In her most traditional appearance."

"That's a paradox, isn't it?" Fix pushed back. "Her most traditional appearance is as the Unseen, without an image. The New Moon is the invisible moon. Is this a riddle? Are you testing us?"

"Things that appear are visible," Oleandra said. "Her most traditional *appearance* is as a woman with no face."

"No head, in fact," Indrajit said. "I've seen that image."

"It's often scratched on the lintel-posts of shopkeepers to ward off theft." Oleandra nodded.

"Not assassination?" Fix asked.

A hint of a smile played at the edge of the shadow within the hood.

"Okay, you deposited a statue of a headless woman,"

Indrajit said. "What, twenty years ago? Don't be offended, but . . . maybe even thirty years ago?" It was hard to tell from just the voice and the chin.

"Among the other votive sculptures standing within my family's sacred niche," Oleandra continued, "I saw the famed gift left by my great-great-grandmother."

"An even fancier statuette," Indrajit guessed.

Oleandra shook her head. "In fact, it was a much *less* elaborate statue. My granddam found a stone, a chunk of black, smooth rock, while she was journeying around the Sea of Rains. It was a stone that had never known a chisel, but nevertheless was a clear image of the kneeling goddess. A natural idol, and obviously an item of great power."

"Obviously," Indrajit said.

Fix's jaw clenched.

"That statuette brought great power to my granddam and to our family," Oleandra continued. "We waxed wealthy, and the Lords of Kish began to give us heed."

"You attribute this to the statue," Fix said.

"To the goddess," Oleandra countered, "whom we honored with the gift of the idol."

"This is all interesting," Indrajit said. "Indeed, I'm already considering how to capture it in a pithy, moving, yet thrilling fashion, in a few lines for the Blaatshi Epic."

"You don't have to," Fix said.

Indrajit shrugged. "But I have not yet heard anything that explains to me why you need our help."

"I am but an acolyte." Oleandra's tail swished, disturbing her cloak. "I serve the goddess in ritual ways only, and only for discrete periods of time. When it is my turn, I am permitted briefly into the temple, and when my time of service is past, I am ushered out again. My worship is genuine, but my appointment is social."

"You're not an assassin," Fix suggested, "you just go to the assassins' club with your friends."

"That's glib," she said.

"Yes, it is," Indrajit said, "and I'm the one who's supposed to make the glib observations."

"Are glib observations really consonant with the somber calling of an epic poet?" Fix asked.

"I'm wounded," Indrajit said. "And I take your point."

"Your description," Oleandra said, "however glib, is not wrong. And my appointment means that, although I am regularly allowed inside the Unnamed's temple, I have little freedom within its walls, and little time."

Indrajit rested his hand on the pommel of Vacho, his leaf-bladed sword, and nodded. "Go on."

"My grandmother's votive has been moved from its place."

"Stolen?" Fix's gaze was cool and piercing. "Ironic."

"I think not," Oleandra said. "The family niche became too crowded when my niece was initiated, two new moons ago, and I believe that the temple staff made room by throwing out older votives, including that of my granddam."

"What, thrown out into the trash?" Indrajit gulped. "That seems like a poor way to dispose of an item of power."

"Or, at least, a poor way to show respect to your own tradition," Fix suggested.

"Casting out sacrifices into the trash would incur the

wrath of the goddess." Oleandra shook her head, and the hood shifted slightly. The top of her skull seemed to be square, and to have pointed corners. "Offered food is eaten by the priestesses, in the place of the goddess herself."

"That sounds pretty typical," Fix said.

"Old votive statues are thrown into a pit," Oleandra said.

"And we are back to the garbage heap again." Indrajit shook his head. "Why doesn't your goddess of assassins strike dead people who disrespect her in this fashion? Mother Blaat is a peaceful goddess of the sea and its life—"

"That's Indrajit's granddam," Fix said. "That's why he looks like a koi with legs."

Indrajit ignored his partner. "—and I would never spurn her so."

"The pit is a holy pit, in consecrated ground. I have seen it only once; I asked about my granddam's votive, and a priestess took me to see the pit. The pit lies beneath the temple, and is therefore itself a sacred and appropriate receptacle into which to throw such consecrated items as old votives, worn-out ritual garb, and successfully-used assassins' blades."

"You saw your granddam's votive?" Indrajit asked. "Lying in this pit?"

"I saw the pit, in the shaky light of a lantern. I saw many sacred items. Before I could see my granddam's idol, I was led away. But the statuette must lie close to the surface of the mound of items in the pit, since it has only recently been removed."

"I begin to understand the picture," Fix said. "You don't

have the time while you're in the temple to go after the idol yourself, so you want us to recover it."

"I can let you in," Oleandra said, "by a secret entrance. But I only have time to open the door, I can't stand in the pit and search, or my absence will be noticed."

"A secret passage?" Fix asked. "Where's the temple? It's rumored to exist somewhere in the Dregs, but even the building is a secret. Much less some back door."

Oleandra only smiled.

"All this makes sense," Indrajit conded. "But if we break into the temple and steal an idol, won't the goddess feel ... discomfited?"

"You really worry that she might feel vengeful," Oleandra guessed.

"Of course," Indrajit said.

"Or perhaps there are no gods," Fix countered. "Not really. Perhaps they're just stories, and if you and I go into that pit, my long-limbed, green-skinned friend, we can find items of value to sell."

"Green is just one of the tones of my skin color," Indrajit said. "I am more mahogany than green."

"You're brown," Fix said. "We're both brown. That's a good shade, you don't need to be any fancier than that."

"Let's focus on the possibility that there is a real goddess here," Indrajit countered, "and a goddess of assassins, at that."

"Assassins and thieves," Oleandra pointed out.

"What are you saying, that she'll look the other way for us because she favors burglars?" That didn't sound ... impossible.

"Yes," Oleandra said. "But also, you won't steal the idol.

You'll find it, and hide it just within the door by which I admit you. You will just have moved the idol within the temple's sanctified grounds."

"Downgraded from burglars to trespassers," Fix said.

"Also, I'll give you sacred garb to disguise yourselves with. The goddess won't even see you."

"If the sacred garb disguises us from other believers, that's enough for me," Fix said.

Indrajit's stomach felt unsettled. "This feels like we're really tempting fate."

Oleandra set a purse on the table. "One hundred Imperials, paid now. Another hundred Imperials when I have the statuette in my possession."

"But the story doesn't quite add up," Fix said. "You're so religious that you want this statuette of the goddess back, but so impious that you will go ahead and trick the goddess to get it?"

Oleandra hesitated. "The idol is important to my family because of our history with it."

"I still don't believe it." Fix shook his head, but without taking his eyes from the woman. "You're risking some pretty big consequences for a few memories and a warm feeling."

Oleandra wrapped her fingers around the purse and gripped it tightly, until her knuckles whitened. "You're investigators, as you say. Very well. Scratched onto the underside of the idol is secret information that my family needs."

"Ah-ha." Indrajit leaned forward. "Now we have a real story going."

Oleandra said nothing.

"What is it?" Fix asked. "A bank account password? A map to treasure? A dirty secret to hold over the Lord Stargazer?"

Oleandra pressed her lips together.

"Does the nature of this secret make the job more dangerous for us?" Fix asked.

"The temple staff don't know the secret," Oleandra said. "They couldn't read the secret information, even if they saw it."

"Reading." Indrajit snorted, but he did wonder what the information could be.

"If they knew what they held in their hands, they would never have thrown the lady into the pit." Oleandra spoke as if her words were final.

They sat in silence a moment. Fix turned to his partner. "And think how much more fun this is than trying to enforce the regulations of the Paper Sook."

That clinched the argument. Indrajit barely understood the language of the merchants of the Paper Sook. When the Lord Chamberlain and his spymaster, Grit Wopal, gave Indrajit and Fix tasks among those merchants, which was often, Indrajit found himself repeating back to Fix the words his partner said, usually without comprehending them at all. "I'm in."

Fix leaned forward. "Your friend who recommended us . . . she isn't a devotee of the Unnamed."

"But she is my close friend." Oleandra smiled warmly. "And she will hear of this bold exploit and be pleased."

"Show us where this secret door is," Indrajit said, "and tell us when to meet you."

~~~~~~~~~~

There was no moon. The Spike rose in the middle distance, blocking out a chunk of the night sky with its knuckle of rock gripping the temples of the city's five acknowledged gods. Light from lamps and torches splashed up in yellow streaks against the tall walls of the buildings of the Crown, Kish's most elegant and exclusive quarter. The Crown was home to the palaces of the rich and the buildings of government as well as the temple district. Indrajit and Fix stood beside a small, unimportant-looking wooden door, on a dull, untrafficked side street.

"Strange," Indrajit said. "The temple to Kish's secret sixth god is located awfully close to the temples of the other five."

"Don't get cold feet," Fix said.

"I don't have cold feet. I'm just marveling at how much I still have to learn about this rotten old city."

"We're close enough to the Spike that the temple of the Unnamed could be on the Spike itself," Fix said. "Right alongside the other five."

"Hmm." Indrajit frowned.

"Or underneath it."

Kish was an ancient city, perched on a knob of rock riddled with catacombs, in turn stuffed with ruins, strange beasts, ancient machinery, poisons, and peril. It was not an insane thought that the goddess of thieves and assassins might make her home down in that warren. But it wasn't a comforting thought, either.

Indrajit pointed. "Also, this looks more like a side entrance into that dry goods shop than a secret back door into the temple of the New Moon."

"What should a secret back door into the temple look like, then?"

"Point taken. But maybe the temple isn't on the Spike, it's inside that shop. And, you know, it might be that the best possible outcome for us here is that Oleandra never shows up, we don't trespass on sacred ground, and you and I get to keep the hundred Imperials."

"But then you wouldn't accomplish any mighty deeds worth recounting in the Epic," Fix countered.

They were dressed in simple kilts and sandals, given the warm night. Indrajit wore Vacho at his belt, and Fix wore his falchion, his hand ax, and two long knives. He favored fighting with a spear when possible, but he'd left his spear behind, saying it might become awkward in narrow hallways. In a pocket in his kilt, Indrajit had a few items—a lantern, a flask of oil, flint and steel, and chalk.

Munahim, lurking in a shadowed doorway farther along the street, had his long, straight sword strapped to his back and carried a bow. He also had a two-handed wood ax in his possession, but it wasn't for fighting.

Munahim's role was protection. He was a selling of risk, in the language of the Paper Sook. He hung back because Indrajit couldn't quite bring himself to trust Oleandra Holt. Despite his enflamed and stricken looks, neither could Fix.

Indrajit stroked his chin. "You make a good point."

There was a triple rap on the inside of the door. Indrajit checked to be certain they were alone in the quiet street, then responded with the countersign, which was two double knocks, with a pause between.

Oleandra opened the door. She again wore her black cloak, with its hood up. "Quickly, please."

Indrajit and Fix stepped inside. The door was sturdy, and bound with iron bars. Indrajit pulled the door to, deliberately not quite shutting it, while attempting to look careless at the same time.

Oleandra yanked the door completely shut. A narrow passage descended immediately over brick steps into darkness. An oil lamp sat flickering at the top step beside a tall orange clay jar. From beneath her cloak, Oleandra produced a bundle of cloth, which she peeled apart into two smaller bundles, handing one to each man.

"Wear these to stay unobserved by the goddess." She kept her voice to a whisper.

They unrolled the fabric.

"This is a woman's dress," Indrajit said. It was the same style of dress Oleandra herself wore.

"I don't have access to the men's garb." Oleandra took down her hood, revealing a pale face with large eyes. She had no hair on her head, and four inwardly curving horns protruded from the top of her skull, making four corners. "I got the largest that I could find."

Fix pulled the dress on over his kilt. After a moment's hesitation, Indrajit did the same. The dresses were white and sleeveless. Fix's was long enough for him, but not big enough to accommodate his muscular chest, so the seams of his dress squeaked out a brief complaint and then split apart. Indrajit's dress was big enough, but short, so its waist rode halfway between his armpits and his hips, and his kilt protruded below the dress.

"Oh, we look *fine*," Fix said.

"You look right to the goddess," Oleandra said.

"When you tell your friend this part," Fix told her, "you

could emphasize to her the heroism and downplay how ridiculous I look."

"That's certainly how *I* will recite this episode," Indrajit said. "Also, you will be tall."

Oleandra picked up the jar and moved it to the corner behind the door. "This is big enough for the statuette. You can leave the dresses here too, when you're finished."

"You have little time," Fix said. "Show us the pit."

Oleandra took the lamp and led them down the stairs. The air vibrated with a sound that Indrajit could not quite hear. He pressed his cheek to the wall and could make out chanting. He heard each syllable clearly, seemed to feel them in his bones, and he even felt that the syllables were familiar . . . but somehow, they didn't add up to words he could understand.

"Worship is beginning," Oleandra said. "The sacrifices are only a few minutes away, and I will be missed." She quickened her pace.

"We must be beneath the Spike about now," Fix said.

They made several turns and Oleandra didn't slow down for them. Trying not to attract attention to himself, Indrajit took the chalk from his pocket and marked the turnings. Was it a desecration to write on the temple's walls? He didn't know what sacred gesture to make to placate the goddess in case it was, but he pressed his palms together in an attitude of prayer, bowing and looking up in the general direction of where the moon might be.

Then they arrived, and he made one last mark before putting the chalk away.

The room was much larger than Indrajit had imagined

it would be, and so was the pit. Seven pillars carved like headless women were spaced evenly about the walls, supporting the vaulted ceiling with their shoulders. Each of the women held a different item before her: a dagger, a garotte, a vial, a caltrop, a sword, a crossbow, and a spiked cestus. Between every pair of pillars gaped an opening and a hallway. Around all sides of the room, two paces' worth of open floor separated the walls from the pit.

The sides of the pit were steep but scalable. Within the pit lay a tangled heap of objects, including blades, trophies, clothing, and idols. There were also bones.

"This will take us some time," Fix noted.

"I'll leave my lamp," she said. "The statuette should be near the edge. Items are dropped in, not thrown into the center."

She set down the light and left them, circling around the pit to leave by a different exit.

"Is it my imagination," Indrajit asked, "or is the chanting getting louder?"

Fix cocked his head to one side. "I think you're wrong."

Indrajit eyed the shadows with suspicion. "Okay, let's do this."

They let themselves down into the pit. The climb was half again Indrajit's height, maybe seven cubits, and the handholds were generous, so Indrajit could climb down while carrying the lamp. When Indrajit stepped into the heap of objects filling the pit, he sank up to his knees.

"There are a lot more bones down here than our client led me to expect," he grumbled.

Fix arrived beside him. "What kind of bones?"

Indrajit pointed. "The bones of men. I mean, of all kinds. Look, that must have been a Luzzazza, you can see the sockets for four arms. And these little ones everywhere are probably Zalaptings."

"Let's keep our eyes on the prize." Fix slogged inward two steps, putting himself between Indrajit and the center of the pit. Oleandra had been right that objects cast into the hole were thrown in from the sides, so the heap sank to a depression in its center. "We walk side by side, slowly, around the pit. We're looking for a black stone that looks like a headless idol. Use your imagination, people can see images in rocks and clouds with very little provocation. Anything made of black or blackish stone, we at least pick it up and look at it."

"Agreed," Indrajit said.

"If we see anything else valuable, I say we steal it."

Would that enrage the goddess? But they were helping one of her acolytes. "Yes," he said weakly.

They combed their way around the edge of the pit. Indrajit held the lamp high, because he was taller, but he occasionally passed it to Fix when the shorter partner needed to examine some object.

He noticed that the ceiling above them was pierced by a circular hole. He could see a few stars winking through it. How must that hole be disguised on the surface? Was it unseen because it was surrounded by buildings? Or within the courtyard of one of the Crown's palaces? Or a temple disguised as a palace?

Indrajit also took what opportunity he had to study the skeletons. They were wrapped in layers of rotting cloth, but not with the care that a mummy would be. He saw smashed skulls and deeply nicked neck bones, and three times he saw rib cages with crossbow bolts lodged between the ribs.

When he looked up to see how much progress they had made, he was disappointed.

"We're a quarter of the way around." His voice sounded huge, and it echoed. "What time is it?"

Fix shrugged.

"Where's Munahim?"

Fix shrugged again.

Indrajit grumbled, but carried on.

Fix plucked jewelry from the heap, and even picked up a codex to examine it. Indrajit didn't have the nerve, and contented himself with scouring the pile of discarded temple items for any sign of the black stone idol.

Then they encountered the first body with flesh on its bones. It was a Grokonk Third, of middling height and rotting from yellow to a limpid gray. It had been strangled to death—the gashes left by a wire circled its neck, and the skin around the gashes was rotting black and peeling away from the corpse.

The second fleshly corpse was a furred Wixit, whose tongue was black and bloated in his mouth. The third, in quick succession, was a Zalapting whose chest was feathered with crossbow bolts. All three wore white dresses, rotting as quickly as the bodies were.

White dresses.

"We're getting out of here right now." Indrajit turned to climb up the wall of the pit—

and saw Oleandra standing at the top.

"Too late." Her voice was hollow.

To either side of her stood two men. All four wore black trousers and shirt and a black cloak over the top, hoods hiding their faces. All four held crossbows in their hands, and they all aimed at Indrajit.

"Do you not know . . . ?" Fix's voice was anguished. "You didn't . . . There is no friend who recommended us, is there?"

Oleandra shook her head.

An arrow struck one of the four men in the chest with a *twang* and a wet slapping sound. He fell into a puddle of his own cloak with a soft grunt, and then Munahim came crashing out of the dark, long sword raised over his head.

Indrajit sprang forward. He jammed his foot into a depression in the stone and threw himself upward. The remaining three cloaked men turned to face Munahim, and Indrajit grabbed the man in the middle by his ankles.

Oleandra turned and ran.

Munahim slashed through the crossbow of the man in front and Indrajit yanked the second down into the pit. The man lost his grip on his crossbow and Indrajit pulled him down over himself as a shield.

He felt a satisfying thud as a crossbow bolt buried itself in the man's back.

Indrajit landed flat and hard on a knobby pile of statues and bones, all the wind knocked out of him. His peripheral vision was excellent, so despite feeling stunned, he saw Fix scoop up the dropped crossbow and shoot one of their attackers with it. By the time Indrajit rolled the dead man off himself and stood, all four attackers had been shot or cut down.

"Munahim," he grumbled. "Glad you could make it."

"Your timing was perfect," Fix said.

By a stroke of good fortune, the lamp had not been extinguished in the fracas. They climbed out of the pit.

Munahim was wounded. Blood seeped from cuts on both arms, and he had a long scratch along the side of his doglike muzzle. "They have men behind us in the tunnels. I was traveling without light, following you by your scent, so they didn't see me coming. But I don't advise going back that way."

"There have to be other exits," Indrajit said.

Fix stared at his feet.

"Okay," Indrajit said. "The woman—can you follow her scent?"

Munahim nodded.

"Then we follow her out," Indrajit said. "She clearly led us into a trap here, so for all we know, she might now lead us into another. But probably not. Probably, she's running for her life and will head for the nearest exit."

Munahim grinned. "Frightened of the Protagonists."

Indrajit clapped the dog-headed warrior—the first recruit into the Protagonists since he and Fix had formed the jobber company—on the shoulder. "Frightened of *you*. Lead out, Munahim. I'll bring up the rear."

Munahim stooped to sniff at the bricks, and then quickly jogged into one of the room's seven exits. Not, Indrajit noted, the one that he had marked with chalk.

Indrajit pushed Fix to get him in motion. Once the small man was moving, he went quickly, but he still seemed distracted.

"There's no idol," he murmured, shuddering down a staircase into a wide gallery.

"If there is, we were never meant to get it." Indrajit hesitated at the top of the stairs and shielded the lamp with his body to look back. Was that a glimmer of light behind them?

"Why?" Fix asked.

"Maybe someone took out a contract," Indrajit said. "Any number of people might want us killed, starting with Mote Gannon, who can't use his own men to do it without getting into trouble. This whole thing was clearly a trap."

"Maybe you were meant to be sacrifices?" Munahim called back over his shoulder. His voice, when asking questions, sounded like the mournful yodeling of a hunting dog to the moon.

"The bodies in the pit," Fix said.

"Maybe they were earlier sacrifices." Indrajit tried to think through what he'd seen. "Maybe we were next. Maybe these aren't really priestly dresses we're wearing. Maybe they mark us as offerings."

"I don't think 'maybe,'" Fix said.

"I don't think maybe, either."

Flowing water crossed the end of the gallery. Munahim splashed through the stream, sniffing at the opposite bank, and then picked up the scent again at the leftmost of three circular openings.

As he and Fix raced on, Indrajit pressed himself into the curve of the arch. A light appeared at the far end of the gallery. He heard slapping feet, too, but the men pursuing them wore soft-soled shoes and they had the knack of treading lightly. He couldn't make out how many were coming.

He ran to catch up to the other Protagonists.

"We're followed," he hissed.

"It could be both." Fix's voice was glum.

"Both . . . meaning, maybe someone took out a contract on us with the priests of the Unnamed, and the temple is trying to carry out the contract by sacrificing us?" It was not a comforting thought. "Uh . . . how do we terminate a hit on us?"

Munahim led them across an octagonal chamber whose floor was an iron lattice. Green light glowed beneath their feet. Indrajit had seen such light several times before, and generally thought it was a sign of ancient Druvash sorcery at work. At the far end of the chamber, they climbed a groaning iron staircase bolted into the wall. At the top, they stopped to catch their breath, and Indrajit and Fix both shucked off their white dresses.

"Oleandra is a fast runner." Munahim was panting.

"Help me get rid of these stairs," Indrajit said.

Munahim had left his great ax on the street after chopping through the door with it, but Fix had his smaller hatchet. The iron of the staircase was rusted, but solid— but when Indrajit threw his weight against the stairs, he discovered that the brick around the screws bolting the stairs to the wall was crumbling. He lay on his back and kicked repeatedly, until the stairs curled away from the wall and fell.

As the stairs crashed to the brick below, the lights of their pursuers entered the other side of the room. "Hey," Indrajit suggested to Munahim. "Let's make them put out those lights, shall we?"

Munahim fired three arrows at their pursuers,

forcing them to scatter and douse their lamps. Then the Protagonists ran.

"Why does it feel like people always want to kill us?" Indrajit asked.

"Because people always want to kill us," Fix said.

"I don't think that pit was the garbage heap for old votives," Indrajit said. "I mean, everything Oleandra told us seems to have been a lie, but that in particular."

"That was the altar," Fix said.

"That's what I think, too."

They passed through an open door into a room lit by torches. The sudden flickering flames burned Indrajit's eyes like bonfires and he blinked away tears. The chamber was furnished with four thickly upholstered divans facing a low, square table in the center. Opposite, Indrajit saw through an archway into a stone-flagged room with large double doors. High, paneless windows let in cool air. They must be aboveground again.

Oleandra stood beside the low table. Her cloak was gone. She seemed to be on the tips of her toes, and it took Indrajit a moment to realize that there was a man behind her, holding her up. He wore black from head to foot, including a cloak. Silver stitching around the edges of the cloak might represent writing of some sort. He also wore a black mask that showed no skin beneath, or teeth or anything, giving him the impression of being headless.

He held a long, thin blade to Oleandra's throat.

Fix shut the door behind them. Indrajit drew Vacho from its sheath and he heard the sound of Fix sliding a bolt into place.

"You're going to let us pass," Indrajit said. "But first, you're going to give us information."

"I will hurt the woman if you move," the man in black said.

"She's on *your* side," Indrajit said. "What kind of threat is that?"

"She's dressed as a sacrifice," Fix added. His mild voice contained a strained note. Fear? Preoccupation?

"It's a threat because you *care*," the masked man said.

"We're going to leave," Indrajit said. He looked for a moment of inattention on the man's part, so he could leap in and free Oleandra. Such a bold move could make for several good minutes of Epic recitation: a description of tensed muscles and sweat trickling down his back, a reminder of the weapons he bore, a call back to his heroic ancestry. "We never picked a fight with you."

"The goddess claims sacrifices," the masked man said. "The goddess herself chooses. This moon, when we consulted her, she said we should take *you*."

"We don't want trouble in the future," Indrajit said. "Live and let live. Unless you commit fraud in the Paper Sook. Or anger the Lord Chamberlain, I guess. Otherwise, we'll leave you alone."

"I will trade," the man in black said. "Her life for yours."

Oleandra's expression was unreadable. Her lips moved as if she were singing or reciting, but her eyes were glazed over. She might have been in a trance, or drugged, except that she must have been sprinting away from them only moments earlier.

Fix produced jewelry from the pocket of his kilt. "We'll

give you these back, for her life." His voice was pitched too high, even for Fix.

"You know this woman is not your lover," Indrajit murmured.

Fix didn't answer.

The masked man spat. "What is sacrificed is dead and gone, and nothing to me, or to the goddess. The true jewels are on the moon. What you hold are mere husks."

"Did your oracle say you must actually sacrifice us?" Indrajit asked. "Or just try to? Because you've gone and given it a good try. Best efforts. Maybe now it would be okay to accept failure. Maybe the Unnamed just wants you to make the attempt."

"And did your divination mention me at all?" Munahim asked. "I'm new, and maybe your goddess really had Indrajit and Fix personally in mind."

Hammering sounds at their backs suggested that their pursuers had caught up, and were beating against the door.

"I'll take any one of you," the masked man said. "Even the dog-head, I don't care."

"Hey," Munahim said.

Indrajit sheathed Vacho. He walked slowly toward the masked man, preparing to grab him by the wrist, disarm him, trip him, or do whatever was necessary to save Oleandra. Not that she deserved it, since she had lured them into this place to sacrifice them to her goddess, but . . . well, a hero would save her, and Indrajit wanted to be that hero.

Also, Fix stared at her as if he were staring at his former lover. He must know that this woman was not the same woman who had jilted him, but in his head, he seemed to have made a connection that he couldn't shake.

And then again, Oleandra herself appeared to be a victim.

Indrajit raised his hands to show that they were empty. The hammering on the door was joined by muffled shouting noises.

"Just let her go," Indrajit said.

Three things happened so quickly, so closely together, that to Indrajit they seemed to happen simultaneously. The masked man leaped forward, lunging at Indrajit with his knife, stabbing for the throat. At the same moment, Oleandra's haze of uncertainty and her mumbling fell away like a veil cast aside, and she hurled herself into the masked man's path. Finally, his thrusting blade struck her in the back of her neck and passed completely through, the tip of the dagger stabbing out the front of her throat. Blood spurted down her white sacrificial gown.

She fell forward, dead on the table.

Fix leaped upon the masked man with fury in his face. His ax was in his hand, and before the man in black could even turn to face him, Fix had shattered his skull. A second blow nearly severed one of the man's arms and a third took his head completely off.

Fix screamed.

"Hey," Indrajit said.

Fix took a swing at Indrajit with his ax, and only Indrajit's quick reflexes let him dodge the attack.

"We should get out of here," Munahim muttered.

"It wasn't her," Indrajit said.

The dog-headed Protagonist knelt and scooped up

jewelry that Fix had dropped. He led the way to the archway into the next room, but stood waiting.

Fix dropped his ax. He knelt beside Oleandra's corpse, cradling her in his arms.

"You know that's not your love," Indrajit said, slowly and firmly.

Fix blinked and rubbed his eyes with his fists, smearing blood all over his face in the process. He looked at Oleandra one last time, then laid her back on the table. "It could have been, though. It could have been her. And someone should have loved her the way I love . . . If she'd had the love in her life that she deserved, she might not have ended this way."

The knocking and yelling had stopped.

"We should go," Munahim said. "They'll find a way around."

Fix took a small book from his kilt. Indrajit didn't recognize the volume—his partner must have found it in the pit. He tore a page from it and took a bit of writing charcoal from his pocket. He wrote, face tight in concentration, and then he took the dead man's dagger and used it to pin the note to the man's chest, sinking the blade in all the way to the hilt.

The double doors in the next room opened onto the street. Fix was shaking as they walked out.

"We got this jewelry," Munahim said.

"There's also the hundred Imperials." Fix spoke mechanically, as if without thought. "We'll divide it all by shares."

They took several turns in quick succession, to throw off pursuit. Once Indrajit realized that they had emerged in the Spill, he took the lead and directed their path back to the inn that served as both home and office.

"What did you write?" he asked his partner. The sea breeze was cooling the sweat that poured off him and filling his lungs with stiff, bracing air. The lurid chambers beneath the city, the skeletons, and the heap of sacrificed loot were beginning to fade and to seem unreal. Would the assassin cult come after them another day? It seemed impossible to predict, but, for the moment, it didn't feel imminent.

"I told them we know where their temple is now." Fix ground out the words through clenched teeth. "I told them that, if we ever see them again, the Lord Chamberlain will kill every single one of them, scorch their cult from off the face of the earth. And I told them that, for this moon, enough sacrifices have been thrown into the pit."

Welcome to Kish

❧ Part One: The Name of the Monster ❧

"My daughter is a poet." As the green-skinned shipowner spoke, the mass of thin tentacles hanging off the front of his face beneath his nose danced. The voice emerging from the worm-like strands was deep and monotone.

Indrajit cocked his head. "Poet?"

"Oh, *now* Indrajit is listening," Fix said.

"I was listening before." Indrajit snorted. "I am very concerned for Melitzanda's safety."

They stood in the shipowner's office, a single wooden room whose walls were lined with shelves. The shelves sagged under the weight of ledgers, boxes, and stacks of paper. The office crouched at the head of a long wharf in the Shelf. Outside, Indrajit heard the crying of seagulls and a squeaking sound that he thought was made by the Sobelian Lamprey. That made sense; autumn was arriving, and the lamprey's migration patterns meant it should now be starting to swim around the rocky beaches of Kish. Soon, it would swim south, toward the Free Cities.

"Oritria." The face-tentacles circled slightly and flexed. The shipowner's golden eyes flared wide open and his nose flattened into his face, leaving behind only two narrow slits. Indrajit didn't know this race of man, and had no idea how to read the facial expression. Grit Wopal—the head of the Lord Chamberlain's Ears, and sometimes Indrajit and Fix's boss—would have known what the shipowner was thinking. He would have *seen* it, with the third eye set into his forehead.

But Indrajit and Fix were working for their own account, today, and Grit Wopal was nowhere in sight.

"Yes, Oritria." Indrajit cleared his throat. "I said 'Melitzanda' because I was thinking of an important incident in the Blaatshi Epic, involving a kidnapped princess named Melitzanda. Who is also a great poet. Naturally, the similarities to your daughter's situation brought that episode to mind."

"My daughter is not a princess," the shipowner said. "I am not a king. I sail in the Serpent Sea trade."

"But princess-*like*." Indrajit smiled.

"In what respect?" The tentacles quivered.

"In deserving to be rescued," Indrajit suggested.

"I don't want you to *rescue* her," the shipowner said. "The little vixen ran away with her filthy Yeziot lover and, as far as I'm concerned, he can have her. But she took important documents with her, and I want you to get them back."

"I don't know the Yeziot." Fix's coppery-brown face brightened, his eyebrows lifting high enough almost to touch the straight hair spilling over his forehead. Fix loved nothing more than learning, unless possibly it was learning from a *book*, the pervert. "Tell me about them."

"They're ravenous maneaters," the green man said. "They're really excellent sailors, practically a one-man crew, huge capacity for work and they never get tired, but you have to keep feeding them man-flesh or they go berserk."

Indrajit now worried he had forgotten the man's name, and he checked his memory palace. There, standing on a tussock of grass beneath the steep gray cliff from which Indrajit had dived as a boy, were four frogs. Four frogs.

"Forfa," he said, "we'll get your daughter back."

"I'm vexed." Forfa's voice continued to be flat. The tentacles were curling more tightly, so apparently the curl reflected negative emotion. Or tension. "You don't appear to be listening to me."

"You don't want your daughter back," Fix said. "You want the documents."

"Yes," Indrajit agreed. "I meant we'd bring her back, with the documents. What *are* the documents, by the way?" He hoped they contained merely pictures, with no words. Fix got entirely too much approbation for his literacy as it was.

"First, demand the return of the documents," Forfa said. "Wopal said you'd be the right jobbers for the task. He said you work complex and sensitive jobs in the Paper Sook. Jobs involving contracts and so on."

Indrajit harrumphed.

"I presume she took them because they have value." Fix's voice was melodic, high-pitched, almost feminine in tone, though it emerged from the barrel chest of a muscle-bound jobber.

"Of course."

"So we'll demand them back," Fix said. "And what if she offers to sell them to us, instead?"

"I'll reimburse you," the shipowner said. "Up to fifty Imperials."

"Which happens to be our fee, conveniently," Fix said. "If you pay us in advance, we'll have the cash to negotiate."

A sound like wordless mumbling bubbled from behind the tentacles, but Forfa retrieved a brass-bound casket from a shelf behind him, unlocked it, and counted out fifty gold coins.

"What kind of poetry?" Indrajit asked.

"Eh?" The merchant grunted.

"What kind of poetry does your daughter compose?" Indrajit clarified. "Or write?" He hoped she didn't write it, but that was probably a vain wish.

"The foolish stuff," Forfa grumbled. "You know, swords and heroes and love."

"That's the *best* stuff," Indrajit said.

Forfa glared at him.

"We'll demand the documents back," Fix said, "then offer to pay for them if she says no, then steal them, if we have to."

Forfa nodded curtly. "As a last resort, bring back the girl."

"That seems clear enough," Fix said.

"You have to tell us what the documents are," Indrajit reminded their client. "So we can identify them."

"They're not documents such as you would recognize," Forfa droned. "They aren't written on parchment or carved into clay."

"Good." Indrajit smiled.

Fix shook his head.

"They're four long strips of leather, as wide as your thumb. Each is punched with a series of holes and has knots tied along its length."

"So . . . not documents at all," Fix said.

"If you prefer." Forfa's face-worms bounced.

"How long are they?" Indrajit asked.

"Each is about as long as a man is tall." Forfa looked from Indrajit to Fix and back. "About as tall as you, with the long face-bone. Not your short friend."

"Short is a matter of context." Fix frowned.

"I usually call it my 'nose,'" Indrajit said, "rather than my 'face-bone.'"

Forfa shrugged. "You'll admit that it's long and prominent, and goes somewhat farther up your face than most noses do. Also, your eyes are rather far apart."

"And you have a plate of noodles glued to your cheeks," Indrajit said.

"Noodles?"

Fix stepped forward, putting himself between the other two men. "What can you tell us about where your daughter might have gone?"

"I'll have you know," Forfa said, "that my grandmother chose my grandfather from the Mating Run precisely *because* of his thick, luxurious beard."

"A beard is made of hair," Indrajit said.

"Not all beards!"

"It's true, I have seen face-tentacles before," Indrajit admitted. "But I recall them being on men who were very short, and gray, with triangular faces. Sort of like a cross between you and a Visp. Do you know the race of man I'm talking about? Are they kin of yours?"

Forfa's eyes bulged.

"Your daughter," Fix said. "Oritria. And the secret messages. How do we find them?"

"I never said the strip-writing contained secret messages." Forfa snorted.

"Fine." Fix nodded amiably. "The cryptic dots and knots embedded in four leather strips the length of an itinerant Blaatshi bard."

"I'm not itinerant." Indrajit sniffed. "You'll be calling me 'shiftless' next."

"The nature of the documents should not concern you," Forfa said.

"Fix is just jealous of any book he can't actually read," Indrajit said.

"I'm not concerned with the nature of the documents," Fix replied mildly, "or their contents. My question was, how do we find them? How do we find your daughter and the Yeziot?"

"You don't have to *find* them." Forfa shook his head as if he were sluicing away water. "They're aboard a ship called the *Duke's Mistress*." He stepped to the door, opened it, and pointed at a two-masted, lateen-rigged ship within bowshot. "The brazen thieves. Oritria and the monster she's making off with. They sail tomorrow with the morning tide."

"Why not go take your documents back?" Indrajit asked. "You have sailors."

"I can't lose any of my sailors," Forfa said. "And my sailors might not be as cautious as I'd like around the documents. And worse, if the harbormaster were to hear I had started a fight in port, it would get back to the Lord Chamberlain—"

"I'm pretty sure the Lord Stargazer has the contract for the ports," Fix said.

"Fine, the Lord Stargazer." Forfa nodded. "But whichever of the great families is administering the port these days, if I get banned from docking here, the trade is useless to me."

"Not useless, surely," Indrajit objected. "The Serpent Sea trade has four legs, doesn't it? You could still trade in the other three—Pelth, Boné, and Xiba'alb." He grinned at Fix.

"Except," Fix said immediately, "the spices you buy in Xiba'alb you sell in Kish, to be resold to buyers from Ukel and Karth and Ildarion. Ildarion won't buy directly from Xiba'alb because of the political tensions, and the others are too far."

"And the Pelthites don't care about spice!" Forfa sputtered. "Or they use all the wrong ones. They put rosemary on lamb!"

Indrajit nodded. "Of course. So if you can't sell here, you'd have to sail farther or lose the entire trade."

"Farther, and across rougher seas!" Forfa snapped. "My costs would go up for the time alone, and then there's the cost of selling the risk!"

At the mention of risk-merchantry, Indrajit closed his eyes and willed the conversation to go elsewhere.

"Grit Wopal said you were discreet." The shipowner's eyes sagged with fatigue.

"How do we recognize the Yeziot?" Indrajit asked.

"He'll be the biggest man on the ship," Forfa grunted. "You won't be able to miss him."

"What's the name of the monster?" Fix pressed. "And what do we do if he tries to stop us?"

"Squite." Forfa nodded, his tentacles wiggling excitedly. "Feel free to kill him. Indeed, I want him dead. Bring back his corpse, and I'll pay you an additional ten Imperials. I could sell tickets to passersby to see it."

"Do you feel like we never get quite *all* the information we'd like to have up front?" Indrajit asked.

The two men pushed their way along the busy boardwalk. Indrajit gnawed at the fried leg of a Kishi fowl gripped in his left hand and kept his right hand near the hilt of his legendary sword, Vacho. Trying to appear nonchalant, he scanned the wharf where the *Duke's Mistress* was moored. Sailors loaded merchandise, and a large, four-armed, scaly-looking man directed their movements.

Fix sauntered, his thumbs hooked into his wide leather belt, keeping his hands near his falchion and his ax. For real fighting jobs, he'd bring a spear, but if you carried a spear around in your hand, you announced you were ready for combat, and you attracted attention. Even in Kish.

"We'll be able to identify the documents on sight," Fix said, "and Oritria must look at least *something* like her father."

"Not sure about that. Grokonk males and females look radically different, for instance."

"Like tadpoles and frogs." Fix nodded. "But most likely, we'll spot Oritria easily."

"She should at least be green."

"So the thing we don't really know is what a Yeziot is."

"The thing *you* don't really know." Indrajit cast the bone, gnawed clean of flesh, into the water. A lavender-skinned Zalapting who had narrowly missed being struck glared at him. "Mmm, I would really like some fried tamarind right now. Maybe on a bed of kelp."

"The Yeziot appear in the Blaatshi Epic?"

"How many times must I tell you," Indrajit asked, "that the Epic contains all the best knowledge of the Blaatshi? *Everything* worth knowing is in the Epic. This is why knowledge of the Epic not only enlightens the mind, it necessarily edifies the soul. One becomes a better person merely by listening."

"The Epic doesn't tell you how to find a successor Recital Thane. Or you'd have done it by now."

"Touché. This is also why, naturally, I'm interested in talking with Oritria, who is *not* a princess, but who *is* a poet. I wish to see what … edification … may be had from *her* poems."

"What do you know about the Yeziot, then?"

"Shall I declaim?" Indrajit wiped grease from his mouth with the back of his forearm. He wore a sleeveless and baggy tunic and a kilt; Fix wore a kilt only. Both men had sandals on their feet. Even in winter, Kish would experience cold rain, but would not freeze.

"Just say the line."

"Yes, I will declaim." Indrajit looked around for a platform and saw a chunk of stone carved roughly with the features of a horned skull, lying beside a brick wall at the corner of an alley. Not roughly, he realized; the sculpture had once been very fine, its cuts deep and its lines subtly curved, but it had crumbled under the teeth of wind, rain, and time into its present state. He stepped up onto the skull and turned to face Fix and the street. "Auspicious that I should have for a stage the image of our patron." The heraldic symbol of Orem Thrush, the Lord Chamberlain, was a horned skull.

"Or his great-great-great-grandfather."

Indrajit raised his arms and struck the third combat pose; that was the one in which his left arm imitated a stabbing spear and his right pantomimed the motions it would make if bearing a shield. *"Yeziot the growler, eater of the flesh of men,"* he chanted, *"swords in his mouth and spearheads for fingers."*

A passing sailor with rope sandals and canvas trousers threw a rock and hit Indrajit in the shoulder.

Fix stroked his beardless chin. "Those are picturesque details."

"Picturesque? Perhaps you missed the part about 'swords in his mouth.'"

"Yes, yes, and spearheads for fingers. But Forfa had already told us that the Yeziot were eaters of men, so you'd expect that sort of thing. And 'growler' tells us something, I suppose. But a man may growl, and so may a dog, and have little else in common. Is there another epithet for them, or anything else that would give us more... *specific* information? Such as... I don't know, their color?"

Indrajit switched to the seventh combat post, a crouch with an imaginary spear braced to receive an attack. *"Long-limbed Yeziot, drinking blood in darkness."*

A waddling merchant with a green turban wrapped around her head hissed. "Shut up and go away!"

"You see that the burden of poetry lies heavy upon me," Indrajit said.

"'Long-limbed,'" Fix mused. "That's a little vague. I suppose it means tall."

"Prominent limbs," Indrajit suggested.

"Hmm."

"If I were Squite and Oritria, I'd hide belowdecks," Indrajit said. "At least until the ship left port."

"We could pretend we want to buy passage. Bluff our way aboard."

"Or pretend we want to ship cargo."

"Or that we're inspectors on behalf of the Lord Stargazer."

"That one would come back and bite us," Indrajit said. "We could tell the captain who we are and say we're investigating for the Lord Chamberlain. Make out that some kind of Paper Sook misbehavior has taken place. Fraud or off-book risk-merchantry or trade indoors."

"You mean insider trading. But we have no uniforms and there are only the two of us, so the captain could easily tell us to go away."

"Right. Or we could disguise ourselves as sailors. Or leave our weapons and swim."

"I don't think leaving our weapons is a good idea. The Yeziot have prominent limbs, after all. Maybe the Epic's epithets call attention to their limbs because they're unusually strong."

"Forfa said it's like having a one-man crew, so the Yeziot are likely strong and very fast. I say we just walk on board," Indrajit said. "And if anyone stops us, we tell them we're looking for Melitzanda. Or Oritria, rather."

"What, to collect a debt?"

Indrajit stepped down off the weathered skull. "No. We'll say we want to hear her poetry. Which happens to be true."

Fix nodded and they turned their steps toward the *Duke's Mistress*.

The ship was moored at the far end of a long, sagging wharf. Sailors with undyed cloth wrapped around their legs to form something resembling baggy trousers marched along it with baskets and large clay jars on their shoulders to trudge up a splintered gangplank and deposit their burdens in various corners of the ship, mostly belowdecks. A big man, covered with a patchwork of scales and fur, directed their motion with movements of a long, coiled whip. Indrajit and Fix walked purposefully alongside the line of sailors and then, when a gap presented itself, slipped up the gangplank.

At the top, a cracking whip stopped them.

The big man loomed over them. His scales were red, orange, and yellow, in a repeating diamond-shaped pattern. His fur, which sprouted in irregular patches, was black and oily. His legs curved back and forward again, like an exaggerated caricature of the hind legs of a dog. Or like a frog's legs, much more dramatic even than the legs of the Grokonk Indrajit had seen. He wore a harness of broad, thick leather straps. Of the man's four arms, one held a long whip and the other a falchion, a curving, one-edged sword like Fix's, only twice the size.

"Businessss?" the big scaly man asked.

"Pleasure," Indrajit said. "We have come seeking a poet."

"A poet?" The scaly man's eyes narrowed and the

nostrils at the end of his long snout flared. "Thiss is a merchant ship."

"I'm Indrajit Twang," Indrajit said. "I'm the four hundred twenty-seventh Recital Thane of the Blaatshi people, and keeper of their sacred epic. You may not have heard of me, but, as a man of culture, you've no doubt heard of the poem."

"Anaxssimander Sskink mentioned you." The big red man chuckled. "You were trying to pay your tab at the Blind Ssurgeon with poetry."

"Yes." Was this big fellow a Yeziot? Indrajit didn't dare ask, nor did he dare meet the gaze of Fix, who must surely be asking himself the same question. The man's nails were long and sharp, as were his teeth. He was large and strong; was he large and strong enough to crew a ship entirely by himself? Or had that been mere hyperbole? "I'm all paid up now, though. In fact, I have cash, and, look, I'll pay you. I'll give you a shiny gold Imperial if you let us go belowdecks to talk to Oritria."

The scaly man's eyes narrowed further. "You take me for a ssilly child."

"We take you for a big man with a sword and a whip," Fix said. "What race of man did you say you are?"

The scaly man growled.

Fix hesitated, then nodded. "Five Imperials. This is easy money. We'll be gone before you know it, and we won't cause trouble."

The big man held out one of his hands. Fix, who always handled the money because he didn't trust Indrajit to do so, dropped five yellow coins into the scaly red palm, and then the brute with the whip stepped aside.

Indrajit followed Fix toward an open hatch in the deck, near the front of the ship. He saw two more hatches, farther back. "That could be Squite."

"He'll watch us go belowdecks in any case, so don't look back at him."

Indrajit forced himself to keep his eyes on the plank ladder at his feet as he climbed down into the hold. "I don't want to fight that guy. I'd rather jump into the water and swim, if it comes to it."

"Fortunately, we're looking for documents that aren't water soluble."

"Documents, I feel obligated to point out, that might be hidden under the leather straps wrapped around that fellow's large, long-limbed body."

Fix nodded. "Let's find the girl before we tackle the monster."

"I wish he'd told you his name."

Light filtered down through a grate overhead, revealing a broad central open space, piled high with stacks of loose rope of a greenish fiber. The sailors carrying casks and jars descended to a second level below this one, from which arose an unpleasant odor reminiscent of a latrine. Fore, hammocks hung close together lined the walls, and left and right—starboard and port, Indrajit reminded himself—were rows of doors, close together so as to imply tiny cabins. Aft, two doors farther apart might belong to the captain or his principal officers. Indrajit's people were fishermen, but they rode the waves in small boats, and the details of a ship this large were a little beyond him.

"I guess we knock," Indrajit said.

They started at one end and rapped on the door. When it didn't open, Indrajit cracked the door and took a look inside, finding no one. Then the second door, and then the third.

"This reminds me a little bit of my youth in the ashrama," Fix said. "We'd go door to door sometimes."

"Salish-Bozar the White has a proselytizing operation?" Indrajit shook his head. "That surprises me. What did you say to people—'Come join us for the glory of memorizing useless nonsense'?"

"Basically."

"I'm shocked Salish-Bozar hasn't converted everyone."

Two irascible Zalaptings waved them away from one narrow cabin, and a sleepy Luzzazza grunted from his cot in another. A third cabin held something that looked like a sloth, gripped to a beam overhead and staring with eyes like bone-white saucers. Otherwise, the starboard cabins were empty.

"Passengers haven't boarded yet," Fix suggested.

"Or they won't fill these cabins with passengers, and will stack cargo in them eventually," Indrajit countered. "Or maybe the ship's officers have cabins. Did something just move in the pile of ropes?"

"Most likely a rat," Fix said. "Ships have rats."

They crossed the central space, pausing to let sailors emerging from the hold below to pass them.

"The ropes are pretty disordered, aren't they?" Indrajit asked. "Isn't that a point of pride for sailors, to always make sure your ropes are tightly coiled and neatly stowed?"

"Did you learn that from the Epic?" Fix asked.

Indrajit nodded. "It's an epithet of ships. *All ropes tightly coiled, all sails furled tight.*"

"Maybe this captain is just less epic than the Blaatshi captains were."

They knocked at the first port cabin door, and there was no answer. Fix pushed the door open.

A woman sat on the cot inside, staring at them with golden eyes. She had green skin, and strands like tentacles hung off the front of her face. She was wrapped in a toga, and she held a wax writing tablet on her lap.

"Oritria," Indrajit said. "You have a—" He caught himself. He had almost said "beard," but he didn't feel comfortable finishing the sentence that way. "Tablet. Writing tablet. You write your poems down, of course you do."

He felt a little disappointed.

The green-skinned woman blinked. "Are you sailors?"

"Your father sent us." Fix kept his hands away from his weapons, but both ax and falchion were clearly visible. "We've come for the documents you took."

"What documents?" She held up her writing tablet. "This is for writing poems."

Fix sighed.

"Maybe keep an eye out for Squite, coming down the ladder and surprising us," Indrajit suggested. "Let me talk to Melitzanda, poet to poet."

Fix stepped back into the larger chamber and turned to watch the stairs.

"Melitzanda is a princess of Blaatshi legend," Oritria said. "My name is Oritria."

Indrajit leaned against the wall. He felt light-headed. "What do you know about Blaatshi legend?"

"I've read summaries of stories. The Epic itself isn't written down, of course, but in Zilander's *Ninety-Nine Riddles*, he retells a dozen or so of the tales. Including the one about Melitzanda and the harp that knew how to tell time."

"Wait, wait . . . what is ninety-nine riddles?"

"It's a book." The green woman's brow furrowed. "Are you Blaatshi?"

A wave of nausea hit Indrajit. "The Epic is *written down*?"

"Only some stories," Oritria said. "And in Kishi, not in the original Blaatshi. And, of course, the real experience of the Epic is engaging with a Recital Thane who performs it, composing it as he goes from his stock of epic epithets. So the true Blaatshi Epic is never exactly the same twice, as no two men live exactly the same life."

"I . . . I'm sorry, may I sit down?"

Oritria scrambled to her feet and Indrajit fell heavily on her cot.

"Indrajit?" Fix called.

"I'm fine," Indrajit said. "Just. Is the scaly red guy coming?"

"Not yet."

Indrajit took deep breaths. "Okay, sorry, I'm a little overwhelmed. It's just . . . I've been here . . . months, I'm not sure how many, I've lost track of the time, and no one has ever heard of my people, or wants to hear the Epic, or understand what it's about, and here you are . . . practically *teaching* me!"

"I *am* a poet."

"Yeah." Indrajit exhaled slowly, trying to stop his head

from spinning. "Listen, we're here to get the documents you took from your father."

"I didn't take any documents."

"They looked like four leather strips, with knots tied into them and holes punched through."

"I've seen those." Oritria nodded. "I didn't take them. I'm just leaving Kish, and I have to sneak out so my father doesn't stop me. He thinks the world is dangerous."

"He's right."

"Yes, but I'll never write my own epic if I don't try to live an epic life first."

Indrajit clapped his hands to his forehead. Thoughts raced through his mind faster than he could catch them. Had he finally stumbled, in the hold of this ship and trying to escape Kish, upon an appropriate apprentice to become his successor as Recital Thane? She wasn't Blaatshi. On the other hand, her greenish skin and the generally... oceanic... appearance of her features suggested she might be some sort of distant cousin. Fix teased Indrajit that he looked like a fish; Oritria looked like an octopus. A little.

But she wanted to leave. Indrajit could leave with her, of course, and they could travel the world together as he passed on the Epic and its many arts. On the other hand, where would that leave Fix? But was that any of Indrajit's concern? Fix would be fine, he would be no worse off than he had been before he and Indrajit had met and become partners. If Fix could reunite with his lost lady love by leaving Kish, wouldn't he do so in a heartbeat?

But they were here for something else. What had they come for?

"Indrajit!" Fix snapped.

Indrajit took a deep breath and stood. "We need those two documents. Four documents. The leather strips. We don't have any instruction to bring you back, so I guess your father thinks it's okay for you to travel the world."

"He does?" Oritria blinked.

Indrajit shrugged. "Anyway, listen, let us buy the documents from you. Fifty Imperials."

Fix groaned and stepped in close to the door. "At least *try* to bargain."

"It's just money," Indrajit said.

"*Everything* is just money!"

"Fifty Imperials," Indrajit repeated. "You could use the cash if you're really going to travel. And listen, maybe I could come with you."

"That's too much." Oritria took a step backward, pressing herself against the wall. "Why would you want to come with me?"

He had come on too strong. "To be poets together, on the road. You could hear the Epic, maybe even learn Blaatshi." Her eyes looked more skeptical by the second. "Also, I'm armed, so I could protect you against dangers on the road."

"I have protection," she said. "This is why I am traveling with Squite."

Indrajit sighed. He wanted to run away with this girl and explore poetry. Instead, he was going to do his job. "My instructions are to ask for the documents, then offer to buy them, then take them from you."

"I don't have them," she said again.

"Keep watching," Indrajit reminded Fix. He searched

the little cabin. It took all of a minute, and he found no leather straps. Standing, he faced Oritria again and put his hand on the hilt of Vacho to look menacing. "Take off your toga." He hated himself, but it was what the job required.

"You can't torture any information out of me because I don't have the documents."

"I'm not going to torture you. I have to make sure you're not hiding them under your clothes."

She stripped and Indrajit checked her toga. She didn't have the documents.

"You can get dressed again." He stepped back, standing in the doorway.

She left the toga on the floor where it lay.

"The captain could have them locked away," Fix said.

"Or Squite has them." Indrajit sighed. "I guess we have to go talk to the big guy."

"Let's search his room first," Fix said. "Where is Squite sleeping?"

"Right where you first saw him," she said. "It takes a lot of effort to move, and he can operate the ship from where he is right now, so he just plans to stay there until it's time to disembark."

Indrajit stared at Oritria and blinked. Something wasn't adding up.

"What does Squite look like?" Fix asked.

Then greenish cords wrapped around Fix and whipped him sideways, out of Indrajit's sight.

The thing in the center of the deck, the thing that Indrajit had taken for a pile of disordered ropes, now shuddered. It contracted, and a forest of eyestalks sprouted in its center. Indrajit drew his sword. He heard a crash and Fix cursing, somewhere off to his left and out of sight. Sailors dropped their crates and scampered back up the ladder.

Then a mass of the green ropes sprang toward Indrajit, like darts fired from crossbows.

He slammed the door shut. A hail of simultaneous thudding sounds erupted from the door as most of the ropes—they were really tentacles—struck the wood. Two of the tentacles slipped in through the door before it shut, and now squirmed, pinned between wood and wood.

The tips of the tentacles bore curved talons. Where they scratched the wood, they cut deep furrows, slicing easily through the planks.

Indrajit took a step deeper into the room to give himself space, and sliced the tips off the two tentacles. Thick green ichor sprayed in wedge-shaped spatters across the wall.

Outside, he heard a noise that was ear-piercing shriek and deafening bellow at the same time. Then a thud. Then he heard Fix shouting, "The Protagonists!" That was a battle cry of sorts, as it was the name of the jobber company of which Indrajit and Fix were both the owners and the sole employees.

Indrajit stepped forward to open the door and join the fray, and something seized him by the throat.

It felt like a single finger, and the sudden backward tug caused him to lose his grip on Vacho. The sword clattered to the floor and his flow of air disappeared. Indrajit staggered backward, slapping at the choking strand around his neck.

It was tightly twisted cloth.

A toga.

Of course it was. Was Oritria innocent? Or at least relatively innocent, a woman trying to escape her father and now trying to defend her friend?

Squite the Yeziot, who looked like a tangled pile of green ropes.

Was it possible she had some darker part in this affair? She was, after all, choking him.

But she was a *poet*.

He struggled, but couldn't bring himself to smash the woman in the face with his elbow. His vision spun and was beginning to turn black, and then he heard words in his ear.

Blaatshi words.

"Softheaded Indrajit, eyes and heart blinded, he'll die and let his friend die, before he will see clearly."

The Blaatshi was grammatically perfect, perfectly intoned and accented. The lines rhymed and scanned and had impressive internal rhyme.

Indrajit swung his head back. With a crack, the back of his skull connected with something hard and heavy, and then he was lurching away forward, sucking in the humid, close air of the *Duke's Mistress's* lower decks.

He heard a heavy thud outside the little chamber and spun around to face Oritria. She stood, wrapping the fabric of the toga around her left arm; in her right hand, she held a long, thin dagger.

"Who taught you that line?" Indrajit demanded. The room swung left and right beneath his feet, as if the ship were cresting an enormous wave.

"I *wrote* it!" Oritria stabbed with the knife.

Indrajit's senses returned to crisp clarity at the last possible moment. He slapped the blade aside and swooped forward, slamming Oritria in the face with his forehead. With his long face bone, in fact.

Blood spurted from her nose and poured into her tentacles. Perversely, disgustingly, the bright red blood over the waving face-appendages reminded Indrajit of a bowl of spicy noodles.

"Liar!" he shouted.

"Blind fool Recital Thane, death now comes calling!" she howled, again in Blaatshi.

She couldn't have memorized lines, could she? Her accent was too perfect.

But what was the alternative? That a previous Recital Thane, someone of whom Indrajit was unaware, had come to Kish and taken an apprentice? And now the apprentice was attacking Indrajit?

Or could she have encountered a Blaatshi poet somewhere else, sailing with her father? Was there a Blaatshi village in Pelth, or in Xiba'alb?

But then why was she trying to kill him?

"Who taught you this?" he demanded.

She stabbed him in the side.

He pushed, knocking her to the floor. "Stop doing that!"

"Indrajit!" Fix yelled, outside the door.

Indrajit scooped up his sword and rushed out into the larger space belowdecks. Tentacles whipped and flailed in all directions. Some whipped themselves through portholes or around railings, bracing the Yeziot, while others snatched up weapons—a boathook, a metal rod, an ax—and fell in a mass toward Fix, crouched in a corner with his falchion in one hand and his ax in the other.

Indrajit rushed in, sword first. Oritria was right—he would only one day be worthy of his epic poetry if he had lived an epic life in the meantime. Vacho sliced through one tentacle and then another, dropping a cudgel to the floorboards and then a huge chunk of pumice and then an iron pot.

Pain lanced through his back.

He turned, his motion ripping the dagger from his flesh and sending it spinning along the floor. Oritria crouched like a wrestler, naked, face-tentacles writhing. "I'll let you live, Blaatshi!" she shrieked. "But you will be mine!"

Only moments earlier she had seemed coy, retiring, put off by Indrajit's forwardness. Had that all been an act?

Clearly, she wasn't made of the right stuff to be an apprentice Recital Thane.

"The documents!" he bellowed, waving his sword.

"Squite!" she yelled.

The tentacles that rushed Indrajit didn't seize him so much as *push* him, faster than a running pace, lifting him off his feet and hurling him against the wall. He managed to raise his arms at the last possible moment to protect his face and he bounced off the wood, falling to the floor.

Indrajit heard a thick growl that elevated instantly into a roar, and then he felt the heat of flame on his cheek. He raised his head, saw that a fire burned in the midst of the all the ropelike tentacles and eyestalks, and then Oritria kicked him in the face.

He rolled over onto his back, groaning.

"Squite!" Oritria shrieked. "Kill the other one!"

"I'm trying!" Squite's voice sounded like the thick buzz of a saw cutting through hardwood, accented with a barrelful of rattling stones. Tentacles ripped open the doors of the ship's small cabins and dragged blankets out, trying to dampen the flames.

Oritria was looking at the fire, and Indrajit took the opportunity to grab both her ankles. He rolled toward the flames, pulling her to the ground and sending her bouncing away across the wood. He managed to find Vacho and gripped it in his hand as he stood.

"Fire!" The alarm was bellowed by the large red scaly man—who was not, after all, Squite—who now stood at the bottom of the ladder, long, curved scimitar naked in his hand.

Squite launched four tentacles at the scaled man. They wrapped around his legs, one tentacle on each, and two further tentacles whipped themselves around his sword arm. How many tentacles did Squite have, anyway?

And how many did he have *left*?

Indrajit left Oritria on the floor. One thing he was fairly certain of was that she did not possess the documents he and Fix were looking for. As four more tentacles lashed at Fix, ripping the ax from his hand and dragging him to the floor, Indrajit took two long steps and leaped forward, diving into the center of the Yeziot's body.

He felt the tentacles bunched up beneath him like corded rope. As he landed, the tentacles tensed, and stalk-mounted eyes swiveled to look Indrajit in the face.

"Drop my friend!" Indrajit howled, raising his blade.

Tentacles seized him from behind—

He swung the sword, chopping through the eyestalks entirely.

Squite squealed. A thin, soupy, warm liquid that smelled of minerals and brine sprayed from the severed stalks and washed Indrajit's face. The tentacles wrapped around him dragged him away, but they lacked coordination, and as one pulled in one direction and one pulled in another, Indrajit swung again. Like a farmer who hadn't cut the grain close enough to the ground, like a woodsman who had left too tall a stump, he mowed through the stalks a second time, cutting right above the massed central bunch of tentacles.

Squite howled and threw him against the wall again.

"You!" The scaly red-skinned man stomped across the deck and stooped to grip Indrajit by his sword belt. He raised Indrajit into the air with one arm and shook him. "Causing trouble!"

"Me!" Indrajit's vision swam in circles. He realized that he'd lost his sword, but he wasn't exactly sure where. "I'm not here for trouble, I came for"—he felt faint—"the poet. And the rope-beast."

"Attacking passengers?" The four-armed man punched Indrajit in the face simultaneously with two enormous fists. His head rocked back so hard he felt his neck nearly snap, and for a moment he lost consciousness.

"Don't kill the Blaatshi!" he heard Oritria yelling, and her words woke him. "I need him!"

Needed him? For what?

Indrajit heard thumping behind him. Fix, fighting the enormous bundle of tentacles that was the Yeziot?

They were losing. They might be defeated already.

Indrajit needed a way to take some of his enemies out of the fight, immediately.

"*Need* him?" The scaly man snarled, echoing Indrajit's own thoughts. "For what?"

"That's my affair, Chark!" Oritria snapped.

Chark. Was that the scaly man's name? Or his race?

Indrajit kicked the scaly man. It wasn't much of a kick, because Indrajit's lungs were deflated and his limbs heavy, but he put all the force he could into the blow and struck Chark in the knee.

Chark hurled Indrajit to the floor and roared.

"Squite!" Oritria screamed.

Indrajit heard a louder thud and then tentacles surged over him. Oritria was screaming and Chark ripped tentacles apart with his bare hands and slashed with his huge saber. Indrajit dragged himself out of the middle of the storm of noise and movement. He patted the floor, looking for Vacho—

And found a knotted leather strip instead.

And then another.

He gathered them together and squinted. Fire had engulfed one wall of the chamber and it gave more than enough light for him to see that, as described, he held two lengths of leather, about his own height, holed and knotted irregularly.

And there were two more on the floor.

He was on his knees in the center of the space, where Squite had . . . lain? Been heaped up?

The Yeziot had been lying on the documents.

Indrajit gathered up the strips and looked behind him; Squite was massive and strong, but he fought blind and his tentacles crashed aimlessly against the ladder and wall behind Chark. Or *the* chark. Oritria was focused on the fight, screaming directions at Squite, and Chark waded into the sea of tentacles, slashing and cutting.

Indrajit spotted Vacho at the base of a wall and scooped it up with his free hand. Then he went looking for Fix in the shadowy depths of the room and found him, crumpled in a heap and bleeding from his nose. Indrajit prodded his friend.

"Can you hear me?"

"Mmmm . . . urggg . . ."

"One of the more miraculous properties of the Epic is its restorative virtue," Indrajit said. "The Recital Thane is obligated to sing over the sick and wounded, to accelerate their recovery."

"By all your ugly gods, no." Fix grunted and dragged himself onto all fours. "I'm fine. No singing." Fix gathered up his ax and falchion from where they lay on the deck.

"You see that even the *mention* of the Epic has healing properties," Indrajit said.

"It's not the Epic, it's the fire. I don't want to burn to death on a ship in port."

"You started the fire. What did you do, hit Squite with a torch?"

"I threw an oil lamp." Fix shrugged. "It seemed like a good idea at the time."

Indrajit raised his friend with an arm under Fix's shoulder and they limped toward the back of the ship, where he was reasonably confident they'd find another ladder and hatch. "Still, since I'm the one who will be composing the account of today's events . . . it will be the Epic that caused you to revive."

Fix growled.

"Be careful," Indrajit said. "You are growling, and you have noteworthy limbs. I may mistake you for a Yeziot."

"We didn't find the documents," Fix grunted.

"I have them," Indrajit said. "Squite was sitting on them. But after I blinded him, he moved off them to try to kill Chark."

"Who's Chark?" Fix mumbled.

"Well," Indrajit said, as the climbed the ladder toward a square of daylight, "I think it's the name of the big four-armed fellow with red scales. Or possibly he is *a* chark."

"I didn't imagine today would be so educational."

"So much to work into the Epic." Indrajit nodded. They emerged onto the deck past sailors with leather buckets full of sand and water, rushing below. "Too bad for you the knowledge is all strictly useful and professional information. You'll never qualify to be one of the Pointless by learning the names of monsters."

They turned toward the gangplank and the wharf, moving slowly but steadily.

"Selfless," Fix murmured. "The priests of Salish-Bozar are called the Selfless. And I gave that up long ago."

Welcome to Kish

~

The office door was closed, and no one answered when Indrajit knocked.

It was early morning, the sky a gray and sunless slate reflecting the shrill accusations of the wheeling gulls. The *Duke's Mistress* smoldered still, alongside the wharf where it lay at anchor. Indrajit and Fix had set fire to the ship the day before; really, Fix had done it, throwing an oil lamp onto a hulking tentacled man named Squite. Indrajit and Fix had recovered four punched and knotted leather straps, each the length of a tall man's height, from Squite and his companion, the poetess Oritria, at the behest of Oritria's father, a merchant named Forfa in the Serpent Sea trade. Indrajit and Fix had gotten quite battered in the encounter, and Squite had lost a number of limbs and also eyestalks. They last seen Oritria facing off with a four-armed, scaly man named Chark, and then Indrajit and Fix had returned to their inn-room

headquarters to lick their wounds and lie low for the
night. Now it was morning, and they'd come to Forfa's
office to return the straps.

Only no one answered, and the door was locked.

Indrajit scanned the docks, squinting at each jar-
lugging stevedore and loitering seaman to make sure he
didn't see the face-tentacle beard that Oritria and Forfa
both had.

"We've already been paid," he said. "It's hard to care
too much."

"There is the ethical question," Fix said. "We need to
return the texts to him." Forfa had claimed that the
punched and knotted straps were writing, of all things.

Indrajit grunted. "Remarkable. I've just discovered an
actual use for writing. We could leave him a note saying
we have the straps, and to come back to our place to get
them."

"Oritria's still out there," Fix pointed out. "And we
know she can read."

Oritria had written her poetry on a wax tablet. "She
might read the note and come after us, you're saying."
Indrajit rubbed his chin. She had intriguingly known a
number of Blaatshi epic epithets. She had even chanted
lines to Indrajit about his own death, like a warrior in the
Blaatshi Epic. It had been both disconcerting and
fascinating. "I'm not so frightened of her."

"She might bring that pile of bladed rope with her," Fix
said. "Squite."

Squite was a Yeziot, a race that turned out to resemble
giant piles of living green rope, with blades on the end of
each strand and eyestalks in the middle of the heap. Until

Fix had lit the ship on fire, it had looked as if Squite might singlehandedly kill Fix and Indrajit both, putting an end to their young jobber company, the Protagonists.

"Good point." Indrajit examined the office building. It was a single-story cube made of mud bricks plastered white, with a tarred roof. It had shuttered windows on all sides, and the shutters were closed. "Then we'll just have to break in."

"And leave the strands here for Forfa?" Fix asked. "Does that really absolve us of our duty?"

"In light of the possibility that the Yeziot might this very minute be crouched on that rooftop, ready to pounce on us?" Indrajit drew his leaf-bladed sword, Vacho, and examined the shutters. "It resolves the ethical question for me."

He eased Vacho's blade between the shutters. The steel was fine and thin; this wasn't great for the blade, but it needed sharpening anyway. He slid the weapon up until he found the latch, and pushed it open.

He looked up and down the wharf; no one was watching them.

"Shall we just toss them in the window?" he asked his partner.

Fix sighed. "Let's at least go inside. I'll leave him a note."

"Wait by the door," Indrajit told him. "I'll let you in."

He hoisted himself up onto the windowsill and into Forfa's office. He saw the same sagging shelves as the day before, the same ledgers, the same counter.

But today, Forfa himself lay dead on the floor. His head was almost entirely severed, the white bone of his spinal column showing through the wound. He lay in a dried puddle of his own blood, his face tentacles stained brown.

"Frozen hells." Indrajit pulled the shutters nearly closed. "No more Serpent Sea trade for you." He opened the door and pulled Fix inside, shutting and barring it again after.

"Well, no wonder he didn't answer," Fix murmured.

Indrajit sheathed his sword and pulled the knotted leather from the pocket of his kilt. "We were paid in advance. We can leave this and walk."

"Who killed him?" Fix asked.

"Does it matter?" Indrajit tossed the straps onto the counter. "People get killed in Kish every day. Welcome to Kish, watch your back! Robbers killed him. Blackmailers. Muggers. A former business partner, an old lover, someone he cheated in a card game. It's not entirely crazy to think that maybe his daughter killed him."

"Or her tentacled lover."

"We have no reason to think they were lovers." Indrajit shuddered. "But yes, maybe the Yeziot did it."

"Maybe he was killed for the texts." Fix folded his arms across his chest and raised his eyebrows.

"That should warn us to stay away from the written word in the future," Indrajit suggested. "Even when the writing in question is a knotted thong. And if someone is willing to kill for whatever is written on those straps, I say let them have them. I don't think any written words are worth a man's life. Not Forfa's life, and certainly, to be clear, not mine."

"You raise an interesting point," Fix said.

"Yes," Indrajit said. "Now let's get out of here."

"Whoever killed Forfa may be looking for the texts and he may think we have them."

"We'll leave the thongs here. The killer can have them."

"The killer has already been here." Fix tapped Forfa's shoulder with the toe of his sandal. "He, or she, didn't find the strings. He's not coming back."

"You're saying we have to watch our backs." Indrajit shrugged. "I knew that already. What do you think I am, new in town?"

"I'm saying that we should investigate the texts," Fix said. "Knowing what they are will help us understand why someone would want them, who that person might be, and will help us defend ourselves."

"Before I met you," Indrajit said, "I never had to think about books. Do you know that? I didn't read them, didn't see them, wasn't troubled at all."

"Your life is so much richer now."

"I miss the days of my poverty."

"Besides," Fix said. "A murder on the wharf? The Lord Stargazer has the contract to keep the peace down here. Even if you and I aren't ethically obligated to investigate the murder, we can do Bolo Bit Sodani a favor, and I'd like him to owe us one for a change."

"The translucent bastard." Indrajit grunted, and then gathered the leather strands back into his kilt pocket. Also, it occurred to him, Forfa had said that Grit Wopal had recommended hiring them. That meant that Wopal was Forfa's friend, and Wopal was head of the Lord Chamberlain's Ears. In that capacity, he sometimes gave

Indrajit and Fix sensitive work for the Lord Chamberlain. It couldn't hurt to find out why Wopal's friend had been killed. "Okay. But why do I have the feeling that I'm going to regret this?"

"Well," Fix said slowly, "maybe it's because we're going to have to go do research."

"The Hall of Guesses?" Indrajit sighed.

"I don't think they'll let us in," Fix said. "But I have a hunch they wouldn't be able to tell us anything, anyway, and there's somewhere else I want to try first."

"This is the ashrama of Salish-Bozar the White?" Indrajit gazed on the edifice in question. It was an unadorned, blocky building of gray stone with an extra-wide entrance. He might have taken it for a warehouse, if Fix had not identified it for him.

Also, it was located in the Spill. The city's main temples were in the Crown, the district of palaces and government buildings and large institutions. The Spill was mostly occupied by merchants' shops and the related buildings: inns, taverns, apartments, warehouses, stables, factories, and so on. And, apparently, the ashrama of Salish-Bozar the White.

The two Protagonists stood in a light drizzle across the street from the ashrama, in front of a pungent shop selling tea and spices.

"Why doesn't your god have a proper temple?" Indrajit asked. "What's an ashrama?"

"He's not my god," Fix said. "The Selfless of the ashrama raised me."

"Very selfless of them." Indrajit nodded.

"And Salish-Bozar is worshipped in the dedication of the thoughts of his acolytes. The ashrama is where the worshippers live, meet, and work."

"The Useless and the Miniscules."

"The Selfless and the Trivals."

"Right. And you're thinking that some of these worshippers of Salish-Bozar may have dedicated their thoughts to these knotted straps, and may be able to tell us something about them."

"Exactly."

"But doesn't that force us into another ethical question?" Indrajit asked.

Fix frowned.

"If some Trivial's knowledge of this knotted-rope matter helps us, say, solve a murder," Indrajit said, "or save our own lives, then it's not useless information. And we'll have revealed that the Trivial's efforts have been in vain. We strip away the sacral value of his knowledge."

Fix nodded. "We'll have to talk about the matter indirectly. Maybe it's best if I do most of the talking."

"As in the Paper Sook." Indrajit yawned. "Interest rites and funding sinks and so on."

"Interest *rates* and sinking funds. Never mind, follow my lead."

Fix headed to the ashrama's gate and Indrajit came one step behind him. In the gate, sheltered from the steady falling mist, stood two women in dirty white robes. One was a long-snouted, lavender-skinned Zalapting and the other was a coppery Kishi like Fix, with short black hair. They made a gesture of greeting by splitting their fingers left and right, and Fix repeated it back to them. Indrajit tried, couldn't get his fingers to move in quite the right way, and finally just bowed.

"We've brought a gift for the White," Fix said. "A mystery, found in the world."

The women's faces lit up.

"The world, and all its mysteries," they said together.

"May we see the Selfless Bonk?" Fix asked.

"Come this way." The Zalapting opened a door within the gate and led them; her Kishi companion stayed on door duty.

"What's a Bonk?" Indrajit whispered as he walked down a hallway behind Fix. At first, he took it for a narrow hall, but then he realized that a wide hallway had been subdivided by running tall, freestanding shelves down its middle as well as by standing shelves against both walls. The shelves stood pregnant with scrolls and codices.

"Bonk is a person's name," Fix whispered back. "The Selfless Bonk is the head of this ashrama."

Indrajit nodded.

The Zalapting Trivial left them in a shaft-like room that was narrow in two dimensions but rose up three stories to the height of the building. The room's ceiling was a skylight; water leaked in around the edges of that light and trickled down the plaster of the walls. A thin man with skin so pale that Indrajit thought he could see the man's organs sat cross-legged on a small mat on the brick floor. He had large, shell-like ears, no hair, and skinny shanks wrapped up in puffy pantaloons.

"Fix, my son!" he cried.

"Are you kin to the Lord Stargazer?" Indrajit blurted out. He'd met the Lord Stargazer once, and the man had been similarly translucent. "Or the same race of man, anyway?"

The Selfless Bonk grinned, revealing a complete absence of teeth. "I'm kin. Wonderfully, that knowledge is useless to you, as I have absolutely no influence over my cousin, Bolo Bit Sodani."

"Why is that wonderful?" Indrajit asked.

"Because today you have learned at least one useless piece of information," the Selfless said. "That is one step on the road to a mind of complete and restful contemplation, in tune with the glory of Salish-Bozar."

"Be careful," Fix warned Indrajit. He greeted the Selfless by kneeling and bowing to the floor, making the split-fingers gesture as he did so.

Indrajit tried to imitate the bow, at least.

"I have a theory," Indrajit said as he climbed to his feet. "Though this may be useless information."

"A theory isn't actually information," Fix said. "It's an attempt to *explain* information."

"Tell us your theory," the Selfless said.

"You're not a religion about information at all," Indrajit said.

The other two men both looked at him as if he'd said something shocking. Maybe even rude.

"Salish-Bozar is really a god of beauty," Indrajit said.

Fix scowled.

"What do you mean?" Bonk asked.

"Information that is useless is information that no one understands," Indrajit said. "Which means that it's not really information at all. Or it may as well not be information. It's just patterns, or images, or parallels.

What you like is weird patterns, strange things that should have an explanation, but don't. Or the explanation is unknown. Pretty colors, shining lights, weird syllables, forgotten tongues—you like the strange beauty of the world."

Bonk stood with the spryness of a child and took Indrajit by the elbow. "Have you considered a life in the ashrama?"

"We've brought a gift," Fix said, shooting Indrajit a sour look. "We asked to see you first so as to know which of the Selfless or the Trivials we should share it with."

The Selfless Bonk seated himself again, smiling benignly. "Tell me the mystery you have seen."

Fix gestured to Indrajit, who brought the knotted lengths out from his pocket.

Bonk's face lit up. "Ah," he said. "I have seen such strands before."

Fix nodded, a satisfied look on his face. "Are they studied by one of the Selfless?"

"Yes. If you leave them with me, I will pass them on."

"We can't leave them, unfortunately," Fix said.

Bonk's smile collapsed. "You have a use for them?"

Fix hesitated.

"No one has a use for them," Indrajit said, "but we promised to give them to someone. Only we thought we should show them to you first. Perhaps you could make a replica, or draw a picture. Aren't they beautiful?"

The Selfless Bonk sighed and shook himself, like a dog sloughing off worry. "Do you remember Meroit, Fix?"

Fix nodded. "I remember the Trivial Meroit well. Does he still sell his paintings in the market? He worked hard on the geometric patterns of damage caused to stone buildings by rubble. The falling directions of ruined walls, the cuts made by wind as opposed to the cuts made by water."

"Until the risk-merchants of the Paper Sook learned of his work." The Selfless shook his head, eyes drooping heavily. "They delighted in the knowledge, which they said would allow them to write more precise risk-selling contracts. They offered Meroit large sums of money and employment in the Paper Sook."

"He didn't take it?" Fix asked.

"He tried to take his own life instead. Years of study wasted, because it turned out that the subject of his study had practical value. We had to watch him closely for months, to stop him from simply walking into the sea."

"Perhaps he should have been an artist," Fix murmured, "and left the mystery of the world to others."

"So the study wasn't *wasted*," Indrajit said, "it just wasn't the right kind of beautiful for Salish-Bozar."

Bonk bobbled his head, a gesture that circled around and became a nod. "But then, on one occasion when we thought we had to rescue him from the waves, we found him staring in great fascination at the sea-kelp."

"Ah." Indrajit nodded, as if remembering the beauty of kelp.

"Meroit undertook then to learn all he could about the kelp," Bonk said. "Its thickness at different depths, its length at different times of the year, the changes in color and texture the plant undergoes at different proximities to the habitations of man. And, in particular, man's sewers."

Indrajit and Fix nodded. Fix seemed genuinely

interested, but Indrajit had long since degenerated into a state of complete pretense.

"To the astonishment of the entire ashrama," the Selfless continued, "the Lord Archer turns out to have large kelp farms. They're on the southern coasts, managed by Fanchee sea-farmers, and none of us was aware of them."

"You're focused on useless information," Indrajit said, "but kelp turns out to be useful. No wonder you were astonished."

"It feeds many people." The Selfless shrugged. "Meroit had memorized ten thousand pieces of information and was preparing to defend his knowledge and seek to ascend to Selflessness when one of the Lord Archer's Fanchee came and offered him a job managing kelp plantations."

"How did Meroit take that?" Indrajit asked.

"He ran to the Crown and climbed the Spike. The only thing that stopped him from throwing himself off and plummeting to his death was that a group of dried-goods merchants up there, preparing to consecrate their annual accounts to Spilkar, saw him."

"They saved him?" Fix asked.

"They saw him running up and assumed he was a criminal, come to rob them." Bonk frowned. "Their bodyguards subdued him."

"Lucky Meroit," Indrajit said.

The other men nodded.

"The good news for me," Indrajit added, "is that I have absorbed several hundred useless facts about the life of Meroit this morning. I'm well on my way to becoming a Selfless!"

Bonk frowned and Fix shook his head.

"Caveat number seven," the Selfless said. "'The deeds of no man's life can ever be considered useless.'"

"Wow," Indrajit said, "you guys are really strict."

Fix glared at him.

"Sorry," Indrajit said, "bad joke. Please continue. I think we had yet to hear about how Meroit became involved in the study of knotted thongs."

"I don't know how that happened," the Selfless said. "You can ask Meroit himself, if you like. But after the incident on the Spike, he took to his pallet for a month. When he arose, he showed me the first of his knotted strands, to be weighted."

"Weighted?" Indrajit asked.

"Caveat number three," the Selfless said. "'All useless facts shall be accounted according to the weight assigned to them by the Hierophant Selfless.'"

"Bonk is not merely Selfless," Fix said. "He is the Hierophant Selfless, the senior priest of the ashrama."

Bonk shrugged modestly.

"I understand." Indrajit stretched out one of the strands with his fingers. "And someone has to decide how many facts can be extracted from a strand such as this."

"Length," Fix said. "Weight. Elasticity, strength. Number and size and position of knots and piercings. Color, texture, taste."

"Sure," Indrajit agreed. "So Meroit wouldn't have to commit ten thousand of these things to memory. But how many? A thousand?"

The Selfless Bonk flared his nostrils and arched his

eyebrows. "That number is within the sole purview of the Hierophant Selfless to decide."

"I don't want to argue," Indrajit said. "Just trying to understand. The beauty of the world interests me. And the beauty of the followers of Salish-Bozar the White, too."

"Caveat number four," Bonk said. "'No fact about the organization of the followers of Salish-Bozar shall ever be deemed useless.'"

"Makes sense." Indrajit nodded. "That and the deeds one prevent an aspirant from *creating* ten thousand useless facts."

"Exactly how many of these strands Meroit shall have to know will depend on the strands themselves," Bonk said. "But it will be nearer to one hundred than one thousand."

Indrajit nodded. "Wonderful."

Bonk chuckled. "The mystery of the world is indeed wonderful. Fix, do you remember where Meroit sleeps? I believe he is there now, reflecting on the mystery."

They took their leave of the Selfless. They passed through a long chamber containing cubbies full of stones, sorted by color and size, along the walls. At a staircase at the end, Indrajit expected to climb, but instead they descended.

Beneath the ashrama spread a maze, winding and radial like the roots of a tree. Indrajit followed Fix out along a narrow, low-ceilinged root that ended in a circular room bristling with doors.

"What is a Fanchee sea-farmer?" Indrajit asked.

"I assume Fanchee is a race of man," Fix said. "Do you not know any epithets for them?"

Indrajit did not. "We're not under the building anymore," he observed.

Fix shrugged and knocked on a door. Without waiting, he opened it.

Inside, a lone man sat on a straw pallet. He had a bulbous, rootlike head, pointed and covered with thick bristles of hair and impaled by a bulbous, rootlike nose. His skin was a weedy yellow and what seemed to be his ears were two little flowerlike buds attached beneath his jaw. The buds curled forward and swiveled slowly to face the direction of any sound as he listened. No eyes were visible in his face.

A lattice of wood crossed the room just below the ceiling. From it hung dozens of knotted and punched leather strands. The four strings in Indrajit's pocket would have fit instantly and perfectly among them. The walls were hung with paintings of complex buildings. They looked like temples, with multiple stories, windows, gables, and columns, each scene dotted with dozens of men and women in togas of various colors.

"Are we not disturbing meditation?" Indrajit murmured.

"Meroit!" Fix bellowed.

Two black beads rose to visibility from beneath the surface of Meroit's skin. "Fix? Have you returned?" The voice was dull and blurred, the mouth a tiny crescent in danger of being filled entirely, should the nose ever slip from its position.

"Not in the way you mean." Fix made the Salish-Bozar greeting gesture and Meroit echoed it instantly. "We wanted to come show you something. A gift for the White."

Meroit held very still. "What?" His voice was tiny.

Fix gestured at the strands hanging overhead. "We came across four of these, and we're trying to understand them. I thought that the ashrama might be the right place to come, and I was right."

"Well you know, I . . . I don't *understand* them," Meroit said.

"If you understood them," Indrajit said, "they wouldn't do you any good. Wait . . . is there a caveat that says helping one to achieve the status of Selfless doesn't count as being useful?"

"There is," Fix said.

"That's the second caveat," Meroit added.

"See?" Indrajit grinned. "I'm getting this."

"Next thing you know, you'll be reading," Fix said.

"Let's not go crazy." Indrajit cleared his throat and addressed Meroit. "But you've got quite a collection there. Forty? Fifty?"

"Something like that," Meroit agreed.

"The Hierophant Selfless suggested you might be up for consideration when you get to a hundred or so," Indrajit said.

Meroit nodded. "May I see yours?"

Indrajit fished a strand from his pocket and handed it over. Fix shot him a quizzical look, and Indrajit winked.

Meroit took the strap in hand and ran it through his fingers slowly. He started at one end, where there was a triple knot, and caressed the entire length from that end to the other. His lips moved slightly as he touched each knot and divot. Once or twice, he backtracked to run his fingers over a particular section a second time.

"Where did you find this?" he asked when he had finished.

"We came across it in a brothel," Fix said quickly. "So many corpses from a fight that had just happened, we couldn't even tell who had dropped it."

"How about you?" Indrajit asked. "You have fifty of these. The Trivials of Salish-Bozar can't spend *that* much time with harlots."

Meroit turned a slightly darker shade, and his eyes sank into his puffy flesh almost to the point of disappearing. "I found the first one. I . . . don't remember where. On the beach. And then I put out the word that I would pay money if people found more of them. They just come to me."

"You don't worry that putting the word out causes people to just *make* these for you?" Indrajit asked. "There's got to be a caveat there, somewhere."

"I think I can tell the real ones," Meroit said.

"What do you mean, *real* ones?" Indrajit asked. "Real strands of knotted leather? I can make you a thousand real leather strips, just give me a week."

"I mean strands that weren't just faked for me. That would have existed without me." Meroit shook his head. "You know what I mean."

"One thing that has to really worry you," Indrajit said, "is that you can't be sure there will be enough of these for you to get to your ten thousand useless facts."

Meroit nodded. "The path of the White is hedged about by peril."

"So you can't tell us where these come from," Fix said, "or even where they're usually found, can you?"

Meroit chuckled. "Just the useless knowledge here, I'm afraid."

Indrajit noticed the question that Fix was scrupulously avoiding: *You can't read these strings, can you?* He kept his own mouth shut, too.

"You said you had four," Meroit reminded them.

"The others are back at our room," Indrajit said. "We just brought the one."

"Room?" Meroit asked. "I mean, ah, are you sleeping at the ashrama?"

"We're in an inn," Fix said casually. "Doesn't have a name, actually, but it's next to a big camel merchant off the Crooked Mile."

Meroit handed the string back to Indrajit. "I see, I see."

"Don't you want to write something down?" Indrajit asked. "Paint a picture of the string, count out its knots or something?"

"Ah, yes." Meroit rummaged around in the corner behind his pallet and came up with a roll of paper, inkpot, and pen. He stretched the string out across the floor and laboriously scratched a series of marks on the paper, presumably recording all the information the Selfless Bonk had said he would have to know.

Indrajit stood humming an old tune and raising his eyebrows at Fix.

When Meroit had finished, he handed the strap back to Indrajit. "When can I, ah, see the others?"

Indrajit and Fix shrugged at each other. "Next week?" Fix suggested.

Meroit's hand shook. "No sooner? What if I came to your room to look at them?"

"No rush, right?" Indrajit said. "You're still dozens of strings short of your hundred. Besides, we're not actually going back now. We have to be elsewhere."

"Deeds of derring-do for the Lord Chamberlain," Fix said. "Makes me miss the days of contemplation in the ashrama."

"You never missed us." Meroit laughed. "Did you marry that lady of yours, Fix?"

Fix shook his head slowly. "I did miss the ashrama, Meroit. Still do. And I'm afraid the lady went another way."

"Meroit's not telling us the truth," Indrajit said as they left the ashrama. "At least not the whole truth. Did you see the way he trembled?"

"He's not telling us any of the truth," Fix said. "He can read that string. He read it right in front of us."

"That's what reading is supposed to look like?" Indrajit asked. "Moving your mouth like that?"

"He's not a very *good* reader," Fix said.

"We should tell on him," Indrajit said. "We tell Selfless Bonk he's reading messages, and that guy never makes Selfless. They probably throw him right out of the ashrama. How many tries do you get before they kick you out?"

"He started at the end with three knots," Fix said. "Do all four have an end with three knots?"

Indrajit pulled the string out and looked. "Yes."

"He's reading messages," Fix said. "They're secret. And he's hiding them in plain sight, by pretending he's studying some kind of mysterious phenomenon. Maybe he does pay people to bring him strings they find, and those who want to send him a message just leave the strings lying about."

"This sounds like thief- and assassin-craft," Indrajit said. As he said it, he turned his head slightly to one side. His eyes, set far apart in his head, gave him good peripheral vision. As they ascended the hill above the ashrama, toward the long street called the Crooked Mile, he saw a flash of red and yellow scales behind them.

Just a flash, and then whatever it was dipped out of sight.

"I would say spies," Fix suggested. "This sounds like a system for transmitting stolen information to foreign powers."

"That makes it a matter for Grit Wopal." There was altogether too much reading and writing going on here, and Indrajit was happy to have what looked like a way out.

"Let's learn a little more about it first," Fix said. "Let's be sure we're bringing him something real."

"How did you guess that we should go to the ashrama to look for information?" Indrajit asked.

Fix hesitated. "I go back to the ashrama from time to time. I'm generally aware of what the Trivials are researching. I thought I remembered seeing one of these strands there."

"You go back . . . because you miss it?" Indrajit asked.

"That's not it."

"Because you think the woman you love might go back there looking for you?"

Fix shook his head. "Almost, though. I . . . just feel close to her there. I can remember my times with her. And it's safer than standing outside her house at night, watching her bedroom window."

"Well, if Meroit is going to try to seize the other three strings, surely he'll do it now." Indrajit yawned. He'd missed most of a night's sleep from pain, after battling on the *Duke's Mistress*. "He'll think we're elsewhere."

"You should go back to the inn and lie in wait, then," Fix suggested. "See what turns up. Don't get into any fights unless you're sure you can win."

"When do I not win fights?" Indrajit asked.

"Just be discreet. I'm going to go back to the docks."

"What for?"

"I want to dig around a little into Forfa. See if he was real."

They parted ways, Fix turning left at the next alley and heading to the water. Indrajit reached the Crooked Mile and followed it straight down. He stopped twice to pretend he was shopping and look for pursuit, but he didn't see anyone.

The rain stopped, leaving a cool afternoon with a general blanket of humidity lying over the city, begging for a breeze to lift it.

At the nameless inn that served as the Protagonists' headquarters, he avoided the front door. He reasoned that if Meroit came or sent someone to search their room, he might ask the innkeeper before trying to break in. So instead of alerting the innkeeper to his return, Indrajit climbed a bakery that backed onto the inn. From the bakery's roof, he dragged himself over the wall and onto the roof of the inn's stables, then forced his way up the corner of the building onto the rooftop. Lying on his belly, he peered over the lip of the roof and watched the door to their chambers from the inside.

He also watched the courtyard and the stables; anyone looking up from that direction would be hard pressed to miss seeing him, lying on the roof.

He tried to think about the events of the day before and this morning, but in his fatigue and recumbent position, he quickly dozed off.

A loud click awakened him. Peering into the room, he saw the lock to the door rotate, pulling the bar from its socket in the wall. He held his breath as the door pushed open, and then bit his tongue as the four-armed, red-and-yellow-scaled man named Chark entered.

Chark had been some sort of officer on the *Duke's Mistress*, the ship he and Fix had just burned down. Indrajit had last seen him locked in battle with Squite the rope-monster.

Which Indrajit had taken as a sign of Chark's noninvolvement. So what was he doing here?

Indrajit eased a few fingers back from the edge of the roof without losing his view of the interior. Chark proceeded to toss their quarters with a vengeance. He shredded mattresses, ripped off table legs, pulled at loose bricks, and even shattered the chamber pot. He came away looking dissatisfied.

For the first time, Indrajit was happy he'd agreed to let Fix put their money in a bank, rather than hidden in their rooms.

Chark had torn apart two spare kilts belonging to Indrajit and was beginning to circle the room, as if for a second look at everything, when Indrajit heard voices at the door. They were muffled and Indrajit couldn't make out words, but Chark heard enough to make him bolt for the window.

Indrajit pushed himself slightly farther back and gripped the hilt of his sword, ready to draw and fight if the scaly man climbed up the wall. Instead, Chark dropped down into the courtyard. Indrajit kept out of sight until he heard the scratching sounds of the man's taloned feet running, and then he peeped over just enough to see Chark's back disappearing out the stable doors, running toward the Crooked Mile.

He looked into the Protagonists' chambers as the door opened again.

"Oh, my," the innkeeper said. "Oh, my."

The person standing with the innkeeper was Meroit. The little Trivial seemed not so much disturbed as annoyed. "I take it this is not just bad housekeeping?"

"Something has happened," the innkeeper gasped. "I don't know. I can't. Maybe you shouldn't."

"Maybe I shouldn't wait here for my old friend, Fix the Trivial," Meroit said, nodding. "He'll have enough to do to clean this up without dealing with me, too. Perhaps I can leave him a note?"

The innkeeper leaned against the wall, gasping for breath and nodding.

Meroit walked through the chambers. Indrajit watched him through one window and then a second; the little acolyte of Salish-Bozar didn't leave a note at any point, but searched briskly through the trashed remains of the rooms.

Looking for the other three knotted thongs.

"Thank you," Meroit said to the innkeeper. He

produced a couple of copper coins. They didn't stop the innkeeper's hyperventilation, but they produced a smile and a nervous laugh.

They closed the door.

Indrajit had never in his life more than this moment wanted to be able to write. If he could have left Fix a letter, it would have said, *Meroit came and I am following him.*

But Indrajit could not write. He climbed down through the window into their chambers. He found an inkpot, but couldn't find any of Fix's scraps of paper—they were probably on his person. So he located the biggest scrap he could of his slashed pallet. He spread the fabric out on the floor, and using his own finger as a rough pen, he drew a picture of Meroit. Root head, root nose, beady eyes. Surely, Fix would recognize the picture.

Then he drew a rough picture of himself, a man-shaped image who was mostly stick, but had a long, bony nose ridge and held a leaf-bladed sword. He did a careful job, he thought, of drawing himself following Meroit, even though he hacked out the entire picture, both images, in under two minutes.

Then he took a cloak from the mess on his floor and hurled himself down the wall into the courtyard. He took the ink bottle with him, not entirely sure what he was going to do with it. Stepping around fresh camel dung, he crept to the door to the street, in time to see the little root-headed man in dirty white walking away down the Crooked Mile.

Indrajit followed, wrapping the cloak about him to hide his distinctive facial features. Mercifully, the cool, damp afternoon meant that many other pedestrians on the street were hooded.

He splashed a line of ink with one finger on a doorpost as he started out, at the level of his own eyes. He wanted to stop and draw a little picture of Meroit, but there was no time for that.

Then he slouched, kept his eyes down, and tried generally to make himself smaller and less conspicuous as he followed the little acolyte across the Spill.

It wasn't difficult. Meroit looked over his shoulder from time to time, but he did so awkwardly, bouncing and stopping before he looked back. Indrajit was able to adjust his position, drifting back, pulling closer, or turning sideways, and he was confident Meroit didn't see him.

He'd have liked to be able to trade off following with Fix, and he blotted his path with ink dots as he went. His trailblazing earned him glares and kicks and more than once an evil eye. A grain merchant even shouted, "Witch!" and chased him past her shop, but if Meroit heard, he didn't turn around.

The Trivial left the Spill and headed into the Dregs. The shops ended at the wall, replaced abruptly with gambling dens, taverns, bordellos, squalid tenements, and ruins. Indrajit nodded warily at the jobber crew handling security at the gate—he recognized them as some of Mote Gannon's Handlers: Zalaptings, a Luzzazza, and a Thûlian powder priest. He and Fix had an uneasy truce with the Handlers, who had tried to kill them, and he would have preferred to run into them with Fix at his side.

He didn't look closely to see whether the Luzzazza was missing an arm (which would have been Indrajit's fault), or if the powder priest was a woman under all the swaddling (which would make her the priest he had wrestled with in an earlier scuffle). He just put his hand on Vacho's hilt and hoped for the best.

But the Handlers just bared their teeth, spat on the ground, and let him through.

Meroit walked into a seedy coffee shop and took a seat at a small table. He sat with his back facing the street.

Was he hiding his identity? Was he waiting for someone who expected to be able to sit with his back to the corner?

A server consulted with Meroit about his coffee and Indrajit looked for a place to hide. The coffee shop squatted in the corner of a small, muddy plaza. Indrajit backed to the opposite corner of the square and positioned himself on the far side of a cart selling fried tamarind. He bought a handful, wrapped in flat bread and topped with hot sauce, and took his first bite while watching Meroit.

A sharp point poked him in the back. Then a hand pulled Vacho from its sheath.

"Pull down your hood," a thick voice muttered, "and turn around. Slowly."

Indrajit swallowed his mouthful of tamarind and complied. The man holding a knife on him was green-skinned, noseless, and had a thicket of tentacles falling from the lower half of his face. Indrajit sighed.

The crowd on the street continued drifting sluggishly past, ignoring the knife in broad daylight: *Welcome to Kish; mind your business!*

"The only reason I don't kill you now is that I want you to tell me who you are first," the green-faced man hissed.

Then he collapsed.

Fix stood behind him, a rock in his hand. He tossed the

rock aside, took the knife, handed Vacho back to Indrajit, and dragged the green man to his feet.

"Right," Fix said. "You yourself already explained why I haven't killed you yet. Start talking."

The green man spat in Fix's face; Fix dragged him past the tamarind seller and thumped his shoulder blades against a mud-brick wall.

"Did you arrange this meeting?" Indrajit asked. "Or did the Trivial?" The green man turned his face toward Indrajit, and Indrajit clapped a hand over his mouth. "No spitting." He wolfed down the rest of the fried tamarind and flat bread.

The prisoner growled.

"Meroit did," Fix said.

Indrajit looked up and down the street for any sign of jobbers who might interfere, and saw none. The Dregs was notoriously under-policed, though, and organized criminal gangs sometimes stepped in to fill the gap.

"Here's what we know," Fix said. "You're Fanchee."

When had Fix learned anything about the Fanchee?

"You and Forfa are part of the Fanchee clan that farms kelp for the Lord Archer," Fix continued. "You've been sending information to our friend Meroit in the form of knotted ropes. The fact that he's a Trivial makes it easy; you leave the strands in public places, and people take them to the ashrama, knowing they'll be paid. None of your people gets exposed to Meroit, or vice versa. Only now some of the messages have gotten lost, and Meroit wants a meeting. What's the information about? Is it about the farms themselves? Or is there some secret information about the Lord Archer or his other holdings that you're smuggling out?"

Indrajit removed his hand. The Fanchee only hissed.

Indrajit grabbed the Fanchee's face tentacles and yanked; the Fanchee yowled and squirmed. Fix dragged the green man down a narrow alley, stepping over two drunkards in a puddle.

Indrajit looked over at the coffee shop to be certain that Meroit was still there and then joined Fix.

Something nagged at the back of his mind, and he couldn't focus on it.

"Who pays you?" Indrajit barked.

"Good question," Fix growled. "Who gets this information? Pelth? The Paper Sultanates? The Free Cities?"

The Fanchee laughed. "Why do you think I would know?"

And then Indrajit understood.

He shook his head. There was no point in interrogating this Fanchee. "You've given away everything, you fool!" Fix shot him a quizzical look. "We've got an appointment, Fix. Time to leave this pawn."

Indrajit pushed the Fanchee to the ground and turned away, dragging Fix with him.

"What are you doing?" Fix asked. "What do you know?"

"What do *you* know?" Indrajit shot back.

"Forfa's body is gone," Fix said. "But I checked those ledgers, and they aren't about the Serpent Sea trade at all."

Indrajit nodded. "Forfa was lying to us from the beginning. And he was using someone else's building. Any idea whose building that is?"

"No. And I asked around the docks to see whether anyone knew Forfa, and no one did. But when I described him, several people called him a Fanchee."

"I have a bet," Indrajit said. He directed their footsteps uphill, toward the Crown. "I bet that building belongs to the Lord Chamberlain."

Fix was silent for a moment. "You think that this spy ring that we've stumbled upon is part of the Lord Chamberlain's Ears. And that it is spying on the Lord Archer."

"Yes," Indrajit said.

"How does Meroit pass the information on, and to whom?"

"My guess is that it's something indirect, like the knotted strings." Indrajit shrugged. "Does he still sell his paintings? Maybe the paintings are a way to pass the information on."

"Likely." Fix's voice was flat.

"It would be deeply ironic if the Lord Chamberlain's spies killed us," Indrajit suggested, "since we also work for the Lord Chamberlain. So to avoid that unfortunate fate, I want to shortcut all the confusion and just deliver the four knotted strands to Grit Wopal himself."

They climbed through the gate into the wealthiest part of Kish. They were heading for the Lord Chamberlain's palace, which was not the only place to find Grit Wopal, but it was a good place.

"Tell me why you think this," Fix said.

"Your problem is that you read," Indrajit said.

"Your problem is that you *don't*," Fix responded. "I almost didn't arrive in time to save your life because I couldn't figure out that terrible triangle-headed cartoon of yours was meant to be a picture of Meroit."

"It's an excellent likeness," Indrajit said.

"It's an excellent likeness of a bulbous root."

"Meroit looks like a vegetable. Anyway, it took me a minute to recall the information, but as we were discussing the situation with our Fanchee friend back there, I finally found the spot in my memory palace. It's a little protrusion of earth, framed by rounded gray stones and lapped at by the water."

"What?"

"My memory. I had to consult it, but I found the information I was looking for."

"Your memory is a picture?"

"Yes. Isn't yours?"

Fix shook his head. They turned down a side street—in the Crown, there were no true alleys—and headed for the tradesman's entrance to the Lord Chamberlain's palace. "Go on."

"And I saw there a picture of Grit Wopal, recommending us to Forfa."

Fix stopped and stared at the Lord Chamberlain's door. "Yes," he said slowly. "Forfa said that Grit Wopal recommended us to help recover these knotted strands."

Indrajit knocked at the door. "I don't think that's a coincidence. I don't think that was one old friend recommending a reliable service to another, as a kindness. I think Wopal was sending us in to repair a breach in one of his spy rings. Without telling us."

The door opened. Inside stood Grit Wopal, a short man wearing a yellow turban.

"It's about time," he said.

Welcome to Kish

"As you have surmised, it is I who was purchasing information from the Lord Archer's Fanchee administrators about the kelp farms they run." Grit Wopal nodded as if in salute to his own cleverness, the dirty yellow turban bobbing neatly. "On behalf of the Lord Chamberlain, of course. As the head of the Lord Chamberlain's Ears."

Wopal stood in a sparely furnished room in the palace of the Lord Chamberlain, Orem Thrush. Indrajit Twang and Fix each sat on a low sofa; sitting, they were nearly as tall as the Yifft spymaster. The Yifft's famous third eye was shut and invisible.

"We did surmise that," Indrajit agreed. "But not until we almost got killed by a Yeziot, and a Chark, and an angry Fanchee."

"I wouldn't think a single Fanchee would be much of a threat to you two." Wopal smiled. "They're kelp farmers, not renowned for their martial prowess."

"This one was really angry," Indrajit said. "The point is that you could have told us more up front."

"I could have." Wopal smiled. "I didn't want to."

Indrajit ground his teeth. "Do you know what I'm remembering, and with pleasure?"

"Punching me in my third eye?" Wopal suggested. "Twice?"

Indrajit nodded.

"Savor the memory." Wopal shrugged. "I know I think of it often."

"You didn't want to reveal to any unnecessary person anything about your information-gathering operation," Fix said. "We understand. But now we've recovered the stolen information, so that's it. That's the end of the story."

"The stolen information, please." Wopal held out a hand, palm up.

Indrajit extracted four knotted leather straps from his kilt pocket. Apparently, they were written documents, containing information about the Lord Archer's kelp farms. And Grit Wopal had bought that information from the Lord Archer's Fanchee kelp farmers. It had been intercepted by the poetess Oritria and her accomplices, and the Protagonists—Indrajit and Fix—had recovered it. In the process, they had learned that the conspiracy of kelp-farm information sharers gave their strings to one of the Trivials of Salish-Bozar the White, a small man named Meroit. Meroit passed the information on to other agents of the Lord Chamberlain by painting it in symbolic form in pictures of buildings.

Indrajit handed over the documents.

"It's not quite the end of the story," Grit Wopal said.

"The girl," Indrajit guessed. "The poetess Oritria."

"She stole the information from her father, who was your spy," Fix said. "You want to know who hired her."

"Of course," Wopal said. "The Lord Chamberlain trades on the stolen information. If there is some third party availing itself of the same data, he could get fleeced. And what if the poetess's employer was a hostile foreign power?"

"Maybe it's better if someone else handles this job," Fix said.

"As you pointed out, I strongly prefer not to spread knowledge of these activities any farther than is absolutely necessary." Wopal smiled.

"Then just send me," Fix suggested. "Indrajit has feelings for Oritria."

"I do not," Indrajit said. "And besides, you have feelings for all written texts, and that didn't stop you from going after the kelp strap writings with me."

Fix sighed and shook his head.

"You two," Wopal said. "Both of you. That's who's going to track Oritria and find out who has employed her."

"Her and the Yeziot, Squite," Fix said.

"And Chark," Indrajit pointed out. "Big scaly guy, four arms, nasty claws? Remember him?"

"The Yeziot is dead," Grit Wopal said.

"Are we certain Chark is in league with Oritria?" Fix asked. "Perhaps it was the confusion belowdecks on the *Duke's Mistress*, but I thought maybe Chark and Squite were battling."

"They were." Indrajit shrugged. "But she knew his name, and they seemed to me to be disagreeing over tactics rather than fighting as enemies. And then Chark destroyed our chambers."

"If Chark is not in league with Oritria," Wopal said, "then I want to know who employs him, as well."

"Who do you think employs them?" Fix asked. "Shouldn't you be testing hypotheses?"

"Indeed, I will be testing hypotheses," Wopal said. "But I don't plan to share them with you."

"You think you know," Indrajit said, interpreting the conversation for himself, "but you're not going to tell us. Even though knowing what you think you know might help us prove whether what you think you know is right or not."

"Look at you, Recital Thane," Fix said. "You're fit for the Hall of Guesses now."

Wopal nodded.

"Ah, good," Indrajit said. "Blind and ignorant, that's how I'm most comfortable. If someone actually told me what was going on for once, I'd feel downright out of sorts."

"Like a fish out of water?" Fix suggested.

Indrajit ignored his partner. "How do you know the Yeziot is dead?"

Wopal nodded. "His body is on display at the Blind Surgeon."

"Something about that bothers me," Indrajit said.

"Perhaps that you owed the Blind Surgeon's publican, Anaximander Skink, a prodigious debt before entering the Lord Chamberlain's service?" Grit Wopal suggested.

"No."

Wopal frowned. "Perhaps that you were humiliated in

hand-to-hand combat at the Surgeon first by Skink's bouncers and then by Yashta Hossarian, a jobber in the employ of Holy-Pot Diaphernes?"

Indrajit shuddered at the memory of the bird-legged man. "No, but I feel we're getting closer."

"The four-armed scaly fellow," Fix said. "Chark. He mentioned the Blind Surgeon."

"That's it." Indrajit closed his eyes and could visualize the encounter, complete with Chark's sibilant hiss and his disdain for the Blaatshi Epic. "He knew I had once been a regular there. And, ah, some unflattering financial details."

"Welcome to Kish," Fix said. "It's a small town when you need a big one."

"And a maze when you need a crossroads." Indrajit sighed.

Indrajit inhaled damp sea air as he and Fix strolled down the ramp from the Spill onto the West Flats. The air reeked of the exhalations, bodily odors, and effluvia of all the thousand races of man, but the cool salt of the sea on the breeze gave it a bracing metallic edge. They passed two carts, creaking with the day's pungent take from the sea, and pushed away a troop of men with shaven heads and yellow-green robes, chanting a song about how the wind heard all the words ever spoken.

"What are the odds," he asked Fix, "that Grit Wopal is withholding information you and I would actually like to know?"

"One hundred percent," Fix said. "Perhaps that is because you and I are unusually curious fellows."

Indrajit bobbled his head from side to side. "In this profession . . . you make a good point."

"But I doubt he would get nearly as much value out of men who were less curious."

"Another good point," Indrajit said. "When I compose epic epithets for you, one of them shall certainly reference your curiosity."

"I am disappointed to hear that the epithets do not already exist," Fix said. "But pleased that they will be plural."

"Multiple," Indrajit said. "Many. And mostly not overlapping with my own."

Fix slowed his step as they neared the end of the ramp. "Anaximander Skink doesn't know me," he said. "We should go in separately. Would you feel safer if I went in first, so you're not in there without backup?"

"Safer?" Indrajit snorted. "A hero is safe at all times. If you enter first and unnoticed, though, perhaps you'll be able to identify possible sources of trouble before I even arrive. You can wait, armed and unnoticed, to leap like a bolt of lightning into the fray when needed."

Fix nodded. At the foot of the ramp, Indrajit turned right and slowed his pace. He drifted down to the sea, where he stood, listening to the cries of the gulls, the slap of the waves, and the whistles of the fishermen plying the trade that sustained the East Flats, the West Flats, and the Shelf alike. From this angle, he saw that the northern rim of the Blind Surgeon squatted over a narrow canal that connected directly with the sea; a long wooden boat lay there, tied to a post. The tide was beginning to go out, and the boat bobbed steadily lower as he watched it.

He gave Fix five minutes, a time he could accurately

estimate because it was the length of time it took him to recite a dry account, with no embellishments or physical articulation, of the Taking of the Bone Tower. When he reached the line in which clever Gondahar, long of thew, took the Mistress of the Keys astride his dolphin mount, he stopped.

Then he turned back, climbed up the pebbly beach, littered with refuse and scarred by the hulls of boats, and into the Blind Surgeon.

The corpse of the Yeziot Squite hung from ropes lashing it to the ceiling. Strictly speaking, Indrajit had no idea whether it was in fact Squite, as opposed to some other Yeziot; all he could really tell was that it looked like a heaped mass of mildewed rope, each strand joining in a central clump that was accented with eyestalks and split by a gaping mouth filled with multiple rows of teeth. But since Squite was the only Yeziot Indrajit had ever seen, it seemed likely that the living man and the corpse were the same. Customers of the public house yanked on the Yeziot's tentacles and touched the sharp tips of its teeth with cautious fingers.

"Indrajit Twang!" Anaximander Skink howled. The barkeep and owner of the Blind Surgeon was a Wixit, a furry bipedal race of man with a muzzle like a little wild dog's. On the ground, he would only have come to Indrajit's knee, so he stood on a rough catwalk nailed to the backside of the bar.

"Don't let him recite!" a customer bellowed. Indrajit glared back at the man, a fur-wrapped Yuchak with three axes hanging from a broad belt.

"Now, now." Skink made a clicking noise with his

tongue. "That's no way to treat an old friend. Besides, Twang's credit is restored. Old Bird Legs wiped it clean, didn't he?"

"I don't need credit." Indrajit smiled. "I have cash now."

"Ah good." The Wixit pointed at the dead Yeziot. "Because that's two bits already. Price of admission to see the dead monster."

The crowd inside the Blind Surgeon jeered. A dozen of the races of man thrust their faces in Indrajit's direction to hiss and boo. A Zalapting made obscene gestures in the direction of the Yeziot.

Indrajit didn't see Fix. His partner would have his face down on a table somewhere, or would be lurking behind some burly patron of the bar to keep himself unseen until he was needed. Indrajit didn't look too hard; no sense finding his partner, only to give him away.

Indrajit strode up to the bar. "Wine. And none of that Ylakka piss you like to pass off as beer, either. Give me the good stuff."

The Wixit hauled on a short rope to pull a bottle from beneath the counter, sloshing dark red liquor into a stone cup.

And then Indrajit realized that Fix had the money. This was at Fix's insistence; his partner swore that Indrajit had no sense of economy or fiscal prudence, and should only be allowed to touch coin as a last resort.

"Actually," he murmured to Skink, "I seem to have left my purse at home."

"Your credit's good here now," the Wixit growled. "Just don't try to pay me back in poetry."

"I wouldn't dream of it." Indrajit took the stone cup

and sipped; the wine was sour, but he liked the aftertaste, and he found himself thirsty. He drained the cup and beckoned for more, which the Wixit promptly poured. "Who sold you the Yeziot?"

"No one *sold* it to me." Skink sniffed. "He was a customer with a large tab. He died before I could collect, so I claimed the body."

"Died in the common room, did he?" Indrajit asked. "Or did you drag him here from the Shelf all on your own?"

"What do you think you know, Twang?"

Indrajit took another sip. "The Yeziot was named Squite."

The Wixit sneered. "Next you're going to tell me about his starving wife and pups."

"I killed him." Indrajit pointed at the visible scorch marks around Squite's mouth and eyes. "Lit him on fire."

"Smork droppings," Skink said.

"Ah yes," Indrajit said. "I remember this about you."

"My tough-minded, skeptical approach to life?"

"Your obsession with Smork feces. Shall I recite to you the tale of my battle with the Yeziot?"

"Kill me first."

"I'll tell you how you got the Yeziot's corpse," Indrajit said. He finished the cup of wine again. Was this a Wixit-sized cup, that he was draining it so easily? "You just fill in the blanks, and I'll pay you for it."

"On credit?"

"Yes."

Skink frowned. "Okay. Tell me how I got the Yeziot's corpse."

"A Fanchee woman," Indrajit said. "Green, with face tentacles. Quite pretty. You might have noticed her carrying a wax writing tablet, and you might have heard her using the name Oritria."

"Go on." Anaximander Skink's eyes narrowed.

"She ran up quite the bill here," Indrajit suggested. "Maybe you rented a room to her or to her Yeziot pal, or both. Or you sold them a horse. Maybe a Yeziot drinks a lot of wine."

"Raki," Skink said. "A Yeziot puts away a lot of raki, it turns out."

"Expensive," Indrajit said.

"And a room," Skink added. "They both slept in my supply room downstairs."

Indrajit nodded.

"That much information was free," Skink said. "The next thing I tell you costs you money."

"She came to you last night," Indrajit said. "She needed something, or she would have just run away. What did she need?"

"Two bits," Skink said.

"What about two orichalks, or two terces?"

"I prefer Imperial coin. Even chopped up."

"Agreed."

"She needed a place to stay. Said her business in Kish wasn't done yet."

"And she offered you the Yeziot's body to pay off her bill."

"Two bits."

"Agreed."

"Yes, she offered me the body."

Indrajit growled, leaning over the bar to look menacing.

"Okay, okay, yeah, she gave me the body. She needed a place to stay for a couple more nights, and I told her if the Yeziot brought in enough cash, she could stick around here."

Indrajit frowned. "And enough of your patrons are willing to pay two bits for a glimpse of a dead Yeziot to pay off a big raki tab?"

Anaximander Skink shrugged. "For a full Imperial, I let people cut off one of the limbs and take it with them. No one's paid the two Imperials for a tooth yet, but at this rate, I'll be burning the thing's head by morning, with a coin-fat purse to hide away."

"That *thing* is a man," Indrajit muttered.

"That you killed." Skink shrugged. "Smork droppings, now. I might as well make a few coins."

Indrajit swallowed a long diatribe studded with reproach and condemnation. "And where is she now? The Fanchee woman?"

"That's a full Imperial," Skink said.

"Making the total . . ."

"Call it an even two Imperials."

Indrajit wished he had started by simply asking where Oritria was. Maybe his indirect approach had helped open the Wixit up. "Two Imperials it is."

"She's in my supply room downstairs," Skink said.

"I'm not going to ask you how to get there," Indrajit said in his most commanding Recital Thane tones. "I've paid you enough, and now you're just going to tell me."

"Back around in the kitchen," Skink said. "There's a trapdoor and a ladder."

"Lead me."

Indrajit followed the Wixit behind the bar and under a rotting brick arch into the kitchen. A pot of something meaty bubbled over a fire in one corner of the room; tottering stacks of shelves held pots, kegs, bottles, barrels, and eating utensils over most of the floor.

Another Wixit crouched over a heap of dirty mugs and plates, wiping the food and drink from them with a greasy cloth.

"What possessed you to dig a hole under this place?" Indrajit asked.

"We didn't dig anything. Neither did the fellow who sold me the Blind Surgeon; he built over a natural cave."

"Just a cave?"

"Nothing strange down there. No walking dead or Druvash mutants or anything." Skink held a finger in front of his muzzle to call for silence, and Indrajit held his tongue. With careful motions, the Wixit rolled a threadbare square of carpet away from the floor, revealing a rectangular trapdoor underneath.

"Give me a taper," Skink whispered to the other Wixit. She set down a gravy-smeared bowl, tossing her wiping rag on top of it, and lit a short, fat taper.

"Is she alone down there?" Indrajit felt a little slow; perhaps he'd had a bit too much wine. But he didn't worry about facing Oritria alone.

Skink took the taper and nodded. "I'm to awaken her at nightfall. Let me go first; if she sleeps still, I will signal you. And if she's awake, I'll maneuver her so that her back is to the ladder."

"You are cunning, Skink. I shall have to be more careful

of you in the future." Indrajit drew his heroic sword, Vacho, and steeled himself. Should he call for Fix? But Fix hadn't seen fit to make himself visible, so perhaps he was watching other dangers. Perhaps he had found the four-armed and red-scaled man Chark and was tailing him. All in all, he decided to leave Fix hidden.

Skink crouched beside the trapdoor as the other Wixit retreated across the room. "If you lift the door, I'll descend."

The trapdoor had an iron ring for a handle, sunk into a circular groove cut into wood polished smooth by years of hands. Indrajit spread his legs wide to lower his body. Holding his sword up and to one side and breathing in a calm, controlled fashion to avoid accidental grunting, he hoisted the trapdoor.

Below, darkness, and the soft lapping sound of water.

Two enormous hands seized Indrajit by the right wrist. He spun, twisting his arm and torso to try to claw his arm free, but in vain.

The hands that gripped him were at the end of two enormous, muscular right arms. They were covered with red scales, patched here and there with brown fur, and they corresponded to two left arms, all attached to the same huge torso.

Indrajit stumbled and lost his balance. Chark, the four-armed, scaly accomplice of the poetess Oritria, hurled Indrajit down into the darkness.

He wasn't sure what part of his body hit the floor first, but he survived. Pain exploded across multiple points in his chest, back, and ribs. But the loud metallic clanging told him that Vacho had fallen down into the pit with him.

Lying on stone, hearing the ring, he groped in darkness toward the sound and found his weapon's hilt.

Lifting it was an effort that caused his breath to come short, but the sword felt the right weight; it hadn't snapped in two, at least.

Was this, after all, a storeroom? Or did Anaximander Skink's public house conceal some sort of dungeon, or murder hole?

"Fear to come at me, fell monsters," he grunted. "I am armed."

"I am not," Fix said in the darkness. "On the other hand, I don't think there are monsters down here."

"Frozen hells. What happened?"

"I was grabbed from behind," Fix said. "Outnumbered. They disarmed me and threw me down in this hole."

"What's down here?" Indrajit knew that Fix would have begun exploring the moment he was conscious.

"Boxes," Fix said. "I haven't finished poking around."

"Did you find the canal?" Indrajit asked. "There should be a water channel. A sluice of water runs right up to the building."

"I hear the water," Fix said. "I haven't found it yet."

"You hear it slapping?" Indrajit said. "That's the action of the tides. It means the water in this room connects to the sea."

Fix cursed mildly.

Indrajit patted around on hands and knees and had just found the lip of the channel when the tide suddenly dropped enough to admit light through the groove. It was the pale northern light of an autumn afternoon, but after a couple of minutes of darkness, it nearly blinded Indrajit.

And then it was gone, as the water returned.

"We'll get more of that," Indrajit said. "Let me get down in the water and see if there's a way out of here. You dig around in the boxes. Look for raki. It's a very hard liquor, double-distilled grape."

"I know what raki is. I assume you don't just want to get drunk."

"Wine won't burn," Indrajit said. "Raki will."

He lowered himself into the cold water, feeling the push as a long wave came in and then the pull as it dragged out. The water dragged him forward with it, but then he abruptly stopped; the channel was blocked off by an iron grate beneath the wall of the Blind Surgeon.

He took a breath and dove.

The iron bars descended all the way to the stone floor of the channel, and from wall to wall, completely blocking off the passage. When the tide reached its ebb point, he got several seconds of light, and could see both the boat bobbing just on the other side, and the heavy iron lock on the bars.

"It's locked," he told Fix. "Can you pick locks?"

"No. You?"

Indrajit climbed out of the channel, sloshing water on the stone floor. In the few seconds of light, he could see that they were indeed in a natural cave, with rough walls and a floor of cold, hard-packed, pebbly dirt.

"Picking locks is one of the few skills not illuminated in the Blaatshi Epic," Indrajit said.

"Seems like an oversight now," Fix said. "Perhaps you should compose a few verses."

"If we escape by picking the lock," Indrajit said, "I will. But I intend to get out of here by lighting a fire."

"Burning ourselves to death," Fix guessed.

"We will crouch in the channel, while the water is still high."

"If the Blind Surgeon collapses, we will still be killed."

"I don't think Anaximander Skink will allow the Surgeon to collapse. And also, I don't think Oritria will allow me to be killed."

"You romanticize a spy who probably murdered her father."

"She told Chark she needed me," Indrajit said. "Back on the *Duke's Mistress*. And not to kill me. And indeed, today, when Chark could easily have murdered me today, he knocked me down into this hole instead."

"It seems a thin reed," Fix said, "but I see no other."

Working in spurts as they had light, they broke down a crate of raki. The straw inside, and the board of the crate, they piled against a stack of other crates, containing various dried goods—beans and rice and tamarind. They shattered several bottles of raki, soaking all the crates and the tinder.

Then Indrajit struck the hilt of Vacho against a rock until he produced a spark.

Blue flame leaped up, engulfing the heap of crates.

"Truly, Vacho is the hidden lightning." Fix lowered himself into the watery slot, arms at the lip so as to be able to quickly emerge.

"The Voice of Lightning," Indrajit said. "Which is to say, thunder. And this is an abuse I have heaped upon Vacho. I shall have to make up for it by plying him with raki later."

"You will drink it for him, of course."

"I will do him this service." Indrajit lowered himself into the channel with his partner. He laid Vacho on the cave floor, in easy reach so he could leap out of the canal, instantly armed for the fray. "For being the Voice of Lightning, he is surprisingly not possessed of a mouth."

With the stack of crates in flames, Indrajit now saw a pile of lumber behind it, and a rolled bundle of cloth—an unused curtain, or blankets?—on wooden shelves. He considered climbing out again, to push other flammable material into the fire, but the flames leaped well enough on their own that, in moments, the cave was a burning hell.

"My head might bake," Fix complained.

"Keep dunking yourself," Indrajit suggested.

"I also might suffocate."

"We knew there were risks."

Indrajit heard stampeding feet overhead. The ladder leading out of the cave, visible now in the firelight, was a series of iron rungs bolted into stone, leading up to the underside of the trapdoor. The trapdoor opened to the sound of several voices yelling. Anaximander Skink lowered a foot to climb down the ladder, and then immediately pulled it back with a pained shriek.

"The ladder is hot!"

"I didn't think about that one," Indrajit said.

"You morons!" Anaximander Skink squealed.

"Come on," Fix suggested, "let's grab that curtain."

They snaked between two burning columns of wood to seize the rolled-up cloth. It smoldered, so they tossed it into the channel and jumped down in with it. The water was now only waist-high and dropping at the height of the

tide, but they trampled the fabric deep into the water to
thoroughly soak and chill it.

Then they threw the wet curtain over the iron rungs of
the ladder and climbed.

Indrajit went first, climbing with one hand and pushing
ahead of him with Vacho to clear the path. He dragged
himself through the trapdoor into a kitchen filled with
smoke. Chark lunged for him with his falchion, but it was
a half-hearted attack, and Indrajit drove him away with
the sharp tip of the leaf-bladed sword, and then gave Fix
a hand.

Oritria stood in the door, a short, thin blade in her
hand.

Skink was yelling something so shrill and wild that
Indrajit couldn't make out the words. "Listen, you should
go around," he told the Wixit. "Unlock the canal gate, and
then slosh water onto the flames."

"I've already lost a fortune in wine and raki!" the Wixit
wailed.

"You're losing more fortune by the minute," Fix
pointed out.

The Wixit skittered away, leaving the Protagonists
standing with Oritria and Chark. Without any spoken
agreement to hold off hostilities, they all stumbled out onto
the street. Fire raced up several walls. The Yeziot had been
stripped of limbs and sagged like a bushel of teeth from the
ceiling of the Blind Surgeon, which was aflame.

The tavern's customers had evaporated, other than the
handful who were trying to help fishermen sling water
onto the burning building.

Indrajit kept a tight grip on his sword. Chark had a

leather bag slung over his shoulder and stood crouched, as if prepared to spring into battle.

"If you want the leather straps," Indrajit said, "they're gone."

"Our patron will be displeased," Chark growled.

"I don't know whether I should care about that or not," Indrajit said. "Here's what I'm prepared to offer. You tell us who your patron is, and in exchange, I will listen to you explain what it is you need from me."

"I need nothing from you," Chark said.

"Her." Indrajit pointed at Oritria with his sword. "What *she* needs from me."

Chark snarled.

Oritria turned to Fix. "I will offer *you* a trade. Give us the Blaatshi, and we will tell you the identity of our employer and give you your weapons back."

Fix addressed Chark. "Give us the girl, and we'll let you go."

Chark laughed, a sound like metal being folded. "I have all your weapons, you impudent sack of meat."

"I see we are at an impasse," Indrajit said.

"I want to be your apprentice," Oritria said.

Indrajit stared.

"Nonsense," Chark rumbled.

"Terrible idea," Fix said.

Indrajit raised a hand. "Wait a minute."

"You can't be serious," Fix said.

"You want to learn the Epic," Indrajit said to the poetess. She already composed like a Recital Thane. She had sung to him perfectly composed lines about his own death, as she had attacked him.

"I want to finish learning it," she said. "My grandmother sang many songs to me from the Epic. I would learn the rest."

Indrajit's head swam. "Why?"

"Because it is beautiful," she said. "Because it is the truest thing known to all the races of man."

"Oh no," Fix muttered.

"Was your grandmother Blaatshi?" Indrajit stumbled at the idea. "I don't understand."

"She loved a wandering Blaatshi singer," Oritria said. "He had been apprenticed to become Recital Thane, but had fled the responsibility. But he carried the Epic with him. He could not escape it, and neither could she. And neither can I."

"And neither can I," Indrajit murmured.

"When you say *loved*," Fix said. "Do you mean . . . *loved*?"

"I am full-blooded Fanchee," Oritria said. "My grandmother wed my grandfather, but she cherished the secret of her youthful love, and passed it on to me."

Indrajit heard his own heart pounding in his ears. He felt as if he were living an episode of the Epic.

"Are you aware of this runaway apprentice Recital Thane character?" Fix asked.

"No," Indrajit said. "This is a tale of the generation it will be my privilege to add to the Epic. The goddess has brought this girl to me."

"She tried to choke you," Fix said. "And stab you. She imprisoned you in a basement."

"What was the apprentice Recital Thane's name?" Indrajit asked.

"Rupavar," she said.

"I do not care to be gutted by the Lord Archer for this nonsense!" Chark roared.

The Lord Archer.

Indrajit shook his head. "Arda Ne'eku? That's your employer?"

"It seems reasonable," Fix murmured. "Plugging the leak in his own organization. I wonder if that's one of Wopal's hypotheses."

"What does the Lord Archer want?" Indrajit asked.

"The four texts you stole from us," Chark roared.

"We can't get them," Indrajit said.

"Unless . . ." Fix frowned.

Was Fix contemplating assaulting Orem Thrush's palace to take the strings back? But why would he do that, when there were authentic knotted cord-messages to be had elsewhere? "Frozen hells," Indrajit said. "I believe I'm going to do something impious."

"Poor Meroit," Fix said.

"He's faking anyway," Indrajit pointed out. "He knows the strings contain information. He reads them."

"What are you talking about?" Oritria asked.

Indrajit sheathed his sword. "We'll get you back the four strings. Then you'll be in the good graces of the Lord Archer, right? And Chark, you can go on your way, eating babies, or whatever it is you do normally. And Oritria, you can get paid, and will be freed to study the Epic with me. Right?"

Fix grumbled without words. Chark nodded hesitantly and Oritria sprang to Indrajit, kissing him on the cheek.

"Where shall we bring you the strings?" Indrajit asked.

Oritria hesitated.

"Do you know Salt Alley?" Fix asked.

"In the Dregs?" Chark growled.

"There's a well on Salt Alley," Fix said. "Can you meet us there at moonrise?"

"That's about six hours." Indrajit nodded. "It should be enough time."

"We'll be there," Oritria said. Chark pulled Fix's weapons from his bag and handed them over, and then he and Oritria disappeared into the shacks of the West Flats.

The fire in the Blind Surgeon was nearly out. "I owe Anaximander Skink two Imperials," Indrajit said.

"After what he attempted?" Fix snorted, and they headed back up toward the Spill.

"Why Salt Alley?" Indrajit asked.

"I don't trust them." Fix shrugged. "I don't want them to choose the location, and Salt Alley is . . . well, it's a place I know well. From my youth. We'll get there early and we'll watch."

Indrajit had difficulty focusing on his steps. Was he, after all and in spite of his efforts, about to find the apprentice Recital Thane he had come to Kish seeking? But their relationship had had such an inauspicious beginning—she had stolen documents from her father, and Indrajit had been hired to recover them.

And she had attacked him, at one point.

They hiked up into the Spill and quickly to the ashrama of Salish-Bozar. A row of Trivials in white tunics filled the street in front of the rectangular building, stopping passersby to talk.

A woman with chalky white skin and four stubby horns

on her forehead gripped Indrajit gently by the wrist. "Have you ever felt exploited?" she asked, her voice gravelly and seductive.

"Sometimes." Indrajit shrugged. "Mostly, I feel ignored."

The chalk-colored woman opened her mouth to say more, but Indrajit and Fix pushed on, into the ashrama. They found Meroit in his cell underground, sitting at a small easel and painting a large building. He swiveled his yellow, rootlike head to look at them as they approached.

"Look." He pointed at the painting.

"The Palace of Shadow and Joy." Indrajit shut the door behind himself.

"You know it?" the Trivial asked.

"The opera house," Fix said. "We've been there."

"Think of all the drama that happens inside." Meroit sighed.

"Quite boring, really," Fix said.

"Listen, Meroit," Indrajit said. "We're going to take four of your strings."

"What?" Meroit's skin was normally the color of a rotting potato, but it grew white. "No. No, you said you were going to give me four more. The four you had, you were going to give them to me."

"We're going to do this one way or the other," Indrajit said. "Are you going to force me to brutally rip away your disguise?"

"I don't know what you're talking about."

"Brutal it is," Fix said.

Indrajit pointed at the painting. "This painting right here. You're recording in it the data that you read on the string we brought in here, the one we let you touch. The one you read."

Meroit's mouth fell open.

"The information on the strings is not useless, and you know it. It contains data about the kelp farms of the Lord Archer, smuggled out by Fanchee double agents. And you know that, too."

"You don't have to tell anyone," Meroit said.

"The god would know," Fix said.

"But the Selfless wouldn't! And it would be all the same, I could finally become one of the Selfless! You know what a worthy goal that is, Fix. Remember when you were one of us, a Trivial like me!"

"You would cheat the god." Fix stared, as if by vision alone he could drill holes into Meroit's forehead.

"I don't know what the information is!" Meroit squeaked. "Yes, I know it comes from the kelp farms, but I don't know what it says! Yield, plantings, territory covered, price, strains, pests, labor—I have no idea! The patterns are abstract to me, they might as well be useless information!" Sweat poured down the conical head of the little Trivial.

"How do you get paid, Meroit?" Indrajit asked.

Meroit shut up again.

"Is coin slipped to you by the Hierophant Selfless?" Fix's voice was bitter. "Or are your paintings purchased for surprisingly large sums of money by strangers, who then transmit the information onward!"

"I sell the paintings!" Meroit squeaked. "And half of the proceeds go to the ashrama!"

"And the other half on wine, women, and song?" Indrajit guessed.

"Caveat number one." Fix's voice was flat and hard. "'No information that can be sold for money is useless.'"

Indrajit drew his sword. Meroit scooted away from his easel, pressing his back against the far wall.

"You wouldn't take the easy way," Indrajit said. "The easy way would have been that you pretended to be innocent but let us take four of your strings. Now you have to choose between the hard way, and the really hard way. I've drawn my sword in case you choose the really hard way."

Meroit plucked four strings from his collection and handed them over. Fix took them and tucked them into his kilt pocket.

"Will you return them?" the Trivial asked.

"Probably not," Indrajit said.

"Will you tell anyone?" Meroit pressed.

"As of now, I think it's in all our interests that this whole episode stays quiet." The hardness in Fix's voice and stance had softened. "If you recorded the knot sequence, or can reconstruct it, you may be able to talk the Selfless Bonk into letting you include these in your ten thousand useless pieces of information."

Meroit said nothing, and his lower lip trembled.

Indrajit and Fix left.

"I don't feel very good about that," Indrajit said. "If you're wondering."

"I don't feel so bad," Fix said. "If you're going to go around professing a god, eating at that god's table, sleeping in his ashrama, and seeking the company and praise of his devotees, you should live your life accordingly. You should at least try."

"You'd have been a good priest, Fix. Ironically." They

emerged into a street full of cold rain, and Indrajit took a deep breath. "Well, I did try to do it the easy way."

They crossed the Crooked Mile and took the street heading into the Dregs. Indrajit didn't recognize the jobbers on guard at the gate, but he thought they nodded at him with deference.

The Dregs was smaller than the Spill by quite a bit, but it had far more alleys. Every block seemed to have a single stone or brick building at its heart, five hovels of wood or clay nailed to its sides, and seven alleyways cutting through and around it on all sides. Salt Alley turned out to be a winding path that ran along the wall of a large brothel, between a gambling den and an ironmonger, past a small square surrounded on three sides by cramped temples to foreign gods, and then into the courtyard of a hostler's.

The well was in the plaza surrounded by temples.

"Who are these gods?" Indrajit asked.

"The one on the left is Aileric. Technically, he's a saint, not a god, so that means he isn't worshipped, he's revered. Or maybe contemplated."

"Karthing?"

"Ildarian. That's him, distributing food to the poor in that painting. You can tell he's a saint by the horns on his head."

"Ah, I assumed that was one of the races of man I didn't recognize. I know the Ildarians, they're practically neighbors."

"The one in the middle is Tlacepetl," Fix said.

"Xiba'albi," Indrajit said.

"Is he in the Epic?"

"He's a sorcerer who sends dead men marching over the mountains against his enemies."

"And, in fact, he is the Guide. Here in the Dregs, he leads the misfortunate through the mazes of their lives, but he also blazes the trail for the dead through the multiple underworlds. And sometimes, he brings them back."

"The one on the right is gruesome. Her face is a skull and her hair is snakes."

"Sharazat the Kind."

"What does she do?"

"She kills you."

"How is that kind?"

"She kills you when your life can never get better, at the moment from which your life takes a permanent turn for the worse. Her priestesses visit the sick to dispense the blessings of the goddess, but the goddess herself distributes death much more widely."

"The gods of mankind are many and strange," Indrajit said.

"Men are many and strange," Fix answered. "Where shall we hide?"

"The hostler's," Indrajit said. "I don't want to get in Aileric's way, and the other two frighten me. Let's see if we can get up on that wall."

They passed through the hostler's gate, and pulled up short at the sight of a powder priest of Thûl, pointing his musket at Indrajit's face. Except that, looking at the way the loose robes and scarves hung over the priest's frame, Indrajit was pretty certain she was a woman.

And she wore a tunic marking her as one of Gannon's Handlers.

As did the three Yuchaks with scimitars and shields who crowded in on Indrajit's and Fix's sides.

"Don't move," the Thûlian said, "and I won't shoot."

"I thought we were friends," Fix said. "Or basically even."

"Or at least at peace," Indrajit suggested.

One of the Yuchaks raised a horn and blew it; it was a wild sound, a noise that would have been at home on the steppes, but rang false and alien within the walls of the decadent old city.

Indrajit looked uneasily over his shoulder and saw the doors of all three temples open. Gannon's Handlers slowly came out: the Zalaptings; the Luzzazza with only three arms; the Sword Brother; others he didn't know.

Not the Grokonk, because Indrajit and Fix had killed them.

And there was Tall Gannon himself, the Ildarian-looking man who was the public face of the jobber company's true leader, a one-cubit-tall green midget.

"We're friends, Fix," Gannon said. "You're going to want to come into this stable now, and meet with some other friends."

"Most of my friends don't point muskets and swords at me," Fix said.

"You're right, it's time to end the misunderstandings." Gannon waved a hand and the powder priest lowered her weapon. The Handlers moving across the square blocked Indrajit and Fix from retreat, forcing them to follow Gannon into a stable to the right.

The stable had been emptied of horses and also mucked out, so that it stank considerably less than stables usually did. Oritria waited there, fists clenched and eyes narrowed. She stood beside Chark, who scratched at the earth floor of the stable with the talons of his feet and gnashed his teeth from time to time. There was a third person with them, too.

"My Lord Archer," Indrajit said.

Arda Ne'eku did not look like an archer. He was imposing, a tall, broadly built, violet-skinned man with a heavy jaw and a stubby nose. A bit like some artist had tried to render a Zalapting and had gotten every descriptor other than the color backward. He wore a wooden breastplate and a kilt of studded leather, both stained yellow.

"The Protagonists," the Lord Archer said. "Forgive me for forgetting your names."

"I'm Indrajit," Indrajit said, and Ne'eku raised a hand to stop him.

"I don't care," the Lord Archer said. "Listen, this whole thing has gone far enough, and I have called this meeting to put an end to it."

"I thought *we* arranged this meeting," Fix protested.

"I know you did." Ne'eku grinned, all his teeth visible past thick, rubbery lips. "Let me tell you a story. I learned from a loyal Fanchee servant, who was willing to betray his own family, that information about my sea-farming enterprises was being recorded and transmitted to parties unknown. Certain purchases in the Paper Sook suggested to me that the buyer of the information might be the Lord Chamberlain, my colleague and rival. I decided to test the hypothesis."

"This again," Indrajit said.

"I was fortunate enough to know that among the

Fanchee of my plantations was a lovelorn, idealistic, somewhat unhinged young poetess named Oritria, enamored of the idea of foreign travel, and song, and all the usual romantic nonsense. I knew of her infatuation with the Blaatshi Epic in particular. I also knew that Orem Thrush, the Lord Chamberlain, had a Blaatshi poet on his payroll, working in fact for his spymaster, head of the Lord Chamberlain's Ears. From there it was all obvious and easy."

"You told her to steal those strands," Fix said, "and said it would bring the Recital Thane here running."

"Which would prove my hypothesis that Orem Thrush was behind the espionage." Arda Ne'eku smiled.

"Why use the girl?" Indrajit asked. "Why not use . . . I don't know, Mote Gannon?"

"I didn't want to disturb the Fanchee," Ne'eku said. "I'd rather have them think there's a mad poetess running around, causing havoc, than know the truth. Those who are spying should continue to spy. Those who are loyal should stay blissfully unaware that they are being spied on—unless I choose to inform them."

"And if someone other than us showed up to investigate the issue?" Indrajit asked.

The Lord Archer sighed. "Well, you see, it was always going to end the same way for Oritria, no matter how right or wrong my hypothesis turned out to be."

"Don't kill her," Indrajit said.

Oritria jerked, as if making a break toward the door, and Chark grabbed her with all four arms.

Ne'eku chuckled. "No, nothing like that. But she can't go home. That would rather undermine the point. Fortunately, she doesn't want to go back to the plantation."

"I hate farming," Oritria said. "I want the heroic life."

"Farming's not so bad," Indrajit said. "It's honest work."

"I'll send her to join the household of a Bonean noble family that is friendly to me," Ne'eku said. "Chark will accompany her. She'll study poetry, and be treated well. Like a curiosity and perhaps like a pet, but well."

"But she won't study the Blaatshi Epic," Indrajit pointed out. "She was going to be my apprentice."

"Ah, yes. Well, that was never going to work out, either." Ne'eku smiled. "She's a little mad, you see. Did you know that she seduced the Yeziot Squite? Squite was a plantation worker; I have quite a few Yeziot who work for me. Their ability to breathe underwater is a real boon, not to mention their strong resemblance to the kelp itself. Good for hiding, they make excellent guards on a kelp plantation. I asked her to work with Chark—he's no jobber, he's on my permanent staff. She didn't quite trust him, so she seduced Squite."

"She does seem . . . very intense," Fix pointed out. "She tried to kill you. Her apprenticeship might have looked a lot like an imprisonment for you."

Indrajit shook his head. "But then I'm back where I started."

Ne'eku sighed. "Well, there was always only going to be one outcome for you, too."

Indrajit grabbed Vacho's hilt. "We've beaten the Handlers before."

In his peripheral vision, he saw Fix preparing to draw ax and falchion.

"We've never fought in a fair fight before," Tall Gannon growled. "Are you ready to try your luck now, fish-head?"

"No, no, no," the Lord Archer said. "Nothing like that. You Protagonists go home now."

"But . . . we caught you," Indrajit said.

"And *I* caught *you*," Ne'eku pointed out. "So you will tell Grit Wopal what you learned, and we will continue as before. And now Orem knows that I know he's spying, so maybe he'll be a little more circumspect. And I'll be a little more careful when I have truly sensitive information, so that Orem doesn't get it. And I'll be aware that he's trading on knowledge about my farming. And maybe, at some point in the future, when Orem catches one of my agents with unauthorized fingers in one of the Lord Chamberlain's pastries, he'll remember this day, and the peace between us will continue."

"Frozen hells," Indrajit said. "The Yeziot died. He died so that you could confirm what you were pretty sure you already knew."

"Don't forget," Fix threw in, "Grit Wopal also wanted to confirm what he thought he already knew."

"We broke a . . . a religious votary," Indrajit said. "He wasn't a very good one, but he was trying, in his way. We took away all his dignity. Our chambers were turned upside down. A ship was burned to the waterline. A tavern . . . the Blind Surgeon mostly burned up, too, with a whole lot of raki and wine in its basement. Oritria's getting exiled. All that for . . . what? Nothing? Just to keep the city's great families comfortable in their usual corrupt competition? Just to maintain the status quo? The rich get richer, and the poor get crushed?"

Arda Ne'eku nodded as he strode toward the stable's exit. "Welcome to Kish."

Good Boy

"Good boy," Fix said. He was the shorter of the two principals of the small jobber company known as the Protagonists. He was a muscular, bronze-skinned Kishi who carried an array of knives as well as a hatchet and a falchion hanging from his broad belt. He generally leaned on a spear, as he did now.

"Don't say that to him, he's not a dog." The poet Indrajit Twang was taller than his partner. He was similarly dressed in a kilt and broad belt, but his belt carried only the leaf-bladed sword he was so fond of. Indrajit's head was long and his face was divided in two by a bony nose ridge that pushed his eyes far out to the sides.

Fix shrugged. "He says it himself."

"I'm a Kyone. I *look* like a dog." Munahim wanted peace between his two bosses; his stomach curdled when they argued.

They argued a lot.

Fix shrugged. "And *you* look like a *fish*," he said to Indrajit.

Indrajit growled. "You see? You're just throwing fuel on the fire."

Munahim hunched down to hide from the poet's irritation. Since he was as tall as Indrajit, this didn't make him any less visible.

"There's no shame in your appearances," Fix said. "*I* look like an *ape*."

"Agh!" Indrajit clapped his hands to his ears. "Munahim, if you admit to looking like a dog again, I will let Fix here teach you how to read. I swear, by all your self-licking gods, that will ruin your life."

"I don't have self-licking gods," Munahim said mildly. "I could come with you."

"The only problem with that," Indrajit said, "is that you're terrible at lying."

Munahim hung his head. "Is lying so important?"

"Today it is," Indrajit told him. "We have to surprise this guy."

"So follow us at a distance," Fix said. "Bring your bow and that enormous sword and be prepared to intervene if something goes wrong."

"This should be simple," Indrajit added. "It's just an arrest. You're the backup, just in case."

Munahim nodded and his two bosses set out, crossing the mercantile bustle of the Spill and heading toward the stink of the Dregs. Munahim let them get a stone's throw ahead of him and then followed.

"I'm a Kyone," he said, mumbling to himself. "We don't have gods anymore. Not since we killed them." His long sword slapped comfortingly across his back and his quiver pressed snug against his thigh. Pushing his way through the sweaty crowd of the Crooked Mile, the longest street in the Spill, was easy with his long, muscular arms. He was a head taller than most men—other than men of the enormous races, of course, like the Luzzazza and the Grokonks and the sexless Gunds—and so was Indrajit, so following his bosses was an easy exercise in watching Indrajit's fishlike head bob along above the crowd.

Three camels burst from a courtyard into the street, bleating and kicking. The green-skinned, bug-eyed merchant who chased them cursed and struck at his beasts with a long-handled whisk. Munahim stopped while the animals were rounded up and then saw Indrajit's head again, now as a mere brownish-greenish dot.

He lengthened his stride to catch up.

He much preferred Kish to Ildarion, where he had spent several years trying to make a living. Ildarians were a tallish, pale, and rather bland race of men, and Ildarion was full of them. In Ildarion, Munahim stood out like a freak and collected constant stares. In Kish—decadent, old, rotten Kish—all thousand races of men mixed in a frothy, constant foam, and Munahim was far from the most unusual-looking fellow in almost any crowd.

Also, among the Protagonists, he was valued for his skills. Indrajit wished he were a better liar, but Munahim's bosses esteemed him as a tracker. Indrajit and Fix had hired him specifically for his sense of smell. The Ildarians had treated him as just a hired sword.

And as a Protagonist, he earned a share, not a wage. It made him feel much better about himself.

"Good boy," he said.

An arrest was a simple job for the Protagonists. Usually,

their tasks involved policing merchants or ferreting out spies. When they contracted privately, they might do anything from bodyguard work to rescuing kidnapped maidens, but the fact that they were marching to arrest someone meant that their employer was Orem Thrush, the Lord Chamberlain.

Who paid less than other clients, generally, but provided a lot of work, as well as a certain amount of protection. In a city of mercenaries, it was good to have a patron.

Munahim's ancestors had killed their gods when the gods had become too demanding. They had given too little food and no shelter, and so Kyone heroes of the time had risen up. They had slain the gods, shattering the pack, and forming a new pack, of only Kyones. Naturally, out of gratitude and prudence, Munahim and his people reverenced their victorious ancestors, remembering them with short invocations and averting their wrath with simple charms.

"Much better than having gods."

He could see Indrajit and Fix, and he could, just barely, smell them. Time and distance were not the complicating factors in smelling his bosses; the challenge was the roiling sea of mankind that bubbled around them, concealing the distinctive odor of each man beneath a mask of cinnamon, roasting fish, camel's dung, perfume, and a hundred other smells.

Two Kishi men slapped a wooden crate into the middle of the road just a few paces in front of Munahim, and a bawdy show sprang into being around them. Actors in masks and togas swarmed the low stand, and two bang-harp players plopped themselves right into Munahim's path.

This was a bit like the games his sire, Garuna, had played with him when he had been a boy on the King of Thunder Steppes, leaving young Munahim behind the pack and ordering him not to follow until the sun set. Garuna would then deliberately confuse the scent by provoking elk and deer into crossing the trail, or would march the pack in circles.

Munahim always found the pack.

Indrajit and Fix passed through the gate into the Dregs. The Dregs could not obviously be said to be the worst part of Kish, but only because it had serious competition. The Dregs' claim was that it was the zone with the most street-robbery, purse-cutting, throat-slitting, streetwalking, and daylight assault. The Lee probably offered more burglary, and the Spill more usury, but those were less colorful crimes.

Munahim gripped his bow tight. He was tempted to put an arrow to the string just in case, but that would draw attention.

From gate to gate, the passage across the Dregs was a brief march, *cutting the short corner*, as it was sometimes named by locals. To *cut the long corner* was to march the direct route across the Dregs from the Spill to the Crown. The Dregs proper, sometimes called the Filth, was the half of the Dregs with no gate, and which no casual traveler had any reason to enter, ever. Only desperation ever brought anyone into the Filth.

Munahim avoided looking toward the Filth. He spat on the packed earth to flush the thought of the place from his heart, and then Indrajit and Fix finished cutting the short corner, moving down the filthy slope of the Dregs, and passed through the gate into the East Flats.

Munahim didn't meet the gaze of the jobbers working the gate. He didn't recognize them, but there were far too many jobbers in Kish for him to know them all. Half of this crew were Xiba'albi with their characteristic obsidian-edged swords, which was in itself curious; Xiba'albi were rarely jobbers, and though Xiba'alb was not distant, its people were an uncommon sight in Kish. Tensions with the Ildarians, or perhaps the blandishments of the Free Cities, kept most Xiba'albi from making it this far.

Or perhaps they simply didn't like to travel.

There was a commotion on the other side of the gate. Munahim heard the clash of metal and thudding sounds. He edged forward, in case his bosses were falling afoul of violence, but two of the Xiba'albi stepped into his path before he could pass through, one raising a forbidding palm and the other hefting his stone-bladed club.

Munahim didn't have to stand on tiptoes to look over the jobbers' heads. He still couldn't make out the source of the noise, but saw tall Rover wagons, one painted with some kind of winged Ylakka on its side and another featuring an intricate pattern of interlocking snails. The images were different for every wagon; Munahim thought they represented the Rovers' ancestral totems, something closer to the spirits his own people reverenced than to the gods whose temples clung to the Spike at the top of Kish.

He tapped his booted foot impatiently on the packed earth, but less than a minute passed before a wordless whoop came from the other side of the gate. The Rover wagons continued onward, rolling south, and the Xiba'albi stepped aside.

Munahim jogged through, onto the East Flats.

This was one of Kish's three coast-hugging slums. All three were plagued by the stink of fish, sweat, and cheap beer. The hard-packed earth of the Dregs gave way to churned mud, sometimes alleviated by layers of straw strewn on top, or, around the least repulsive taverns and warehouses, sagging boardwalks.

The ground beneath Munahim's feet descended slightly, along roads running north, east, and south. The slope and his height gave him an excellent vantage point, but no matter how he strained, he could no longer see Indrajit's bobbing head.

His heart sank.

But no matter; he sniffed.

He caught the faint scent of both men. The trail was slightly confusing and he stalked in a tight circle as he tried to follow it, enduring the hard jostling of a scab-eyed Gund and the jeers of a pack of gray-skinned Visps. The scent of his bosses was mixed with the thick smell of rotting fish and with the smoke-and-spices smell that clung to every Rover wagon, but he eventually found a trail that emerged from the noxious cloud and ran east.

He took a deep breath, and felt fear fall away like a discarded cloak.

None too soon. "Get moving," one of the Xiba'albi growled.

Munahim growled back, without words, and loped down toward the water.

The smell of his bosses was faint. There was a light

breeze, now that he was outside the city's walls. Perhaps that was causing the dispersal of the scent. Or perhaps the waves of brine and fish smells were covering up the more subtle odors of musk and sweat. He quickened his pace; he'd be more comfortable once he had the other Protagonists in sight again.

The smell disappeared and he doubled back, walking in a small circle through a crowded intersection. Stooping to sniff at the ground didn't make the scent any clearer, but after a few spins around the well through a grumbling crowd, he caught a whiff off to the north and he followed it.

He didn't dare run. He was the backup force, the hidden reserve. It was a role he'd played before. His sense of smell let him stay out of sight so that forces watching for pursuit didn't see him until too late.

Only now it seemed that he might become separated from Indrajit and Fix by the sea breeze, and arrive when it was too late for the Protagonists.

Except, of course, that he was just the backup. He might not even be needed. Indrajit and Fix were good fighters, competent and clever, so they would probably be all right even if Munahim got lost along the way.

"You're not lost, though," he mumbled. "You're still on the trail. Good boy."

And then the scent was gone.

Munahim shook his head. He hadn't even passed an intersection. He stopped and looked at the buildings around him: a net weaver, a ropemaker, a seller of sailcloth, a shipwright, two leaning taverns, a leatherworker, three buildings that might be residences.

He traced his steps back until suddenly he smelled

Indrajit and Fix again. He sniffed at the air and prowled up and down the straw-stamped street, examining the scents of the doorways.

No sign that his bosses had gone into any of the buildings.

Had he turned wrong back at the last intersection? Was he following a phantom scent? He snorted, clearing his nostrils.

The street was packed with foot traffic and a small number of beasts of burden. Munahim crept back the other direction again, sniffing each person and animal. A stray Grokonk Third honked at him and a four-legged Shamb hissed, its tongue slithering over sharp yellow teeth.

Then Munahim sniffed the heavy leather sacks strapped across the back of a two-humped Drogger, and smelled his bosses.

The Drogger plodded at the end of a lead string held by a thin-bearded Zalapting. Munahim stepped past the good-natured beast and hoisted the little Zalapting into the air with one hand.

The Zalapting squealed. "I'll call the constables!"

"I'm on the job myself," Munahim said. "What have you got in the bags?"

"I don't have to show you!" The Zalapting's feet scrabbled at the air and found no purchase. "You don't have a warrant!"

"I can get one." Munahim wasn't actually sure how to go about that, but he thought Grit Wopal, the Lord Chamberlain's chief spy, could probably arrange it. Maybe the arrest papers Indrajit and Fix carried even included a warrant. Kyones had very simple ideas about law, which did not include written court orders. Mostly, for any important issue, the pack considered, the pack debated, and the pack came to a decision. Once in a while, a fight was necessary. "Do you want to come with me up to the Crown to sort it out?"

"Beans!" the Zalapting cried. "You can look, it's just beans!"

Munahim set the lavender-skinned man down and undid the clasps. Opening the sacks, he found that they were indeed full of dried beans.

Except that, in the top of one sack, atop white beans the size of his thumbnail, he found two kilts, a leaf-bladed broadsword, and a pile of other weapons: three knives, a hatchet, and a falchion.

He knew these weapons by sight as the ones Indrajit and Fix carried everywhere, except that Fix's spear was missing. And by smell, he knew instantly that he was looking at his bosses' kilts.

"Frozen hells," he muttered. His people didn't have any profanity, so he borrowed Indrajit's favorite curse.

"See?" the Zalapting snapped. "All I have is beans!"

Munahim dragged out the kilts and weapons. "Then these must belong to someone else."

The Zalapting paled to a pinkish shade. "Yes. Those aren't mine. I don't know where they came from."

Munahim could smell fear, and he smelled it now on the Zalapting. He wished he could smell lying, but he was pretty certain the little man was telling the truth. Without another word, he took his bosses' gear and marched back the way he'd come.

The pungent odor of the sweat-impregnated kilts, the tang of the metal, the thickness of the cured wood in the ax's handle, and the oiled leathers of the various scabbards made a heady bouquet. Twice Munahim plunged his face into the mass. Didn't he need to remind himself of what Indrajit and Fix smelled like?

But he was blocking other scents from reaching him. With an effort of will, he balled the fabric and weapons up and clenched the mass under his left arm, the right holding his bow.

He forced himself to think.

Indrajit and Fix might have been stripped of their gear and diverted at any point along the path he had walked. But he had last seen them at the gate connecting the Dregs to the East Flats, where he had been forced to stop and wait for the passage of Rover wagons. And there had been a commotion. And then, when Munahim had finally emerged from the gate, they had been gone.

He had followed their scent, but it seemed likely that he had followed the scent of their kilts, stuffed after the hubbub into the sack on the Drogger's back. Probably without the bean-merchant even knowing.

The commotion he had heard at the gate. Wasn't it likely that that had been the sound of the two senior Protagonists being beaten and spirited away?

He broke into a determined trot, all his accouterments clanking and swishing as he ran. Whom had Indrajit and Fix set out to arrest? If he knew that, Munahim could go to that person and seize him. Maybe make a trade.

Except that Indrajit and Fix had many enemies. Not to mention professional rivals. Gannon's Handlers might have seized them, or the secret agents of one of Orem Thrush's rivals, or the heirs of some merchant criminal they had previously arrested or overthrown.

And in any case, Munahim didn't know whom they sought to capture.

He stopped just below the gate. The jobbers had changed.

He now wished he had noticed the uniforms on the other jobbers; he closed his eyes and tried to remember, but he was much better at noticing and remembering smells than visual images. His memory conjured up the raw-meat smell of Xiba'albi, and even the specific odors of the man with the raised palm and his companion hefting his club, but not the color of what they had been wearing.

But these men were not Xiba'albi. Ukelings, Karthing, and Yuchaks, with a single scaly, four-legged Shamb. Munahim made himself look and notice the black tunics they wore. They were a jobber company, and not in the permanent employ of one of the great families.

He approached a mailed Karthing with two long swords strapped to his back. The man stood slightly apart from the rest of the company, leaning against the wall and chewing dip weed as he watched the crowd.

"Excuse me." Munahim tried his most polite words. "Could you please tell me who were the jobbers here earlier today?"

The Karthing shook his blond, shaggy head. "No other jobbers here today. Just us."

"There were Xiba'albi," Munahim said mildly.

The Karthing bellied forward, pushing into Munahim

with his torso like a bull and knocking him back. "Wrong. We were here all day. Bjurn's Bruisers, under contract with the Lord Archer."

"There's been a mistake," Munahim said.

"Yes." The Karthing nodded. "And you made it. And if you keep insisting, that will be your second mistake. I'm Bjurn, and I don't let people make three mistakes."

Munahim hesitated. Bjurn was lying, and they both knew it. Did that mean that he had conspired with whoever had seized Indrajit and Fix?

But he didn't have to have conspired very much. Maybe all he did was order his men to stand aside for a short time while the Xiba'albi watched the gate. That was a very ordinary sort of corruption in Kish, looking the other way.

But however much the Bruisers had conspired, that definitely meant that the Xiba'albi had been where they hadn't belonged.

Munahim scratched his nose to hide the fact that he was sniffing. The trail he wanted wasn't here.

"My mistake," he said. "You're right. I was thinking of a different gate."

Bjurn grunted. Munahim drooped his shoulders, trying to look unthreatening, and walked through the gate. The Ukelings and Karthings jeered at him, but the Yuchaks stared warily; like the Ildarians, their lands bordered on the King of Thunder Steppes, and they may have had dealings with Kyones before.

Munahim slouched and dropped his chin.

On the far side of the gate, he smelled the trail he was seeking: Xiba'albi, half a dozen of them, crossing the

Dregs and marching up into the Crown. This was the third leg of the main thoroughfares traversing the Dregs, and was sometimes referred to as *walking it straight*. Munahim walked it straight now, climbing steeply from the lowest, most rotting section of Kish through its most heavily defended gate (by a wall of blue Luzzazza holding spears and glaring), and into the part of the city where all the most wealthy and noble citizens lived.

The Crown. He smelled fruit and blossoms and delicate perfumes, and no sign of Indrajit and Fix. He felt a hard, cold knot in the pit of his stomach, but at least he could still smell the Xiba'albi.

He followed the trail.

They marched due west to the edge of the Spike. There, under the looming knuckled rock and the lurching temples of the city's five gods, they turned left. They stuck strictly to the boulevards, the widest streets where the traffic flow was heavy but the channel of traffic was unimpeded. Munahim had moved fast and was moving fast still, and yet he didn't see them. Had they let him move through the gate and then immediately turned and raced this direction? They must have, to have gained such a head start.

And then, suddenly, the smell of them grew stronger.

Munahim stopped and sniffed. He stood near the mouth of an alley, a narrow, cobbled lane that separated two large brick palaces from each other. Beyond the alley, a flower vendor shouted names and prices beside his green-varnished wooden cart. Across the street, another cart-merchant hawked tea. Two ladies in togas carrying parasols stood and sipped wooden cups of the steaming beverage.

The Xiba'albi were waiting in the alleyway. Munahim was certain of it. He could smell the wood of their clubs and hear their breathing.

Had they detected him yet, or were they waiting for him to pass in front of the alley?

He backed away, watching the alley's mouth. A blue-uniformed doorman in front of the palace aimed a kick at him, but Munahim bit back a growl and kept moving until he had reached the edge of the building.

Then he slipped around behind. Crossing a fountained plaza at the back of the building, he crept up the far end of the alleyway, toward six Xiba'albi at the mouth. The Xiba'albi crouched together, staring out into the street. They were obscured from view on the boulevard by a pile of garbage timbers, and they held their stone-edged clubs in their hands, muttering to one another.

Munahim looked for a place to hide. There were balconies that would have afforded an excellent view of the alley and the plaza both, but they were on the second story or higher, and he was a very ordinary climber. But all along the base of a pink-brick-built palace clustered a thick hedge of bushes with broad, dark green leaves and white berries. He pushed himself into the hedge and waited.

Long minutes passed. Had he made the wrong choice? Was there a better scent he should be following, a scent that was now growing cold because he had wasted his time pursuing these Xiba'albi thugs?

But they did seem to be waiting for him.

His skin began to itch, where it was pressed against the leaves. He sniffed, but the smell of the bushes told him nothing.

And then he saw that the skin of his arms and shoulders, where the leaves pressed against it, was red and raw. Blistering, in fact.

Blister-berry bush.

"Frozen hells," he muttered.

And then the Xiba'albi moved.

Munahim froze. The itch immediately seemed to swell ten times in effect. He felt as if his arms and shoulders were aflame. He wanted to burst from the hedge, rush forward, and hurl himself into the fountain, scratching his skin furiously.

He held still, and managed not to whimper.

Four of the Xiba'albi stood and walked in his direction. Munahim held his breath and prepared to draw an arrow, but they passed him, entering into the mouth of another alleyway and disappearing.

He took a deep breath. "Good boy."

The other two settled back into their vigil. Munahim waited a few minutes and then crept from the bush. His skin was patched red and raw, and wept in several places from open, blistering sores. Resisting the urge to leap into the water, he peered after the four departed Xiba'albi; they had gone, disappeared around a bend in the little side street they had taken.

He laid down Indrajit's and Fix's gear and his own bow beside the fountain, drew his long sword, and crept toward the two men lying in wait.

The sword could be used with either one hand or two. Munahim was no sword brother, but years of fighting for Ildarian marcher barons against other Ildarians, Yuchak men's societies, Karthing raiding parties, and the wagon nomads of the Steppes had made him a proficient swordsman, maybe even a good one.

He didn't want to kill the men, though. He wanted them to lead him to Indrajit and Fix.

He crept up with silent steps. Both men faced away from him. The nearer squatted and leaned forward, poised almost on all fours to stay low and in the shadow. The farther stood, pressing himself against the pink-brick wall.

Munahim slammed a boot down on the back of the croucher's neck, to pin him to the cobbles. The man squealed. At the same time, Munahim raised his long sword, gripped in both hands and prepared to slash downward. It was a pose he had found terrible and frightening when he had seen other warriors adopt it.

"Hold!" he snarled.

But the Xiba'albi did not hold.

The man beneath Munahim's boot rolled sideways. He gasped for breath and choked, but his move was abrupt and swift. Munahim had put his weight on the Xiba'albi's neck to pin him, and the sudden removal of his footing sent Munahim stumbling back.

Instead of gripping his sword heroically in two hands, preparing to slash, he now found himself juggling and trying to catch it.

The second Xiba'albi leaped forward, swinging his club.

Xiba'albi clubs were made of a heavy hard wood that didn't grow in Kish itself, sometimes called ironwood. The wood alone made the clubs lethal, and this club was swung with all the force of a leaping Ylakka. Staggering backward, Munahim lurched out of the way of the first blow, and then the second.

And then he backed into a brick wall.

Beyond his attacker, he saw the other Xiba'albi rise to his feet, drawing stone knives. The warrior with the club bent his elbow, preparing to swing again.

But the wall gathered the force of Munahim's motion and hurled him back the other way. He missed his catch, and winced at the loud rattle his sword made, clanging onto the cobblestones. But abruptly, he was within the Xiba'albi warrior's guard and moving forward.

He seized the man by the wrist and spun him. He was taller and stronger, and he used his body as a lever, winging the short fighter and his club into a circle.

The Xiba'albi with two knives ran forward, and directly into the stone blades of his friend's club.

Munahim released his grip. The knife-wielder dropped to his knees, suddenly headless. The man with the club spun once more in a circle as he tried to catch his balance; Munahim used the spare moments to regain his own poise, scoop, and pick up his blade.

The dead man's head thudded to the cobblestones behind him.

Beyond the Xiba'albi, on the boulevard, someone was screaming. Constables—which was to say, whichever jobbers currently had the contract for law and order in the Crown—would arrive shortly.

"Tell me where Indrajit and Fix are," Munahim said. "Otherwise, I cannot let you live."

It was a direct statement and without deceit, befitting a Kyone. The Xiba'albi roared and charged.

The Xiba'albi club was hard and sharp, but Munahim's sword was longer, and so were his arms. He stabbed the Xiba'albi through his neck, then wiped the blood off his blade on the man's kilt and ran.

He sheathed his sword, snatched up his bow and his bosses' things from beside the fountain, and charged down the alleyway after the other four Xiba'albi jobbers.

Four men left a strong enough scent to follow at a dead run, but he didn't want to run into an ambush, so Munahim sprinted only for a minute and then stopped to look around. He wasn't being followed, that he could see, so he continued his pursuit.

He exited the Crown into the Lee. The Lee was home to racetracks and high-end brothels and wealthy merchants, and Munahim expected the tracks of the Xiba'albi to rush right through and out into the Caravanserai, the giant, permanent tent-city beyond Kish's south wall.

Instead, the scent-trail of the men turned left, and then abruptly ended at the door of a brick rectangle. The rectangle sat at one corner of a rough triangle, smashed up against a two-story-tall inn that leaned outward in three directions, and a building split between a clothier and a cooper. The other two buildings had windows and balconies, but the rectangle was a solid mass like a single brick, the only distinguishing feature of which was a slightly recessed door.

In the street beside the rectangle waited three Rover wagons. Two Rover men stood between the first two wagons, slowly playing some card game on the foremost wagon's tailboard. Each man had two pistols tucked into the sash at his waist. Munahim was unsure exactly how the pistols worked, except that there was part on top of them that had to be moved before firing, a part that made a loud click. Sometimes they required more preparation than that, but sometimes they didn't, and it was safest to assume the latter.

Each wagon was pulled by a single horse. The images on the sides of two of the vehicles looked familiar; Munahim squinted and tried to think. Snails and a winged lizard. His memory was tied to smells more than images, and he couldn't quite remember his connection with these vehicles.

But then the wind shifted and the scent of the wagons came to his nostrils. He had smelled this mixture of smoke, spice, sweat, and dung before, in the gate between the Dregs and the East Flats.

These wagons had blocked him off from following Indrajit and Fix.

He sniffed, concentrated, and found a faint odor of his two bosses on the wagons. They weren't in the wagons now, but they had been.

He faded back around the corner, pressing himself against the wall behind a cart piled high with lychee fruit. He tried to think. Someone had seized Indrajit and Fix. Whoever it was had expected that Indrajit and Fix would have backup and had twice taken steps to stop that backup from coming to the rescue: with the blocked gate, and then with the Xiba'albi rear guard.

Did those enemies know that the backup consisted only of Munahim? They might, because they had marked out a false trail with his bosses' kilts, as if they expected someone with a good sense of smell to be following. On the other hand, they might have been marking out that trail to mislead someone following with more magical powers, a witch or a scryer of some kind.

And if they had thought that Munahim alone was following, wouldn't they have simply seized him at the gate, too?

On balance, it seemed likely that the kidnappers expected a rescue attempt, but didn't know that Munahim was the whole reserve force.

Munahim considered plans, and found that he hated all of them.

He could climb onto the roof of the building, but there was no guarantee that there was an entrance into the building from above, and every likelihood of attracting attention in the climb.

He could find a privy or a basement nearby and try to let himself into the labyrinth that ran beneath the city, but it would take him time to find such an entrance, and there was no guarantee that the rectangular building could be accessed from below.

He entertained the idea of lighting the door on fire, but if there were an exit underground, the kidnappers would likely simply take it and flee. Also, the Rovers might simply put the fire out. Also, if the fire did burn the building down, it might kill Indrajit and Fix in the process.

He had no reinforcements to summon; he *was* the reinforcements.

Munahim dropped his bundle at the street corner and bought a lamp with a clipped quarter of an Imperial. The vendor, a portly Zalapting, ostentatiously filled the clay vessel with oil before handing it over. Munahim shifted his bow into his left hand to take the lamp in his right. "Will you light this?"

"Are you crazy?" The Zalapting gestured at the empty sky. "It's broad daylight!"

Munahim nodded. "Please."

He brushed past a pair of Pelthites and a Kishi beggar rounding the corner again. The Rovers didn't even look up until Munahim hurled his lamp against the side of the first wagon. The clay shattered, the oil splashed across the brightly painted wood, and the men cursed.

By the time they turned their attention to Munahim, he had an arrow to the string of his bow and was aiming at the larger of the two men.

"I hope you will get in your wagons and leave," Munahim said. "Put the fire out, go away, mind your own business. I will only kill you if I have to."

The big Rover snarled, his thick mustachios curling up in hatred, and tried to draw his pistols. Munahim shot him in the heart and he dropped.

The second Rover raised his hands. "There's a bucket of sand inside the wagon," he said. "Let me put the fire out, and then I'll leave."

"Pistols on the ground first," Munahim said.

The Rover laid down his guns. He climbed onto the tailboard and disappeared into the back of the wagon.

Click.

Munahim loosed his second arrow, shooting through the wagon's wall. He heard a cry, but he shot again and again, jogging to his right as he shot until he could see into the open back of the wagon. The Rover had three arrows in his chest, but was still trying feebly to raise a long musket to fire at Munahim.

Munahim pulled the Rover's feet out from under him. He crashed to the boards, and Munahim tossed the musket across the street.

Startled passersby looked once, then averted their eyes and fled.

Welcome to Kish, Indrajit would say. *Mind your own business*.

"I told you to leave," Munahim said.

Munahim gathered his bosses' things and his own bow into a bundle and tucked it under his left arm, holding his sword in his right hand. The door into the building was heavy, and it didn't budge when he tested it; barred. There was no peephole. He could apply fire, or hack away at the wood with Fix's ax, but either method would take much more time than he felt he had.

He knocked politely.

The door opened. He was surprised that it did, but he was poised and prepared, so when the door pulled in a crack and a pale face appeared in the gap, he kicked the door in.

Alarmed shouts rose from behind the door. Munahim threw his bundle into the open doorway and charged in.

The pale man drew a dagger. Munahim slapped it out of his grip with an open hand and then bashed the man in his forehead, knocking him to the ground. The man tried once more to rise, and Munahim stomped on his chest.

That left him still and whimpering.

Munahim was in a small cloakroom. Boots stood in pairs on the floor, and heavy gloves lay in pairs on a shelf, and canvas smocks hung from pegs. The air was thick with motes and the floor was covered with grains that felt metallic under the soles of his boots and added crunch to every step.

Two steps brought him over the body of the pale man to the cloakroom exit. A Gund loomed up in the doorway. It was a civilized Gund, with four of its six eyes gouged out to prevent the madness that overcame the wild members of the tribe. It grabbed for Munahim's throat with its two hands, while the thicket of insectoid limbs sprouting from its shoulders reached out and groped toward him, too.

Munahim lowered his shoulder and slammed it into the Gund's sternum. The Gund stumbled backward, but its bug-legs snapped sideways and caught the doorframe, keeping it from falling. The Gund grabbed Munahim by the throat, cutting off all his air instantly. With its enormous muscles, it would crush Munahim's larynx in seconds.

Munahim bit the Gund's wrist, hard.

The Gund pulled his hand back, and Munahim bit harder. He felt his teeth rip through sinew and vein, plowing ragged furrows across the bone itself. The Gund tore itself free, shrieking. It grabbed its left wrist with its right hand.

Munahim still feared the bug-legs. He stepped in toward the Gund again, swinging his long sword in a two-handed sweep that sliced off all the legs on one side. Yellow pools of lamplight and deep brown shadows dappled the Gund as it staggered away, and Munahim threw back his head to howl.

It was an instinctive move, not a planned one. But in

the boxy space he entered now, he heard his own war cry echo with great satisfaction.

The building was a single large room. Scaffolding created a mezzanine floor of thick timbers, and heavy tables lay in two parallel lines across the floor. The thick air made Munahim's eyes water and his nose twitch, but he could still see Indrajit and Fix lying side by side on a table, perfectly still, naked, surrounded by a knot of men.

Two Xiba'albi warriors charged.

Munahim leaped left, putting himself out of reach of one of the warriors, and keeping both warriors between himself and the rest of the men. He slid his long sword neatly under the arm of the Xiba'albi, between two ribs. The man sank without launching a blow, bloody foam erupting from his lips. When the second Xiba'albi bent his path to try to return and attack Munahim, Munahim snarled at him; the Xiba'albi dropped his club and fled.

Munahim surveyed the scene, his sword up in a two-handed guard position. The Gund lay weeping in the corner. The blood that flowed from its wounds was soaked up by the crystal grains on the floor, which swelled as they drank the liquid. Two Xiba'albi warriors remained, clubs trembling slightly in their grip, and behind them stood a dark-skinned man in a long silk tunic and silk pants. The toes of his shoes curled upward and back, and he wore a short cylindrical cap. He held an open vial in one hand.

The Xiba'albi and the man in silk all stood on the near side of the long tables.

"I am from Togu," the man in silk said.

"Are you a sorcerer?" Munahim snarled.

"Yes."

"Are you deadly and evil?" Munahim growled, snapping his teeth for emphasis.

"I am deadly. Evil is a matter of—"

"Are you prepared to die?" Munahim roared.

"Beware, dog-man," the sorcerer murmured. He raised the vial over his head as if he might throw it.

"I am a Kyone," Munahim said. "I do not lie and I do not fear."

"You are not the first Kyone I have known."

"Your Rovers are dead," Munahim continued, "and their wagons burn. Your Xiba'albi are dead, or broken in spirit."

"You do not frighten me," the sorcerer insisted.

The two remaining Xiba'albi drifted slightly apart, creating an open avenue between Munahim and the sorcerer. Indrajit stirred, raising one arm slightly.

So Munahim's bosses still lived.

"Your Gund is crippled," he said. "Do you think your little glass bottle is going to stop me?"

"What do you want?" the sorcerer asked. "Money?"

"I am a Kyone," Munahim said. "I do not negotiate."

"So you want a *lot* of money, then."

"I cannot be bought."

"You have no sense of humor," the sorcerer grumbled. "Don't mistake that for heroism."

Munahim roared and leaped at the nearest of the two remaining Xiba'albi. He didn't raise his club fast enough and took a deep slashing wound across the forearm. He staggered away sideways, and he and the other Xiba'albi raced for the exit, nearly knocking one another over in the process.

Munahim raised his sword back into guard position. "Ha-ha."

The sorcerer still held his bottle high. Did it contain an acid? A poison? Some sort of Druvash transformation magic? Munahim was loath to turn his back on the sorcerer, but Indrajit was just beginning to stir and Fix still lay catatonic.

"You're not the hero," the sorcerer said. "You are interfering with justice."

"And you are interfering with my pack."

"Leave now," the sorcerer said, "or this potion will kill you all."

Munahim threw his sword. It was not a throw that might impale the sorcerer; the weapon was far too big for that. But neither was it an awkward, spinning throw. The weapon was balanced and Munahim was experienced and he hurled it with sudden force, sending the pommel straight at the sorcerer's face.

The sorcerer ducked, and Munahim leaped forward.

The long sword flew across the room, over the tables, missing the sorcerer. The sorcerer dropped into a crouch, and Munahim grabbed his wrist with both hands, slamming his forearm against the table.

The sorcerer screamed, and Munahim grabbed the bottle. Thick smoke rose from the vial's glass, which was hot to the touch. Munahim ripped the bottle free and threw it into the corner of the room.

BOOM!

Smoke and flame erupted from the vial. The Gund bellowed—had Munahim hit it with the sorcerer's potion? Munahim felt all the air drawn from his lungs in one whoosh and he fell down, choking.

Blackness.

Munahim opened his eyes. His ears rang and his lungs hurt. He smelled smoke and heard coughing.

He stood and found himself still inside the rectangular building. Indrajit was lowering himself from the table to the floor, coughing fiercely. Fix was attempting to roll over, but having difficulty moving.

He could now see that both his bosses were bruised and bloodied.

And Munahim realized that he was coughing, too.

His eyes watered from the smoke. Scaffolding along two of the walls burned.

The Gund lay scorched and still. The sorcerer was gone.

"Munahim." Indrajit retched, trying to talk. "Who was that?"

"I don't know." Munahim found and sheathed his sword and then grabbed Fix. Breathing was difficult, but he managed to sling the smallest Protagonist over his shoulder. "They said they wanted justice."

"They meant revenge," Indrajit said.

Munahim grunted.

"Believe it or not," Indrajit said, "that dandy from Togu isn't even the man we set out to arrest. We still have work to do."

Munahim nodded. "I'm ready."

"My sword?" Indrajit asked. "And, uh, kilt?"

"By the door." Munahim pointed.

Indrajit nodded and limped toward the exit. "Good boy," he said. "Good boy."

The Politics of Wizards

⦃ Chapter One ⦄

"I need you to rescue my son," the Wixit said.

Indrajit nodded. He sat drinking lang-lang berry tea, sweetened with lemon and honey and thickened with cream, with his partner Fix. The tea shop was owned by the Wixit, whose name was Hector Thoat. Outside, the late-morning sun spilled down on the traffic along the Crooked Mile, steadily building toward noon. Over the scent of his tea, Indrajit smelled camel and Drogger musk.

Indrajit and Fix sat on stools around an upended barrel serving as a table. On a third stool, Thoat stood. Like all Wixits, Thoat was two cubits tall and furry. Indrajit and Fix wore kilts alone, given the summer heat. Their weapons hung on their belts, other than Fix's spear, which leaned against the wall. The Wixit was naked and unarmed.

"We sort of specialize in princesses," Indrajit said.

"We do not specialize," Fix said. "We don't specialize in princesses, or in kidnappings, or in anything else. We're broadly skilled generalists. And we're happy to rescue your son."

"We can certainly extend our activities to recover the stray prince." Indrajit smiled.

"He wasn't kidnapped," Thoat said.

Fix frowned. "Then why does he need rescuing?"

"He won't come home," Thoat said.

"Ah." Indrajit folded his arms across his chest. "This is a different matter."

"A different kettle of fish, you might say?" Fix smiled mildly.

"Fish have nothing to do with it," Indrajit said.

"Hmm."

"I can pay." Thoat unslung a small purse from around his shoulder and poured coins onto the barrel. Without counting, Indrajit estimated that the pile contained some thirty Imperials. Bright, yellow, gold coins. "Consider this a deposit," Thoat said. "A retainer. Call it half, shall we?"

"A child who has run away is a lot like a child who has been kidnapped," Fix said. "In some ways, the dangers are greater."

"A child who has been kidnapped usually has a roof over his head," Indrajit pointed out. "And food."

Out of the corner of his wide peripheral vision, he saw Munahim's back. The third member of the jobber company, and in theory the only one who wasn't a partner, stood with his back to the tea shop's window. Indrajit saw his long sword slung there, beside the bow that snapped into a taut copper bracket. He saw the black fur along the back of Munahim's head, and his doglike ears as he looked from side to side, standing watch.

Munahim hadn't been paid in weeks. None of them had eaten for two days.

"Do you ever take biscuits with your tea?" he asked Thoat. "Or a nice bit of cake?"

"Sometimes." The Wixit wasn't taking the hint. "When you say 'child,' though ... you understand that my son is an adult."

"Finding and reconnecting with a long-lost loved one can be a trial," Fix said. "Sometimes it's as fraught with challenges as rescuing a kidnap victim."

"I know exactly where to find him," Thoat said.

"Perhaps you'd better explain exactly where your son is," Indrajit suggested.

"Also, help us understand why you can't just get him yourself," Fix added.

"He's at the Collegium Arcanum," Thoat said.

Indrajit fell silent.

Fix sipped his tea.

"Maybe you'd like a little cake," Thoat said.

Indrajit frowned. The Collegium Arcanum was a secret organization of wizards. Did it train new wizards? Did it regulate magicians? Did it serve as a cartel of wizardry to keep the prices of magic high? No one could say for certain, because there was no building such as, for instance, the Hall of Charters occupied, where a person could make inquiries. The Collegium was completely secret.

If it existed at all.

The Wixit brought two little seed cakes on a silver tray.

"How do you know he's at the Collegium?" Fix asked.

Indrajit ate a cake quickly, before Thoat could take it back. He had a terrible feeling that the job offer was going to evaporate and the coins on the barrelhead disappear, but at least if he had a nice little cake, he wouldn't have come here completely in vain.

It wasn't a nice little cake. It was heavy and oily and he gagged choking it down, but Indrajit was hungry. He ate the cake and tried not to stare at its mate, sitting innocently on the tray.

"He asked for his inheritance early." Thoat scratched his belly and shifted from paw to paw. "We'd quarreled, you see."

"Go on," Fix said.

"Did he spend it on magical tools?" Indrajit asked. "A ceremonial dagger? An alembic?"

"Are those in the Epic?" Fix asked.

Indrajit shrugged. "Common knowledge."

"No," Thoat admitted. "Or maybe. I don't know what he spent it on."

"Perhaps the Collegium requires the payment of tuition," Indrajit said. "Or a licensing fee."

"The point is that he cut me off," Thoat said, "so I wouldn't know where he went. But he'd always dreamed of becoming a sorcerer."

"Any particular kind of sorcery?" Indrajit asked.

"The magical kind," Thoat said.

"So no preference for, say, necromancy? Or scrying?"

"Druvash spellcraft?" Fix piled on. "Temple thaumaturgy? Bonean stargazing? Yuchak spiritwalking? Alchemy?"

"He liked the idea of getting rich," Thoat said. "He despised the tea business. He never could tell his mint from his marmalade, and perhaps I drove the boy too far."

"So he took the money," Indrajit said, "and he always dreamed of being a wizard, and can we help you find him now. Is that about the size of it?" He eyed the pile of coins, afraid it was still liable to slip away. "Is there nothing more to go on?"

"I received a note last night." Thoat cleared his throat.

"Sounds fishy," Fix said.

As an act of revenge, Indrajit ate the second cake. He instantly regretted it; his hunger had sufficiently sauced the first cake to make it palatable, but wasn't enough to make the second go down. It lodged in his throat like a beam turned sideways. He sucked at his tea, trying to sluice it down his gullet.

"It wasn't signed," Thoat added.

Indrajit swallowed. The cake stayed where it was, an awkward lump, but he could breathe and talk around it. "That's the problem with writing. If I say something to you face-to-face, you know who spoke the words. You can look at me and judge whether I'm trustworthy and whether I know what I'm talking about. But a written message— pfagh! You have no idea who made it, when it's not signed."

"Even when it is signed you might not know," Fix admitted. "Signatures can be faked."

"I don't know why you hold with the practice." Indrajit snorted.

"So I was saying," Thoat continued, "I received an unsigned note. It was there, on the floor behind the door. Someone had pushed it under the door in the night."

He held up a scrap of parchment, offering it to Indrajit. Fix reached over and took the note.

"What's on the back, there?" Indrajit asked.

Fix examined both sides of the scrap. "There's a note on one side. On the other, more writing, but it's in a language I can't identify. And it accompanies drawings."

"Art?" Indrajit asked.

"It looks more like technical schematics," Fix said.

"I couldn't read that side, either," Thoat admitted. "Maybe your Kyone could give it a look."

"Munahim is an honest Kyone, unsullied by the greasy art of ciphering letters." Indrajit sniffed.

Thoat looked dismayed.

"Don't worry," Fix said. "Someone is just reusing a scrap of parchment. Parchment and paper and all other writing materials are expensive, so a prudent writer never lets any go to waste."

Indrajit snorted. "A prudent *writer*."

"The note," Thoat said.

Fix held up the scrap of parchment. "It's written in ink."

"What else would it be written in?" the Wixit asked.

"There are many possibilities," Fix said. "Paint. Pencil lead."

"Charcoal," Indrajit suggested, embarrassed that the idea occurred to him.

"The fact that the note is written in ink suggests that the writer is preparing the note in a study or a library," Fix reasoned. "No one carries a bottle of ink with him to, say, the wharf, or to the market."

Thoat nodded, eyes gleaming. "Yes, I see."

"'I know your son, Adakles,'" Fix read. "'He is a disciple of the third degree in the Collegium Arcanum.'"

"What's a disciple of the third degree?" Thoat asked.

"I don't know anything about the Collegium's structure, as such," Fix said.

"But a disciple is a student," Indrajit added. "It probably just means a student. Since he just started, presumably the 'third degree' part means he's just a beginner."

Thoat nodded. "Adakles would be new there. It makes sense that he would be a lesser disciple."

"Unless he used his inheritance to buy a greater station," Indrajit pointed. "So . . . he didn't do that."

"Is that how it works among the Blaatshi?" Fix asked. "Would an aspiring apprentice Recital Thane, for instance, give the old Recital Thane a large cash gift to be advanced in her studies?"

"I'm not an old Recital Thane," Indrajit said.

"But you know what I mean."

"And no, a Recital Thane would do no such thing. In the first instance, an apprentice doesn't buy his position, he is admitted to it by the Recital Thane after careful examination." Indrajit shuddered at the thought of bribery. "Indeed, he's adopted by the old . . . by the *incumbent* Recital Thane as a son."

"The family of the apprentice never gives gifts?" Fix asked.

"The family might give gifts," Indrajit acknowledged, "but only because these would ultimately be bestowed on the apprentice himself, in the form of food, lodging, tuition, and other kinds of support. But a Blaatshi could never buy rank as a Recital Thane with money or any other payment. A Recital Thane must above all be able to perform, so it's imperative that apprentices and thanes alike have actual ability, that they meet all requisite standards."

"Yes, yes," Thoat said. "A disciple of the third degree. But the other part is more important."

Fix looked back at the parchment. "'Adakles has failed his examination to become a disciple of the second degree. He believes that he will be allowed to continue as a disciple, and retake his examination. He is mistaken. Tomorrow, he'll be killed.'"

"Not technically kidnapped," Indrajit said. "But now we see what the problem actually is."

Thoast shifted from paw to paw and made a whimpering noise in his throat. "It's not finished yet."

"'I cannot tell him,'" Fix read, "'so I am telling you. I will meet you at sunset tonight at Headless Took. I will wear red so that you recognize me. I'll tell you where to find your son tonight so you can bring him home. You will want to have prepared a fast way to get him out of the city.'"

"That wasn't a note," Indrajit said, "it was a novel."

Fix frowned.

"I don't even know where Headless Took is." Thoat's voice was strained and squeaky.

"Headless Took is a statue in the Crown," Indrajit said. "Some people worship it as a god."

Fix shook his head. "Some people believe that the Took represents the spirit that descended upon Imperial Kish's emperors upon coronation. And that the statue's headlessness represents . . . or relates to . . . the fact that Kish is no longer an empire. And that the reappearance of the statue's head will be a prophetic sign of the imminent return of the empire."

"Reappearance?" Indrajit asked. "Does that mean that the head used to be there and disappeared? As in, vanished? Not knocked off the statue, but just ceased to be visible?"

Fix shrugged. "I'm more troubled by the fact that this would-be helper is unable to notify Adakles himself. What does that mean?"

Indrajit shook his head. "They're separated somehow. In a different order or dormitory. Surely the person will tell us tonight."

"Does that mean you'll help?" Thoat asked.

Indrajit scooped the coins off the barrelhead. "Yes."

◦〈 Chapter Two 〉◦

"It isn't fair that the Kyone has a better sense of smell and also a better sense of hearing than other men," Indrajit said. "The gods should have been more evenhanded in distributing their gifts."

"Well, a fish rots from the head," Fix said.

"What does that mean?"

"Kish is rotten," Fix explained. "Perhaps her gods are rotten, too."

Indrajit and Fix crouched atop the ceiling of a tailor's shop, two stories above a narrow, stone-cobbled lane. The lane ended in a square, in the center of which stood a statue of a headless man, dressed in a toga and wearing rings on all its fingers. Water bubbled up in a spring between the Headless Took's feet, and the circular trough that caught the water was filled with flower petals.

Thoat stood beside the statue, a basket of flowers slung over one arm. He picked petals from the flowers and dropped them one by one into the water, murmuring what might have been prayers. Other pilgrims also threw flowers, or circumambulated about the statue, or did both.

Munahim sat on a stone bench in the corner of the square, slumped back against the wall and feigning sleep as he kept an eye on the Wixit. Indrajit had urged the Kyone to hold a wineskin and pretend to be drunk, but Munahim had protested that he wasn't drunk. Wasn't much of a drinker, in fact. Never had been.

"Now that I think of it," Indrajit said, "the gods have notably deprived the Kyone of the ability to lie. Sight and hearing notwithstanding, I find it astonishing that the race still exists."

"Not everyone is a liar," Fix said.

"On the King of Thunder Steppes, perhaps not. In Kish . . . ?"

"In Kish, even the epic poets become liars."

"We do not become liars," Indrajit said. "We have always been the best liars."

"I thought the purpose of the Blaatshi Epic was to tell important truths," Fix said.

"Not just important truths. *The* important truths. *All* of them. The high and holy calling of a Blaatshi Recital Thane is to tell all the truths a young Blaatshi must know to understand his place in the universe and to pass successfully through life. Which he does, in a very important sense, by lying."

"Look." Fix pointed.

A Fanchee woman wearing a red toga cautiously entered the square from the far side. She was green-skinned, with the mass of noodle-like appendages hanging off the lower half of her face that gave all Fanchee, male and female alike, a vaguely bearded appearance.

"Fanchee shouldn't wear red," Indrajit said. "Their skin is such an uncompromising shade of green, it really doesn't match."

"The assault on the eye does make for an effective signal," Fix pointed out.

Munahim was doing an admirable job of restraining himself. The guileless Kyone no doubt wanted to leap up and seize the Fanchee immediately, but he lay still with his mouth hanging slightly open, tongue lolling to one side. His role was just to observe, to hear what was said, and then, if necessary, to track.

Thoat dumped the flowers on the street and bounded to meet the Fanchee.

"He doesn't look very pious," Indrajit said.

"Let us hope the Took doesn't punish him."

The Wixit shook as he confronted the green woman. He leaped up and down, his arms waving. Indrajit could hear squeaking sounds, but couldn't make out any words.

Then Thoat sprang up onto the Fanchee. His jaws were splayed wide, much wider than Indrajit would have guessed possible, and his teeth were large enough to be visible from here. He gripped the front of the Fanchee's toga and sank his teeth into her neck.

Except then the Wixit fell to the ground. He shuddered violently, back arching, and foam boiled up from his throat.

Munahim leaped to his feet and drew his long sword in a single fluid motion. Cripplingly honest or not, the dog-headed man was an impressive, even a terrifying, sight. He bore down on the Fanchee, snarling and raising his weapon.

Then Munahim pitched forward and crashed to the cobblestones.

The other worshippers of the Headless Took scattered, melting into alleys and rushing away into the Crown. The Fanchee stripped off her toga, but when she did, she was no longer Fanchee. Or a woman. Her body took on a gelatinous, translucent appearance and an arachnoid shape. Six legs instead of eight, but she—it—resembled a see-through spider more than anything else.

Indrajit drew his famous sword Vacho, the Voice of Lightning.

Fix held him by the arm. "Wait."

"While it kills Munahim?"

"I don't think it will."

The spider rolled Thoat toward itself with two limbs and then raised Thoat bodily, placing the Wixit on its back. Thoat remained there, arms and legs to his side, as if he had become sticky.

Then the translucent spider took up the toga again and skittered toward an exiting alley. As it reached the alley mouth, its steps became longer and taller and its body rose, and then it was bipedal and whitish and sprouted insectoid arms out its shoulders. It raised the red fabric of the toga and threw it over its own shoulders, concealing Thoat from sight, just as it disappeared from the square.

"Munahim!" Indrajit cried.

They had climbed to this rooftop by a lead pipe on the other side of the building, but Indrajit had no time for that now. Sheathing his sword again, he lowered himself over the side of the building. Stretched to his full height, his feet were only eight or nine cubits from the ground. He dropped, rolled, and then rushed to the Kyone.

Munahim lay facedown, not breathing. Indrajit flipped him over and found his face thick with a transparent slime that covered his eyes and filled his mouth. Indrajit was about to wipe the slime off with his hand, but stopped. Had the slime knocked Munahim unconscious? Had the same slime reduced Thoat to a shuddering wreck?

He pulled up the edge of Munahim's tunic and wiped the Kyone's face. Munahim still didn't breathe.

Fix rushed to Indrajit's side.

"He's dead," Indrajit said.

"Not yet, he isn't." Fix knelt and pounded the Kyone in the chest with his joined hands.

Munahim coughed, spat up translucent goo, and inhaled.

"What was that thing?" Fix asked.

"A Fanchee." Munahim retched, fighting to get breath.

"It was no Fanchee." Fix shook his head. "It was bigger. And it had too many arms."

"It started as a Fanchee," Indrajit said. "Then it became an invisible spider."

"It was never invisible," Fix said.

"Practically." Indrajit stood, scanning the alleyways. "In dim light, we wouldn't have seen it. Then it knocked out two men, transformed itself into a Gund, and walked away. Obviously, it was a sorcerer."

"You can tell because of its sorcerous power of walking away," Fix said.

"Unscathed!" Indrajit snapped. "It was attacked by two men, and walked away unscathed!"

Munahim dragged himself to his feet, leaning on Fix. "I never attacked it. Not for lack of trying, but I charged and then . . . that's all I remember." He stooped to pick up his long sword.

"We have to follow it," Indrajit said, "sorcerer or no. On top of the threat to young Adakles, now Thoat is kidnapped. Still not a princess, but close enough."

"Given that Thoat has the money, he *is* the princess." Fix gripped Munahim by the elbow. "Can you track the creature?"

Munahim sniffed, making a thick, clotted, snorting

sound. "One moment," he said. "You might want to look away."

Indrajit failed to take the warning. Munahim leaned forward, hands on his knees, and exhaled sharply through his nose. Streams of thick goo spattered on the cobblestones and then the Kyone staggered to the fountain, immersing his face in the water and scrubbing himself vigorously with both hands.

"Welcome to Kish," Indrajit said. "Everyone here is disgusting."

"Except the Recital Thane," Fix countered. "He's disgust*ed*."

"A man must have standards," Indrajit said. "Or a poet must, in any case."

Munahim shook himself, splashing water all over the two senior Protagonists. Then he leaned forward, sniffing at the cobblestones. "There's no Fanchee smell here."

"There was no Fanchee," Fix said.

"There was," Indrajit said. "But it changed shape."

"I can smell the Wixit," Munahim said. "He also smells strongly of lang-lang berry tea."

"That will do," Indrajit said. "Follow the spoor of Thoat."

"And if there's a consistent accompanying musk," Fix suggested, "remember it. That's the monster."

"Sorcerer," Indrajit said. "Who may also have the power of changing scents."

Munahim loped quickly down one of the alleys. Indrajit held his head high as he followed, worried they'd round the corner and bump into the Gund-Fanchee-spider-sorcerer at a pace that wouldn't permit Indrajit to arm himself. But as Munahim turned the corner and emerged from the alley, they entered the Avenue of Golden Chariots, and plunged into heavy traffic.

Chariots passed them. So did rickshaws and carts and carriages. A lord in lacquered wooden armor rode at the head of a train of ladies in silk, all mounted on horses. Three Zalaptings led a string of Droggers against the flow of traffic, cursing as the clumsy, six-legged beasts bumped their shoulders against wagons and knocked a pot-bellied man in green to the stones. Tea and coffee shops shouted prices to lure in customers—here in the Crown, Kish's most expensive quarter, they sometimes shouted *higher* prices as lures. A princeling with a feather in his felt cap led a group of seven other children on some sort of hunt, ducking and dodging among the many vehicles and pointing their fingers like weapons. A choir of initiates of Salish-Bozar the White, god of useless knowledge, stood against one wall, reciting a long series of facts. "Fresh shipment today!" a jeweler cried. "Pearls from Malik! Very rare, exclusive to Zump's!"

Munahim slowed. He took more deliberate steps now, and at each step he sniffed several times.

"Focus," Fix murmured. "Find the smell of Thoat."

"We should have asked for more money up front," Indrajit said. "We could have eaten, at least."

"One of us ate two cakes," Fix said mildly.

"They were terrible, though."

"Was the whole thing about Adakles a trick?" Fix asked.

"You mean, was the letter faked? Did the sender really just want to kidnap Thoat?"

"Perhaps Adakles didn't join the Collegium Arcanum at all." Fix shrugged. "Maybe he signed on as a rower on a trading vessel and now he's diving for pearls off Malik."

"You see now?" Indrajit shook his head. "You can't trust a written document."

Munahim stopped in front of a door. "Thoat and the sour-smelling thing that has him went into this doorway."

Indrajit examined the entrance. It didn't look . . . right, somehow. The wall was the side of a large palace, one of the big palaces dotting the Crown. Often, they belonged to a single family, or to a guild, and they could comprise an entire city block, as this one seemed to. Generally, the palaces had no windows on the ground floor, and one or two entrances at most. The entrances were usually big enough to drive a wagon into, and gave access to an inner courtyard, and passed the office of a doorman or some similar official.

This was a simple wooden door, just big enough to accommodate a stooping Gund.

"Tradesman's entrance?" Fix suggested.

"Wouldn't it be on a side street, then?" Indrajit gestured at a passing carriage, and at a tea vendor across the street who carried his supply of piping-hot drink in a tank strapped to his back. "Rather than the avenue?"

"You're saying magicians are strange." Fix tried the handle of the door and it turned.

"Do we draw our weapons?" Munahim asked.

Indrajit looked at Fix and they both shrugged.

"Be prepared to draw," Fix said. He opened the door and entered.

Munahim followed.

Indrajit scanned the street once, looking for any sign of pursuit or observation, and he saw none. Gripping the hilt of Vacho with one hand, he stepped through the doorway.

⊰ Chapter Three ⊱

"Do you smell the sea?" Munahim asked.

Indrajit sniffed; to his astonishment, he did.

He spun about, reaching to push open again the door through which he'd entered . . . but the door was gone. His hand on Vacho's hilt became a white-knuckled claw.

"I still smell the Wixit," Munahim said.

Indrajit breathed deeply through his nostrils, trying to slow his racing heart. Turning slowly, he examined the room. Its four walls were of white plaster and bare of any decoration. Heavy timbers served as roof-beams. One tall, wide window, with a sill at waist height, admitted warm yellow light and the cry of seabirds. In another was sunk a doorway with a green-painted wooden door.

A man in a red robe stood in the back of the room. His hands were behind his back, the top of his pate was bald, and white hair was tied in a queue at the base of his skull. Indrajit realized with a start that he wasn't standing on the floor, but above it, floating a good cubit off the worn wooden planks. The floating man was short; so short that, even with the extra cubit provided by his levitation, he was shorter than any of the three Protagonists.

"The Gund sorcerer," Indrajit muttered.

"No," Munahim said.

"Where is the Gund?" Fix asked. "Or spider, or whatever?"

"I've lost the scent." The Kyone bent his knees and flexed his hands open and shut.

"Everyone, stay calm." Indrajit spoke for his benefit as much as for Munahim's. "What about this fellow?"

"Hail," the short man in red said.

"Hail?" Fix frowned.

"It's an archaic greeting," Indrajit said. "It means hello."

"I know what it means," Fix said. "Who says it anymore?"

"He's not here," Munahim said.

Indrajit felt a shiver run up his spine.

Munahim shook his head. "This little man in red. He's not here."

Indrajit growled and drew Vacho. He took one long step forward and swung his blade through the man in red. It passed through without slowing.

The little man smiled. "I said, 'Hail.'"

"What game is this?" Fix asked.

"It's sorcery, of course." Indrajit shook his head.

"Hmm."

"Are you ready to talk now?" the man in red asked. "Have you exorcised your preference for violence by your attack on me? Have you, as we say of children, got the wiggles out?"

"Condescending midget," Indrajit said.

"Child," the levitating man replied.

"Stop," Fix said. "Everyone."

Indrajit sniffed.

"You." Fix pointed at the little man. "What's your name?"

"Theophilus Bolt," the little man said. "Recondite second class."

"A magician," Munahim said.

"You Kyones are delightful," Bolt said. "Even your thinking lies on the surface of your skin."

"Our client has been kidnapped," Indrajit said. "A Wixit named Thoat. He came through here not moments ago."

"He came through here." Bolt shrugged.

"You can help us," Indrajit said. "Or you can suffer the consequences."

"Will you chop me in half again?" the magician asked.

"Let's not focus on the consequences right now," Fix suggested. "Maybe tell us what you want."

Indrajit stepped to the window, turning his back on the magician and gritting his teeth. Below the window, an exterior wall dropped three stories to a slope covered with black stones the size of a man's head. The slope groaned and shuddered its way down a blue sea.

Too blue. The wrong color entirely.

"We're not in Kish anymore," he said.

At the edge of the water stood a tower. A rectangular window faced Indrajit, and through the window he could make out a man in red.

"You're not in Kish anymore," the magician said.

"You magicians," Fix said. "You wear your thinking on your skin."

The magician harrumphed. "Do you want to learn how to get your friend back or not?"

"Not our friend," Fix said. "Our client. But yes."

"A client is much more important than a friend." Indrajit gestured subtly to Munahim to join him at the window. "A client gives you money."

The gesture was too subtle. Munahim stood where he was.

"The Collegium needs your help," Bolt said.

"Really?" Indrajit folded his arms across his chest. "Our swords go right through you with no effect, and you need *our* help?"

"You might say that a duke has no need of paupers," Bolt said.

"And yet the duke will hire paupers to dig ditches," Fix said. "Yes, yes."

"I was going to say, work in his garden." Bolt sniffed.

Indrajit gestured to Munahim again. This time, the Kyone saw him. He nodded, and began slowly drifting across the room.

"Imagine that the ditches are in the garden," Fix said. "We understand the metaphor."

"We resent it a little," Indrajit said, "but we know what you mean."

"A tyrant has seized control of the Collegium," Bolt said. "This is a grave threat to all of Kish."

"A tyrant?" Fix said. "Does the tyrant have a name?"

"He is called Megistos," Bolt said, "but that is only a title. He is Lord Dean of the Collegium Arcanum. None of us has ever seen him."

"Is it a grave threat to this place?" Indrajit asked. "By the color of the sea, I'll go ahead and guess that we're in the south. Hith, maybe? Easha?"

A flash of surprise crossed the little magician's face. Indrajit managed not to laugh in triumph.

"How do you know that?" Bolt asked.

Munahim had reached Indrajit and stood by the window, looking out.

"*A race across the south lands, where warm breezes*

blow," Indrajit recited. "*The fair and sunny south lands, where the seas are green.*"

"The seas are not green," Bolt objected.

"But close," Indrajit said. "Green*ish.*"

"It's poetry," Fix said. "It lacks precision."

"But pleases the ladies," Indrajit said. "You should try it."

"The ladies like financial security," Fix argued.

"You could be a financially secure poet."

"I'm not sure such a thing exists."

"Usurpation of control of the Collegium Arcanum is, as it happens, a threat to the entire world," Bolt said. "Including . . . including whatever place we are in now. The Collegium Arcanum is the greatest single power on Earth, and should not be in the hands of a madman."

While the little magician spoke, Indrajit murmured a few quick words and indicated what he was thinking to Munahim. The Kyone nodded.

"Well, that is a fine kettle of fish," Fix said.

"You're grasping at straws," Indrajit said. "Really scraping the bottom of the barrel."

"*You're* the poet." Fix shrugged. "I'm a fish out of water."

"Your friend *does* look like a fish." Bolt grinned. "You're mocking him, right?"

Munahim removed his bow from its copper bracket and eased an arrow from his quiver. He stood at the far corner of the window. If Bolt had perceptive senses centered on the phantasm as he could from his physical body, then Munahim was in the extreme edge of his peripheral vision, or even beyond it.

"I can't resist." Fix shrugged. "I fish in troubled waters."

"Be careful." Bolt chortled. "He'll give you the fish eye."

"Thanks," Indrajit said. "Maybe you could teach everyone we meet to mock me. Maybe you could teach the Lord Chamberlain to call me a fish."

"He already does," Fix said.

Bolt was laughing so hard that he clutched his belly and leaned back. Indrajit wished he felt that much mirth about anything.

"Now," he said.

Munahim put the arrow to the string, raised his bow, pulled the string back, and released, in one motion that was so fast that it was almost invisible. The arrow leaped across the space between the two windows, passing inside the tower at the edge of the water.

The arrow reappeared within the room where they all stood, for just a moment, as it flashed past the magician. Bolt leaped and disappeared, and Indrajit heard a loud snap and a clatter.

Now Fix laughed.

"Oh my," Indrajit said. "The gardeners have a longbow."

"That was rude." Bolt's voice spoke, but he did not appear.

"We're not going to shoot you," Indrajit said. "But I think it's good that you know that we *can* shoot you. Feels fairer, don't you think?"

Bolt reappeared where he had been before. He arrived foot-first, as if stepping into the space.

"We have other spells," Bolt said.

"We have other arrows," Indrajit told him. "And swords, and an ax, and more."

"So tell us how we get our client back," Fix said. "If you've forgotten, that's a Wixit named Thoat."

"We'll give him to you," Bolt said. "Once you do a little job for us."

"This is always how it goes for us," Indrajit said. "Why is that? Is it because we're a small jobber company? The whole world feels entitled to harass us?"

"Maybe you're just sensitive," Fix said.

"No, we're constantly being forced into jobs." Indrajit snorted. "We were set up by the Holy-Pot to be killed in that risk-merchantry scheme. That scholar in the Hall of Guesses tried to murder us. The Lord Archer and the Lord Chamberlain, Orem Thrush himself, marched us around like pawns in the game between themselves over . . . what was it?"

"Kelp farming."

"Kelp farming. And now this. Doesn't it feel personal?"

"When you put it that way," Fix said, "it starts to."

"Maybe we should change our name to the Patsies. If that's the work we're going to get, we may as well advertise for it."

"I like the Protagonists," Munahim said.

"You could walk away," Bolt said.

"We could," Indrajit agreed. "We could start by shooting you. It would take Munahim all of two seconds to end your life."

"I am impervious to your weapons," Bolt said.

"If you were impervious to our weapons," Fix said, "you'd be standing here with us, instead of projecting your image from that room to this."

"You don't know that," Bolt said.

"It's a pretty good guess, though," Indrajit said. "Then we'd just march north for . . . I don't know, a few weeks."

"The Epic doesn't spell out how many leagues Hith is distant?" Fix asked.

"The Epic is not a map." Indrajit cleared his throat. "So, we need Thoat back, and his son. Before we do anything."

"I can't do that." Bolt's hands trembled. "What hold would we have on you?"

"Our word," Munahim said.

"There you go," Indrajit said. "Our word. The word of a Kyone, whose thoughts are all worn openly on his skin. But all three of us, we match our words to our deeds. It's one of the great lessons of the Epic."

"Thank you," Fix said.

Bolt hesitated. "I can give you the boy now. The father later."

Indrajit looked to Fix and shrugged. Fix nodded.

"Sounds good," Indrajit said. "What's the one little job? Something to do with the high lord mage tyrant of the Collegium Arcanum, I suppose?"

"You're to kill him," Bolt said.

Several long seconds of silence passed.

"You were telling us just moments ago," Indrajit said slowly, "how this tyrant Megistos wields more power than anyone else in the world."

"I'm not sure that's exactly what I said." Bolt cleared his throat. "But, more or less, yes. He's very powerful."

"And you're going to send us. And why won't he just kill us out of hand?" Fix asked.

"He might," Bolt admitted. "But he probably won't."

"Because we're the gardeners," Indrajit said. "Except that we're not *his* gardeners. We're a trio of jobbers he's never heard of."

"Hopefully," Munahim said.

"Hopefully," Indrajit agreed. "But you've got a plan."

"You're going to steal an artifact," Bolt said. "From a Hithite summoner."

"Oh, good, a summoner," Fix said.

"You are doing so at our instruction," Bolt continued. "You will return the artifact to Kish, where you will deliver it to the Collegium. There, you will kill the tyrant."

"Easy," Fix said.

"At least there's a plan." Munahim shrugged.

"What artifact are we going to steal?" Indrajit asked.

"A bottle imp," Bolt said. "A devil bound into a flask."

"The conjurer has hidden it in a secret room in his fortress, naturally," Fix said.

"He wears it on a chain around his neck." Bolt pointed. "Out the door, you will find a path. The path leads to the conjurer's home. His name is Adunummú. Halfway up the path, you will find young Adakles, son of Thoat. He will have two things you will need on your quest. One is a Dagger of Slaying, which will kill a magician with the slightest scratch. The other is a Band of Distance. Pressed into a door, it turns an ordinary doorway into a portal that will bring you back to Kish, and the Collegium."

"Anything else we need to know?" Fix asked.

"Young Adakles may be a bit disoriented," Bolt said.

"I'm glad it's not just me." Indrajit opened the green door.

᛭ Chapter Four ᛭

A rocky path led from the door of the plaster-walled room along the top of a rocky cliff. Standing in the open air, the view greatly resembled what Indrajit had seen through the window—turquoise sea, black rocks, and clear sky— except that there was no second tower.

"Can we have a policy of not working for or against magicians?" Indrajit asked.

"We'd lose work," Fix said. "Also, are we going to ask every potential client to warranty he or she is not a magician? Post a bond to cover damages resulting from breach?"

"I leave that end to you," Indrajit grumbled.

"There are Yuchak tribes who kill magicians on sight," Munahim said. "I had never understood why."

"We don't have to like this," Fix said. "We just have to get Adakles, then keep him safe while we rob the conjurer and then assassinate Megistos."

"Whose real name and location we don't know," Indrajit pointed out.

"They'll obviously have to tell us something," Fix said.

"Who is 'they'?" Indrajit asked. "I don't know a 'they.' I know a Bolt. Technically, I know the *image* of Bolt."

"Bolt and his allies," Fix said. "But we worry about that when we get to it. One thing at a time."

Indrajit sighed. "One thing at a time. We kill the conjurer."

"No. We find Adakles."

"There he is." Munahim pointed.

"Wait . . ." Indrajit shook his head. "Are you saying your eyesight is better than mine, too?"

"Well, you do have eyes on the sides of your head," Fix said.

"That's an exaggeration. They're a little farther apart than yours."

"A lot farther."

"I can smell Wixit," Munahim said. "I'm pointing where I think the Wixit is."

They lengthened their stride to reach that point. Indrajit took perverse pleasure in taking the longest possible steps; Munahim, who was his height, kept up without complaint, but Fix was forced to jog.

Which he also did, annoyingly, without complaint.

The Wixit stood right where the path veered away from the top of the cliff and turned inland. The soil here was dark and powdery, resembling charcoal that had been pounded into dust. The path was crowded on either side by ferns and by plants Indrajit didn't know, with spiny branches and broad, shield-shaped leaves.

The Wixit shifted from one hind paw slowly to the other and back as the Protagonists approached. In his front paws, he held a black velvet sack streaked with gray dust. His jaw worked and his mouth opened and shut several times, but no words came out.

"Adakles?" Indrajit asked.

The Wixit stared.

"Son of Thoat?" Indrajit tried to clarify.

Still no answer.

"He's under a spell," Indrajit said.

"He might just be an idiot," Munahim suggested.

"Or drugged," Fix added.

Fix took the sack from Adakles and showed the contents. The first item was a flat bar of material that looked like brass but had the flexibility of leather. Spikes and clamps protruded from one side of it. The other thing in the bag was a long, narrow dagger in a sheath. Fix took it in his hands and slid the dagger from its sheath a finger's width, revealing a blue steel blade.

"Don't touch it," Indrajit said.

"Do you really believe in a Dagger of Slaying?" Fix asked.

"It doesn't have to actually be a Dagger of Slaying," Indrajit said, "whatever that may be. It could just have venom on the blade."

"Good point." Fix strapped the weapon to his belt alongside his other knives, and hung the bag beside them.

"What do we do with the Wixit?" Munahim asked. "If he holds this still all the time, we could just hide him in the bushes and come back for him."

"Except that he might start moving," Fix pointed out. "Or get eaten by thylacodons."

"Or we might not be able to return this way," Indrajit said.

"I'll carry him," Munahim said.

Indrajit stepped between the Kyone and the Wixit. He scooped Adakles up and slung him over a shoulder. "No, I think I want you to have full use of your hands. We need your sword or bow in any fight we get into."

"What about *your* sword?" Munahim asked.

"Indrajit's preferred weapon is his mouth."

"Yes," Indrajit agreed. "Yes, it is."

He led the way, Fix following and Munahim bringing up the rear. The trail climbed slowly up a rolling prairie of ash. As the sea fell behind them, the air dried out and the plants changed. Ferns and shield-leafed bushes gave way to brush-tipped grasses whose smell reminded Indrajit of roasted lamb. With jelly and mint. And hot, fresh-baked rolls.

"I'm hungry," he announced.

"Don't eat the Wixit," Fix said.

"Wait here a moment." Munahim waded out into the herb-smelling ground cover, bent to pluck something from the ground, and returned with a handful of gray grasses that curled into a hook at the tip.

"Horngrass." Fix took one and popped it between his teeth, chewing to release the juice that took the edge off hunger and produced a very mild sense of well-being. "How did you see it?"

"He smelled it." Indrajit took some too.

"Of course, I did."

They chewed grass and marched in silence briefly.

"I do sort of want to eat the Wixit, though," Indrajit said.

The vegetation ended abruptly, leaving a flat circle of ashy earth that was packed hard and surrounded with a thin border of white stones. More white stones curled across and through the circular space, producing patterns whose complexity grew as Indrajit looked at them. Spirals and loops of the same proportion repeated themselves again and again at smaller and smaller scale, and Indrajit slid his gaze along them. A curl descended into a curl and again into another curl and—

"Wake up!" Munahim punched Indrajit in the arm.

Indrajit staggered, almost dropped Adakles, and recovered his balance. He saw Fix, rubbing his own bicep and scowling.

"What happened?" Indrajit asked.

"You two both fell asleep, standing still," Munahim said.

"Ensorcelled?" Indrajit asked.

"Maybe," Munahim said. "I don't know. You were staring at the white stones."

Indrajit turned to look at the pattern again, but pulled himself away. "The stones? The pattern? But why should that put us to sleep? And if that is its sorcery, why didn't it work on you, when you looked at the pattern?"

"I didn't look at the pattern." Munahim shrugged. "It doesn't smell like anything."

"Keep your eyes off the ground," Fix warned. Then he pointed into the center of the pattern of white stones, where a black tower rose from the ash. "Look!"

At the tower's base, ragged holes were bored into its structure. They opened instantly into darkness, and were crusted with greenish lichen around their edges. Indrajit followed Fix's indication, and saw thylacodons emerging from the caves.

Their heads were long and triangular, their jaws heavy, their teeth ragged and yellow. Each was the size of a man, though they moved like a man hunched over and crawling. Their bodies were nearly spherical, with long limbs, all covered by brownish fur streaked gray by ash. Their noses and long, curling tails were all obscenely pink, and also looked wet.

"They think we're ensorcelled," Fix said. "This is the tower's defense. It hypnotizes anyone who approaches, and then the thylacodons eat them."

Indrajit pointed. "There is the gate. See how a path rises from the field of stones to that portcullis?"

"If we move, will we startle the thylacodons?" Fix asked. "Perhaps they'll simply flee, once they realize that we won't be passive, easily destroyed prey."

"Perhaps we should kill them," Indrajit suggested. "And see if we can enter the tower through their warren."

"Agreed," Fix said.

Munahim took his bow into hand and set to work. He shot the thylacodons in back first, most dropping dead with a single arrow in the neck or chest, though a couple of the beasts took a second arrow to dispatch them. Indrajit laid Adakles on the ground, and when the foremost thylacodons realized that their packmates had been killed and charged forward in a panicked frenzy, swords and axes made quick work of them.

"The bodies?" Indrajit asked.

"You two go to the cave openings," Munahim suggested. "Take the Wixit with you. Don't look at the stone patterns, and I will deal with the bodies."

Indrajit looked up and toward the tower as he walked, to keep himself from being entrapped again, though the thylacodons had in their death throes often disturbed the stone pattern. Perhaps the charm had been broken now? But he had no wish to make the experiment.

They reached the cave mouths and sheltered at the

edge of the light, swords in their hands. The caves stank of filth and beast and rot, and even within paces of the openings, Indrajit saw the skulls and rib cages of men, flesh long gnawed away.

Munahim recovered most of his arrows, and then dragged the dead thylacodons to the base of the tower. One twitched slightly, and he dispatched it definitively with a sword blow to the neck. He dragged their corpses one at a time into the darkness.

"The smell of this tunnel puts me off," Indrajit said.

"Smell is our friend," Munahim said. "Smell and hearing."

"Are you saying there are no living beasts in the warren?" Fix asked.

Munahim nodded. "I'm saying that's probably the case."

Fix fashioned a torch from a dry thigh bone. He wrapped one end thoroughly in bleached fabric and then lit it with a flint and steel from the pocket of his kilt. Holding the torch raised over his head, he led the way into the caves.

The bones littering the tunnels' floors didn't all belong to men. Indrajit picked his path forward through the bones of animals as well, and even bones that were likely the bones of children—though skulls and rib cages of that size might belong to, say, a Wixit, or something of a similar size.

They found heaped garbage and nests made of grasses and branches. Fix fed more strips of clothing they found to his torch as they progressed, wrapping new flammable layers into the fire as the old ones were consumed.

"Someone is ahead of us," Munahim murmured. "Not a thylacodon, but a man."

"Keep your eyes open," Fix said.

The tunnel floors were irregular at first, strewn with rocks and occasionally interrupted by stalagmites. As they moved forward, the floor become smooth, and the natural walls gave way to large stones and mortar. Finally, they entered a circular chamber with stairs wrapping their way around the walls and ascending up and out of sight; Indrajit couldn't see the roof or an exit.

In the center of the chamber, a pillar rose from the floor. It was stone, and covered with obscured characters carved or scratched into its surface. Pairs of iron brackets were sunk into the stone encircling the column, and chains hung from the brackets, ending in iron manacles.

"Here," Munahim whispered.

Indrajit looked around. "Where?"

"I'm right here!" a voice called, apparently from the column. Indrajit drew his sword and circled the pillar slowly. On its far side, both hands manacled, feet on the floor, knees slightly bent, hung a man. He had lavender-colored skin and thick fur clumped about his shoulders, and he wore only a loincloth.

He spoke, and as the mouth in his face opened and closed to form and express the words, a second mouth set into his chest opened and closed in exactly the same patterns. "Thank you for rescuing me," he said in a soft voice. "I am Adunummu the Conjurer."

⸙ Chapter Five ⸕

"Why have the thylacodons not eaten you?" Fix asked.

"Shhh," Adunummu said. "Keep your voice down, please."

"Munahim, watch the stairs," Indrajit murmured. "It's a good question, though, Conjurer." He set Adakles on his feet. The Wixit stood and stared at the wall.

"You call me Conjurer and yet you wonder why the beasts have not eaten me?" Adunummu tsked. "You doubt my ability to conjure."

"And yet you are chained to a post," Fix said. "If you are so great a magician as to defend yourself against a pack of beasts that regularly kills men, how do you remain chained? Why not simply conjure yourself back to the upper floors of the tower?"

"Are you a conjurer yourself, then, to express such an opinion so confidently?" Adunummu asked.

Fix shrugged. "Every guild wants to obfuscate its own subject matter, to keep out the outsiders and protect revenues. Notaries, apothecaries, risk-merchants, all of them. Why should magicians be any different?"

Adunummu cocked his head to one side and curled his lip into a reckless smile. "Because it's magic!"

Fix shrugged.

"Who will come down the stairs?" Indrajit asked. "If you don't fear the thylacodons, what is it that gives you pause?"

321

"Perhaps you would care to unchain me, so that we may discuss these questions better."

"As it happens," Indrajit said, "I think we'll leave you chained. At least for the minute."

"You are cruel."

"You are evading the question."

"My apprentice has chained me here," Adunummu said.

"You have an apprentice?" Fix asked. "Not a disciple-ordinary, third class?"

"I am trying to minimize my use of jargon," Adunummu said. "As you seem to prefer."

"You fear your apprentice," Indrajit said. "That seems rather a perversion of the idea of apprenticeship."

"Yes." Adunummu nodded. "He is indeed a pervert."

"Tell us more about this apprentice," Indrajit said. "I am attempting to find a good apprentice myself. Perhaps your example of a bad apprenticeship will teach me valuable lessons."

"Also," Fix added, "tell us how you came to be chained. Which may have something to do with your apprentice."

"It does, it does." Adunummu nodded vigorously. "But perhaps you would care to give me some food first, to strengthen my storytelling capacities. Or perhaps you have water to spare."

"We don't have either," Indrajit said. "We were walking on the streets of Kish only this morning, certainly not planning to come to Hith at all. We were not prepared with provisions."

"Kish!" Adunummu's eyes opened wide. "That's a million leagues from here!"

"I gather that mathematics and geography are not part of the curriculum of the Collegium," Fix said.

"What?"

"It isn't a million leagues from Kish to Hith," Fix explained. "I doubt it's a thousand. A few hundred, yes."

"Give a magician license for a little hyperbole," Adunummu said.

"Hmm."

"The apprenticeship," Indrajit prompted the bound man. "Tell us how you came here."

"You mean, how my apprentice came."

"Ah, yes." Indrajit nodded. "Also, tell us about the apprentice."

"He's fierce." Adunummu writhed in his chains as if to communicate ferocity. "He came to me, starving and wastrel, in this desert place, seeking food."

"This desert place, Hith," Fix said.

"If you say it is." Adunummu shrugged. "We magicians care little for the names and buildings and politics and fashion of the mortal world."

"So you fed him?" Indrajit asked.

"I offered him food in exchange for his bound service as my apprentice," Adunummu said, "which he accepted. But then he was a bad apprentice. He tried to learn magics beyond what I taught him, like a thief. And when he stole from me an item of great power, I confronted him."

"What sort of magics?" Fix asked. "Conjuring? Druvash sorcery? Theurgy? Weather-witching?"

"Conjuring!" Adunummu snapped. "As you said."

"But when you confronted him," Indrajit continued the

thought, "you were unable to defeat him. With his pilfered magics and his borrowed item of great power, he was able to put you here in this dungeon, chained to this post."

"You see my tragedy."

"I'm not sure tragedy is the genre," Indrajit mused.

"Eh?"

"What was the item?" Indrajit asked. "A medallion?"

Adunummu hesitated. "A bracer. A jeweled bracer."

"Tell us more about the apprentice," Fix said. "Maybe we can go upstairs and defeat him for you. What sort of man is he?"

"I told you, he's bad and a thief."

Fix sighed. "I'm not asking about his moral character. Is he a Wixit? A Pelthite? A Zalapting? Is he of your same race? We need to recognize him, if we're to defeat him."

"For you," Indrajit said. "Defeat him for you."

"I have a question," Munahim said.

"Is anyone coming down the stairs?" Indrajit asked.

"No," Munahim said.

"Good," Indrajit said. "Stay focused."

"But my question—" the Kyone insisted.

"Later," Indrajit said. "Shush now."

"Does the Wixit not talk?" Adunummu asked.

"He's a former enemy," Indrajit said. "He dared go against us, and we used our formidable powers to defeat him."

"Are you wizards also, then?" Adunummu asked.

"After our fashion." Fix shrugged.

"You were about to describe your rebel apprentice," Indrajit reminded the prisoner.

"He's big," Adunummu said. "He has a head something

like a walrus, with tusks and whiskers and a thick, blubbery neck."

"He sounds frightening," Fix said. "I'm impressed you were brave enough to take him in."

"I am a conjurer of renown," Adunummu pointed out.

"Go on."

"He has a big chest and shoulders. One arm ends in a hand like yours or mine. The other ends in a flipper."

Fix looked to Indrajit with raised eyebrows. "What race of man is that? Any ideas?"

Indrajit cleared his throat. "Let me consult my magical lore. Perhaps it's the *one-handed Siskaloo, teeth like downward daggers?*"

"Sounds right to me. And does the magical lore tell us anything else about the Siskaloo?"

Indrajit considered. The Siskaloo only had the one epithet. *"In the Epic, the Siskaloo lives in a tower near the sea."*

"Epic?" Adunummu asked.

"Sounds right," Fix said. "How is the Siskaloo defeated?"

"He isn't," Indrajit said. "He knows and sees many things, and he's not defeated."

"Who *are* you guys?" Adunummu asked.

"Good question. Who are *you*?" Indrajit asked.

"Adunummu the Conjurer," Adunummu said.

"Liar," Fix said.

"I have a question," Munahim said.

"Okay," Indrajit told him. "You can ask your question now."

"Why don't you have a flask on a chain around your neck?" the Kyone asked.

"There it is," Fix said. "Because you see, Munahim, this is not the conjurer Adunummu."

"Yes, I am," the chained man said.

"You're the bad apprentice, if you're anyone in the story," Indrajit said. "Which I suspect you are, because it's easier to tell a true story and switch your role in it than to make up a new story entirely. So tell us your name."

"Also, what did you come here to steal?" Fix asked. "Was it the bracer? Or was it the flask on the chain around the conjurer's neck?"

"What are you going to do to me?" the prisoner asked.

"That's a very good question," Indrajit said. "We're still thinking about it."

"Personally," Fix said, "I'm just as happy to kill you. But my partner here has a soft heart. So if you keep him happy, he'll probably want to let you live."

"Who *are* you guys?"

"No no, we'll get to that," Indrajit said. "Tell us your name, or we'll have to name you ourselves. And then we'll be calling you something embarrassing, like Hey, Stupid."

"My name is Shafi," the chained man said. "I'm a thief."

"You heard of the wealth of the conjurer and you traveled here to rob him," Fix said.

"No, I was shipwrecked, while on a voyage from the Free Cities to Boné. I'm not sure where we are. That part is true. As you said, it's easier to keep a story straight in your head if it's mostly true."

"You were shipwrecked and saw the tower," Indrajit said. "Did you offer yourself as an apprentice?"

"I even did that. I was hungry."

"But once you had eaten," Fix concluded, "you decided

you'd like to try your luck stealing something and running."

"I was a thief before I got here," Shafi admitted. "It seemed like an easy snatch-and-run job."

"What magic powers did Adunummu use to stop you?" Indrajit asked.

"Or what ancient technologies?" Fix suggested.

"None. I doctored his wine to make it stronger, so he'd sleep through anything I did. Then, while he was sleeping, I tried to remove the bracer. And he woke up."

"No magical powers at all?" Indrajit felt disappointed.

"He hit me very hard."

"Perhaps there are no magical powers," Fix said.

"You have personally been healed by Druvash sorcery," Indrajit said.

"By Druvash art," Fix agreed. "Whether or not it was sorcery is an interesting question."

"And here we are, hundreds of leagues from Kish, a distance we leaped instantaneously, walking through a door." Indrajit shook his head. "And you're going to tell me you don't believe in magic?"

Fix spread his hands. "Some things that look like magic are just craft that we don't understand."

"But you rendered that Wixit an idiot," Shafi said. "You're magicians yourselves."

"Ah, sad," Fix said.

"What's sad?"

"You're not just a thief," Indrajit explained, "you're a stupid thief. We're not magicians. The Wixit came like that."

"But someone made him an idiot," Shafi said.

"Good point."

"I concede that it sounds much more romantic to do battle against Adunummu the Conjurer than against Adunummu Who Can Take His Liquor and Also Hits Pretty Hard," Fix said.

"Good. In the Epic, I'll definitely make him the Conjurer, regardless of how this works out."

"In either case, we need the flask." Fix glared sternly at Shafi. "Adunummu does wear a flask around his neck, doesn't he?"

Shafi nodded. "He talks to it, caresses it like it's a woman."

"Perhaps in the Epic he can also be Adunummu the Insane," Fix suggested.

"Perhaps he is talking to a demon in the bottle," Indrajit suggested.

"Or he thinks he is."

"But the real question," Shafi said, "is, how are you going to get me out of these chains?"

"Easiest thing is to rip your arms off," Fix suggested. "The Kyone can do it."

"Hey," Shafi said.

"So Adunummu put you down here to give you a horrible death," Indrajit said. "Maybe you could scare away the thylacodons for a while by shaking your chains or yelling or something, but sooner or later you'd fall asleep or be weak from starvation, and then they'd eat you. Is that about the size of it?"

"Yes. I was thinking, if you had some grease, like some nice animal fat or butter, you could coat my wrists and that would probably be enough for me to slip out."

"I told you," Indrajit said. "No provisions. But there's another question to ask, which is, what can you do to help us get Adunummu?"

"I can choose not to yell to alert him to your presence," Shafi said.

"We can solve that problem by killing you," Fix said. "You really don't want to push us very far down that road."

"Or just gag you," Indrajit countered.

"See?" Fix said. "Softhearted."

"I can help," Shafi said.

"Now we're talking." Indrajit nodded to encourage the thief. "What would you suggest for a plan?"

Shafi considered. "I could scream like I was being eaten by thylacadons. Then when he came to collect my bones, we could jump him."

"Only he might not collect your bones at all," Fix said. "He might find your screams unpersuasive. He might be perfectly happy leaving your bones down here forever, unwitnessed."

"I could tell you what I said to persuade him to take me in," Shafi said. "Then you could make a similar appeal."

"Surely, he would find a band of three armed men asking to be his apprentices suspicious." Indrajit shook his head. "What else?"

"That's all I can think of."

"What if we wait until dark," Fix suggested, "and then you lead us to where the conjurer sleeps?"

"I . . . would rather not," Shafi said.

"Because you're afraid he'd capture you and put you back in this pit," Indrajit said. "With the bird of freedom in your hand, you don't want to trade it for anything uncertain that might be in the bush. You want to run away while you can."

"Yes. For that reason."

"But remember that we might not let you go at all," Indrajit pointed out. "And if you help us get what we need from Adunummu, we won't stand in the way of your taking that bracer you wanted."

Shafi slumped in his chains, then nodded slowly. "Agreed."

◈ Chapter Six ◈

As a gesture of good faith, they smashed Shafi's chains and freed him. Fix argued in favor of leaving the thief chained until the last possible moment, but eventually, and with much grumbling, gave in.

Shafi asked for a weapon. Again they debated, and eventually agreed that he would remain unarmed.

They climbed the stairs, Indrajit once again shouldering the Wixit. Fix's torch finally consumed the last of the flammable material he'd gathered as they were several stories' height above the floor. Fix laid down the charred thigh bone and they proceeded in single file, hugging the wall.

After another minute or so of climbing, Indrajit realized that he could see a yellow glow coming down from above. Eventually, they climbed into the light and saw that it poured through the barred window set in the door at the top of the stairs, on a narrow landing.

Indrajit crept ahead and peered through the window. Beyond, he saw a hall. He couldn't find the source of light, but its tenor suggested that it was daylight, filtering in through some unseen window. He pushed at the door, a moment of truth, and found it unlocked.

So Adunummu didn't fear that the thylacodons would creep through the doorway, and trusted the chains to hold his erring apprentice in place.

They settled on the landing and the first few steps to

wait for sunset. In the meantime, Shafi quietly described the tower. "This floor has a refectory and a dining hall. The floor above that is a library."

Indrajit spat.

"Above that," Shafi continued, "is the floor where Adunummu sleeps."

"Where did you sleep?" Indrajit asked.

"Beside the fire in the refectory," Shafi said. "Using an old bolster for a pillow."

"The upper floors are accessed by stairs?" Fix asked.

"It's the continuation of the same staircase," Shafi said. "Rising around the outside of each floor."

"Is his bedroom the top floor?" Indrajit pressed.

"The stairs rise above that," Shafi said, "but that's as high as I ever went."

"What other servants does he have?" Indrajit asked.

"None visible."

Fix harrumphed. "Forget about invisible servants. What you need to think about is that our best chances of survival will result if we ambush the wizard, killing him before he can do anything to us."

"Before he can cast any spells, you mean?"

"Or hit us hard. Or use strange Druvash weapons on us."

"But if we're in a position to just grab the bottle around his neck," Indrajit said, "we should do that. And then run."

Fix was silent.

"We should grab the flask and run," Indrajit said again.

"Maybe," Fix conceded. "If that seems within reach."

Night fell outside the tower. Indrajit watched the light on the other side of the door fill with the pinks and golds and oranges of a lush sunset, and then dim into blue and gray. When he could barely see the outlines of the hall any longer, he pushed open the door and led the way.

Standing in the hall, he could see that he was between the dining hall and the kitchen. He peered into the dining hall, seeking to fix the layout of the place in his mind as well as to see Adunummu Who Can Take His Liquor and Also Hits Pretty Hard before Adunummu saw him. Starlight drifted down in gentle flakes from high, glassless windows. Statues stood around the half-moon-shaped hall at regular intervals; thirty or forty, he thought, without actually counting. Every third statue was enormous, a standing figure three times the height of a man, and all the colossi bore on their shoulders a stone ledge that ran around the entire room, beneath the windows on the curving side of the chamber, and bearing pots overflowing with vines and other green tendrils. Every statue was unique—he saw two men embracing, and a woman holding a sheaf of wheat, and strange beasts. The shorter statues were set in niches sunk into the wall. The whole arrangement tugged at the back of Indrajit's memory, but he was unsure of its meaning or where he had seen it before. A massive slab of stone table sat centered in the room, surrounded by chairs with tall backs, thick legs, and upholstered cushions for seats.

The refectory had a similar slab of a table, shelves laden with food, running water sluicing endlessly through several stone basins, and a massive fireplace. A cylindrical bolster lay squashed and dirty with ash on the stones before the fireplace. Within the refectory, stairs climbed up the wall toward the next story.

Indrajit drew his sword and the other Protagonists did the same. Shafi drew a long, triangular knife from a wooden block sitting on a table, and then Indrajit again went first up the stairs. "Brace yourself," he couldn't resist whispering to Munahim, "next comes the library. Be prepared to catch Fix if he faints."

Munahim responded with a puzzled whimper in the back of his throat.

Indrajit passed two rectangular windows just before crossing up through the floor into the next story. Moisture whipped in through the openings on a stiffening breeze, and a creeping shield of gray cloud was eating up the stars.

The library was a single enormous room. Light emanated from two silvery-green spheres standing atop pillars about Indrajit's height, one near where they entered the room and the other on the far side. Two short walls near the center sheltered a desk on which lay two open codices.

"Load-bearing walls," Fix murmured.

"Sure," Indrajit said.

The outward-facing sides of the load-bearing walls were plated with shelves and burdened with writing. Indrajit cringed at the sight of all the scrolls, sheaves of paper, stacks of paper, charts, codices, and books. More shelves stood free about the room, and more were bolted into the outer walls.

Fix stood and stared.

Indrajit wanted to make a joke at his partner's expense, but he was aware that Adunummu was likely sleeping just one floor above their heads. He settled for briefly pantomiming striking fire to the nearest shelf of papers with flint and steel, and then headed up.

Shafi's hands shook as they climbed.

The library had no windows, but the room they climbed into now did. These were set into the wall regularly—large, open rectangles through which a wind blew that was now furious and wet. Lightning struck outside, a sheet of pure white, and then the gongs of thunder burst through the open windows and across the chamber.

In the lightning's flash, Indrajit saw a bedchamber. An open firepit sat between two walls near the center of the room, low coals burning dull red, smoke lazily wafting up into a crack in the ceiling, against one wall. Beside the firepit, a marble tub was sunk into the floor; water sloshed from a spigot at one end and the tub somehow didn't overflow; there must be a drain sluicing the water away as fast as it came in. Shelves contained stacked linen, scent bottles, and other toiletry articles. Stairs continued up into the ceiling and darkness. A bed big enough to support two Droggers in heat stood near the room's center.

In the bed, a heap of furs.

He wanted to ask his companions what they had seen, but didn't dare.

He wanted to sneak forward and pat down the bed, find the flask and run with it. He didn't relish the idea of assassinating anyone in their sleep, wizard or no.

Although this magician had been happy to tie Shafi up and leave him to be eaten by wild beasts.

According to Shafi. Who was, by his own admission, a thief.

But having come this far, Indrajit didn't see another choice. His client was kidnapped, the client's son was still in a trance, this was the way forward. He hissed in disappointment at the evil of the world.

He crept forward, Vacho raised and ready. The size of the shadow to his left told him that Munahim was with him. Indrajit stopped and stood the Wixit in a corner, away from the tub and the fire, then swung his blade to feel its weight. A second shadow crept forward; it was too big to be Fix, and had a slight carrion smell to it, carried up from the thylacodon pit. Shafi.

Shafi, who was now armed with a big kitchen knife.

He crept forward and they came with him.

He had to risk a little noise if he wanted to coordinate. "On three," he whispered. He raised Vacho above his head. "One . . . two . . . three."

He sprang forward and stabbed down, sinking his knife into the mound of furs. He struck flesh and smelled the hot stink of gushing blood. Kneeling on the furs, he felt a huge body beneath his knees shake, lift its arms and legs, and then let them drop. Munahim leaped onto the body with him, slashing repeatedly at what must be the body's head.

Lightning flashed again and brought with it simultaneous thunder. Indrajit saw Munahim slash at the bedding, and as Munahim's sword came away, a head came with it. Indrajit saw the flash of lightning on two long tusks, and then a spherical head swung away into the darkness.

"The hand!" Shafi shrieked. "Where's the hand?" He plunged his knife into the bed.

"Stop stabbing!" Indrajit hissed.

Shafi stabbed at the bed again, and this time Indrajit punched him, knocking him to the floor.

The body lay still.

"A light," Indrajit said. "We need a light in here. Can anyone find a lantern?"

He heard the sharp rasp of steel on stone, and then saw a faint flicker of light in the darkness. It grew in brightness and size until Indrajit realized what it was; Fix had struck fire to one end of a rolled scroll, and now held it up like a torch.

"You're coming around to my view of the written word." Indrajit chuckled.

Fix shrugged. "I couldn't read it, anyway. I don't even know what language it was in." He held the torch high and poked about the room until he found a lamp. That lit, a mellow golden glow filled the chamber.

"This isn't him," Shafi gasped.

Indrajit pulled away the furs and blankets. They were dark purple with blood; he tossed them all into a heap. Beneath lay a massive body, sexless like a Gund's but without the insectoid arms. Instead of a right hand, the corpse had a flipper.

Munahim lifted the severed head. He gripped it by a tusk; the head answered to Shafi's previous description.

"What do you mean, this isn't him?" Indrajit asked. "Because there's no bracer on the arm, and no flask on a chain around his neck? Maybe he sleeps naked."

Shafi shook his head. "Adunummu's right hand is a flipper. This . . . person's got a flipper, too, but look at it."

Indrajit looked. The flipper was the left hand.

"Are you sure?" he asked.

"Is this some other Siskaloo, then?" Munahim asked.

Shafi shook his head. "Look, I . . . Look how this thing is sexless."

"Yes," Indrajit said.

"It's not Adunummu," Shafi said. "I'm pretty sure it's not a Siskaloo at all, or any other kind of mortal man."

"Adakles!" Fix yelled.

Indrajit wheeled about in time to see Adakles disappearing up the steps into the room above.

He rushed to the foot of the stairs and peered in vain up into the darkness.

"Adakles?" he called. He would be heard if anyone were on the floor above, but they'd already screamed and banged about enough to warn anyone up there that they were here.

"Come up," a voice called back. "Let us talk."

It didn't sound like a Wixit.

⊰ Chapter Seven ⊱

"So much for surprise," Fix said.

"So much for killing the conjurer before he could attack us," Indrajit added. He felt relief like a cold wave through his body; he hadn't, after all, killed a man in cold blood. On the other hand, he had certainly done everything that would have been necessary to kill that man, except that he had been tricked. Did that mean he bore the guilt of the murder, anyway?

To atone for the guilt, he sheathed his sword and started up the stairs.

"Indrajit, wait," Fix said softly.

"Get my back," Indrajit said. "Please."

He didn't wait for a response. Did he feel he owed this to the magician he'd tried to kill? Did he owe it to the Epic, somehow, or to his future apprentice?

"I'm coming up, Adunummu!"

He could see nothing in the dark opening above his head. Lightning crashed again outside the tower, so close it might have been inside the room, and still there was no flicker of light in the room above. Windowless, then. Unlit. And probably Adunummu could see in the dark. And Indrajit's sword was in his sheath.

This was an excellent idea.

The skin on the back of his neck prickled as he walked up into the darkness. He smelled a burning, lightning-like odor. His knees trembled slightly.

Then he rose to the next story and stepped onto the floor, and suddenly he could see.

He stood on the top floor of a tower, on the battlements, and it was broad daylight. Below and around the tower stretched a carpet of fluffy white clouds. An apparatus stood on a pole at one end of the circular tower-top. Beside it stood an enormous man with a tusked and whiskered head, wrapped in a blue silk robe and resting one hand on the device. It was his right hand, and the hand wasn't a hand at all, but a flipper. On his left wrist, Indrajit saw a gold bracer, and hanging from a chain around his neck, a glass flask.

Adakles stood at the apparatus, with his face pressed against it.

"You are the one they call Indrajit." The Siskaloo's voice was a deep rumble.

"Indrajit Twang," Indrajit said.

"I don't think your head resembles a fish's head."

"Right? Thank you."

"Not very much, anyway."

"So, ah, you know more about me than I know about you," Indrajit said.

"Curious, isn't it?" Adunummu chuckled. "And interesting that your ignorance correlates with a willingness to kill me, while my knowledge correlates with a preference for your survival. Mind you, our sample size is very small."

Indrajit wasn't entirely sure that he followed the magician's meaning. "I think you're saying you don't plan to kill me."

"I don't plan to kill you. Or your companions." The Siskaloo smiled. "Yet."

Indrajit chuckled uneasily. "Can they come up, then?"

"Oh, they've come up," Adunummu said. "Only they came up to the other place at the top of the same stairs. Would you like to see them?"

Indrajit reflected on all the stories of magicians in the Epic. Magicians could be devious, cunning, deceitful, sadistic, and many other things. Above all, they were always surprising. Was this a trick? Would agreement that he'd like to see his friends cause him to be catapulted into a shared hell with them?

"Given your, ah, goodwill toward us," he said, shifting from foot to foot, "I'd be happy to see them."

"Adakles," Adunummu said. "Give this fellow Indrajit a turn, will you?"

Adakles stepped away from the device, stepping down in the process from a series of rungs attached to the pole on which the device was mounted. "He's been watching us, you see," Adakles said.

"Right." Indrajit nodded. "Of course, he has."

"You don't have to shove your face into the visor," Adunummu said. "But pressing your face close enough to be completely under the brass hood tends to shut out the light, and I find that gives me the best views."

A pane of glass was framed with a skirt of brass, whose edges were blunted with a strip of white rubber. Indrajit pressed his face into the viewer, feeling a semicircle of rubber gripping his forehead, the embrace rendered a little awkward by Indrajit's prominent bony nose ridge.

"What do I have to—oh." He stopped talking as the visor filled with an image. He saw Fix, Munahim, and Shafi, in a dark chamber. He saw the three men as if they were painted in shades of red, while the shelves, tables, and glass and brass instruments in the room were all painted blue and gray.

"What is this sorcery?" Indrajit pulled his face from the device.

"It's a simple viewer." Adunummu shrugged. "If this astounds you, you must live a life of daily astonishment."

"I do," Indrajit said. "And . . . did this device restore Adakles?"

"I did that by other means," the Siskaloo said. "Shall I put him back?"

"No," Adakles said. "Please."

"No," Indrajit said. "No, he's just . . . he's fine."

"You have been sent by magicians to kill me," Adunummu said.

"Technically, just to rob you," Indrajit clarified. "We're to take that bottle you carry on your chest."

"Interesting." Adunummu made a sound like purring in his chest. "And do what with the bottle?"

"So I guess you couldn't see us during our meeting with Theophilus Bolt?" Indrajit asked.

"And do what with the bottle?" Adunummu asked again.

Indrajit shrugged. "I guess it's sort of our ticket. Or maybe it's a distraction. Or both. It's to get us in the door to see someone else."

"Hmm."

"Where are we?" Indrajit asked. "Are we at the . . . are we in the same tower here as . . . as is down below?"

"Well, the answer to that rather has to be yes, doesn't it?"

"But I mean..." Indrajit struggled. "I came up one tower, and it all seemed to be a certain way, a single structure. Am I now in the same structure I was in while I was ascending?"

Adunummu laughed, a rich sound that Indrajit found surprisingly fruity. "You're above the clouds."

"You're not answering my question."

"Who hired you?" Adunummu asked. "What are the terms of your engagement? Do you intend to attack and rob me now?"

"I...killed your...the other you," Indrajit said.

"And now you confess." Adunummu laughed. "I saw you do it. The synthetic felt no pain."

"I feel pain," Indrajit said. "I feel guilt."

"Good. Expunge your guilt by answering my questions."

"I want to look again," Adakles said.

Indrajit stepped aside. "Our client is Adakles's father. We were engaged to rescue Adakles, which seems to be mostly accomplished. Although he's here with me, and not at home. But then his father, Thoat, was kidnapped. So we aim to rescue Thoat. The people who kidnapped Thoat—"

"Theophilus Bolt."

"And company, I believe," Indrajit said. "They promised to return Bolt to us if we took your flask and took it to the Collegium Arcanum. We would say that we had recovered the flask from you, for the Collegium, and this would get us access to the Collegium's tyrant. Whom we would then kill. That was the job: kill the man who has made himself leader of the Collegium Arcanum."

"Interesting," Adunummu said.

"Why do I feel so comfortable telling you everything?" Indrajit asked. "I feel like Munahim."

"It's my craft," Adunummu said. "I'm doing things that encourage you to talk."

"I have no desire to help Bolt," Indrajit said. "And I don't want to assassinate anyone, least of all a magician whose apprentices and familiars might come after me. I just want to rescue my client. And also, I suppose, protect myself from reprisals from Bolt and his friends."

"I won't reveal to you the inner political workings of the Collegium Arcanum," Adunummu said.

"I don't want to know them," Indrajit said. "They don't cross the history of my people, and I feel safer in ignorance."

"And yet you are going to play a part," Adunummu said. "Here is my proposal. I'll give you my flask, and the bottle-imp inside it. It is indeed coveted by my rivals in the Collegium. I'll also teach you a set of instructions by which you will deploy the imp in accordance with my will. I will also make you a gift of this bracer I wear. You will say that you stole it from me, and give it to Bolt. His greed will not allow him to do anything other than accept it, but the gift will then destroy him."

"And the result of all of this?" Indrajit asked.

"I shall gain power. Why else would I do anything?"

"And my client?"

"I'll free him. That's what's in it for you."

Indrajit considered. "Shafi wants your bracer very much."

"Shafi is a thief, and I intend to kill him."

"I wouldn't want that to happen," Indrajit said.

"Interesting." Adunummu stroked his thick neck with his flipper. "Why not?"

Indrajit sighed. "I'm the softhearted one, I suppose."

"Even toward a thief?"

"Yes."

"What if I told you that he wished you ill?"

"I would believe it."

Adunummu chuckled. "Adakles, let Indrajit have another turn."

The Wixit stepped aside, and Indrajit looked into the viewer. To his surprise, he saw himself, climbing the stairs from the kitchen. Behind him came Shafi, a knife in his hand. He saw himself arrive in the library, and Shafi creep forward, as if planning to stab Indrajit in the back.

But then Munahim loped up the steps, and at the last second, Shafi turned aside and examined books on a shelf.

"I could kill him," Adunummu said. "No judge in the world would deny that I was doing justice."

"Some might." Indrajit sighed. "But that's not the point. If you can show mercy, you should."

"Did you show mercy to my synthetic?" Adunummu asked. "Whom you took to be me, sleeping in my bed?"

"I made a mistake," Indrajit said. "I made a terrible mistake, but fortunately, you outwitted me then. You outwitted me, and there were no consequences to my error."

"There were consequences. My synthetic bore them."

"You outwitted me then," Indrajit said. "Be wiser than me now. Let Shafi go."

"Magicians are not famous for their wisdom."

"You could be the first," Indrajit said. "I would put you into the Blaatshi Epic. The tale of your wisdom and nobility might outlive you."

"Might it?" Adunummu mused. "Some magicians live very long lives."

"The Blaatshi Epic is millennia old," Indrajit told him. "With a little luck, it will continue for millennia still."

"Very well," Adunummu said. "Go downstairs to your friends and summon them up to be instructed."

"And Shafi?"

"I will deal with him."

"You will deal with him . . ."

"Mercifully."

Indrajit climbed down the steps. As he descended, light came with him, spilling over the staircase and emanating from it, and when he reached the floor below, he found Munahim and Fix blinking at the illumination. The room around them was free of furniture, had no windows, and was enclosed within blank stone walls.

Shafi lay on the floor before them, snoring.

"You disappeared," Munahim said. "No scent, even."

"Come up with me." Indrajit extended a hand of invitation. "You'll understand . . . well, not everything. But more. Maybe sheathe your swords first."

"Is it safe?" Munahim asked.

"Well, there are wizards in the mix," Indrajit said. "So no, it isn't safe. On the other hand, it's interesting."

ᛃ Chapter Eight ᛁ

The synthetic raged.

It looked just like Adunummu, though it roared a lot and spoke in simple sentences. "Robbers!" it howled. "Give back what you have stolen!"

The interior of Adunummu's tower had a marked lack of doors, so Indrajit and his companions had returned to the door to the thylacodon pit. Indrajit had pulled the door shut and was now spreading the flexible brass bar across the bottom, pressing its tacks and clamps into the heavy wood. They sank in easily; magic?

The synthetic, wrapped in a blue robe that hid its sexlessness, roared. The real Adunummu stood crouched behind it, his non-flipper hand wrapped in a smooth white ceramic knuckle-duster.

"Louder," Adunummu said softly.

But was he, after all, the real Adunummu? How would Indrajit even know that this Adunummu was not also a simulacrum of some kind? Or a projection, as Bolt had turned out to be? Magicians seemed to have the knack for presenting false reality.

Which probably made this plan to capture a wizard, and apparently a powerful one, a terrible idea.

"Ready," Indrajit murmured.

He wore the flask hanging around his own neck and carried the golden bracer in his kilt pocket.

"Thief!" the synthetic bellowed.

Indrajit pulled the door open. A crackling sheet of light hung in the doorway. Beyond, his memory told him, should lie a narrow landing and then a long fall into the thylacodon pit. His senses detected neither, but he planned to move cautiously, just in case.

Adunummu raised his ceramic-wrapped fist and pumped his elbow. A beam of red light shot past Indrajit, narrowly missing his head and striking the sheet of light. His cheek felt scorched by the heat of the passing ray. The light in the door briefly turned red and a wave radiated out from the point of impact.

"Run!" Fix yelled.

Indrajit stepped through the light curtain. His step was careful, because he half-expected to step into darkness and a potential fall, but Munahim, Adakles, and Fix crashed through immediately after him, piling onto him and knocking him down.

He braced himself for a fatal fall, but tumbled onto a stone floor in a well-lit room at the bottom of a pile of Protagonists. Another red beam passed overhead. He smelled burning wood and heard a sizzling sound.

"Shut the door!" The voice belonged to Theophilus Bolt. Booted feet thudded on stone, hands grabbed Indrajit and dragged him across the floor, scraping skin off his knees and elbows. A door banged against his ankle as it was slammed shut. Indrajit rolled away from the legs of manic men as they slammed a brass bar across the inside of the door, a bar much like the one Indrajit had put onto the door's other side.

"Clear!" one of them shouted.

The men wore heavy boots and were covered from

head to toe. They looked something like the powder priests of Thûl, except the Thûlians were wrapped in scarves, shawls, and cloaks, to protect themselves from profane gazes; these men wore single garments that covered them entirely. They lacked even holes for eyes, and Indrajit saw no buttons or clasps for closing the garments. For all he could tell, the clothing had been woven directly onto the men.

"Wait," he said. "I pulled the door open from the other side, and then you pushed it shut from this side."

Theophilus Bolt laughed. The magician stood beside Indrajit, hovering in the air—which probably meant that this Bolt was a mere projection. "Yes."

"That makes no logical sense." Fix disentangled himself from the pile of men, climbing to his feet and straightening his kilt.

Munahim grunted and rolled into a sitting position. His instruction from Adunummu had been to keep his mouth shut and do as he was told.

"It makes all the logical sense in the world," Bolt said. "It's just a logic with which you are not perfectly acquainted."

"Yet," Fix said.

Bolt bowed as if conceding a point; he looked amused. "Not *yet* acquainted."

"What's burning?" Munahim asked.

"The building." Bolt shrugged. "The men will handle it."

The men in featureless suits rushed the other way across the room. Indrajit now saw a heavy timber, one of several matching beams running across the roof, on fire. The men aimed a hose at the flames and gray powder sprayed all over the fire, quenching it instantly.

"Come," Bolt said. "Breathing will be unpleasant in here for a time. Let's go upstairs."

Bolt pointed at a green-painted door, but he himself walked to a rectangular window and clasped his hands behind his back. He smiled at the Protagonists as they passed through the door into a stairwell. Munahim carried Adakles on his shoulder; the Wixit was lucid, if not especially conversational. At Adunummu's suggestion, he was pretending to be dazed and dumb still.

"Make sure to close the door behind you," Bolt called.

Indrajit wanted to comment on their surroundings, but his experience with Adunummu made him fear he was being observed. He shut the door behind his companions, then duly trudged up a flight of stairs behind them to a second green door.

On the other side of this door, they found another plaster-walled room with heavy rafters and a single window. Bolt stood beside this window as well, with his hands behind his back and a smile on his face. In the wall to their right was set a door that looked familiar.

Munahim made a low growling sound in his throat and shook his head.

"I know, noble Kyone," Bolt said. "You are weary of the strangeness of magicians. But you are nearly at the road's end."

Indrajit didn't like the way that sounded. "We just want our client back."

"The Wixit Thoat," Bolt said. "Yes, as soon as you've overthrown the tyrant Megistos."

"'Overthrown the tyrant' sounds like a lot of work," Indrajit said. "We're going to assassinate one wizard and be finished. Whatever's left of the overthrowing business is your problem."

Bolt bowed and smiled again.

"And we want Thoat back now," Fix said.

Indrajit hesitated. This was not the plan.

Bolt smiled. "Well, that's not going to happen."

"We'll trade," Fix said.

Bolt frowned. "You think you can just put your foot down and refuse to go forward? You've obtained the flask, why would I not simply take it from you?"

"Because you need someone to assassinate Megistos," Indrajit said. "The flask is just the way in. But we're men of honor, we'll do what we agreed to do. We're offering you something else."

Bolt's eyes narrowed. "Go on."

"We've obtained a treasure from Adunummu's tower," Fix said. "Beyond just the flask, of course."

"Interesting," Bolt said. "And why would I not just take it from you?"

"Well," Indrajit said, "for several reasons, I suppose. One, Munahim might shoot you. And this time, not choose to miss. Two, Fix might stab you with the Dagger of Slaying. We'd have to run down the slope to get to you, but unless you can fly, that won't take long. And three, we might just opt out of this whole assassination thing. I don't like it very much in any case, to be honest. We're fighters, but we're not killers."

Bolt chewed his lower lip. "What's the treasure?"

Indrajit removed the golden bracer from his kilt pocket.

"Why not keep it for yourself?" Bolt asked.

"And risk a wizard's curse?" Indrajit shuddered, a genuine reaction.

"I will think about it," Bolt said. "You make an interesting offer."

"No," Indrajit said. "We'll go out your door, wherever it leads, and carry out our appointed task. But we take Thoat with us. You can produce him, just as easily as you produced Adakles."

"I produced Adakles outside the tower," Bolt pointed out.

"Fine," Indrajit said. "So we go through that door, and if Thoat's on the other side, great, we'll give you the bracer. Hand it to you in person, deliver it to your instruction, whatever you like. If he's not, then we take the bracer and sell it, before we go carry out your plan."

"I'm sure the Lord Chamberlain would pay us for the artifact," Fix said. "Or the Hall of Guesses."

"Or the Vin Dalu," Indrajit said. "Or one of the temples."

"Stop," Bolt said. "I agree. Go through the door and you'll find yourselves in Kish."

"I knew it looked familiar," Indrajit muttered.

"I'll see that Thoat is returned to the plaza of the Headless Took," Bolt continued. "He will be in a stupor like his son's. A messenger will be there to take delivery of what you offer. The messenger will also tell you where to meet and slay the tyrant. Once the slaying is accomplished, we will restore both Wixits to their full minds. Is that agreeable to you?"

Indrajit looked at Fix, and his partner nodded.

"Agreed," Indrajit said.

"Will the messenger be wearing red?" Fix asked.

Bolt nodded.

Fix passed through the door first, followed by Munahim, and Indrajit came last. They emerged onto the Avenue of Golden Chariots, in the darkness of night. Light from windows in the upper stories of the Crown's palaces and towers threw golden puddles here and there, and travelers in togas were preceded by servants with torches and followed by armed guards.

Indrajit looked over his shoulder. The door by which they had come had vanished.

"The Headless Took?" he suggested.

They walked for a minute before Fix spoke, and then in a low voice. "What possessed you to negotiate for Thoat? We hadn't discussed that."

"I hate the feeling of passivity," Indrajit said. "I want to be the hero, not the hapless fool in the grip of fate. We couldn't have discussed it in Adunummu's presence without involving him in the planning. And I don't want to be Adunummu's puppet any more than I want to be Bolt's."

"It was a good move," Fix said. "They might have withheld Thoat and tried to force us to do more, or to betray Adunummu."

"And if Bolt's party refuses to remove the stupor from Thoat, we know that Adunummu can do it just as easily." Indrajit sighed. "Though we may find ourselves negotiating with the two parties to get one of them to do it."

"You can set me down now," Adakles said.

"I don't think we can," Fix said. "And you need to

continue to play dumb, as long as anyone might be watching."

Indrajit thought about Adunummu's viewing device. "Which might be a long time."

They were nearing the alley to the plaza of the Headless Took. "What do you think the odds are that any of this is real?" Fix asked.

"What? Kish?" Indrajit asked. "Kish is real. Kish has caused me far too much pain to be anything but real."

"Hmm. In fact, I could be persuaded that Kish was an illusion, too." Fix shook his head. "No, I mean everything else. The tower by the sea, the sunshine. The tower on the plain of ash, the thylacodons. I don't believe in being instantaneously transported from one land to another, across hundreds of leagues."

"And yet we were transported," Indrajit said.

Munahim made a low growling sound in his throat.

"We perceived that we were," Fix said. "That's my point. What if instead we were lying in a room off the Avenue of Golden Chariots the entire time? Under the influence of some drug, say. Or the odd power of some unknown race of man. And we believed we were transported to faraway places, and instead Adakles was simply returned to us along with the dagger and the bracer and the bottle."

"You resist the idea of magic."

"Yes. Of course, I do."

"Why could it not have been craft that moved us?" Indrajit suggested. "I mean a technique, a device. Druvash sorcery, or something similar."

"It could have been, I suppose," Fix said. "But what

difference is there between saying, 'oh, by magic I was transported to a faraway realm,' and saying, 'oh, by means of mysterious technology I was transported'?"

They turned down the alley.

"That's exactly my point," Indrajit said.

"Shh," Fix said. "Look for a messenger dressed in red."

"And Thoat," Indrajit added.

◈ Chapter Nine ◈

No windows overlooked the plaza where the Headless Took stood. What light there was shone down directly from the moon overhead, filling the center of the square, painting the statue and the well beneath its feet with a ghostly nimbus.

Beside the fountain stood two figures. Indrajit approached, followed by the other Protagonists.

"Remember to play stupid," he whispered to Adakles.

The Wixit slumped further, melting over Indrajit's shoulder.

Thoat stood beside the fountain. Slightly in front of and blocking access to the little tea merchant was a Fanchee woman in a toga. Under the light of the moon, the toga could have been red, purple, or even blue.

It had to be the same Fanchee. Which was to say, not a Fanchee at all, but a sorcerer or a shape-changer of some unknown race.

"You are Indrajit and Fix," the Fanchee said. Her voice was high-pitched and rasping, and didn't sound like a Fanchee's at all. "And the dog-man."

"We're here to make a trade," Fix said. "And to get your directions."

The Fanchee handed Indrajit a folded sheet of paper. Indrajit took it, resisting the urge to tear it into shreds.

"Frozen hells, you too?" he muttered.

"They *are* the magicians' guild," Fix pointed out.

"Yes, magicians," Indrajit snapped. "So they could send little talking images to tell us what we need to know. Or plant the ideas in our minds directly. Or cause the Headless Took to speak and address us."

"The Headless Took has no mouth," Fix said.

"It was just an example," Indrajit grumbled.

"And paper is cheaper."

"Paper is cheap," Indrajit said. "But that rationale will cause it to replace everything, everywhere—paper houses, paper clothes, paper food, paper shoes."

"Those things might serve perfectly well," Fix pointed out.

"Do you two fight all the time?" the Fanchee asked.

"Sometimes we fight other people," Indrajit said. "Not that it's any business of yours."

"The bracer." The Fanchee held out her hand.

Indrajit drew the jewel-encrusted gold from his pocket.

"Bolt told us to warn you," Fix said.

The Fanchee and Indrajit both paused.

"About what?" the Fanchee asked.

"He said that you absolutely should not try to wear or use this armband," Fix said.

"Right," Indrajit added. "Under no circumstances."

"It might be dangerous," Fix said.

"Dangerous . . . how?" the Fanchee asked.

"He didn't say." Fix shrugged. "He just said it was dangerous."

"He said to bring it straight to him," Indrajit said. "No delay."

"His very words." Fix nodded. "No delay."

"I run all my errands without delay," the Fanchee said. "Not that it's any business of *yours*."

"Good," Indrajit said. "So hand over the Wixit."

The Fanchee stood still.

"The Wixit," Fix said. "Thoat."

"Did he say anything else about the bracer?" the Fanchee asked.

"No," Indrajit said.

"Nothing." Fix shrugged.

"Do you know where it came from?"

"We stole it," Fix said. "From a very powerful wizard."

"A wealthy wizard," Indrajit said, "more to the point. A wizard with large piles of gold and jewels."

"Rich," Fix said. "Hand over the Wixit."

With a single motion, the Fanchee reached back, grabbed Thoat by his furry shoulder, and tossed him stumbling toward Fix, snatching the armband from Indrajit at the same time. Fix picked up the stupefied tea merchant.

"Good luck." The Fanchee spun about and marched into the dark alley at the back of the plaza. At the last moment, the red toga rose and the Fanchee seem to inflate into something large and misshapen. Then she disappeared.

"You hope she tries the bracer on and it punishes her," Indrajit said.

"Yes. I took the initiative mostly because it seemed like a good thing to do."

"Yeah, I agree. What does the paper say?"

Indrajit lowered Adakles to the ground. The young Wixit examined his father, pinching his cheek, shaking him by the elbows, and shouting into his face. Thoat didn't respond.

Fix unfolded the paper and read out loud. "'We have bound a portal using the front door of Thoat's tea shop. The portal opens into the hidden palace of Megistos, Lord Dean of the Collegium Arcanum. He expects your delivery of the bottle-imp.'"

"Unspoken," Indrajit said, "*we* expect your delivery of the Dagger of Slaying."

"I don't like it," Fix said, "but I don't see how else we rescue Thoat here."

Indrajit nodded. "Ironic that they'd use Thoat's door."

"It makes sense, maybe," Fix said, "if the magicians needed to use a door that wasn't going to be inadvertently opened by someone else. You wouldn't want random street traffic just walking into the Lord Dean's palace, and Thoat's tea shop is closed."

"What do we do with the Wixits?" Munahim added. "It's not safe to bring them with us."

"It's not safe to leave them anywhere else, either," Indrajit said. "Especially with Thoat in a stupor. I think we have to carry them with us and protect them."

"I can walk, at least," Adakles said.

"Safest if you don't," Fix said. "In case we're observed. But we'll set you down out of the way before any fighting starts."

"If I have a choice," Adakles said, "I want the Kyone to carry me. It's nice to snuggle against his fur."

"That's what they all say," Indrajit said.

"Like a mama Wixit," Fix suggested.

The three Protagonists hoisted the two Wixits and they

began their trudge toward the Spill. "You have the dagger?" Indrajit asked.

"I do," Fix said. "You have the bottle?"

"I do, and I remember how to use it."

With brief whispered coordination, they chose an indirect route. It allowed them to take smaller streets and even alleys—though alleys in the Crown were as wide as streets in the other quarters and as wide as a boulevard in the Dregs—to double back on their trail and watch for anyone following them. They saw jobbers on patrol as constables, very elegant streetwalkers, and even a second-story man, creeping across the peak of a high rooftop, but no tails.

The jobbers at the gate waved them through into the Spill without comment, not even asking about the apparently unconscious Wixits.

"If none of this is real," Indrajit said, "if none of the events of the past day actually happened, but instead we imagined them in a drugged state . . . why is our client unconscious?"

"Our client is drugged," Fix said. "If anything, that's evidence that we might also have been drugged."

"But who did it?" Indrajit asked. "Why would someone drug poor Thoat?"

"Remember what brought us here," Fix said. "We were warned that young Adakles was in danger from the Collegium Arcanum. Which certainly seems to have been true. He had been kidnapped and drugged."

"By the Bolt faction."

"If the Bolt faction exists," Fix said. "Put into a stupor by someone. Were you in a stupor, Adakles?"

"I was."

"What was it like?" Indrajit asked. "Were you conscious of things around you? Were you conscious of standing on a clifftop when we found you, for instance?"

"I don't remember that," Adakles said. "I remember coming out of the stupor on Adunummu's tower. That felt like waking up."

"You felt as if you had been asleep," Indrajit pressed.

"Yes."

"See, I never felt as if I were asleep," Indrajit said. "So whatever happened to me, I don't think it's the same thing that happened to Adakles. I've been awake and conscious. And, I think, in Hith."

"Hmm," Fix said. "Perhaps different drugs were used on us."

"Perhaps no drugs," Indrajit suggested.

"Perhaps no drugs," Fix agreed. "But still, the bizarrely flexible nature of reality we've seen today suggests that reality might be something different from what we imagined."

"How so?"

"Reality seems to be something like a stage. Actors walk on and walk off and most of the time we stay in scene, but once in a while, a director or stage manager whisks away all the furniture and scenery and moves us to a different stage."

"Someone is in charge of reality and can just move us around at a whim," Indrajit said.

"Yes."

"The gods."

"No, that's not what I mean." Fix considered. "I mean,

what if the world really is like a play, but it isn't the gods who manipulate us. We're manipulated by more powerful men. Men who can apparently move us from one place to another at whim."

"All you're saying is magicians," Indrajit said. "But again, you're going to tell me, magicians who don't have magic, they have devices. Or skill."

"Yes."

"You see gods and wizards at work in your own life, and you insist that it must be men. Who are just more powerful than you are, and you can't explain how they effect their deeds."

"And you just call those same men gods, and give up trying to explain how they do it."

"Sometimes, I feel we're at an impasse because we're saying the same idea, but you insist on using entirely different words."

Fix laughed. "I would say precisely the same thing."

"I don't care whether it was magic or craft or the gods," Indrajit said. "Something has moved us around multiple times today. And it seems it's going to happen to us at least once more."

"Twice," Fix said. "We're going to come back from seeing the Lord Dean."

"Twice," Indrajit agreed.

"Maybe it's too much," Fix said. "Maybe we should cut our losses now. Leave Thoat to his son. Walk away from the money."

"I don't feel like I'm doing this for the money," Indrajit said. "I don't feel like I'm doing any of it for the money."

"What for, then?" Fix asked. "Good client relations?"

"I don't mind that at all," Indrajit said. "I like that people find us reliable and competent. What bothers me is the part of our reputation according to which, apparently, we are patsies. I don't want to be a patsy."

"You aren't a patsy," Fix said. "You are a noble warrior and a poet, with the soul of a hero."

"Well." Indrajit felt suddenly embarrassed. "Well, yes. That is what I am trying to be. So I am going to save my client, but not because I need to get paid. Or not only because I need to get paid."

"It's nice to eat," Fix said.

"I'm going to save him because that's what a hero would do."

"Have you guys not eaten?" Adakles asked.

"Ah . . . not recently," Indrajit said. "We've been distracted."

"I considered asking Adunummu for food," Munahim said. "But I was afraid I wouldn't be able to trust it."

"Stop here," Adakles said. They stood before a corner tavern. The smell of Pelthite spices on roasting lamb and fish wafted out. "Let's eat."

"But your father," Indrajit said.

"He would want you to eat," Adakles said, raising his head from Munahim's shoulder. "You may need your strength tonight."

Within the tavern, they sat Thoat upright between Fix and his son, on a dark wooden bench circling a booth in the back. Munahim and Indrajit sat on stools; with their larger frames, they shielded the Wixits from view, and between Munahim's hearing and sense of smell and Indrajit's peripheral vision, they could monitor the tavern pretty well. A droggerherd, a ship's captain, and drovers from somewhere on the Endless Road dozed over their own meals, each leaving the others well enough alone.

Indrajit had never tasted more delicious roast lamb in his life. It came with crispy brown bread and root vegetables.

He was careful to restrain himself from overeating, knowing that he had a fight coming up, maybe within the hour.

Adakles paid for the food and bought a skin of wine to take with them.

"Okay." Indrajit swallowed the last bit of bread, soaked in olive oil, lamb fat, and herbs. "Let's go see the Lord Dean."

◁ Chapter Ten ▷

Sure enough, a brass band had been tacked into the tea-shop door, at about the level of Indrajit's knees.

"You see, it's things like these." Fix pointed at the band. "And the dagger and the lamp. Why always the physical things? The fist-guard Adunummu used to launch heat rays, that's another. These things make me think we're seeing an unknown craft, rather than magic."

"Magic *is* an unknown craft." Indrajit shrugged.

"We chase our tail again. Let's go in." Fix pushed the door and it opened inward. He entered and Indrajit followed.

Indrajit wanted to draw his sword, but that would have broken their disguise. They were jobbers, hired by Theophilus Bolt of the Collegium Arcanum to retrieve an artifact from a rogue magician. Now they brought their spoils to the head of the Collegium, a magician named Megistos.

Indrajit had the bottle and its imp. Fix had the Dagger of Slaying, but that was only the backup plan.

Behind the door was no tea shop, but a room with marble walls and a thick carpet. Light came from lamps sitting in niches in the walls; the marble seemed to sparkle and reflect back all the radiance that struck it. A Zalapting in a black robe stood facing them at the bottom of a flight of stairs. He held a silver tray in both hands, extending it toward the jobbers.

"Would my lords care to present themselves?"

Indrajit looked at the tray. "Is there an invisible drink here?" he whispered to Fix.

"He's offering to carry a calling card to his master," Fix whispered back. "This is how the lords and ladies do it. The merchants you and I work with mostly can't be bothered with this stuff, except in extremely formal occasions. Occasions in which they aspire to be more than mere merchants."

"Right." Indrajit drew himself to his full height, barely noticing the weight of the catatonic Wixit on his shoulder. "I'm Indrajit Twang, four hundred twenty-seventh Recital Thane of the Blaatshi and a principal of the Protagonists."

"I'm Fix," Fix said, "also a principal of the Protagonists. We're here to see the Lord Dean Megistos."

"Just Fix, my lord?" the Zalapting asked.

"He used to go by Fiximon Nasoprominentus Fascicular," Indrajit said, "but he calculated that a one-syllable name would save him three hours a day, so he abbreviated himself."

"Just Fix," Fix said.

The Zalapting stepped to one side and pulled a thin cord Indrajit hadn't noticed. He whispered to a stone column, then returned to address the Protagonists. "Follow me."

They followed the lavender-faced, long-snouted man up two flights of stairs. The third floor of the building was a pavilion, with open walls and columns in the shape of giant serpents, holding up a marble roof. A lacquered red handrail ran all around the floor. Beyond the handrail, city lights winked in the darkness. At the far end stood a throne between two ponderous braziers. Flames the height of a tall man rose from the braziers, licking at the stone of the ceiling. To one side of the throne stood a mechanism that resembled Adunummu's viewing device.

A tall, thin man sat on the throne.

He waved them closer.

They set the Wixits down to one side and proceeded.

"Where do you think we are?" Indrajit took slow steps. No need to rush. "Bat? Xiba'alb?"

"Kish," Fix whispered. "Look at the skyline."

"Kish?"

"Disappointed?" Fix asked. "Or just surprised?"

Indrajit stepped to the rail and looked. "It's Kish," he reported, coming back. "We're somewhere in the Crown, I think, though it might be a really tall building in the Lee. The walls aren't always well lit, but I can see where the Spike is, and the five temples."

"You can't tell where we are in the Crown?" Fix continued to pace forward.

Indrajit shook his head. "There's something slippery about the ground. As if it might move at any moment, or as if it were already moving."

"Craft," Fix said. "Strange devices. Magic."

"Well," Indrajit said, "I hope it's not the gods. If this is a god we're about to face, we're in trouble."

"Not necessarily," Munahim said. "My people don't fear the gods."

"Because you never had any," Indrajit said. "Brave-hearted Kyones, honest but godless."

"No," Munahim said. "We had them once."

The bottle and its imp felt very heavy around Indrajit's neck. He smiled, and walked toward the throne.

The man sitting on the throne looked like a blade of grass five cubits tall. His arms were blades sprouting from the same pith, and rather than legs, he had a lower end that was stained brown and split into tendrils like roots. At its middle, the magician's body was not as thick as Indrajit's thigh. Black-dot eyes and a black-slit mouth broke the monotony of the upper half of the stalk, and at its topmost tips, the green man frayed into multiple strands, like a head of bearded wheat.

"The longer I stay in this city," Indrajit said, "the stranger the races of man get."

"Don't tell the wizard that," Fix murmured. "You might hurt his feelings."

They stopped a few paces from the grass-man.

"I am Megistos." The grass-man's voice sounded like the rustle of the wind in a bank of reeds. "Lord Dean of the Collegium Arcanum. You believe you are entering my realm, but the truth is that you have always been in my realm. Welcome, bold Fix. Welcome, Indrajit. Welcome, faithful Munahim."

"Why didn't I get an adjective?" Indrajit murmured.

"Welcome, mouthy Indrajit," Megistos said.

"A palpable hit, O Megistos," Indrajit said. "You honor us with your acknowledgment. We bring you the fruits of our labors in the vineyard of your competitors."

"I have no competitors," Megistos said. "I have no peers. I am the Lord Dean."

"Allow me to clarify," Indrajit said. "We stole a bottle, at the request of one of your subordinates. A Theophilus Bolt."

"Recondite second class," Megistos said.

"That sounds right," Indrajit said. "As directed by Bolt, we're bringing the bottle to you."

"What a sycophant Bolt is," Megistos said. "He hopes that I have no apprentice, and will favor him with the position."

"I am unfamiliar with the politics of the Collegium," Indrajit said.

"Present Bolt's gift."

Indrajit took two long steps forward, trying to appear ceremonious about it. He knelt and removed the flask from his neck. "For you, Lord Dean." He pointed its mouth toward the grass-man, placed his fingers in the grip taught to him by Adunummu, and opened the bottle.

The thing that sprang from the flask's wide mouth could not possibly fit inside the bottle. It began as a mist, but despite being a mist, it didn't slip from the bottle, or ooze or sidle its way out, and once out, it didn't dissipate. The mist sprang out, and when it touched down on the marble, it had a manlike shape. In size it rivaled a Gund or a Luzzazza, and bat-like wings spread out behind it.

"I was promised a magician's blood!" the mist-demon howled.

Megistos the grass-man broke into hysterical giggling. The demon, mist solidifying quickly into sinew, bone, and warty, leatherlike hide, lunged toward the throne.

"I am Megistos!" the grass-man cried. "I am Lord Dean of the Collegium Arcanum! I am the King of Secrets! All Kish is mine!"

Then the demon landed on the throne, and Megistos was promptly shredded into a thousand tiny green strands.

Indrajit stood and backed away. He found Fix and Munahim by his side as the demon, still standing on the seat of the throne, pivoted slowly to face them.

"I was promised a magician's blood!" the demon shrieked. "Such oaths as must be kept, if the universe is not to be ground to dust by the breaking of them!"

"Yes," Indrajit said. "Now you may go."

Just to be on the safe side, he drew his sword. Fix armed himself with falchion and ax, and Munahim took his bow in his hands and put an arrow to the string.

BOOM!

To the right of the throne, just beyond the brazier, a glittering streak of gold light appeared. It looked like lightning, but lightning that struck and then remained in place, shining and twisting, a vertical streak from the marble of the ceiling to the marble of the floor, and thunder rolled from it in a continuous, juddering wave.

Adunummu stepped out of the light, in his blue robe. With him came Shafi, also wearing a blue robe, and holding a large crossbow.

"I am the Lord Dean now!" Adunummu roared. "I defy all to challenge me."

"No one here wants to defy you," Indrajit said slowly. "You remember us. We just want you to restore our client to his wits. Like you did for his son Adakles, you remember. And then we'll get right out of your way."

Adunummu laughed.

"I don't like this," Fix muttered.

"I was promised the blood of a magician!" the demon shrieked. It leaped through the air toward Adunummu.

"Down!" Adunummu bellowed.

Munahim loosed an arrow at the demon, but it struck the creature's shoulder and glanced off. Adunummu swung his enormous flipper. He struck the demon in the face and sent it bowling across the floor.

"You have fed, demon!" Adunummu cried. "Back into the bottle!"

"Liar!" The demon charged again, its maw gaping wide.

Was the demon getting bigger?

The monster put a claw on the throne, scattering green fiber in all directions. It leaped and spread its wings, hurtling through the air toward Adunummu. Shafi stepped to one side, raised his crossbow, and fired. The demon dissipated again into mist, still rocketing through the air.

The bolt passed through the demon.

The demon became flesh again and fell on Adunummu.

"Keep an eye on the Wixits!" Indrajit shouted to Munahim. Then he and Fix charged the demon, weapons raised.

Munahim dropped back two paces. Before the other Protagonists blocked his aim, he sent another arrow into the demon. The beast again vaporized, and Munahim's arrow sank into the flesh of Adunummu's thigh.

Adunummu grunted in pain, but when the demon reappeared, it had lost its grip on the walrus-faced wizard. Adunummu slapped the monster with his flipper again, hurling it against the railing at the edge of the throne room.

"I am here!"

In his wide peripheral vision, Indrajit saw a cloud of smoke burst from the brazier to the left of the throne.

Theophilus Bolt dropped from the cloud, landing and flexing his knees to keep his feet. His right forearm was wrapped in the golden bracer; what had been a bracelet for Adunummu ran from Bolt's wrist to his elbow.

"The throne is mine!" Bolt shrieked.

Indrajit struck the demon across the back of its wings, but it didn't even turn its head. Instead, it leaped toward Bolt. He heard a shrill whining sound from the direction of Theophilus Bolt and saw a short white rod in the wizard's hands. Was this Bolt a projection? But he wasn't floating.

"Watch out!" Fix plowed into Indrajit. They tumbled over the legs of Adunummu as the wizard tried to stand. Adunummu went stumbling sideways, upright but off balance. Indrajit and Fix fell against the handrailing. The upright supports of the railing caught them, but Indrajit almost lost his grip on his sword, and had to catch his breath as a wave of vertigo swept over him. He struggled not to look down.

Fire burst across the throne. It came from Bolt, or from the space around him. Adunummu bellowed and his whiskers evaporated. The clumps of fur around Shafi's shoulders flared into light, and the thief rolled away across the floor, dropping his crossbow and slapping at the flames.

But had he been a thief, after all?

If Adunummu had lied about that, what else had he lied about?

Indrajit took a deep breath and yanked himself to his feet, sword in hand.

"But what a great distraction you would have been," Bolt said. "Then we would have appeared and struck the Lord Dean from behind. Instead, you allied with that miscreant Adunummu, and now my apprentice is dead."

"Your apprentice is dead, but you planned for us to die," Indrajit pointed out. "Let's call it even. You restore Thoat, and we'll go away and leave you alone."

Bolt's lip curled into a sneer. He raised his white wand, pointing it at Indrajit.

An arrow struck the magician in the throat. He staggered backward, and before he hit the ground, two more arrows sank into his chest.

"Well," Fix said, "*some* of our problems are solved."

Indrajit heard the scrape of nails on stone, then the flap of wings, and then the demon dragged itself over the lip of the shelf.

"I was promised the blood of a magician," the demon said.

ᘒ Chapter Twelve ᘓ

"The bottle," Fix said.

He and Indrajit both backed slowly away from the demon.

"Yes," Indrajit said. "I'm pointing the bottle at the monster right now. Sword in the right hand, bottle in the left. If you have any ideas about how to make the demon actually go into the bottle, now is the time to share."

"Enter bottle!" Fix shouted.

Nothing happened.

"The blood of magicians is spilled." Indrajit pointed with Vacho at Bolt's corpse. "Right there. That's a dead magician, still full of blood. Have at him, eat him up. Blood all over the floor, too, it's all yours."

"Do you take me for a carrion-eater, Fish Head?"

"I'm no magician," Indrajit said. "The magicians are all gone. So . . . if you were promised a magician, I'm sorry, that person just broke his promise to you. Good luck to you, I hope you find a tasty sorcerer. This being Kish, it seems that there must be a few."

"You promised me the magician," the demon said, "when you freed me."

The Protagonists continued to back away. Fix held the pointless Dagger of Slaying in one hand and his ax in the other. The demon continued to advance.

"There being no magicians to eat," Indrajit said,

"perhaps you'd like to go back into the bottle and wait until there is one."

The demon leaped. It soared above Indrajit's head, wings wide, front and back legs extended so that Indrajit could see its underbelly and its massive size. It emitted an enormous snarling bellow as it jumped.

Light struck the demon. Indrajit smelled sulfur. His visual perception distorted, and for a moment it seemed to him that the bottle was larger than he was, and he stood beside it, looking through the glass at a landscape of rugged mountains, scorched deserts, thundering waters, and virgin forests. Then he spun about the flask, arcing over its wide mouth even as he reached out, trying to fix his grip on the neck. The marble ceiling was distant, Fix was a bronze giant standing on a faraway horizon, the demon was a mass of muscle bigger than the night sky and orbiting faster.

Then the ceiling collapsed, Fix disappeared, and the demon fell into the bottle. He dropped the flask and it hit the marble floor standing, then spun slowly about as if considering whether it should topple. Yellowish smoke billowed from the wide mouth, and the stink of sulfur clogged Indrajit's nostrils.

"Shut it!" Thoat cried. "Use the grip Adunummu taught you! Shut the bottle now!"

Indrajit was stunned to hear Thoat's voice, and froze. Fix reacted more quickly; he scooped up the bottle in both hands, catching it before it tipped over, and presented it to Indrajit.

Indrajit gripped the bottle as instructed and corked it.

Through the glass, a face mouthed silent curses and shot him angry looks. Indrajit had a strong desire to heave

the bottle right over the platform and let it disappear into
the Kish night, but instead he carefully set the bottle down
and stepped away.

"Thoat," Indrajit said. "You can speak."

"That's not nearly the most interesting thing," Fix
pointed out. "How did you know how to bottle the imp?"

"Thoat is a wizard," Indrajit said.

Both the senior Protagonists stood considering the
import of that statement. Munahim put away his bow and
sat down on the floor. Indrajit considered his options, then
put Vacho up and folded his arms.

"Well," Fix said. "I knew we were being lied to and
manipulated by magicians. Now I see the lying and
manipulation started much earlier than I realized."

Thoat shrugged. The Wixit looked completely lucid
and relaxed. Adakles slapped his father on the shoulder
and grinned, looking for all the world like a coconspirator,
someone who was on the inside of an excellent joke.

"Are you going to explain?" Indrajit asked.

"I don't see why I should," Thoat said. "But I will pay
you."

"For starters," Fix said, "you're Megistos. That grass-
person was some sort of creation, not unlike Bolt's
projection or Adunummu's synthetic."

"The grass-person was in fact a blade of grass," Adakles
said. "Imbued with just enough mirroring capabilities to
be able to fool men into believing it was a man, too."

"And you're not some hapless child entering the
Collegium," Indrajit said. "You're your father's apprentice."

The Wixits nodded together.

"And all this had something to do with settling scores

or ending a rivalry," Indrajit said. "Do you care to tell us more about that?"

"The politics of wizards are too complex to recount to others," Thoat said. "Our lives are long and our grudges are notorious. I may as well recite the Blaatshi Epic to you as try to explain all that has passed under the bridge between me and Adunummu and between me and Theophilus Bolt."

"But they didn't recognize you," Fix said.

"I prefer to be discreet." Thoat shrugged. "Perhaps because I'm a Wixit."

"I've known a lot of Wixits," Indrajit said. "I wouldn't have identified discretion as a signal Wixit virtue. Ferocity, maybe. Business acumen. Persistence."

"How do we know you two are even Wixits?" Fix asked. "We've seen all manner of fake-men and imitation-men. You might be more of the same. Maybe the real wizard and his apprentice are a couple of scab-eyed Gunds sitting on a boat on the Sea of Rains and laughing at us."

"How picturesque your imagination is," Adakles said. "Maybe *you* should be the poet."

"Easy," Indrajit said.

"You manipulated your competitors," Fix said. "Feeding them false information, I suppose. And then you hired us—why?"

"You have a reputation," Thoat said.

"For gullibility," Indrajit said.

"For being men of honor," Thoat said. "For being decent. I entered this contest with every expectation of winning, but I knew I needed men I could trust to be loyal. Men of principle."

"We're not priests," Indrajit mumbled.

"You're sort of a priest," Fix said. "I was almost a priest."

"Men of action who care for the weak and vulnerable," Thoat said. "Men who would stick to a client, even when someone else came along and made a better offer."

"Heroes," Adakles said.

"In a town full of jobbers," Thoat said, "that's no small thing."

"Flattery won't get you a discount," Indrajit said.

"I don't want a discount," Thoat told him. "On the contrary, when you get back to the nameless inn you live in, there on the Crooked Mile above the camel-yard and behind the bakery, you'll find a hundred Imperials in a red purse, waiting on your table beside Fix's inkpot."

Indrajit felt convinced. He nodded his acquiescence and gratitude.

"Do you really own a tea shop?" Fix asked.

"Go to the shop tomorrow and find out," Thoat suggested with a smile.

"Are you in fact the tyrant of the Collegium Arcanum?" Indrajit asked.

"I'm trying to change things," Thoat said. "To those who want to resist, I'm sure I seem like a tyrant."

"I hope one of the things you can change is to give us wings," Indrajit said. "Because it's a long way down, and my only other plan is to let the demon out of the bottle again, and try to ride it to the ground."

"Who needs wings?" Thoat pointed. "The stairs are right over there."

⊰ The End ⊱

TIM POWERS

"Other writers tell tales of magic in the twentieth century, but no one does it like Powers."
—*The Orlando Sentinel*

"Tim Powers is always at the top of the list when folks ask about my favorite authors. His weaving mythology and legend into modern stories that revolve around secret histories of our most mundane landmarks never ever disappoints. This introduction to his new characters Sebastian Vickery and Ingrid Castine is wonderful." —*BoingBoing*

FORCED PERSPECTIVES
HC: 978-1-9821-2440-3 • $25.00 US / $34.00 CAN

STOLEN SKIES
HC: 978-1-9821-2583-7 • $26.00 US / $34.00 CAN
PB: 978-1-9821-9244-0 • $9.99 US / $12.99 CAN

DOWN AND OUT IN PURGATORY
PB: 978-1-4814-8374-2 • $7.99 US / $10.99 CAN
Tales of science fiction and metaphysics from master of the trade Tim Powers, with an introduction by David Drake.

EARTHQUAKE WEATHER
PB: 978-1-9821-2439-7 • $8.99 US / $11.99 CAN
Amongst ghosts and beside a man chased by a god, Janis Plumtree and the many personalities sharing her mind must resurrect the King of the West.

EXPIRATION DATE
TPB: 978-1-4814-8330-8 • $16.00 US / $22.00 CAN
PB: 978-1-4814-8408-4 • $7.99 US / $10.99 CAN
When young Kootie comes to possess the ghost of Thomas Edison, every faction in Los Angeles' supernatural underbelly rushes to capture—or kill—boy and ghost.

MY BROTHER'S KEEPER
TPB: Coming October 2024
Curzon has been working to eradicate the resurgent plague of lycanthropy in Europe and northern England. But forty years ago, a demonic werewolf god was brought to Yorkshire—and it is taking possession of Emily Brontë's foolish brother, putting them at deadly odds.

⇥ Chapter Eleven ⇤

"Let's get the Wixits out of here." Indrajit grabbed Fix and pulled his partner to his feet.

"Agreed." Fix scooped up his ax and his falchion. "We can negotiate with the winner here to get Thoat restored."

Adunummu threw the demon bodily. Bolt yelped and ducked, and the Protagonists leaped across in the demon's wake, trying to put space between themselves and the battling wizards. While Bolt struck the monster repeatedly with his wand, Adunummu pointed his white ceramic fist and fired.

The red beam of light and heat struck the demon and the little wizard alike. Indrajit smelled scorched flesh and something like sulphur. Bolt yelled high-pitched, hysterical gibberish, and Indrajit shot a glance over his shoulder to see what was happening.

Bolt patted around on the floor as if blinded and looking for something. His wand lay just out of reach. Adunummu stood and fired again with his weapon, striking the demon, who sprang into the air and away from Bolt.

But toward the Wixits.

"I was promised blood!" the demon shrieked.

"Adakles!" Fix yelled. "Duck! Get away from your father!"

Munahim stepped into the demon's path, bow whizzing. Arrows struck the beast as it descended, sticking into its hide but not apparently wounding it at all. Indrajit accelerated, stretching his legs into a long, fast pace. He was grateful for the food in his belly, without which he thought he would be unconscious at this point.

The demon alighted, claws slashing downward. Munahim's bow rattled across the stone and his blade flashed from its sheath. He parried the crushing attack, and then Indrajit dove. He grabbed the demon's tail with his left hand and rolled to the right. His momentum spun the monster about, letting Munahim rain unopposed blows around its head and shoulders. Indrajit struck at the creature's ankle. He yelled, not quite managing to form actual words. Then Fix with his shorter stride caught up, in time to hit the demon in the shoulder with his ax, and in the belly with his sword.

The demon squealed and leaped back.

A swarm of insects burst from where Adakles crouched over his father on the floor. They were wasps, but bloodred, and the size of Indrajit's thumb. They weaved left and right to cut around Munahim on both sides and then around Fix's shoulders, giving him a halo like a bloody cloud but not hitting him.

The wasps slammed into the demon's chest and face. Each insect exploded as it hit, and blackish blood sprayed from the monster's body. It leaped up and away, yanking itself free of Indrajit's grip and flipping over backward, toward the dueling magicians.

"Blood!" it howled. "The blood of a magician!"

Bolt had recovered his wand and now crouched to take shelter behind the throne. He launched green lances of fire from his wand, but Adunummu held a shield, resembling a flat copper disk. He caught the stabbing green light, deflecting it right and left and laughing. Shaking his right arm, he unkinked a whiplike device consisting of white spheres linked by short white rods.

"Is your father okay?" Indrajit called to Adakles.

Adakles nodded.

"Are you okay?" Fix asked. "The demon keeps screaming that it wants the blood of a magician. It must have been coming after you."

"I don't know." Adakles's paws trembled.

Swinging the whip once over his head, Adunummu cracked it against the throne.

BOOM!

The throne went flying, split in two flaming halves. Bolt skidded back several steps but rose to his feet at the same time, holding his hands in front of himself in a mystic gesture of defense.

The demon sprang again, falling toward Adunummu.

"No!" Shafi leaped to interpose himself between the monster and the magician. He raised two short swords, and a look of stubborn hopelessness on his lavender face, and Indrajit knew he was doomed.

The demon landed on Shafi and crushed him, reducing him instantly to a lifeless doll that bounced once on the floor and then lay still. One sword rattled back and forth, steel whining on the marble, for several seconds after Shafi was gone.

"I was promised!" the demon wailed. But it didn't linger over Shafi's body. Instead, it hurled itself at Adunummu.

"The demon is a wizard-killer," Fix said. "We should leave now with the Wixits. Urgently."

"Yes." Indrajit scooped up Thoat and tossed him onto his shoulder. "Munahim, can you cover our backs?"

"My arrows seem pointless," Munahim said, but he switched to his bow anyway. "I'll do what I can."

Fix reached to pick up Adakles, but the younger Wixit shook off the offer. "I'll walk."

They shuffled together back toward the stairs that were the only exit from the room.

"What are the residents of the Crown seeing?" Fix asked. "Are we in a tower that appears to be burning? Or is all of this screened from their eyes by magic?"

"Or by mysterious devices we don't otherwise understand?" Indrajit suggested.

He looked back in time to see Adunummu wrap his whip around the demon's waist and then throw the monster at the ceiling. Marble cracked and stone dust fell around the battling magicians. The beast fell, uncoiling from the links of the whip, and Adunummu struck it with his flipper. The demon bowled through the air end over end and crashed into Bolt. They rolled together across the floor. Green flashes of light stuttered in the tight space between the combatants as Bolt stabbed the monster again and again and it bit and clawed at him.

"Shafi!" Adunummu dropped his whip and knelt to cradle the lavender corpse in his arms.

"The stairs!" Fix cried. "Where are they?"

Indrajit pulled his gaze away from the battle and looked. The stairway had disappeared. Were they in the wrong part of the room? He looked around: no, this was where they had emerged, and there was no visible staircase elsewhere.

The stairs had vanished.

He slipped to the edge of the throne room and looked over the railing. "It's still Kish down there," he said. "Can we climb?"

"Without rope?" Fix asked. "Certain death."

"Do you have . . . I don't know, a flying spell?" Indrajit asked Adakles.

Adakles shook. "I can . . . I can . . . translate some things."

"Translate? You can *translate some things*? Frozen hells!" Indrajit roared. "You sound like Fix! You go to wizard school, boy! Can you do nothing useful?"

"Well, you have to be able to read the books first," Adakles muttered.

A high-pitched squeal whipped Indrajit's head back around to look at the fight again.

A cloud of smoke exploded above Adunummu's head, and a Gund fell out of it. The Gund wore a red toga, and as it landed on Adunummu, it collapsed into an amorphous blob, a mass of translucent flesh that swallowed the walrusoid face and melted down over his chest and shoulders.

The demon slashed the blob, and a clear liquid sprayed out.

"Back!" Bolt shouted. "Back!" The short wizard advanced on the demon, stabbing it with green light.

Adunummu lurched to his feet, clawing at the mass on his face. He tore away handfuls of clear gelatinous flesh, but what remained reshaped itself and continued to suffocate him. As Adunummu pivoted, Indrajit saw his face clearly, as if through a window.

Bolt stabbed the demon again, but Adunummu lurched toward the monster and grabbed it.

"Maybe we can do something with the flask," Fix suggested.

Indrajit scanned the room and found the bottle on a chain, lying next to the smoldering remains of the throne.

"Like what?" he asked. "Hit someone with it?"

"Get the demon back inside," Fix suggested. "If it tries to attack us again."

"Right." Indrajit sighed, set Thoat on his feet, and charged back toward the fray.

Adunummu grabbed the demon and pressed it to his head. The beast roared in indignation and pain and slashed at the wizard, but claws and teeth sank into the flesh of the thing wrapped around Adunummu's skull.

Clear blood sprayed. A Fanchee head appeared, momentarily green, and then the white insectoid shoulder-arms of a Gund, and then four arms like a Luzzazza's rose from the translucent mass, darkening momentarily into a slate blue before subsiding again.

Bolt stabbed Adunummu in the side, causing the big magician to spin. He swung his flipper and sent Bolt sprawling with a blow to the head. He clawed at the blob on his head, soaking himself in clear ichor.

Indrajit ducked to grab the bottle and back away, but the demon wasn't looking at him. Intent on the magician in its grasp, or perhaps the two magicians, it raised a crooked arm and plunged its talons into the translucent mass. It stabbed so fiercely and so deep, Indrajit saw the claws pierce all the way through the shape-changing creature and dig into Adunummu's flesh. Red blood rose into and through the shape-changer, puddling in dark clouds within its body, and pumping thinly out around the demon's claws.

Adunummu lurched toward Indrajit. Indrajit staggered backward and fell, dropping the bottle and Vacho alike. Adunummu stared at him, bug-eyed, through the transparent thing on his head, as he gripped it with both hands and tried to rip it free. Indrajit grabbed his sword, just in case.

Adunummu turned and ran. His pace was erratic, his steps wove from side to side. He charged over Bolt, knocking the little wizard down just as he was trying to stand again. He kicked aside a charred chunk of throne as if he hadn't seen it. He hit the handrailing at the edge of the platform and snapped it like a twig, charging straight through it and over the side.

Adunummu fell out of sight, taking the shape-changer and the demon with him.

Indrajit's ears rang from the racket for long seconds after the racket was gone. He took the bottle and stood, feeling weak in the knees and tired in every muscle he had. Fix was there, offering him a hand, and he took it to steady himself. Sheathe the sword, or hold it threateningly? Indrajit decided to put Vacho in its scabbard, and then he cleared his throat.

"Bolt," he said. "Recondite, something, I don't remember. Whatever you are. Magician. We did our part. Time for you to restore our client."

Theophilus Bolt stood. His robe was slashed and charred, his face dusty and streaked with sweat. He held his white wand casually. "*Did* you do your part, then?"

Indrajit nodded.

"As I recall," Bolt said, "your part was to get invited in here with the bottle-imp."

"Which we did," Indrajit said.

"And then your part was to stab Megistos," Bolt said. "Instead, you opened the bottle on him. Didn't you?"

"Why does it matter?" Fix asked. "Megistos is dead."

"It matters," Bolt said, his voice rising in pitch, "because you learned how to open the bottle from Adunummu. Didn't you?"

"So what?" Indrajit shrugged. "You got what you wanted. Megistos is dead."

"So is Adunummu," Fix added, "who was clearly your rival. You win. Help our client."

Bolt shrugged. "No. You didn't do what I wanted. You get nothing more from me. Leave, and be grateful I don't throw you off this tower."

Fix drew the Dagger of Slaying. "Heal Thoat."

Bolt chuckled, drily, once. Then he started to laugh, his laughter growing more and more maniacal until he nearly fell over. "Oh, that's rich."

"He doesn't feel threatened," Indrajit said.

There was a pregnant pause while the Protagonists thought through the implications of that fact.

"The Dagger of Slaying is nothing," Fix said. "It's an ordinary knife."

"You expected us to get killed," Indrajit said to the little wizard. "We'd come in here with the bottle we didn't know how to use, then try to attack and kill the tyrant lord of the Collegium Arcanum with an ordinary little knife. We'd have been ripped to pieces."